He came out of a dream. . . .

Drawing a deep breath, Nicki blew as hard as she could while fanning the length of the candlelit cake.

"Did you make a wish?" someone called.

"Yes, indeed," Nicki announced, her gaze locked on the spot where the new driver was standing. He watched with seeming surprise as she strolled up to him. One thing was clear—he was as handsome a man as she'd ever seen.

"Well, hello," he said in a deep, stirring voice. "I'm—"

"Jack something-or-other," Nicki broke in. "And I'm the girl with the wish." She pulled him down and kissed him with abandon. Passive for a stunned instant, he then put a pair of strong arms around her and pulled her close. . . .

"I said, wake up, sleepyhead."

Waking with a start, Catherine sat up and blinked. Eliot was standing by the bed straightening his tie. . . . Leaning down, he sought her lips. Yet when he found them, Catherine continued to taste the mouth of another man, her cheek tingling with the illusory rub of the dream man's beard. . . .

DREAMSEEKER

Marcia Martin

A SIGNET BOOK

SIGNET
Published by the Penguin Group
Penguin Putnam Inc., 375 Hudson Street,
New York, New York 10014, U.S.A.
Penguin Books Ltd, 27 Wrights Lane,
London W8 5TZ, England
Penguin Books Australia Ltd, Ringwood,
Victoria, Australia
Penguin Books Canada Ltd, 10 Alcorn Avenue,
Toronto, Ontario, Canada M4V 3B2
Penguin Books (N.Z.) Ltd, 182–190 Wairau Road,
Auckland 10, New Zealand

Penguin Books Ltd, Registered Offices:
Harmondsworth, Middlesex, England

First published by Signet, an imprint of Dutton NAL,
a member of Penguin Putnam Inc.

First Printing, November, 1998
10 9 8 7 6 5 4 3 2 1

PUBLISHER'S NOTE
This is a work of fiction. Names, characters, places, and incidents either are
the product of the author's imagination or are used fictitiously, and any
resemblance to actual persons, living or dead, events, or locales is entirely
coincidental.

PART ONE

Into her dream he melted, as the rose,
Blendeth its odour with the violet,—
Solution sweet: meantime the frost-wind
blows . . .

—John Keats

Chapter One

She was getting out.

It was real. It was happening. The phrase pounded along the back roads of her mind with the rhythm of churning hoofbeats: *getting out . . . getting out . . . getting out. . . .*

Catherine opened the final drawer of the dresser and dumped its contents into the suitcase on the bed. Still, she couldn't dispel the fog of disbelief that clouded her actions, nor repress an occasional pang of trepidation that—even now—something could go wrong, and she'd be trapped forever in the tower bedroom of the old house on Legare.

She supposed passersby saw a certain charm in the place. Nestled among ancient, spreading oaks that blocked the sun, Winslow House, 1782, was listed on the historic tour, pointed out as a prime architectural example of the Charleston "single house," and noted for the elaborate wrought iron of the gate in the courtyard.

But for Catherine Winslow the house whose name she bore held no charm. In her eyes it was a prison—its cells filled with shadow and loneliness, its laws dictated by a matron who held the reins on her ward's life just as tightly as she clutched the family purse strings.

For as long as she could remember, Catherine had been convinced of two certainties: one, that she didn't belong here; two, that she would never get away.

With returning wonder she fished in the back pouch of the old, leather-trimmed suitcase and withdrew the paperback novel. *Passionate Bride* by Cat Winslow. Sweet irony. As a lost child she'd found sanctuary in the world of books. As a desperate woman she'd found escape.

She remembered the time as an eight-year-old when she

realized that the ivy-covered trellis outside her bedroom window provided a makeshift ladder to the courtyard below. If she shimmied down at the right time, she could slip through the gate and be gone for a couple of hours without rousing notice. It was then that she first wandered the few blocks to King Street and stepped into Ann Marie Duvall's bookshop. Ann Marie was a young woman who'd lost a husband; Catherine, a waif who'd lost a mother. They adopted each other, and the bookshelves of the Open Window became Catherine's gateway to the shining horizons beyond Winslow House.

Twenty years had passed since then. Today, her own book was featured on those shelves.

Catherine ran her fingers over the title. It had taken three years of secret writing in the back of the bookshop to produce *Passionate Bride*; another year while Ann Marie, her self-appointed agent, sought a New York buyer; still another while the publisher edited, proofed, and finally went to press. Now, after ten weeks in the stores, the historical romance was selling like hotcakes, and—in addition to the promise of royalties—Cat Winslow had received a generous advance for a sequel.

"Mark my words," Ann Marie had always said. "That imagination of yours will pay off one of these days."

And today was payday. She was getting out.

Tucking the novel back in place, Catherine glanced up and caught her reflection in the cheval mirror. She stepped around the foot of the bed and gave herself a sweeping look. Black stockings, gray skirt, white blouse, gray sweater. God, she hated gray . . . and the pinned-up topknot of her hair, which was just as unfashionable as the long braid she'd worn into teenhood.

Inch by inch, day by day, year by year, Aunt Sybil had succeeded in turning her into something that looked as dull and lifeless as a wooden post.

Well, her appearance was the least of all that was about to change. Catherine cast a searching look about the chamber. The little girl's room her mother furnished looked the way it always had—everything in perfect order, for anything less was not to be tolerated. Her gaze settled on the antique dresser. She'd forgotten the cubby.

Crossing the room, Catherine dropped to her knees and

pulled at the base of the dresser, which slid away from the wall to disclose a rough place in the plaster. Prying her fingers along the edges, she dislodged the fragment and reached inside. The cache held a piece of quartz from a long-ago trip to a North Carolina gold mine, several toys she was never supposed to have had, a music box with forbidden earrings inside, and . . . the dream diaries.

She'd kept them in secret for years, then stashed them away when she started writing fiction. She'd hardly been visited by *"the dream"* since then. Settling back on her haunches, Catherine pulled the blue ribbon, opened the first volume, and stifled a smile as she beheld her first entry. It was illustrated with a primitive drawing of Nicki—who, in retrospect, was immediately recognizable as herself, complete with big blue eyes and a blond braid reaching to her waist. *I have a friend who comes at night,* read the careful print of a child.

It was 1973 when she wrote that. The year was emblazoned in her memory: Mother died in a flood, Father suffered a stroke, and his maiden sister took charge of Winslow House. It was the year Catherine's life turned unbearably bleak . . . and Nicki was born.

Catherine turned the page and found a rendering of a white ranch house with pool, stables, flowering lawns, and rolling pasture where horses and cattle grazed. Nicki lived there without parents, but surrounded by a loving cast of characters—her dashing guardian, Austin, who was more like a big brother than an uncle; Malia, the pretty housekeeper, who thought no one knew she was passionately in love with Austin; and grandfatherly Melrose with the silver hair and bushy eyebrows. As president of "the company," he maintained offices in one of the ranch outbuildings.

Over the years Catherine had come to know them all, though Nicki was the dazzling star of the show. Aside from her physically identical appearance, she was, in every other way, Catherine's blatant opposite—the shiny flip side of an otherwise dull coin, Catherine had sometimes thought. Nicki was boisterous, flamboyant, and rebellious; an unmitigated tease, irresistible charmer, and fearless adventurer. Whatever she wanted to happen, she *made* happen . . . often wrapping her uncle, and everyone else, around her finger along the way.

Precious time slipped by as Catherine skimmed through the spiral notebooks comprising the diaries. There were entries she hadn't thought of in years—like the time ten-year-old Nicki scaled her first mountain, stood at the top, and shook her fist at the heavens as though to challenge anything in the universe to unthrone her . . . like the time at fifteen when she locked herself in the bathroom, lopped off her braid, and bleached the pixielike results to platinum.

The flagrant hairstyle had become a lasting fixture—a symbol, to Catherine, of the dare-anything spirit so different from her own oppressed nature. Looking back, it didn't take a genius to see that she'd needed someone, and had created Nicki out of that need. But as a child Catherine hadn't been so clinical. She'd accepted the gift of her dreams with the joy of finding a best friend. As the years passed, and she and Nicki grew up together, Catherine had adored her the same way she idolized the heroines in books.

Returning the other mementos to the cubby, she rose to her feet with the notebooks in hand, and noted the shadows falling into the room. It was after four. Aunt Sybil would be home anytime. A sense of urgency returned, and Catherine hurried back to the bed. She didn't plan on leaving without a good-bye, but she hoped to be on her way out the door when the time arrived.

Settling the diaries on top, Catherine closed the suitcase and latched it. This was it, the last of the belongings she was taking. The rest—a few containers of clothes and knickknacks, plus her mother's prized dishware—was already in Ann Marie's borrowed car, which was parked beneath a secreting drape of Spanish moss by the courtyard.

Catherine had waited until Aunt Sybil left before loading the boxes she'd packed and stored discreetly in the basement. Everything had been planned toward a smooth, swift getaway, for if Aunt Sybil had caught wind of the scheme, she'd have done something to stop it.

Maybe the condominium across the Historic District would have become suddenly *unavailable.* "Miss Sybil" Winslow was a master at swinging the weight of the family name. Or, more likely, she would have stirred Catherine's ailing father into such a state of distress that Catherine would have feared for his life, and her own utter damnation, if she left.

There were many ways to shackle the spirit, and Aunt Sybil knew them all. But for once, it seemed, Catherine was managing to slip past her. The deal on the condo had closed that morning, and an angel must have been at her shoulder when she visited her father's chambers an hour ago. Typically, he preferred to dwell in the past when his wife was still alive. Today he'd been lucid.

"You're all grown up," he observed with surprise.

"Yes, Father. I am."

He shocked her when he moved his good arm and took her hand. "Be happy, then," he added.

The memory pricked at Catherine's eyes and heart. Her father received the attentions of a full-time nurse, a housekeeper who'd been with the family for decades, and a sister who made no bones about the way she sacrificed her life for her brother. Intellectually, Catherine knew there was nothing he could gain by her staying; emotionally, she found it hard to turn a deaf ear to the whispering notion that she was deserting him.

She tried to focus on his parting words. *Be happy. . . .*

The echo was shattered as her aunt stormed into the room—her breasts heaving at the shirtwaist of her dress, her eyes glittering like onyx beneath the chignon of silver hair. "Loaded for bear," Father might have said on one of his good days.

Catherine straightened with practiced calm from the suitcase. Though her gaze never wavered, her attention darted to the brass lock on the bedroom door. She'd been eleven when she was severely switched for bolting that door. She hadn't touched the lock since.

"Constance Monroe was passing this tripe around the society tea today," Sybil announced, and held up a copy of *Passionate Bride.* "Am I to believe that my niece is responsible for it?"

Catherine offered no reply; nor did her aunt wait for one.

"I know you did this," she ranted on. "Don't bother to deny it. What stymies me is how you could lower yourself in such a fashion. *Cat* Winslow." She enunciated with a sneer. "One would think that if you could trouble yourself to alter your Christian name, you might preserve the name of Winslow from such sordidness."

The name of Winslow . . . How many times had Catherine heard the slogan? Her aunt threw the novel to the floor, then wiped her palms as though the touch of it had soiled her fingers.

"Don't just stand there staring, as if you've got no sense—" She halted as she noted Catherine's suitcase. "What's this, then?"

"I'm . . . leaving."

"What do you mean, 'leaving'?" Catherine rolled her shoulders. "Don't slouch!" came the sharp command.

Years of training whipped Catherine's spine to attention, but a fledgling sense of freedom rang in her reply. "It's high time I moved out."

Her aunt emitted a shrill, mocking laugh. "Just who do you think you are to decide such a thing?"

I think I'm the twenty-eight-year-old virgin freak you made me into! Catherine wanted to scream. "I've made my decision," she said instead.

Another ear-piercing laugh. "You've never been able to make a decision in your life. *Who* do you think would have you? *Where* do you think you would go?"

"I bought a place across the District." In the blink of an eye the sarcastic revelry vanished from her aunt's face.

"Bought!" The word exploded like a gunshot. "With what?"

"I have a new contract. My editor thinks my work—"

"Your 'work'!" Sybil interrupted with a scornful kick that sent the paperback skidding across the hardwood floor. "You call such disgraceful indulgence *work*? *Passionate Bride,* indeed! Passionate harlot is more like it!"

"Apparently people enjoy reading about harlots."

Her aunt stepped quickly, threateningly, in her direction. The obvious first impulse was to flinch, but Catherine didn't. Ingrained behavior took hold, and she remained still as stone.

"I always knew you were a sinful girl," Sybil hissed. "This trash proves it."

"Then you should be pleased I'm going."

"And selfish, too!" her aunt accused. "After years of uselessness, now that you're grown and could be worth something, you intend to leave me to take care of this house alone."

"The nurse will be here. And Mamie."

"Mamie! As though she's worth her salt!"

"And I'll visit Father—"

"Aha! Father! Now we've come to it. How do you expect your father to take this?" The question that had curbed a lifetime.

"I've already said my good-byes to him," Catherine responded.

Blotches of scarlet mottled her aunt's face. Together with her white-rimmed black eyes and flaring nostrils, they created a countenance of absolute fury. "I'll just bet you have, you conniving ingrate!" she shrieked. "I suppose I shouldn't be surprised that *I'm* the last to know of this! After all, *I* only devoted my entire life to raising you!"

I never wanted any part *of your entire life,* Catherine thought as her aunt whirled out. After the door slammed behind her, the room filled with contrasting, instant peace. But Catherine knew it was only a lull in the storm. Aunt Sybil would regroup and return stronger than before. Hastily picking up the abused copy of *Passionate Bride,* she grabbed the suitcase and strode to the door.

"Be seeing you," a voice whispered as she crossed the threshold. Catherine shot a startled look down the shadowy hall. But there was no one. Then she realized she'd imagined the voice. *Be seeing you*—it was what Nicki always said. Noiselessly closing the door behind her, Catherine rushed down the stairs and left the house by way of the seldom-used rear exit.

As she pulled away from the curb, a haze of unreality set in once more. The drive across the peninsula passed in a blur, as did her arrival at the stylish building off East Bay. She felt as though she were floating as she ascended the curving stairwell to the second floor and unlocked the door.

After the confinements of a tall, narrow domain structured on the principle of a single chamber's width, the rooms sprawled with openness. Setting down her suitcase, Catherine walked through the L-shaped living area, opened the sliding doors, and was greeted by the view that had sold her on the place.

She stepped onto the iron-trimmed balcony overlooking the waterway. Across the street below, tidewater lapped at a fringe of marsh grass. A ramshackle dock spanned the shallows and tapered to a delapidated end near the channel, where the peninsular floor sheared away and coastal waters merged with the blue Atlantic.

Her thoughts returned to her father. Years ago he'd issued a decree. She would learn to swim. His wife had drowned in a flash flood of the Cooper River; his daughter would swim. Against all the odds of Aunt Sybil's domination, the edict had held.

Catherine had taken private lessons from the best instructors the country club had to offer. She'd been forbidden the "vulgarity" of competing on the swim team, but one thing had been ungovernable, even for Aunt Sybil. Catherine had an uncanny gift. When she entered the water, it received her as its own—lifting, buoying, spiriting her along at speeds that left spectators gaping. When she emerged, she was never exhausted but exhilarated, never depleted but filled.

Catherine gazed across the ocean, felt her spirit swell, and the fog of disbelief finally parted.

For heaven's sake . . . I've made it.

The sun was suddenly bright on the water, the air sparkling with light. A sharp breeze whipped about her, implanting the scent of the sea, stinging her eyes with its salt. The magnitude of the moment hit her, and Catherine began to shake.

"Thank you, God," she whispered, as burning tears filled her eyes.

Hastily wiping them away, she stepped back inside and turned her attention to the few pieces of furniture that had been delivered mere hours ago—a desk to house the secondhand computer and printer Ann Marie was donating, and beyond that the rattan couch and shelving unit for which Catherine had shopped the week before. In the neighboring room was a new queen-size box spring and mattress.

No headboard. No dresser. Just the necessities. Until now, she hadn't been able to embrace the idea of the condo as real, much less allow her imagination to furnish it. Now she could. Walking over to the tall shelves, whose solitary decoration was a clock radio blinking the hour of noon, she set the time and turned on some music—another contrast with solemnly quiet Winslow House.

Catherine spent the next several hours unpacking in a state of joyous awe. There was no forced appearance at the dining table at six-thirty sharp, no stilted "family hour" with Father, which Aunt Sybil generally monopolized with a recitation on what was wrong with the world. Instead, time flowed by on a musical stream of making the bed with crisp new linens, putting away her mother's stemware and dishes in the spacious kitchen cupboards, and munching on fruit and crackers along the way.

When she opened her suitcase, the first things she took out were the dream diaries. Moving thoughtfully to the shelving unit, Catherine stowed them on the top ledge, rested her hand on the blue ribbon, and imagined Nicki . . . bright, effervescent, indomitable Nicki. She'd come into being at a time when life was dark and hopeless, and she'd remained as long as she was needed, a solitary candle glowing through dismal night.

Now that a new dawn was breaking, Catherine suddenly doubted that "the dream" would ever come to her again. Withdrawing her hand, she backed away from the shelves, her gaze upturned.

"Be seeing you," she murmured with a wistful smile, and returned to her unpacking.

Chapter Two

Wednesday, April 20

Each Sunday the Living Section of the *Post* ran a quarter-page story on a local Charlestonian. Since taking over the "Sunday Profile," Marla Sutton had interviewed a gamut of subjects ranging from exotic to eccentric to downright weird. She considered herself seasoned to the unexpected, yet when Ted announced her next assignment, he managed to stun her.

"You mean Catherine Winslow of Legare Street?" she asked.

"I mean *Cat* Winslow, whose first novel just hit number one on the Waldenbooks romance list."

Ted handed over a paperback novel, and Marla peered at the cover. Against a backdrop of Revolutionary warships, a gorgeous man wearing very little was embracing a gorgeous woman just as scantily clad. *Passionate Bride* by Cat Winslow.

"And it's not Legare Street," Ted commented. "She's got a sweet little penthouse off East Bay. Do you know her?"

"I knew a *Catherine*," Marla answered, her memory resurrecting a picture from decades past of a girl in an outdated gray jumper, clutching her books as she darted across the schoolyard. As children, they'd gone to each other's birthday parties and played dolls while their mothers played bridge. But that changed when Mrs. Winslow died and "Miss Sybil" took over. She was stern and cross, and no one wanted to go to Winslow House anymore. As time passed, Catherine had become an outcast.

"I don't think it could be the same person," Marla added.

"Whatever." Ted returned his attention to the page proofs on his desk. "The interview's set for eleven o'clock Saturday morning. Take plenty of pictures."

"Don't I always?" Marla replied on her way out. The only reason she'd landed the Sunday column was because she could handle a 35-millimeter as well as a keyboard. One day her camera was going to launch her career. As she headed back to her terminal, Marla looked once more at the paperback. If the entwined figures on the cover were any indication, there were some sizzling pages inside. No. That just didn't jibe with the image of Catherine Winslow.

Marla recalled the day in sixth grade when she'd been drawn into a taunting group that was trailing Catherine across the schoolyard. She'd been hurrying along, head down as usual, when she unexpectedly turned and looked up with the biggest, bluest, eeriest eyes Marla had ever seen. The group stopped in its tracks. There was something about the way Catherine regarded them—like she wasn't looking *at* them, but *through* them . . . as though they weren't really there at all, or *she* wasn't, or *something*.

Marla never said another taunting word to Catherine Winslow. But neither did she seek Catherine's friendship. No one in the popular circle did. As far as she knew, Catherine had proceeded through the school years in shunned solitude, with the reputation of a "brain" as her only company.

Senior year, she'd won an academic scholarship to the College of Charleston, which Marla also attended. But Catherine didn't live on campus and didn't join in. The few times Marla spotted her, she'd appeared as drab as always.

"Definitely not the same person," Marla muttered to herself.

But in researching the subject of the upcoming interview, she discovered she was wrong. Cat and Catherine—author and outcast—were one.

Saturday morning, Marla still found it hard to believe. If ever she'd taken the time to wonder how Catherine would end up, she'd have imagined the poor thing would simply wither and die within the historic, excruciatingly gloomy confines of Winslow House. Had she really wound up in this stylish residence trimmed with royal palms and wrought iron?

With lingering skepticism Marla climbed a curving staircase to the second floor, rang the bell, and prepared herself for the girl in the gray jumper. A moment later the door swung wide.

"Hello, Marla," she said with a welcoming smile.

Marla blinked with surprise. The sunny creature at the door was wearing a bright yellow shirt and walking shorts. Golden highlights gleamed in her honey-blond hair, which was styled in a chin-length bob with a shock of bangs across the forehead. Her cheeks glowed with rosiness, and her eyes shone.

"It's been a long time," she added. "Won't you come in?"

"Catherine?" The name emerged on a note of blatant doubt.

"Yes. It's me," she confirmed with a lighthearted laugh, and Marla was newly amazed.

The interior of her home was no less cheery. Bright and spacious, with rattan furniture and lots of plants, it had a tropical air. Beyond a receiving area, with a giant aquarium full of angelfish for a centerpiece, the far end of the room had been organized as a workplace complete with computer and printer, and a view toward sliding doors that looked out to sea. The contrast with Winslow House couldn't have been more stark.

"How long have you lived here?" Marla asked.

"Three weeks and two days," came the precise reply.

"It's lovely."

"Thanks," Catherine smilingly replied. "I've splurged more than I intended, but once I got started I couldn't seem to stop."

She led the way into the kitchen, which featured a bay window also facing the sea. While Catherine poured them a cup of coffee. Marla lifted her camera and turned the lens toward her subject, who was slim, blond, and very pretty. However unlikely it might have seemed years ago, the duckling had become a swan.

"Do you mind if I snap a few candid shots as we go along?" she asked when Catherine joined her at the breakfast table.

"The more candid, the better. I tend to freeze up terribly in front of the cameras."

But in contradiction to the warning, Catherine came across with soft-spoken confidence throughout the interview. She was charmingly modest about the success of her first novel, and endearingly hopeful about the new one due to be finished in a couple of months. If she remained a bit reserved, it was in a classy, Grace Kelly sort of way that had nothing to do with the painfully shy girl of yesteryear. Even a direct question about the steamy love scenes in *Passionate Bride* failed to trip her up.

"I'm sorry to report they come purely from imagination," she answered with an intriguing little grin Marla managed to catch on film. If the print turned out the way she expected, it would be the profile portrait.

It was well past noon when Marla packed up her things. "I need to go if I'm going to make my deadline. Hope you like the story."

"I'm sure I will," Catherine replied.

"Want me to reserve some extra copies for you?"

"That would be great."

Marla's gaze settled on Catherine as she cleared the table and crossed to the sink. "Do you mind if I ask you something off the record?"

"Go ahead."

"What in the world happened to you?" She looked around with a quizzical expression. "You're very different from the Catherine Winslow I remember," Marla added.

She leaned back against the counter. "I hope I am."

"You *are*. Believe me. So what happened?"

Catherine glanced aside before lifting her gaze once more, and for the first time Marla saw a ghost of the eerie-eyed girl.

"It took me a long time," she said. "But I finally found a way to break out."

"Out from under Miss Sybil, you mean," Marla supplied. "Everyone knew she was a witch, Catherine."

"Fancy that. And all this time I thought I was the only one."

Marla shook her head. "All the kids knew, and . . . well, I'm sorry I didn't make the effort to be friendlier back then."

"That's okay. I wasn't easy to be friends with in those days."

"How about now? Want to have lunch sometime?"

Catherine smiled, and the ghost from the past vanished. "I'd like that," she said, and insisted on accompanying Marla to her car.

The April afternoon was warm—the sun drenching the street with glimmering light, and the promise of hot summertime days on the way. Across the way a gang of kids was splashing about the water's edge, their hoots filling the air.

"So that's what I kept hearing inside," Marla commented.

"Yes. From what I understand, they've kind of adopted this strip of waterfront."

"Who are they?"

Catherine shrugged. "A neighbor told me they come from around Calhoun Street somewhere." Marla's brows lifted. Some of the most low-rent areas of the city were located around Calhoun Street.

"Apparently it's a summer tradition," Catherine added. "When the weather gets hot, youngsters naturally gravitate to water. I gather these particular ones have no place else to go."

"That's a city property, right?" Marla said. "Why don't you have the cops clear them out?"

The blue eyes turned her way. "They're just kids, Marla."

Marla shielded her gaze as she peered across the sunny street. "*Some* are kids," she affirmed. "*Some* are as big as you and I."

"They don't bother me," Catherine replied. "Unless . . ."

Marla glanced aside in time to see her stiffen. "Unless what?"

"Unless they venture onto the dock like that boy over there. Hey!" she called, lifting her voice. "The dock isn't safe!"

None of the kids heard. They were making too much noise cheering on their companion. He continued along the skeletal structure, occasionally raising a triumphant fist. Catherine took a step into the street.

Marla looked at her, then back to the shoreline . . and it happened. One second the dark-haired youth was perched on the dock; the next second part of it gave way, and he fell. A heartbeat later his flailing arms parted the water.

"He can't swim," Catherine mumbled.

Momentarily speechless, Marla looked her way. Luckily, there were no cars coming as Catherine continued into the street, her eyes locked on the spot where the splashing continued.

"He can't swim," she repeated, and launched into a full run.

"Holy shit," Marla muttered. Yanking off her lens cover, she followed as fast as she could in Catherine's path. By the time she reached the group at the water's edge, Catherine was dashing up the steps to the dock, using the rickety planks as a springboard. Marla lifted the camera, peered through the viewfinder, and started clicking just as Catherine went airborne—her feet fluttering in an expectant kick before she hit the water.

A deathly quiet fell over the onshore group as both the arms of the boy and the bright yellow clothes of his would-be savior disappeared. Then, miraculously, two heads appeared on the surface. The kids gave a deafening cheer. As Catherine pulled the boy toward safety, Marla broke into a smile and continued to click the shutter like a madwoman.

When they reached waist-high depths, they gained their footing, though the teenage boy—who was as tall as Catherine—was still coughing as she led him supportingly to shore. Marla closed in along with the kids.

"What's your name?" Catherine asked as she deposited him safely on the sand.

"Kenny," he managed. "Kenny Black."

"You can't swim, right?"

When he shook his head, she looked up to the dozen youthful faces surrounding her. "Can *any* of you swim?" she demanded.

A few hours later Marla burst into Ted's office.

"You're late," he pronounced without turning from his computer.

"I think you're going to want to bump the 'Sunday Profile' to a two-page spread," she announced breathlessly.

"And I think you're nuts," he mumbled.

"I've got a real-live pictorial exclusive on a real-live hero in action. I call her the 'Charleston mermaid.' "

Ted swiveled in his chair and targeted her over the tops of his bifocals. "This had better be good."

With feelings of pride and triumph, Marla spread the proofsheets across his desk. Never in a million years would she have dreamed her ticket to a feature would turn out to be Catherine Winslow.

Five days after her rescue of Kenny Black, Catherine found herself standing before Charleston's city council. The hearing chamber was cavernous, its vintage eaves and hardwood floors reflecting a solemn echo. The nine-member council was ensconced on an elevated platform, which Catherine hardly thought fair, but she did her best to ignore the fact that they seemed to be looking down from Olympus.

It was only through the grace of Marla's newspaper story that she'd been granted audience, and she was trying hard not to be unnerved by the idea of speaking out. Pausing as she drew near the end of her carefully rehearsed speech, Catherine reminded herself that she had just this one shot. If she couldn't gain the council's support here and now, the idea that had mushroomed into a personal cause over the past several days would cease to exist.

"Ladies and gentlemen of the council," she resumed, "the city owns the shoreline and the dock, which at present provide a picturesque view for tenants like me. What I suggest is that it could provide much more. With a little work this piece of shoreline could become a haven. With a little instruction, which I'm happy to volunteer, this project could safeguard lives."

The heavily jowled Councilman Rudd leaned forward. "I'm sure I speak for the entire council when I say that your actions this past Saturday were most impressive, Miss Winslow. But are you *legally* qualified to oversee such a program as you suggest?"

"My credentials are detailed in the proposal before you, Councilman. I received private swim instruction and coaching for eight years, and although my certification requires updating, I've been fully trained in lifesaving. Also, I've just enrolled in a Red Cross course on CPR. I'll be certified in both by the end of the month."

With lifting brows the councilman settled back in his chair.

"If there are no further questions," Catherine went on, "I'd like to thank you for your time and leave you with a parting thought. These children are among the less fortunate of Charleston. They could use a break, and in this instance it would cost their home city very little to give them one."

Her statement echoed and died. Painful moments elapsed before one of the nine came to his feet and began to applaud. Catherine looked swiftly to his nameplate: Councilman Eliot Reynolds . . . of the fine old blue-blooded Charleston Reynolds . . . youngest official of the group . . . rising Republican star recently nominated to run for the state senate in November.

The rest of the council followed his lead, rose to their feet, and joined the ovation. Flooded with relief, Catherine tendered a shaky smile to the illustrious assembly, her gaze gradually narrowing on the man who had turned the tide with his endorsement.

Clean-cut and impeccably attired, Eliot Reynolds was tall, dark, handsome, and long recognized as one of Charleston's most eligible bachelors. Catherine's eyes widened as he winked down at her from the Olympic platform.

She left the council chamber with the light-headed feeling of walking on air. The hearing had gone better than she'd dared to hope, but that wasn't the reason behind the thrumming heartbeat that struck from time to time through the rest of the day. That night as Catherine lay in bed, her unbridled thoughts hovered on those last few minutes before the council, the memory of a handsome face and seductive wink hastening her dream.

The Frenchman's hands caressed her naked back while his tongue roamed her mouth. Planting her palms on his chest, Nicki tore away from his lips and pushed up to a straddling position.

They moved as one, rider and stallion, their rhythm building with the intensity of their drive. Her mind took flight, and she was home, thundering across the green fields of the Big Island upcountry—the sun pouring over her body, the wind sweeping past her face, the churning muscles of a mount between her legs. When her climax came, it was with a gush of breath flavored by the salty taste of the Pacific.

"Mon Dieu!" Jacques exclaimed, and Nicki felt his explosion deep inside her.

The rocking, gasping contractions gradually subsided. Shifting to her side, she rested her head on his shoulder as he moved a lethargic arm to encircle her.

"However do I manage not to expire of boredom in between these unpredictable sojourns of yours?" he mumbled.

She lazily chuckled. Jacques DuPree was the fourth son of one of the wealthiest families in the French wine country. While his older brothers resided in ancestral splendor at the family chateau in Alsace, Jacques preferred the bohemian setting of an artist's loft in Paris, where he had no responsibilities whatever and was free to immerse himself in the art world that he loved.

He grew his dark hair to his shoulders, dabbled with painting, and was known for throwing some of the most extravagant parties in the city. Nicki had no doubt there was a constant line at his door of hopeful demoiselles.

"I'm sure you manage to fill your time *somehow,*" she replied.

Running his free hand over her short locks, Jacques cupped the side of her face and proceeded to study her in the manner of one examining a portrait.

"In this light your hair is like a halo of moonbeams," he quietly declared. "And your eyes as deeply blue as midnight sky."

"Pretty words," Nicki commented with a smile. "But I believe it's customary for the man to employ that kind of talk *before* the seduction."

Jacques took on an injured look. "I'm trying to be serious."

"Why? We're not good at that, either one of us."

He pursed his lips. "I've said this before, and I say it again now. I'd like to see more of you, Nicki. We met four years ago, and in all that time we've been together a total of only four weeks tacked onto the end of your mountain-climbing adventures in the Alps. Four weeks in as many years."

"Ah, but what a *memorable* four weeks."

"After you leave, I feel as though you were never really here, as though I've rendezvoused with a temptress conjured from some magical place—out of my reach, but never my thoughts."

"If I were around more often, I imagine the magic would wear off *tout de suite*," Nicki quipped.

"Sometimes," Jacques returned with the sharp arch of a brow, "I think I should pinch you to make certain you are real." With that he reached down and gave her bottom a heartfelt European pinch.

"Ow!" she complained, and huffily brushed his hand away. "I'm real enough to know when a cheeky Frenchman tweaks me on the buns."

As he lay back on the pillow and laughed, Nicki climbed out of bed and picked a path across the sprawling loft—which was strewn with canvases, easels, and hastily discarded clothing—to the bank of windows affording an artist's prized north light.

"The sun's coming up," she announced, and hugged herself against a shiver as a draft chilled her naked skin.

The April dawn was heralded by a spring shower that muted the rising sun. Rain drizzled across the city, blurring the lines of monuments and the River Seine, painting landmarks in the watery pastels of a sidewalk artist. Jacques came up behind her and enfolded them in the silken warmth of the bedcovers.

"Nice view, eh?" he said at her ear.

"Mm-hmmm. You know, back home it's still yesterday. The concept of time differences is always so difficult for me to fathom."

"Do you miss it so much? This 'back home' *cow ranch* of yours?"

"That's *cattle* ranch," Nicki corrected in an amused tone. "And yes, I do miss it. After all, I've been on the continent for nearly three months now."

"But with *me* for only a couple of days," Jacques chided.

Turning in his embrace, Nicki tipped her head and smiled up at him. "Eight days qualifies as more than a couple."

"What does that matter? It's not enough. It never is. Must it be *aujourd'hui*? Must you leave today?"

"In a word, *oui*," Nicki answered, and, reaching around Jacques, soundly pinched him on his bare behind. With a quick laugh he pulled her close, captured her chin, and bent toward her.

"Au revoir, cherie," he murmured.

"Be seeing you," Nicki started to whisper, but the words were lost as the Frenchman's mouth covered hers.

Chapter Three

Clasping her shoulder bag in one hand, her camera in the other, Marla hurried along the sunny sidewalk.

"Damn car," she muttered. The damn thing had died some ten or twelve blocks back. She shouldn't be surprised. The flashy sports car Daddy bought her years ago, when he still had money, had never run right. And nowadays she had to pour a can of oil in it every fifty miles to keep it running.

One day, when her career got off the ground, she'd have a new car. But for now, she was struggling, and just when she had a gut feeling that the break she'd been waiting for was under way, she was running late.

Surprising even the media, who were accustomed to fancy footwork, Councilman Reynolds had put personal steam behind the clinic proposition and had set wheels in racing motion. Scarcely a week had passed since Catherine's appearance before the council, and yet first thing this morning Reynolds's publicity people had notified the press of the afternoon's formal groundbreaking for "Waterfront Clinic." Marla had badgered Ted into giving her the assignment.

And now I'm late, she thought once more as she rounded the corner where Catherine's town house building presided. A festive scene greeted her. Reynolds's committee had done it up right. Strings of brightly colored flags outlined a sandy area where a few dozen people milled. A bunch of yellow balloons decorated the face of the old dock, beside which an assortment of bulldozers and trucks were parked, seemingly poised and waiting.

As Marla crossed the lane, she saw Councilman Reynolds

step forward and lift his hands for attention. Reaching the beach, she broke into a run toward the crowd. There was a ripple of applause, and Marla saw that Catherine was walking over to join Reynolds.

Marla moved swiftly around the group to a spot by the water's edge. Dropping heedlessly to one knee on the moist sand, she raised her camera and focused on Reynolds and Catherine. The contrast couldn't have been better. The blonde was wearing a simple sleeveless dress of rich blue color; the raven-haired councilman, a crisp white shirt and dark trousers. Beyond them a bulldozer provided a dramatic backdrop suggesting modern progress; beside them the balloons supplied a celebratory note. It was a great shot.

Marla zoomed in a little tighter and started clicking as the councilman displayed a silver chain sporting a lifeguard whistle. He lifted it over Catherine's head, his gesture drawing another round of applause.

The groundbreaking continued with the symbolic first shovel of sand being moved by a joint effort of Catherine and the councilman. After that a fellow council member stepped up to shake Reynolds's hand, and Catherine seemingly seized the opportunity to escape the spotlight. Marla watched from a distance as she attempted to skirt around the throng, but was quickly waylaid.

Since the interview, the two of them had gotten together several times, and each time Marla liked Catherine more. There was a rich quality of Southern grace about her, but beneath the refined soft-spokenness lay a sharp wit. Sometimes she could be extremely funny. Still, Catherine was not at all the type to relish the public eye now riveted on her. *Hang tough, kid,* Marla thought as the crowd closed ranks about her.

Marla's attention returned to the groundbreaking scene, where Councilman Reynolds was surrounded by a cluster of well-wishers. Her gaze narrowed on the man, tracing with appreciative interest his lean physique and groomed appearance. Eliot Reynolds was one of the best-looking men in town *and* had some of the best credentials. It was said that the governor himself had his eye on Eliot Reynolds.

Dusting off the sandy knee of her slacks, Marla adjusted

her lightweight sweater so that the neckline showed cleavage. The top was a lime-green shade that matched her eyes. More importantly, its clinging fabric called attention to her ample bosom.

As Councilman Reynolds bade smiling farewells to constituents, she ambled his way, watching him closely and noting with satisfaction when she caught his eye. Finally, the last of his attendants moved on. Reynolds glanced in her direction, and Marla walked up to him with a deliberately slow and sexy gait.

"Good afternoon, Councilman Reynolds."

"Afternoon, Marla."

"You know me? How?"

"Charleston is a small town. Most of us natives know each other one way or another."

"I remember you from college days," Marla said. "Sometimes when you were home from Harvard, you dated a sorority sister of mine, Connie Sherwood."

He rocked back on his heels. "Oh, yes. Connie. She was fun."

"So am I," Marla returned.

Eliot smiled. "So I've heard," he responded.

"Oh? What, exactly, have you heard? And from whom?"

Eliot's smile broadened as he tucked his hands in his pockets. "I'm over at the newspaper fairly often, and I've seen you there. The word is, Marla Sutton is an ambitious photographer who's got her heart set on a byline, *and* . . . she likes to party."

"Right on both counts." Shifting her weight, Marla rolled her hips and watched his gaze travel down her body. "So?" she prodded.

"So, it's Friday. Maybe you'd like to party with me tonight at my Kiawah beach house."

Marla's spirits soared. "Well, now," she purred. "That sounds mighty inviting."

"The only thing is, it'll have to start with nightcaps. I'm afraid I have plans for dinner."

"I guess I could settle for a nightcap. *This* time."

"Good. Then meet me at the Kiawah entrance at eleven. I'll try not to be any later than that."

"Try hard," Marla remarked with a wink, and drew a quick grin before the man glanced irritatingly at his watch.

"Sorry to cut out so fast," he said then. "But I've got to be across town in a short while, and I need to say good-bye to the Charleston mermaid before I go. See you to-night, huh?"

With that Councilman Reynolds turned away, and Marla couldn't help but feel a sting of jealousy as he strode purposefully in Catherine's direction.

The silver-haired lady planted a hand on Catherine's arm. "I've been saying it for years. Someone *must* do some-thing about that waterfront. There have been other acci-dents, you know."

"No, I didn't know—" Catherine started to murmur.

"Why, not more than ten years ago there was a dreadful incident—oh, but here comes our handsome councilman!"

Promptly releasing Catherine's arm, the chattering woman stepped swiftly past and extended both pudgy hands, which Eliot Reynolds smilingly grasped in greeting. "Hello, Mrs. Cannon."

"My dear Eliot, I *must* tell you how wonderful it is—what you and this lovely girl are doing together." Without missing a beat, the woman somehow managed to release one of the councilman's hands, latch on to Catherine, and pull her close.

"Goodness," she added with a titter. "That sounded leading, didn't it? But after all, you *have* been running loose too long, young man. It's time you settled down, and you could do worse than our pretty heroine, here."

"I'll keep that in mind," Eliot Reynolds replied while Catherine's cheeks caught fire. They were still burning a minute later when the woman took her leave. Catherine cast a mortified glance to the tall, dark, and handsome councilman, who was gazing at her with a hint of a grin that only piqued her discomfort.

"Are you happy with the way Waterfront Clinic is going so far?" he asked.

"Very happy," she managed to reply in gratifyingly smooth fashion. "How did you manage to make this hap-pen so quickly?"

He shrugged. "I called in a few favors."

"I don't know how to thank you for all your support."

"*I* know how you can thank me."

Catherine met the man's dark eyes and experienced a trilling rush up her spine. "Have supper with me tonight," he added. "I've got a late-night meeting, but if I pick you up at six, we'll still have time for a nice dinner."

She should have been elated. Instead, Catherine was flooded with anxiety as the idea of a *date* conjured dark memories—the oppressive parlor of Winslow House . . . Aunt Sybil hovering nearby . . . and a painfully awkward boy who didn't want to be part of the dismal parody of a mating ritual any more than Catherine did.

She'd been kissed with passion by only one man—an amorous poet named David Sotherby who was passing through Charleston on a book-signing tour and ended up corraling her in the back of Ann Marie's bookshop. Catherine's entire range of experience with men consisted of a half hour of petting, and yet here was one of Charleston's most accomplished and sought-after bachelors—

He startled her out of her thoughts by reaching up and taking hold of the forgotten whistle hanging around her neck.

"Mrs. Cannon is right," he said as he cradled the ornament in long fingers. "You're an awfully pretty lifeguard. I might be tempted to get into trouble just to have you come after me." Catherine glanced aside. "So are you free to celebrate tonight?"

"Celebrate," she repeated, at which point the councilman laughed and released the whistle so that it dropped with a *plink!* to the bodice of her blue dress.

"Celebrate," he confirmed. "Surely you must know the concept."

Catherine's gaze slowly lifted. "What if I don't?" The perfect politician's smile faded as Eliot Reynolds stared into her eyes.

"Then it's time you learned," he replied.

When the doorbell rang at six on the nose, Catherine had changed clothes a half-dozen times, finally deciding on a simple, cap-sleeved sheath in navy and white stripes, which she dressed up with a strand of pearls. Eliot was his typical debonair self in a charcoal-gray suit and silk tie.

"We look good together," he pronounced when he saw

her, and Catherine tried to keep her lips from shaking as she smiled.

It didn't help her nerves that passersby openly stared as he handed her into a silver BMW. Eliot, on the other hand, apparently was accustomed to rousing such notice. He didn't bat an eye as he escorted her, with a firm hand at her elbow, to a reserved table at Magnolias, one of the city's finest restaurants. A dozen early diners were present at scattered tables, and the newly arrived couple became their unquestioned focal point as the waiter delivered an ice bucket with a bottle of champagne.

She'd expected a stilted night with the painful silences of old, but found instead that Eliot was shockingly easy to be with. Throughout an elegant dinner he kept the conversation lively with talk of Waterfront Clinic, which had claimed the position of a pet project. At one point he called the waiter over, requested pencil and paper, and sketched a rendering of the architect's plan.

"The builder has guaranteed me that it will be ready for opening the day after school dismisses for the summer."

"I'm truly amazed by the way you've managed to pull this together," Catherine said.

"It all comes with knowing who's hungry. The builder just relocated here from up north. He wanted the contract, and in order to get it he had to pull out the stops—which is good news for me and you. How about it? Will you be ready to conduct your first lesson in a month?"

She joined him in a smiling look. "Don't worry. I'll be ready to hold up my end of the bargain."

The evening flowed along uninterrupted until the waiter inquired about dessert. "I'm afraid we won't have time for dessert tonight," Eliot answered. "You'd better bring the check."

And so it was ten o'clock, and the night was over. Despite the occasional smiling glance he tossed her way as he drove her home, Catherine was again beset by her earlier case of nerves. A late appointment on a Friday night didn't sound very plausible. Maybe it was just the sort of polite excuse a popular bachelor such as Eliot Reynolds built into a first date—like an escape hatch.

When they parked beside her building, he came around and helped her out of the BMW, but didn't continue to hold her hand. The same mannerly grip of the elbow that had escorted her into Magnolias now steered her through the courtyard and up the stairs.

"I'd ask if you'd like to come in for coffee," she said. "But I know you can't stay." Propping an arm in the portal, he casually blocked her entrance.

"Next time," he replied, and proceeded to look down at her in a way that jolted her heartbeat. Catherine was suddenly aware of the sensual fragrance of masculine cologne. "Did you enjoy yourself tonight, Miss Valedictorian?" he added.

Her brows lifted. "I haven't thought of that in ages. How did you know?"

"That's just the smallest part of what I know. Let's see, you were valedictorian your senior year in high school, won an academic scholarship to College of Charleston, graduated Phi Beta Kappa with a bachelor of arts in literature."

"You certainly seem to have done your homework," she said after a startled instant.

"I make it a habit to find out about things that interest me."

Catherine searched the handsome lines of his face. "That's what perplexes me. I can't imagine what there is about me that you could possibly find interesting."

He gave a short laugh that ended with a shake of his head. "Surely you jest." As she continued to peruse him with a serious expression, his look of levity drained.

"Catherine Winslow," he said, drawing out the name in drawling, ruminating fashion. "Last of the fine old Winslow line dating back to the revolution. She grew up motherless in a Charleston landmark, devoting her time and energies to her ailing father. No wild parties. No indiscretions. Not even a traffic ticket. There isn't a single blemish on her history . . . like a fairy-tale princess growing up in a tower. Untouched. Unspoiled. Perfect. If I'd known what was waiting at the top of that tower, I'd have climbed up long ago. What are you doing Sunday?"

"Working," Catherine answered with a startled smile.

"On a Sunday?"

"If I'm going to be spending my days at Waterfront Clinic in a month, I'd better work while I can. I've got a

deadline in seven weeks." She caught her breath as Eliot
lifted a hand to her cheek.

"Really? What kind of deadline?"

"The manuscript of my new novel."

He leaned close, his fingers caressing the side of her face.
"Even authors have to eat. Have lunch with me at my
parents' house on Sunday. I'd like you to met them. I'd
like *them* to meet *you.*"

"Your parents?" she managed.

"Mm-hmmm," he whispered. "And I won't take no for
an answer." He kissed her—his lips warm, firm, and ex-
ceedingly respectful when compared to David Sotherby.
Expecting the heavy tongue play she recalled from that
experience, Catherine was surprised when Eliot brought the
kiss to a chaste close and backed away.

"I'll pick you up at noon on Sunday," he stated, and
seconds later had disappeared down the stairwell.

Catherine went inside and leaned against the door, tingling from head to toe as she replayed the events of the
night—the lively conversation over champagne, the sweet
kiss at the door, the unforeseen invitation to Sunday
luncheon. . . .

It sure beat hell out of the Winslow House parlor.

A smile spread over her face as she walked into her
bedroom. Maybe, just maybe, she was about to outgrow
Catherine of Legare once and for all. Curling up on the
covers, she slipped unexpectedly into sleep and dreamed of
flying over sunlit hills with the salty air of the sea strong
in her face.

Afternoon sunlight lay like a golden carpet across the
grassy upcountry as Nicki rode toward the ridge that had
been the halfway mark of ranchland rides for as long as
she could remember. The island pony, a chestnut new to
the stables, had the sturdy legs of a bloodline bred to the
rugged diversity of Hawaiian terrain. His canter was
smooth and surefooted, the Pacific air rushing past Nicki's
face cool and fresh.

In the distance cattle grazed, attended by a pair of *paniolos.* She recognized one of the ponies as the black and
white pinto belonging to the foreman's son, Kimo. Shifting
the reins to a single practiced hand, Nicki waved.

Kimo responded by sweeping his hat from his head in salute and pulling the pinto into a theatrical hind-leg rear. He was a superior horseman and a fierce competitor on the radio circuit. It was tradition that Kimo represented Palmer ranch at the huge Fourth of July event in Waimea—which was basically a Parker Ranch town—and succeeded in putting the Parker *paniolos* to shame in their own backyard.

Nicki grinned as she looked ahead once more. There was a good-natured rivalry between the Big Island's two largest ranches, and nowhere was it more evident than the Waimea rodeo. The ranches had been neighbors for generations, their histories stemming back to the early nineteenth century. In 1809, King Kamehameha I granted an upcountry homestead to American John Palmer Parker—no relation to the British adventurer, Barrymore Palmer, who voyaged to the Big Island five years later, fell in love with the lush expanses of the upcountry, and promptly secured a hundred thousand acres northwest of the Parker site.

Parker's son, Samuel, a Hawaiian legend, forged his father's homestead into a cattle kingdom that became the state's biggest producer of beef. Palmer's son, William, established a thriving cattle business that soon took a firm second place; but he also diversified, developing a range of interests in addition to ranching. Parker Ranch went on to become the largest family-owned ranch in the United States. Palmer Ranch became the nucleus of today's multi-million-dollar conglomerate, Palmer International.

Reaching her destination atop the sloping ridge, Nicki reined in the pony and took a sweeping look at the panoramic vista of unfolding grassland, bordered far to the west by a smoky line of mountain, marked in the distant east by a precise white pattern of fences, corrals, and ranch buildings. Her neighboring giant to the south might be bigger, but she'd always thought the manicured expanses of Palmer Ranch more grand.

She peered leeward, where the white house presided. A blend of antebellum and tropical architectures, it featured elegant columns, porticos, and breezeways, and was noted for its rear terrace and hand-tiled swimming pool. Flowering grounds merged with back lawns stretching to a wall of cliffs overlooking the vivid Pacific. Home was so uniquely beautiful. Why she'd felt the impulse to leave it so often over the years, she couldn't say. Perhaps the reason was as simple as restless blood.

"The Palmers have always been adventurers," Austin was fond of commenting—generally just before he took off to hunt some exotic quarry or climb some mountain in a far corner of the world . . . often taking his equally adventurous niece along with him.

Nicki's attention hovered on the remote house as she imagined the people within. Her uncle was probably ushering in the cocktail hour on the lanai, Malia puttering in the kitchen, Melrose wrapping up the day in his ranch-site office before ambling to the house to join Austin for a drink. God, it was good to be home.

Nudging the pony to a moseying walk, she moved along the ridge. Her gaze skimmed over the pastureland, eventually lighting once more on the cattle and Kimo. She thought of riding over, then realized that his partner must be his devoted companion, Peni.

Kimo was six feet worth of muscle—his hair and skin not so dark as a full-blooded Hawaiian's, his blue eyes testifying that he was *hapa haole,* or half white. These meager influences were the only bequests of his European mother, who died when he was a boy. Kimo was his father's son, growing up in the Hawaiian village of the foothills, and following in the tradition of forefathers who had made their living as Palmer ranch *paniolos* for generations.

Peni was from the same village. A full-blooded Hawaiian, her close-cropped hair was black as a raven's wing, and her stature and girth nearly matched that of Kimo, whom she'd always tagged after like a puppy. Having grown up with four older brothers who'd paved the way as cowboys, Peni held the distinction of being the only female *paniolo* on the ranch. She could ride as well as any man, and probably could hold her own in a fight with one.

As children, Nicki, Peni, and Kimo had played together in and around the stables, and learned to ride like the wind. It wasn't until teenhood dawned, and Nicki went off to finishing school in Europe, that the difference in their stations had risen like a great wall—which was further fortified as Austin began taking her along on his wide-ranging travels about the globe.

Now, whenever Nicki was home, she made a point of

renewing the childhood bond with Kimo, who remained
friendly. Peni, on the other hand, took no pains to hide her
hostility. She was in love with Kimo, and had been for
years—although the handsome, *paniolo* bachelor seemed as
blind to her adoration as he was to the bristling jealousy
Peni displayed whenever he and Nicki came within a pasture's length of each other.

And so it was that Nicki momentarily hesitated before
riding their way. *Hell,* she thought. Since returning from
Europe, she hadn't so much as said hello to Kimo. If Peni
couldn't handle it, that was too damn bad. Planting her
heels in the pony's sides, Nicki cantered in their direction.

An unconscious smile spread across Kimo's face. "Nicki's
coming," he announced.

"I've got eyes," Peni dourly countered.

Kimo gave her a frowning glance. "Nicki doesn't spend
much time at the ranch anymore. Maybe you could be
agreeable for once."

"Why bother? Your father's my boss. Not *her*."

"How about for old times' sake, then? You and Nicki
were friends once, remember?"

"Barely," Peni muttered.

"I don't get it. What have you got against her?"

"Men are so dumb."

"Enlighten me."

Peni arched a black brow as she perused him. "All right,
then," she said. "The Palmers are worth millions."

"I know that."

"And one day it will all be hers."

"I know that, too."

"Nicki's out of your league. Always has been. Always
will be."

"You've reminded me of that often enough," Kimo
snapped.

"Then why do you keep mooning over her like a lovesick calf?"

He produced a tight smile that passed almost before it
formed. "I don't *moon* over Nicki. She's an old friend, and
I'm glad to see her. That's all."

"Is that what you tell yourself? You go out with a lot of

girls, Kimo, but it doesn't mean anything because deep down you want Nicki, and nobody else measures up."

Kimo's face took on the dark look of a thundercloud. "You and I are old friends, too, Peni. But some lines shouldn't be crossed. This is one of them."

"Fine!" Peni fired back. "Drool all you like! Just don't expect me to hang around and watch!"

With a hard yank on the reins, she galloped away, kicking up a column of dust in her wake. A scowl furrowed Kimo's brows until he turned and settled his attention on Nicki once more. She sat easy in the saddle as her pony raced his way—her windblown hair shining bright in the sun . . . no brighter, he imagined, than the smile on the face that would soon come into focus.

As he pictured her, Kimo's scowling expression lifted and a fledgling grin took its place. Nicki had always been able to make him smile faster than anyone alive. Coming into her presence was like stepping out of the shadows and into the sunlight. She affected him like no other woman. But Peni was right. Nicki Palmer was out of his league. It was good that she stayed away from the ranch so much. During those times Kimo almost forgot the way his blood quickened when she was around. During those times he didn't lie awake in bed, aching with longing, like he would tonight.

Ten years ago he'd thought it was something he'd outgrow. But now that he was almost thirty, Kimo knew the truth. The older he got, the stronger his passion became, and the greater the pain of fighting it down. Sometimes he wondered how it would all end.

"Aloha," Nicki greeted as she brought the pony to a smart halt.

"Same to you," Kimo replied, his study traveling covertly over her. She was wearing jeans that molded to her legs, and a white top that bared the golden skin of her arms. The shock of short, platinum-blond hair—which had inspired an islandwide trend some years ago—settled in wisps across her forehead and about her flushed cheeks. His memories never did her justice.

"Still breaking all the *wahines'* hearts?" she teased.

Kimo chuckled. "A few here and there. How about you? Still blazing a trail across the seven continents?"

"I suppose I left a few smoldering embers," she returned.

I'll bet, Kimo thought, but let the comment pass. She had a notorious reputation as a femme fatale, and he'd bite off his tongue before he let her know that his heart was among the many she'd carelessly conquered.

"What do you think of the new pony?" he asked.

Nicki reached down and patted the horse's neck. "He's great. I'd wager he could give that pinto of yours a run for the money."

"Let's not get carried away," Kimo challenged with a grin.

"Let's not get *cocky,*" she retorted. "How about a race to the stableyard? *Unless,* that is, you're afraid I'll show you up."

Kimo tugged his hat brim to his brow, though he continued to grin. "Go ahead, then. I'll give you a head start."

"I don't need a head start."

"I'll be the judge of that. After all, I taught you to ride."

"You did *not* teach—"

Kimo interrupted her with a rousing "*Hiyaah!*" accompanied by a whack to her pony's backside. The chestnut took off like a streak of lightning. Kimo broke into laughter as Nicki shrieked something back at him. He let her get fifty yards across the pasture before unleashing his speedy pinto.

They were halfway to the ranch when he caught up to her. Glancing aside, Nicki stuck out her tongue. Once again Kimo laughed, and raced the rest of the way with a smile on his face.

Chapter Four

Lifting the receiver away from his ear, Melrose frowned across the top of his desk. "Yes, Ed. I understand," he broke in finally. "But initial reports are often misleading. I suggest we wait for a full evaluation from our people in Columbia."

Ed launched into an anxious listing of the most dire possibilities that could come to pass. "You didn't get to be president of Pacific B and T by panicking at the first sign of trouble," Melrose said when he finally paused. "I'll talk to Austin, and when we get the facts, the three of us will decide what to do. Until then I suggest you sit tight and keep quiet."

Hanging up the phone, Melrose flopped back in the comforting leather armchair. From beneath furling brows, the CEO of Palmer International scanned the airy rooms, which were more like an apartment than an office suite. Sunlight sifted in golden shafts through louvered windows; from beyond them came the familiar, distant sounds of the *paniolos* returning from a day on the range. *So peaceful,* Melrose thought, especially when compared to the teeming bustle of his Honolulu office.

In the old days he'd flown back and forth to Oahu on a regular basis. Now, with a fax to keep him in touch, he hardly journeyed to company headquarters anymore. His ranch-site office suited him better, and during the dozen years since his wife, Maureen, passed away, it had become more like home than the empty house in Hilo.

Seventy years old. The phrase still seemed to have nothing to do with him, even though his belly had broadened and his silver hair turned mostly white, even though his colleagues of equal age had retired years ago and now spent their days playing golf or yachting. Melrose had no

such aspirations. The quiet splendor of the upcountry was
what called to him. He'd feathered himself quite a retirement nest here at the ranch, and had even thought ahead
to the days when he'd watch Nicki's children grow up
here. . . .

Funny how images that had taken years to form could
turn to smoke in the minutes of a phone call.

Pushing out of the leather chair, Melrose left the out-
building and started along the flower-decked trail to the
main house. Cocktails on the lanai, featuring Malia's hors
d'oeuvres, were a tradition at the ranch. It was half-past
five, and he had no doubt he'd find Austin ensconced on
the fan-cooled veranda.

Melrose thought back to the day three years ago when
Austin returned from safari in South America. While there,
he'd become friendly with a wealthy Colombian widow,
among whose holdings was an emerald mine she wanted
to "unload." *A once-in-a-lifetime opportunity,* Austin had
pronounced with shining eyes.

One of Palmer International's subsidiaries was a producer of coral jewelry. Manufacturing facilities were up and
running. *We can snap up the mine at a steal and use the
coral operation to market pieces. The profit margin will be
staggering. All we need to get started is a little creative
financing.* . . .

As he remembered Austin's words, Melrose grimaced. It
had been a good pitch—good enough to entice both himself
and Ed Coleman into the scheme. That's how Austin was.
He had flashes of brilliance, and the idea of a big score
gave him a charge. Other than that he had no interest in
business—preferring instead to live his life as a thrill-seek-
ing hunter and mountain climber, traveling the world first-
class on the stipend bequeathed by his parents and rejecting
the responsibilities that would have befallen him as a family man. . . .

Rounding the mammoth cluster of banyan trees that cast
a wave of shade toward the lanai, Melrose scaled the steps
to the open porch and found Austin at the patio table in
sneakers, shorts, and shirtsleeves, cocktail glass in hand.
Maybe that's why he looks the way he does, Melrose
thought as he took in Austin's firm, suntanned physique

and wavy, sun-streaked hair. He was nearly fifty-one, but looked ten years younger.

"Hey, old man," he tossed. "You're late."

"I guess it won't do me any harm to be starting on my first Scotch instead of my second." Melrose poured himself a drink at the bar and sat down in his usual chair. Taking a sip, he gazed morosely across the table. "I just had a call from Ed Coleman."

"Oh? What did our friendly banker have to say?"

"There was an earthquake in northwest Colombia last night." Halting in the midst of raising his glass, Austin looked swiftly across the table. "The good news," Melrose continued, "is that everyone had gone home. No lives were lost."

"And the bad news?"

"First reports say the mine is a shambles." If Austin's pleasant mien faltered at all, it was for only an instant.

"That's disappointing," he commented.

Melrose's bushy brows lifted. "Now, *there's* an understatement. Ed was about to come apart at the seams."

"I'll give him a call tomorrow."

"You can't fix this with a phone call, Austin. It's over."

"Nothing's over."

"Without profits we've been counting on, we can't replace—"

"Everything will be all right," Austin broke in. "The emeralds are there. All we need is some time to rebuild—"

"But there *is* no time," Melrose interrupted in turn. "Not the kind we need. Hell, it took a year to get the mine up to a satisfactory production level in the first place, and that was *before* it was leveled by an earthquake."

Austin tendered a smile that was as hard as the sudden glint in his blue eyes. "The question is, are we going to let old Mother Nature beat us?"

"I'd say she's done a fair job at it, yeah."

"You accept defeat too readily," Austin jeered. "I never enter a high-stakes game without an ace up my sleeve. Just tell the boys in Colombia to start rebuilding. Everything will work out."

Melrose studied him with piercing eyes. "You're either very smart or very dumb. I wonder which."

Austin offered a cocky grin. "Do you really care as long as I remedy the situation?"

Melrose gradually succumbed to a smile. "I guess not," he replied as Malia glided up to the table with a platter of iced shellfish accompanied by an assortment of dips.

"Is that red stuff the spicy dip I like?" Melrose asked.

"What do you think?" she returned.

He reached for a plump shrimp. "You're too good to me, Malia."

"She's good to *all* of us," Austin said with a bold once-over of the woman beside him. When she came to work at the ranch at the age of eighteen, Malia had been lithe as a willow. She may have filled out since then, but she was still one of the prettiest women on the island—the long hair coiled atop her head still black as ebony, her skin as smooth and tawny as a skein of caramel.

"You're a lucky devil," Melrose declared.

Austin met his eyes and knew he was referring to Malia. "There's no such thing as luck, old man. Good things come to those who go after what they want."

The three of them looked up as a couple of ponies barreled into the stableyard across the lawn. A kicked-up cloud of dust obscured the forms of Nicki and Kimo as they dismounted, though the sound of their laughter rippled clearly to the lanai.

Melrose chuckled. "Nicki certainly seems happy to be home."

"Kimo's none too displeased about it, either," Austin observed in a neutral tone. It would have been poor form to point out the obvious with his Hawaiian mistress of thirty years standing beside him, but the fact was that despite Hawaii's Americanized status, in the heart of the islands, barriers continued to exist between working-class natives and upper-crust *haoles*.

Kimo simply wasn't an acceptable companion for the heiress of the Palmer empire. But the breach would mean little to wild, headstrong Nicki if she took a notion to have a fling with a *paniolo*. Austin made a mental note to talk to Kimo's father, just before his reverie was shattered by the screech of peeling tires.

"Damn!" Melrose sputtered as he recognized Peni's rusted-out truck speeding up the service drive. "Good thing nobody's on that road. She'd have mowed 'em down. What's wrong with Peni?"

"Good question," Austin chimed in.

"She has a violent temper and a passion to match," Malia stated. The two men looked up at her with questioning expressions. "Passion for Kimo," Malia explained. "One day Peni's jealousy will beget great trouble, I'm afraid."

"The wisewoman of the island speaks," Austin remarked with a teasing grin.

"Make fun if you like, but mark my words. Peni's heart is seething like that of a volcano. And you know what they say . . ." Trailing off, Malia looked into the distance just as Peni's truck crested a hill and passed out of sight.

"All right, I'll bite," Melrose supplied with revived good humor. "What *do* they say?"

"Heaven has no rage like love to hatred turned," Malia softly quoted. "Nor hell a fury like a woman scorned."

Peni drove directly from the ranch to the pool hall, started chugging beer, and managed to put away a half dozen in little more than an hour. By the time she left, the village streets were deserted, everyone presumably having retired for supper.

"Fool," she muttered to herself as she drove along. Why had she allowed herself to hope Kimo would show up at his usual haunt? She'd known he wouldn't be there from the minute she saw Nicki riding toward them in the pasture. He was probably locked inside his apartment at the moment, like some lovesick beast retreating to his den to lick his wounds.

Parking haphazardly in the side yard of the *hale* that had been home all her life, Peni banged her way through the front door. Her mother and father were long dead, her brothers long departed from the islands to find their fortunes elsewhere. The house was empty, silent, and hot as hell.

Peeling her shirt over her head, she strode to the bathroom and took a cool shower. When she emerged, she toweled her short hair and caught sight of herself in the mirror on the back of the door. Tossing the towel aside, she faced the nude reflection. Her body was taut from the rigors of the outdoors, lines of muscle showing clearly in her arms and legs.

"A big, strapping girl," her father used to say, little knowing how much she hated being called "big" . . . little suspecting that once, just once, she longed to hear someone say she was pretty.

Her features were okay. It was her manner that was wrong. Maybe it had to do with the fact that her mother died young, leaving her to grow up in a household of men. She hadn't learned *"girl stuff."*

Peni's gaze scoured the rock-solid length of herself. With broad shoulders, firm breasts, and ample hips, she was a full size fourteen in pants, and a sixteen in shirts. It occurred to her that she'd make two of Nicki, who was probably a perfect size six—just the right size to make Kimo's mouth water.

A deep frown carved its way across Peni's brow. God, she hated Nicki for being pretty and feminine. She despised her for being the rich *haole* princess of the island. She detested her because everything came so damn easy—from being born into the lap of luxury, to horseback riding, mountain climbing, hang gliding, and whatever the hell else she decided to try.

Peni stared into the glittering black eyes of the reflection. But of all the reasons she had to hate, one struck so deeply that sometimes she couldn't breathe. Most of all she loathed Nicki for making Kimo want her.

You were friends once, his remembered words echoed.

In another lifetime, Peni silently answered. Now, when she thought of Nicki Palmer, all she felt was cold, writhing hatred—as though a wicked snake had crawled inside her and was coiling to strike.

The stretch of narrow two-lane road leading to Kiawah Island was lined with overhanging thicket and dark as pitch. Marla's eyes were trained on the beams of her headlights, though her mind was entrenched on the sunlit shore of the afternoon.

Once again Eliot and Catherine's smiling exchange played before her like a silent movie. Once again Marla saw herself wander over when Eliot left, only to find out that it was *Catherine* he'd just invited out for supper. *Catherine!*

Something had made Marla hold her tongue about the late-night date she'd made with the councilman. Maybe it was Catherine's damnably innocent blue eyes; maybe it was her own green-eyed monster. Even now the thought of being passed over for her demure friend made Marla feel like spitting nails.

Reaching spotlit markers that announced "Kiawah" in flowing script, she turned onto a private drive that curved lazily through grounds landscaped with palmetto and pampas. Up ahead a security gate spanned the drive. Beyond it sprawled the country club resort that had long been a haven of the well-to-do. A uniformed guard stepped out of the gatehouse as she slowed to a stop. When she announced that she was meeting Eliot Reynolds, she was briskly informed that "Mr. Reynolds" wasn't on the property; nor had he instructed them to expect a guest.

"I'm to meet him here at eleven o'clock," Marla replied with an edge in her voice. The guard gave her an assessing look.

"You're a few minutes early," he pronounced. "If you'd care to wait, you'll have to pull over to the shoulder."

Marla moved her car to the side of the road, her mood plummeting as time crawled by and she was forced to endure the guard's sidelong glances. Twenty minutes passed before a silver BMW rolled up beside her. Declining to get out of his car, Eliot lowered his passenger window and peered in her direction.

"Can I interest you in a nightcap?" he said.

"That's why I'm here," she returned in a lilting tone that masked a bristling urge to bite his head off.

"Follow me, then," he commanded, and scratched off toward the gatehouse. Shifting the cranky sports car into gear, Marla chugged up behind him just in time to see Eliot slip the guard a bill, at which point the guard waved them through. Like everything else about this late-night rendezvous, the gesture hit her wrong—as though Eliot were buying the guard's discretion or something. Marla pursed her lips as she followed the BMW through the gate.

The Kiawah Island development was huge and grand. They passed signs announcing golf courses and biking trails, as well as innumerable residential complexes, on their way to the established tip of the island, where Eliot finally turned onto a palm-lined drive that led up a hill to a massive house overlooking the beach.

This time he had the grace to approach the car and help her out. Marla's spirits lifted somewhat as he planted a firm arm about her waist and led her into the house—which featured a formal foyer with a black-and-white-tiled floor, a flying staircase to the second level, and richly upholstered furnishings that evoked the air of a mansion rather than a beach house.

"Nice place," Marla said, her quick gaze noting the antiques and objets d'art in the spacious room opening off the foyer.

"Thanks. It's been in the family for years. I'm the only one who comes out here anymore."

"Do you come out often?" she asked.

"Often enough to keep a cleaning lady and a stocked liquor cabinet." He started toward the ornately carved mahogany bar that monopolized the corner of the adjacent room. Marla followed and perched on a leather stool as he stepped behind the bar.

"What's your pleasure?" Eliot asked, his gaze dipping to her décolletage before lifting to her face. "If I had to guess, I'd say you're in the mood for tequila over the rocks."

Marla arched a brow. "Very good. Tequila is exactly what I'm in the mood for." He poured two hefty drinks and lifted his glass.

"To good times," he said, his gaze drifting once more to the cleavage revealed by her scoop-necked top. Marla's mood climbed another notch. She'd chosen the outfit carefully. It was a rich shade of purple that contrasted beautifully with her red hair. The top had a low neckline that enhanced her bosom; the matching short skirt showed off her legs. Feeling more like her confident self, Marla took a sip of tequila and eyed Eliot over her glass.

"I almost didn't come tonight," she remarked.

He took a healthy swallow before saying, "I didn't get any impression of hesitancy at the beach today."

"At the beach today, I didn't know you were on your way to invite my girlfriend to dinner."

He looked mildly surprised. "You and Catherine are friends?"

"Like you said, all us Charleston natives know each other one way or another."

"I assume you didn't tell her we were meeting tonight. Otherwise she'd have said something."

Marla's temper stirred anew. "No, I didn't tell her. Would it have mattered if I had?"

Eliot tendered a small smile. "It might have. You see, I have a plan for Catherine and a plan for you."

"What the hell is that supposed to mean?" Marla flared.

Setting down his glass, he strolled around the bar and came to stand beside her. Marla pivoted on the barstool to face him with a defiant look. Before she had time to react, he grabbed her by the arms, yanked her off the stool, and started kissing her, his mouth hard and demanding, forcing hers to open.

Marla pressed futilely against his chest. He captured her in his arms, one hand moving brazenly over her backside as he continued to ravage her lips. A spark of arousal flickered through her, then fanned to flame. Surrendering to his embrace, Marla started kissing him back. A moment later Eliot broke away.

"I'm in a position to give you something you want," he said.

"So I see," she breathlessly replied.

"But let's get one thing straight here and now—it's Catherine I'm after."

Marla's dreamy state of arousal promptly disintegrated. "What?"

"I'm the Republican candidate for state senate, and in November I fully intend to be moving to the state capital. Linking my name with Catherine Winslow can help me get there. The public is in love with the 'Charleston mermaid,' and I want her on my arm."

"But you want *me* in your bed, is that it?" Marla fired.

"The idea has possibilities."

"You want me to be your—what?—your *back-door piece*?"

Eliot grasped her chin none too gently. "What I want is for us to have our own private party. You didn't seem averse to the idea a minute ago."

"That was before I knew you were planning to parade around town with one of my friends."

"Catherine won't know. It will be our little secret."

Marla tried to yank away, but Eliot's fingers held fast to her jaw. "Why should I?" she challenged.

He bent down and ran his tongue over her lips. "I have a hunch we like the same things, Marla. And if you play your cards right, there might be more in this for you than a good time. I know all about you—that nasty business your father was involved in a few years back, for instance. Fraud, wasn't it?"

"He was acquitted," she blazed.

"But it took all the family money to get him off, didn't it?" Marla violently squirmed. Eliot responded by latching on to her wrist, leading her to an overstuffed couch, and pushing her down.

"And now his little girl is struggling to make it on her own," he went on, his black eyes shining as he sat down beside her. "Like I said, I'm in a position to give you something you want."

"Such as?" Marla warily prodded.

"My father and the publisher of the *Post* have been golfing buddies for years."

Casually lifting a hand, Eliot ran his palm down her throat and under the loose neck of her blouse. Marla gasped as he jerked the lace of her bra below the fullness of her breast, fastened his fingers about her nipple, and squeezed. A shameful shiver of pleasure spread from the spot.

"A word from the right source at the right time could get you that byline you're so hungry for," Eliot added. Shifting down on the couch, he replaced his fingers with his mouth, his teeth grazing her rigid nipple. Marla couldn't suppress a moan.

"Right time?" she rasped. "When might that be?"

"Let's just see how the night goes, shall we?" he mumbled as his hand crawled beneath her skirt. A short time later he jumped to his feet, dragging her with him, and started for the stairs. When she didn't move fast enough to suit him, he hoisted her over his shoulder and transported her to a cavernous bedroom.

Two raucous hours later Eliot fell asleep while Marla

remained stringently awake. Stealing into the neighboring bath, she closed the door, turned on the light, and examined her nakedness in the gilded mirror above the marbleized vanity. There were passion marks on her abdomen and breasts. And her nipples, as well as the flesh between her thighs, were raw from the abrasion of a day's growth of beard.

Her gaze rose to wildly tousled hair, and a mouth still ruddy from the bruising pressure of Eliot's. A slang phrase came to mind: *rough trade*. The distinguished councilman's lovemaking was more brutal than any she'd ever experienced. He controlled. He imprisoned. He violated. And he played to a dark side of her that had never been so aroused.

Plus he promised a byline. Marla studied the reflection of her green eyes, which appeared suddenly sly and smoky with the ways of the world. The paradoxical image of Catherine's eerily innocent orbs came to mind—so wide, so blue, so unknowing.

Poor little star-crossed Catherine of Legare . . . she had no idea of the nature of the beast who had her in his sights.

After that first, mind-blowing interlude, the affair progressed with a series of steamy, covert nights at the Kiawah Island house. Marla found that Eliot dominated her thoughts with the same ferocity as he did her body. It seemed she could put her mind on little else, even at work.

What she felt for him bore no resemblance to love. It was more like an addiction. Sometimes she felt as though she were slipping out of the ordinary world of light she'd always known, and into a murky new reality—that of the secret side of Eliot Reynolds.

In the public arena he courted Catherine. Beginning with Marla's photo of the pair at the groundbreaking ceremony, their picture appeared in the local pages of the *Post* three times in as many weeks. They were Charleston's hot new couple, and sometimes Marla was amazed by now neatly everything—and everyone—was falling into place according to Eliot's plan.

Catherine had called twice since the groundbreaking. The first time Marla declined lunch with the excuse of a headache. The second time she simply didn't return the lighthearted "How ya doin'?" message Catherine left on her machine.

When it came to Catherine, Marla was filled with a clashing mix of guilt and resentment. Part of her still felt the urge to respond to the woman with whom she'd formed such a fast bond after years of estrangement. But, by and large, Marla realized their friendship was over. She'd turned a decadent corner and left Catherine behind. It was done so quickly and irrevocably that Marla couldn't remember a moment of choice—although if she searched her soul, she supposed she could have made the choice never to meet Eliot that first late night. After that, it seemed, there was no going back.

As Marla sank deeper into Eliot's seductive mire, it became easier to dull her senses to the occasional, pricking thought of Catherine. While the Charleston mermaid claimed Eliot in public, Marla began leaving her stamp on their clandestine nest—toiletries and hair dryer in the bath, bathing suit and lingerie in the bedroom dresser, tequila and lime in the refrigerator.

She told herself there was an innate superiority in being Eliot's secret woman. *She* was the one with whom he unleashed his true self. *She* was the one who knew how things truly stood. She'd almost convinced herself that hers was the preferential position, until Memorial Day weekend when Eliot blandly announced that she should pack her "personal things." Catherine was coming to Kiawah.

Marla had never known such burning outrage. She zoomed through the rooms, snatching belongings from drawers and shelves. When she'd collected everything, she stomped to the door and turned to glare at Eliot, who was seated on the couch by the bar, sipping a drink, and watching her with what appeared to be amusement.

"If I were you, I'd open the windows and air the place," Marla blared. "We don't want her catching a whiff of my perfume!"

"Don't worry. I'm having the cleaning lady out tomorrow."

"I should have known!"

"Tsk, tsk," Eliot returned. "Need I remind you of the 'Marla Sutton Gallery' that starts publishing next week?

You're getting what you want out of this little deal, aren't you?"

He was right. With guaranteed space in the "Arts" section every Friday, the "Marla Sutton Gallery" promised to be the opportunity she'd always dreamed of. Each week she would be picking her own theme, showcasing her own photographs. She could hardly wait to see the first issue. Without further word Marla turned on her heel and slammed the door behind her.

Speeding down the palm-lined drive, she merged with the main boulevard leading off Kiawah Island before the stinging in her eyes gave way to scalding tears. God, she hated Eliot for turning her into a whore. But more than that, she hated her rutting, alley-cat self for letting him do it.

There was a dinner dance in the Kiawah Island clubhouse Sunday night, and a Memorial Day brunch at a friend's beachside home the next morning. It only made sense to stay over. That's what Eliot had said, and Catherine mentally repeated his words as she latched her suitcase, which was filled with an array of outfitting that would have sufficed for a weekend abroad, including a selection of sleeping attire ranging from an oversized T-shirt to an ivory silk peignoir trimmed in ecru lace and packed protectively in tissue.

More than likely the peignoir would stay right where it was in the bottom of the case. Catherine couldn't imagine herself getting decked out in the intimate garb—or mindset—of a seductress. But then until a few days ago, she hadn't been able to imagine herself spending the night in a man's bungalow, either.

So much had changed since Eliot came into her life like a whirlwind, sweeping her into a spotlit world of high society, giving her what Ann Marie smilingly called "the rush." In all the times they'd been together, he'd never pushed beyond the level of provocative kisses. But there had been occasions when Catherine read a look in his eyes that promised more to come. And tonight was the night. She could feel it, and consequently was beset by rivaling flashes of excitement and anxiety.

Catherine glanced at the clock by the bed: 7:25. Eliot

would be here any minute. He was never late. She stepped to the mirror and gave herself an appraising look. The two-piece ensemble was in a bold jungle print of dark green leaves slashed with fuchsia and white flowers. It was silky and exotic, the flowing sleeves mimicking the swirling lines of evening pants. With it she wore burnished gold sandals, and as a final accent had pulled back her hair with a comb topped by a single white silk blossom.

Marla would be proud, Catherine thought as she remembered the day weeks ago when they'd been strolling along Market Street, and the ebullient redhead spotted the outfit in a shop window. She'd insisted that Catherine try it on, and then that she buy it.

"But when will I ever have the occasion to wear such a thing?"

"You'll *create* the occasion to wear it," Marla had replied in that bright-eyed, emphatic way of hers.

Catherine slipped into a frown. She was confused and hurt by the way Marla had dropped out of her life the past month or so. They hadn't seen each other since a brief crossing of paths at the clinic's groundbreaking, and although Catherine had left a couple of messages on her machine, Marla hadn't returned the calls. Something was wrong; of that much Catherine was certain. She could sense it sometimes, as though a bleak cloud had stolen over a once bright and cheerful horizon.

The doorbell sounded, and Catherine jumped—her mind swerving back to Eliot and the impending sojourn at Kiawah. As she walked to the door, the hems of silky pants legs swished about her naked ankles, each caressing step seemed to whisper sensually of what the night might hold in store. Tailored as ever in the dark suit, white shirt, and silk tie that were his hallmark, Eliot took on a look of surprise when he beheld her.

"My, don't *you* look tropical tonight."

"Is it inappropriate?" she nervously questioned.

"Nah," he said in a way that didn't quite reassure her. "It's perfect for the island."

Minutes later both her suitcase and herself were loaded in his car, and the unprecedented evening was under way. Although the drive to Kiawah took more than a half hour, it seemed to pass in the blink of an eye. The resort clubhouse was brilliantly lit, its ballroom vibrating with the brass notes of a nine-piece band and the din of a hundred people. As she and Eliot entered the room, Catherine noted a number of prominent faces, as well as the flurry of interest spawned by their appearance. Councilman Rudd and his matronly wife were the first to hurry over.

"Here she is, Penelope." The councilman beamed. "This is the pretty little bombshell I was telling you about."

"My *dear* young lady," Penelope Rudd drawled, and pressed a theatrical hand to her breast. "I was positively *enthralled* by that story about you in the *Post*. The way you saved that poor unfortunate boy—why, even now the thought of it gives me chills. You know, the photographs in the newspaper don't do you justice. Hold on to her, Eliot. She's an absolute pearl!"

"I plan to, Mrs. Rudd," Eliot replied with a proud glance, and planted a possessive arm about Catherine's shoulders.

The Rudds' welcome proved a precursor of the greetings to come from the other guests. The women exclaimed over the Charleston mermaid's heroism and effusively complimented Catherine's appearance. The men clapped Eliot on the back, declaring him a "lucky dog" who'd always had "an eye for beauty." The more they did so, the more Eliot seemed to strut—like a rooster who'd shown up with the prize hen of the barnyard.

Beyond the surprise of being heralded as a "beauty," Catherine witnessed the party scene through a preoccupied haze. As she dutifully smiled through countless introductions, the back of her mind was poised on a single question: *What—dear God—was going to happen when she and Eliot left the clubhouse?*

Typically, when she was on display at his side, time seemed to crawl. But tonight the hours flew, with Catherine's pulse accelerating right along with them. Before she knew it, Eliot was leading her through the ballroom on a round of farewells, spiriting her away, and ultimately ushering her inside a towering house that overlooked a secluded stretch of beach.

He closed the door behind them, his footsteps ringing across the tile floor as he crossed to an antique receiving table. Catherine hung back uncertainly in the foyer, clutching her handbag.

"This is a lovely place," she offered.

"I like it." Eliot shrugged out of his jacket, then peeled off his tie. While he was in the midst of it, his dark eyes fastened on hers, and seemed to speak silent volumes on the topic of clothing removal. When Catherine continued to stand silent as a statue, he grinned and walked over to the bar.

"How about a cognac to sip on while I show you around?"

She started to decline. She'd already had several glasses of wine at the party. On second thought Catherine accepted and took a fortifying swallow of the strong liqueur, which proceeded to burn its way down her unaccustomed throat. Tears gathered in her eyes. Still, she detected Eliot's grinning surveillance as he polished off the contents of his glass and set it aside.

"It's time," he then stated, and Catherine found herself following along as he corraled her elbow, collected her suitcase, and propelled her up the stairs to a huge bedroom with a huge bed. She stood woodenly by while Eliot deposited her case on a luggage rack by the door to an adjoining bath. From there he proceeded to draw heavy drapes and open sliding doors to a terrace.

"Come outside a minute," he said. "It's a nice night."

Catherine moved to join him, her legs feeling stiff and heavy as lead. When they stepped out, the sultriness of the warm seaside night enveloped them. From directly below came the sound of katydids singing from a cloistering screen of thicket; in the distance moonlight glistened on the foam of rippling surf.

"Pretty, isn't it?" Eliot said.

"Um-hmmm."

Turning his back to the balcony rail, he zeroed in on her profile as Catherine stared out to sea. She steeled herself as he reached up, removed the comb from her hair, and tossed it to the surface of a nearby patio table.

"You know, Catherine, the newspapers link us as a couple. So does the public."

"Um-hmmm," she mumbled once more.

"But you and I know we're not *really* linked. Not yet."

Catherine gulped down the last of the cognac and couldn't prevent a wheezing gasp. Plucking the glass from her hand, Eliot put it aside with her comb and took firm hold of her shoulders.

"I want you," he announced. Pressing a quick kiss to her lips, he unzipped the back of her blouse and started to slip it off her shoulders. Catherine caught and clutched it over her breasts.

"I must warn you. I'm not experienced in these matters."

Eliot seemingly ignored the remark as he reached around her once more, this time to the fastening of her evening pants. An instant later they fell with a rustle to Catherine's sandaled feet, in the process revealing the white strip of her bikini underwear. Eliot's gaze lifted, and there was no mistaking the heated look in his eyes. His hand closed about her clenched fingers. One by one, he began prying them loose.

"I don't think you understand," Catherine blurted. "I'm not experienced *at all*."

"If you mean you're a virgin, I figured that. It makes me want you even more." She mutely stared as Eliot wrenched her arms to her sides and freed the blouse so that it slipped down her body to join the silken pile of her pants. She stood before him, stiff as a board, in bra and panties.

"I should think you'd have noticed by now, Catherine," he added huskily. "I'm a man who enjoys coming in first." With that he swept her startlingly up in his arms and stalked into the bedroom.

An hour later Eliot slept in the king-size bed as Catherine stood on the moonlit balcony. The island air was cooler than that of the city. Of course, the chill might have something to do with the fact that she was naked under the filmy robe of the peignoir she'd resurrected from the depths of her suitcase.

She couldn't say that sex was the earth-moving experience of her novels. In *Passionate Bride,* when Alouette gave in to her desires, she was swept beyond reason. Apparently that stuff was fantasy after all. As for reality, Catherine supposed the event she'd built up to monumental proportions had gone pretty well.

And there was no doubt that she felt different. The claim

of a lover's hands was fresh on her body, his scent clung
to her skin, and an erotic sense of power at having brought
a man to such a point warmed her blood. Oh, yeah. She
felt different, all right—kind of lazy and cozy and mellow
to the core . . . like some unknown part of her that had
been twitching in frustration was suddenly ready to settle
down and take a nap. If she'd been a cat, she'd have
been purring.

Propping an elbow on the balcony rail, she smiled into
the moon-gilded night and sensed the last of the old Catherine drifting away on the ocean breeze.

Chapter Five

A steaming shower chased away the vestiges of late nights and free-flowing liquor. As Nicki toweled off, she thought of Paolo and Elena and the rest of the Hawaiian crowd that had pulled her back to its bosom the past few weeks. What began with a polo match at a Kona estate had turned into a progressive party, highlighted by a week aboard Elena's yacht and culminating in a private welcome-home rendezvous at Paolo's seaside hacienda.

Over the years she and Paolo had enjoyed a series of affairs, which were always fun, never serious. They understood each other. He was prince of a coffee empire stretching from Brazil to the Kona Coast; she was heiress to the Palmer fortune. They could afford to play the field, and did so. But from time to time, when circumstances threw them together and the old spark flared, they took advantage of it, as they had the past five days.

Strolling across her bedroom, Nicki opened the double doors to her closet, walked inside, and started looking through the racks. It was after eleven, well past her usual early hour of rising. Yet most of the day lay ahead, and it was the first time she'd had to herself in weeks. What was she going to do with it?

As she pondered, a mood of restlessness overtook her. Lately, when things settled down and she was faced with the privacy of her thoughts, she felt an inkling of something odd—a misgiving that, in her madcap party of a life, she was missing something. The disquieting times were few, but when they struck, she found herself hankering for some down-to-earth pastime to fill her itchy hands. But there was nothing. How anybody could find peace sitting still with something like needlepoint was beyond her.

The one sure thing that soothed her fidgety spirit was the exhilaration of being airborne. The sensation of being wildly alive overpowered everything else when she hung by a rope from a mountain wall, or soared like a bird on the wings of a hang glider, or raced like the wind on a galloping horse. . . .

Suddenly motivated, Nicki grabbed riding boots from the closet floor. Selecting crisp new spring-green culottes with a matching top, she pulled on a pair of thick socks, and then the seasoned black boots that were soft as a second skin.

"Don't you look pretty," Malia offered as she cruised through the kitchen.

Nicki smiled. "You always say that."

"It's always true. There's brunch on the lanai—fruit and muffins, coffee and juice."

"Thanks, but I think I'll eat after I ride. Where's Austin?"

"He was out with some hunting buddies until the wee hours," Malia benignly replied. "What there is of him you'll find parked at the table behind a pair of dark glasses."

Nicki traversed the breezeway to the lanai. Austin looked up from the newspaper as she stepped out, scrutinized her from behind tinted lenses, and proceeded to frown.

"You're going riding?" he questioned.

"Yes. Why?"

"Because I find it positively obscene."

"You find *what* obscene?"

"The way you pop up bright as a daisy in the morning, after carousing your way through an entire week."

"It's hardly morning, Uncle," she pointed out.

"Feels like it to me," he grumbled back.

Nicki reached toward the fruit bowl and plucked a seedless grape. "Anyway, popping up bright as a daisy isn't quite as effortless as it used to be." Tossing the grape in the air, she caught it neatly in her mouth and turned away from the table.

"It doesn't show!" Austin called after her as she ignored the steps and leaped down from the lanai. With a light laugh Nicki waved over her shoulder and cut across the lawn toward the stable.

The late morning scene was quiet, the ranch hands having long since departed for the range. A single *paniolo* was working a pony in the show ring. And Nicki had no doubt Kimo's father, Akamu, was tucked in his foreman's office adjoining the barn. Otherwise, the stableyard was deserted. She proceeded into the cool barn, enjoying the smell of fresh hay and the whinnies of horses peering from their stalls. The chestnut was one of them.

"Feel like getting out, boy?" she said, and drew a nickering toss of his head. Nicki proceeded to the tack room, where the aroma of leather drenched the air. Selecting a bridle, she moved unerringly along the row of posted saddles to the one she sought. She had a newer, fancier saddle, but preferred the one Austin had given her when she was sixteen. After a dozen years the seat was so well broken in that it fairly molded to her backside.

Efficiently saddling the chestnut, Nicki led the high-stepping animal out of the barn, mounted up, and gave him his head. They tore out of the stableyard, the pony gaining speed as he stretched out over the rippling grass of the pasture. Trees and other landmarks flew by in a blur. And as she leaned into the wind, Nicki's spirits rose in familiar fashion.

They were halfway to her lookout ridge when the pony bunched up to jump a gulley, sailed over it, and Nicki found herself—in a split second—tumbling backward off his back, her booted feet still in the stirrups of the falling saddle.

She landed with a thud, her left arm beneath her. There was a cracking sound, and sharp, hot pain shot in all directions from a spot between elbow and wrist.

Catherine shifted up with a yelp and grabbed her left arm. It felt as though it were on fire, the pain searing through flesh and muscle all the way down to bone. She stared at it . . . disoriented . . . trying to gather her wits.

Seconds passed before she became aware of the bathwater sloshing about her midrift. The appointments of tub, faucet, and shower curtain drifted into focus, eventually blotting out the scene of a grassy plain. As the vision dissolved, the pain went with it. Catherine lifted her arm and examined it. The flesh was rosy from a day in the sun, but nothing was amiss—nothing that could explain the excruciating sensation that had jabbed its way from the dream world into the real one.

Dream? How long had she slept? After the tension of opening day at the clinic, she'd gotten into a steaming tub and must have dozed off. Now the water was lukewarm. She cast a hasty look at the clock by the linen closet. Okay. She still had more than an hour before Eliot was due.

After a quick hot shower, Catherine donned a terrycloth robe and walked out on the balcony. It was six o'clock, the sun a big orange ball on the western horizon. Her attention turned to the beachfront across the street. What a difference the power of Councilman Reynolds had made. In barely a month the rustic waterscape had been transformed to a pretty park with graded beach and roped-off swim area, diving dock and lifeguard tower, red-and-white-striped cabanas for changing, plus a pair of shaded shelters with picnic tables and benches.

Eight hours ago she'd stood in this very spot, gazing below with apprehension. She'd been thrilled by the sight of a dozen or so children who assembled at one shelter, and dismayed by the segregated group of adults hovering about the other. Eliot's suave figure was unmistakable, as were the cameras and notepads of the reporters surrounding him.

She'd told him she was nervous about opening day. She'd requested, point-blank, that he do nothing to create fanfare. What if, after all the hoopla about Waterfront Clinic, no kids showed up and the whole thing was a bust? But Eliot had paid her concerns little mind . . . as usual.

The memory came flooding back in stark detail. She remembered exactly what she was thinking as she watched him mingling with the media. She understood that he was caught up in his campaign. Mere months remained before voting day, and in order to be remembered at ballot time a politician had to maintain a high profile. If he'd expressed the sentiment once, he'd said it a hundred times. And after all he'd done to make the clinic a reality—not to mention the dramatic role he now played in her personal life—Catherine felt like a traitor for growing tired of the way "the campaign" seemed to overshadow everything else.

Picking up a clipboard stocked with pens and registration forms, she'd gone down to broach the public arena of the beach. As she waited for a couple of cars to cruise past, she entertained the notion of bypassing Eliot's reporters and the unappealing prospect of yet another interview in the blaring spotlight. It would never do, of course. Eliot fully expected her to come over, and she'd always gone along with what he expected.

But then, as Catherine crossed the street, she'd found herself shockingly in the midst of doing the *un*expected. Lifting her arm in a friendly wave for the adults, she turned her back on them and made a beeline across the sand for the shelter where the kids were gathered. There were fourteen of them, ranging from kindergarten age to teenhood.

The oldest—and the obvious leader of the pack—was Kenny Black, whom she hadn't seen since the day she hauled him out of the surf. As he swaggered to meet her, his dark eyes alight with a flashing smile, he seemed older and taller than a month ago.

"This is the lady who saved my ass," he announced as Catherine stepped up.

"Kenny," she chided in a scolding tone.

"Well, you *did*," he insisted.

She barely had time to say two more words before Eliot strode up, attended by the buzzing group of newspeople, some of whom were snapping pictures.

"Could I speak with you privately for a moment?" he said, and, placing a hand at her elbow, promptly steered her away. "I would have thought you'd stop by, say hello, and give these folks a chance to take a few pictures," he continued as they strolled a few yards from the shelter.

"I'm sorry. I just didn't want to run late on the first day."

"I understand," he returned with a fixed smile. "And I'm willing to let you make it up to me tonight. I'm happy to say I've got a new contributor, a *big* contributor. He and his wife have invited us to supper."

"But we've been out every night this week," Catherine tendered carefully. "Remember my deadline? I've got to work this weekend. We discussed it."

Eliot's eyes drilled into hers. "I know we discussed it, but this is important. They both want to meet my girl. Otherwise, I wouldn't insist. You're not going to let me down, are you?"

She eventually assented and, with a feeling of defeat, watched him stride across the beach, entourage in tow. That was when she noticed Marla in the distance—standing still as stone, camera in hand, staring. Catherine lifted a quick arm in an effort to flag her down, but Marla either didn't see or didn't care to acknowledge the gesture as she hurried toward the street.

After that Catherine had put her mind firmly on the kids, who were both enthusiastic and exuberant. When they became a little *too* exuberant, Kenny stepped in. She could already see that the boy she'd saved was devoted to the idea of being her ally. The day went beautifully, and she'd left the beach in high spirits.

Now, as she stood in the brilliant light of sunset, Catherine wished she could recapture those spirits. The clinic's opening day promised success. She was nearly finished with her second novel. And she had a date with one of the most illustrious men in town. She should feel happy and lighthearted. Instead, her heart was heavy, and her scalp prickled with the sensation that something was dreadfully wrong.

Running an absent hand over her damp hair, Catherine took a parting look at the sea, failed to derive the serenity it usually afforded, and went inside to prepare for Eliot's arrival.

Maneuvering the pinto in a series of tricky turns, Kimo sent an errant calf scurrying back to the fold. With a brief smile he continued his patrol around the southerly skirt of the herd. The noonday sun was brilliant. Tugging the brim of his hat a bit lower, he looked up and spotted the lone, riderless horse barreling across the pasture toward the stables.

The chestnut. Nicki's mount.

Without so much as a whistle to his partners, Kimo dug his heels into the pinto and thundered off in the direction from which the chestnut had appeared. After a fast-paced few minutes, he spotted Nicki walking in the distance and was filled with relief. Galloping up to within mere yards of her, Kimo reined in the pony and dismounted at a run.

"Are you all right?" he shouted. She cast her eyes downward, and he noted that she was cradling her left arm.

"I think my arm is broken," she mumbled.

Kimo dropped to one knee and reached toward her.

"Don't touch it!" Nicki cried. "It hurts like crazy."

He straightened, his gaze sweeping over her in search of additional injuries. Apparently there were none, although she wore streaks of dirt from stem to stern. Producing a handkerchief from his back pocket, Kimo stepped close to wipe a smudge from her cheek. She tipped her face to receive his ministrations, and the old thrill ran through him, narrowly followed by a surge of resentment at the memory of his father's words a few weeks back: *Mr. Palmer thinks you spend too much time with Nicki when she's home. He'd prefer that you keep a respectful distance.* A scowl covered his face as Kimo briskly rubbed the dirt from her cheek and stuffed the handkerchief back in his pocket.

"What the hell happened?" he demanded.

"The damnedest thing. We jumped the gulley, started up the hill at a gallop, and the saddle just fell off with me in it."

Kimo's face remained grim. "Did you forget how to saddle up while you were away?"

Nicki's eyes flashed up at him. "No. I did *not* forget how to saddle up. The girth was perfectly snug when I left the stable."

"Then how—"

"I don't *know* how, Kimo. It was my good old favorite saddle, and it's got a lot of miles on it. Maybe the strap wore through."

"You're supposed to check for things like that."

"Well, I *will* from now on," she retorted. "What the hell's the matter with you? *I'm* the one who's injured."

Kimo studied her a few seconds, directing the full displeasure of his gaze into her belligerent eyes. "Can you ride?" he asked finally.

She cocked her head and gave him a smart-ass look. "As opposed to walking back? Yes. I think I'll give it a try."

Turning on his heel, Kimo strode to the pinto and stripped him of the saddle. When Nicki approached, he silently offered a leg up. Matching his silence, she grabbed a handful of the pony's mane with her good hand and, with his boost, rose to a smooth seat on the pinto's bare back. Kimo vaulted up behind her. Of necessity, his arm went around her as he took up the reins.

"Thanks for rescuing me," she murmured. Settling back on the pony to gain a more secure seat, she ended up lodging her buttocks against him. Kimo rolled his eyes.

"No problem," he muttered, and turned the pinto with a swift lead. Nicki shifted with the move.

"I've only got one good hand here," she announced over her shoulder. "Do you think you could hold me?"

With a hard set of his jaw, Kimo planted his free arm around her rib cage and secured her against him. Sensations smashed into his mind—the caress of her hair against his chin, the scent of her perfume, the feel of her body settling in his embrace like a slim hand in a glove. God, it felt right. Surely Nicki must—

Kimo's spine stiffened as he brought himself up short. Planting his heels in the pinto's sides, he set off at a clip designed to bring the ride to a quick end.

The riderless chestnut had stirred up quite a fuss. By the time they reached the stableyard, Austin Palmer and a posse of other riders were mounting up, presumably to search for Nicki. The group converged on them as Kimo brought the pinto to a halt.

Palmer took immediate, booming charge. Within a half hour of his phone call, the medical helicopter was touching down on the front lawn. Minutes later Nicki was being whisked away to Hilo Medical Center, her uncle at her side.

As the chopper disappeared from view, Kimo remounted the pinto and rode back to the spot where he'd picked up Nicki. After resaddling the pinto, he continued toward the gulley she'd described and located her saddle. Letting the pony graze, Kimo knelt to examine it.

The problem that had caused Nicki's fall was obvious. The billet straps on the right side had come loose at the stitching. Chances were that Nicki had tightened the girth on the left side and never even glanced beneath the saddle flap on the right—where, unbeknownst to her, the stitching had rotted to such a point of weakness that a burst of tension would make it give way.

Kimo's brows furrowed in a puzzled frown. It happened, he guessed. Leather lasted forever; it was the waxed stitches attaching the parts of the saddle that eventually aged. But the frailty usually showed up in the stirrups, not billet straps.

Picking up a stirrup, he turned it over in his hand. The stitching might be a dozen years old, but it was sound as a dollar. Kimo compared the stirrup to the failed billet straps, and that was when he noticed the difference in the looks of the leather. There was a high gloss around the rotted stitching.

Kimo rubbed his finger over the leather and found it as supple as if it had just been oiled. Lifting it to his nose, he detected the familiar smell of neat's-foot oil compound, the preservative dressing used on all the leather in the tack room. Now that he thought about it, neat's-foot had been known to cause premature rot in saddle stitching. But why on the billet straps and nowhere else? It didn't make sense.

Rising to his feet, Kimo hoisted Nicki's saddle, returned to the pinto, and mounted up. As he settled her gear in front of him, his thoughts centered on Nicki. For a veteran rider like she was, a busted stirrup would cause nothing more than inconvenience. But a girth coming suddenly loose would cause even the most experienced rider to take a violent tumble.

She was lucky. People had broken their necks in falls like that. Kimo's train of thought screeched to a halt.

Grabbing the broken saddle straps, he stared at the shiny strip of leather around the severed stitching. A shower of chills swept over him as a fearful theory raised its head. What if the selective high gloss on the billet straps was due to extra treatment with neat's-foot oil compound—*a lot* of extra treatment, enough to rot the wax stitching *purposely*.

God . . . if someone wanted to sabotage Nicki's saddle, he couldn't pick a more dangerous spot, or a more discreet means. Wheeling the pinto around, Kimo returned to the ranch, stowed Nicki's saddle in the tack room, and found reason to stay close the rest of the day.

It was nearly seven when the medical helicopter returned. The other hands had already left for the day. Kimo peered from the deserted stableyard as Austin climbed down and turned to help Nicki, whose arm was in a sling. Malia hurried out on the lawn, and the trio disappeared into the house.

Obviously, Nicki was being well tended, and appeared to be fine except for her arm. Once again Kimo thought how much worse it could have been. Once again he was chilled by the idea that someone might have planned for it to happen.

Stopping by the locker room adjoining his father's office, he washed up in solitude and headed back through the stable. With the onset of dusk, the barn was filled with shadow and was quiet but for the sleepy shuffles of hooves in the stalls. All was peaceful as Kimo neared the twilit doorway . . . until Austin Palmer's silhouette whirled through the center of it.

"Is your father in his office?" he demanded.

Kimo came to a leisurely stop before the man and looked him in the eye. He'd never liked Austin Palmer, especially when he was in an authoritative mode.

"He's gone home for the day," Kimo answered. "Why?"

"Why? I'll tell you why! Because my niece could have broken her neck today just as easily as an arm."

"I agree. But what does that have to do with my father?"

Palmer's eyes blazed through the shadows. "She said the saddle girth broke, and your father is foreman. The tack room falls soundly, if indirectly, among his responsibilities."

"It was the billet straps," Kimo curtly corrected. "And if you're implying that my father has been negligent, you're off the mark. Nobody is more careful with equipment than he is."

"Oh? Then how do you explain a saddle that's been allowed to become so old and neglected that the strap snaps like a twig?"

"It didn't snap. The stitching rotted."

"Whatever!" Palmer exploded.

"There could be another explanation besides negligence. I examined the straps, Mr. Palmer. The result could have been achieved by excessive treatment with neat's-foot."

Palmer stared for a dumbfounded moment. "You're suggesting that someone did this *deliberately*? Give me a break, Kimo."

"None of the other stitching showed anything but normal wear and tear. I suggest you take a look at the saddle."

"And *I* suggest you're trying to cover your daddy's ass."

Kimo's spine went stiff as a rod. "It doesn't need covering. Like I said, he's the best in the business. Everybody knows it."

Palmer blatantly ignored the remarks as he raged onto another topic. "One more thing while we're covering the bases, Kimo. Thanks for bringing Nicki back today, but from now on I expect you to steer clear of her. Everybody else around here might be blind as bats, but I'm not. You're as hot for her as a July firecracker, and if you can't keep your distance, you can consider yourself fired. I don't care how many generations of your people have worked here."

By the time he paused, Kimo was trembling with rage.

"Do I make myself clear?" Palmer barked.

"Perfectly," Kimo returned in a deadly tone. "But you don't have to go to the trouble of firing me, Mr. Palmer. I just quit."

Kimo strode out of the barn and headed blindly for the ranch-hand parking area. An instant behind him Palmer stomped off in the opposite direction of the main house.

Thursday, June 9

"I'm going stir crazy," Nicki announced.

Melrose propped his elbows on his desk and studied her. She was looking out the louvered window toward the stableyard. A sifting pattern of afternoon sunlight shimmered on her platinum pom-pom of hair; shoulders left bare by a slip of a floral muumuu that was so short it hardly could be called a dress; and the crisp white triangle of the sling supporting her left arm.

"The cast comes off in a couple of weeks," he pointed out. "After that you'll get back to feeling like your old self again."

"This goes deeper than the cast."

"You'll change your tune once it's gone. In the meantime, why don't you concentrate on something pleasant? The festival opens tomorrow. You haven't forgotten our date, have you?"

Nicki glanced over her shoulder with a smile. Every year during the second weekend of June, the Hawaiian village in the foothills was transformed by the gala decorations and activities of the *Mauka Ho'olaule'a,* or Upcountry Festival.

There were clowns, acrobats, and carnival rides, booths with local handicrafts of all sorts, exhibits of Polynesian foods, music, and dance. Melrose loved it, and from the time she was six years old, it had been tradition that he took her to the festival on opening night.

"I haven't forgotten," she said. "I'm looking forward to it."

As Nicki turned back to the window, her smile ebbed. *But this goes deeper than the festival, too,* she thought. Since she took the fall, a familiar sense of restlessness had been joined by something new, something of a premonitory nature that stole chillingly over her during the day and haunted her sleep at night. Maybe Melrose was right. Maybe her morbid bent of mind was due to nothing more than the confinement of the cast on her arm.

Across the grounds the stableyard began to fill with *paniolos* returning from the range. Nicki absentmindedly scanned the riders for one on a black and white pinto . . . until she remembered that Kimo wasn't among them anymore. Leaving the window, she strolled toward Melrose with a frown.

"What have you heard about Kimo?" she asked.

"Nothing you wouldn't expect. Parker Ranch snapped him up like a prize plum. I understand he'll be riding for them in the rodeo ring at the festival."

Resting a hip against Melrose's giant desk, Nicki peered down at him. "I mean, why did he leave? He always seemed happy here, and his family has worked at the ranch forever. It's home."

Melrose glanced aside with an unintelligible mutter. An aura of self-consciousness gathered about him, and Nicki thought quite suddenly that there must be more to Kimo's leaving Palmer Ranch than met the eye. "I was told he just decided to make a change," she added. "But there's more. What is it?"

Melrose met her searching gaze with a resigned expression. "Just that he and Austin had words the night Kimo quit."

"The night Kimo quit . . . which was the night I fell. Did the argument have something to do with me? Or the fall? Well, *did* it?" Nicki pressed when Melrose regarded her in silence.

"It had little to do with your fall, Nicki. Your uncle was grateful to Kimo for bringing you back. He just didn't like the looks of him riding in with his arms wrapped around you."

Her eyes loomed wide. "But I *asked* Kimo to hold me! Otherwise I'd have fallen off his damn horse!"

Melrose shrugged. "You asked, so I told you. And frankly, I must agree with Austin. This is best for all concerned."

"How can you say that? Kimo is *part* of Palmer Ranch. He *belongs* here. It isn't best for him to be someplace else just because Austin made something out of nothing." Reaching across the desk, Nicki grabbed a pen and a sheet of stationery. "And I'm going to write him a note and tell him so."

The more she thought about it, the more outraged she became and the faster the pen flew. *Dear Kimo, I just learned you quit the ranch because of some stupid argument with Austin that revolved around me. I can't tell you how sorry I am. Come back, okay? I hear you're riding at the festival this weekend. I'll be there Friday night. Let's talk. Love, Nicki.* Tossing the pen aside, she rose to her feet and briskly folded the paper.

"And what do you intend on doing with that?" Melrose asked.

"Giving it to Kimo's father and asking him to deliver it," Nicki briskly replied. "Even though I don't come into my inheritance for another year, Melrose, we both know that ultimate control of Palmer International, including the ranch, comes down through my father's estate to *me*. If I choose to, I can pull rank on my uncle. And in this instance I choose to rehire Kimo."

"Slow down, and listen," Melrose commanded. "Austin and yourself aren't the only ones to be considered in this matter. I hear Kimo is doing well at the Parkers'. He's building a new life. In short, he's better off where he is."

"I don't believe that," she answered, and started for the door.

"Kimo is in love with you, Nicki. Let the boy go."

Spinning around, she cast a horrified look in her wake. "He is *not* a boy, and he is *not* in love with me. We're friends."

"That's how *you* think of *him*. Now that Kimo has made the break, maybe he won't want to come back."

"If that's the case, then he'll simply disregard my note, won't he?" Nicki retorted.

She made fleet progress across the grassy side yard to the barn. A number of the ranch hands called greetings. Nicki waved as she passed, but didn't slow her pace until she reached the foreman's office.

Kimo's father, Akamu, was seated at his desk, but came quickly to his feet as she walked in. Weathered lines creased his face, his hair was iron gray, and Nicki was struck by how much older he appeared than the last time they'd met face-to-face. Rounding the desk, he took her free hand in a fond shake.

"How's the arm?" he asked with a concerned look at the cast.

Nicki briefly lifted the offended limb and smiled. "When this comes off in a couple of weeks, I'll be good as new."

Akamu raised troubled eyes to hers. "You were lucky. The injury from such a fall could have been much worse. Your uncle had the saddle destroyed, you know."

"So I heard."

"I'm sorry, Nicki. I had no idea—"

"For heaven's sake, Akamu, it wasn't *your* fault. It wasn't anybody's fault. There was a flaw in the stitching. That's all."

"But as ranch foreman, I must take responsibility for the tack room. Your uncle is right about—"

"My uncle is getting too big for his britches, if you ask me," Nicki cut in. "In fact, he's the reason I'm here. I just learned he and Kimo had an argument the night Kimo quit. Furthermore, I understand they argued about *me.* Do you know if that's true?"

Akamu backed away a step and folded his arms. "What if it is?"

Leaning forward, Nicki tucked the note in his shirt pocket. "If it *is,* then I'd like you to give that to Kimo for me."

"A letter?"

Nicki's chin lifted. "An apology for my uncle's behavior, and an invitation for Kimo to come home where he belongs."

Akamu's gaze shifted from his shirtfront to her face. "Maybe it would be best to let sleeping dogs lie."

"Geez!" Nicki exploded. "Why does everybody keep saying that? Will you just see that Kimo gets the note?"

"As you wish," Akamu soberly replied.

"*Mahalo*," she snapped, her curt thank-you ringing with notes of impatience and irritation. Walking swiftly out of the barn, Nicki strode toward the main house with the objective of finding Austin and giving him hell.

As soon as she saw Nicki prance into Akamu's office, Peni started manufacturing a plausible reason for visiting the foreman. It was in place by the time Nicki whirled out. With a precautionary glance toward the blonde's fast-retreating back, Peni strolled through Akamu's doorway.

"Hey, boss. Oko's wife is sick, and I'm gonna take his shift tomorrow. Okay with you?"

"Sure. I'll make a note on the roster."

"What did the princess want?"

Akamu grimaced. "I wish you wouldn't call her that. Nicki Palmer might be high-strung, but her heart's in the right place."

"She's all right, I guess," Peni lied with a shrug. "So what's up? She hasn't darkened the barn doorway since she took the fall. Is something wrong?"

"Nah," Akamu muttered, his gaze shifting in preoccupied fashion to the pile of papers on his desk. "She just wanted me to pass this onto Kimo," he added with a pat of his shirt pocket.

Peni's vision zeroed on the white folds of the letter peeping from his pocket as Akamu took a seat behind his desk. "Looks like you've got a lot of work to do," she observed.

"It's the end of the month. I'll be here all night if I don't get started."

"I'll get out of your hair, then," Peni said and started to turn. "Oh, by the way, boss," she added with the utmost casualness, "I'm meeting Kimo tonight for a few games of pool. Want me to pass that letter along for you?"

His eyes and mind on his desktop, Akamu absently reached to his shirtfront and handed over the missive. "Thanks, Peni."

Biting her lip to keep herself from beaming, Peni stuffed

the letter in the hip pocket of her jeans and walked out to the truck. She could barely restrain herself from ripping the page open as she drove away from the ranch, but made herself wait until she reached the isolation of Nani Lookout, where the wind swept up from the valley with such fierceness that the cliff site was rarely visited, despite its spectacular view.

Rolling up her window as she turned off the main road, Peni confirmed that the bluff was deserted and pulled to the curb. The wind keened about the truck as she tore the paper from her hip pocket and focused on Nicki's bold script: *Dear Kimo . . . Come back, okay? . . . Friday night. Let's talk. Love, Nicki.*

Peni lifted unseeing eyes, the vision of her mind concocting an image of Kimo's face upon reading the words *Love, Nicki.*

Tearing the letter into unidentifiable bits, Peni got out of the truck, carved her way through galelike force to the ledge, and tossed the pieces to the oblivion of the Nani Lookout winds.

Chapter Six

It was a warm, breezy night. Beneath the doming darkness of a Pacific sky spangled with stars, show lights beamed into the rodeo ring, where exhibitions of roping, steer wrestling, and bronco riding had already taken place. Kimo's demonstration of barrel racing was the finale, and his adrenaline was pumping to match the pinto's as they cut around a barrel with inches to spare and took off at a gallop toward the marker at the far end of the ring.

When they finished running the barrels at breakneck speed, they were met with applause from the spectators gathered at the arena. Kimo nudged the pinto into a prancing farewell circle of the ring, halting the pony as a pretty woman leaned over the rail and offered a lei. She had auburn hair and big green eyes. A tourist.

Kimo bent toward her with a flirting grin. "What's your name?"

"Gloria," she answered as she lifted the lei over his hat, then settled the flowers about his neck with a caressing touch.

"That's a pretty name. Are you here alone, Gloria?"

"For tonight I am, honey."

Kimo arched a brow, his smile spreading. "Would you like to meet me out back and go for a drink?"

"I can't think of anything I'd like better," she replied.

Capturing her hand, Kimo pressed a kiss to its back and moved on. He'd nearly completed the full circle when he spotted Melrose near the exit . . . and Nicki.

Kimo's stomach did a familiar flip as his attention zoomed in on her. A week with a cast on her arm didn't seem to have done her any harm. She was more beautiful than ever. Maybe he'd been wrong about the saddle, and her fall was just a freak accident, like everyone said. Maybe his compulsion to sense some kind of threat to Nicki was due to nothing more than his obsession with her.

She waved and looked as though she expected him to stop, as he'd just done with Gloria. But Kimo didn't. In the moment that Nicki gazed at him so expectantly, he saw himself riding over, being received with friendly regard, and then riding away again—having gained nothing but the old, pounding ache of wanting more.

A look of surprise rose to Nicki's face as it became clear he wasn't going to rein in. His eyes leveled on hers, Kimo gave a respectful tug to his hat brim, planted his heels in the pinto's sides, and cantered him out of the ring.

"He must not have gotten my message," Nicki stated as Kimo disappeared behind the rodeo tents. "I'll catch up to him out back." As she started to walk away, Melrose caught her hand. She turned with a questioning look.

"Can't you just let this drop?" he asked.

She snatched her hand away. "Honestly, Melrose. I don't know why you persist in taking such a dark view of this. All I want is for Kimo to get his job back."

"And all I want is for you to look beyond the end of your nose. There are things involved here besides Kimo's job."

Nicki emitted an exasperated sigh. While she did so, Melrose glanced beyond her shoulder and spotted Kimo emerging from the riders' tent. He was swiftly joined by the redhead he'd stopped to speak with in the ring. Obviously, an assignation was under way.

"Turn around and look behind you, Nicki."

"Why?" she questioned, her brows rising in irritated peaks.

"Just look. Kimo's over there."

When Nicki complied and saw Kimo in the distance, putting his arm around the flashy redhead from ringside, the most peculiar feeling swept over her. The closest thing to it she'd ever experienced had occurred a lifetime ago in elementary school, when her best friend had suddenly chosen a new best friend. Only there was an additional edge to the feeling this time. As Nicki realized it was the sting

of losing a man to another woman, she stared after Kimo
with widening eyes.

"He's trying to move on," Melrose remarked. "If you
can't love him, let him go."

Nicki turned, her face a rosy picture of bewilderment and
hurt. Melrose smiled and patted her cheek as he'd done a
thousand times since she was knee-high.

"Come along, then," he said, and planted a comforting
arm about her shoulders. "Let's go see the rest of the
festival."

Someone was watching.

The lights of the carnival continued to glitter, the crowd
to mill, but the bright scene grew dim as the feeling enveloped her like veiling fog. Someone was following . . . his
eyes moving over her inch by inch, sending shivers scurrying in their wake.

"Nicki?" She looked up to find Melrose regarding her
with a worried look. "Are you all right?" he added.

But his voice was drowned out by the pounding in her
ears, and she was locked in a deafening moment of awareness with the voyeur. She'd been stared at by plenty of
men. This was different. There was a threat in these eyes.
A fiery sense of danger flashed along Nicki's limbs as she
stopped and looked around.

Against a backdrop of neon light he moved toward
her . . . a clown in a tuxedo—his face as white as his shirt,
his slicked-back hair as black as his jacket. His brows were
menacing slashes, his mouth a red line. As she helplessly
watched, he stepped up and pressed an orchid in her unre-
sisting hand.

She failed to notice an accompanying note until the scrap
of paper slipped through her fingers and fluttered to the
ground. By the time she bent to retrieve it and straightened, the clown had melted into the throng.

You're mine, the note read. And once again the sensation
of danger showered her like hot rain.

Catherine bolted up, her gaze frantically searching as her
mind's eye replayed a scene of carnival lights . . . which
gradually shrank into pinpoints . . . then blinked into noth-
ingness to present her with the familiar darkness of her

bedroom. She took a shaky breath. Her heart was pounding, her gown damp with perspiration, her memory branded with the frightful face of the clown.

Kicking off the covers, she swung her legs over the side of the bed. It wasn't just his face that was frightening, it was the aura of evil that radiated about him like a dark halo. With a lingering shiver, she glanced at the clock: 3:50. Dawn was hours away, but the sensation of having brushed up against the devil had scared her out of any inclination to sleep.

She felt better after a shower. Slipping into a comfortable robe, she made a cup of tea, curled up on the sofa, and gazed into the glowing depths of the aquarium. The angelfish sailed in tranquil arcs, their bright blues and yellows fanning through the iridescence. They were beautiful and peaceful, and watching them was soothing to the soul, though on this particular occasion Catherine couldn't be entirely soothed.

First, she dreamed of Nicki taking a dangerous fall; now, of a nightmarish clown whose threat had pierced Catherine's waking moments as sharply as the pain of a breaking limb. "The dream" had never been so intense. Nor had it ever been macabre.

Catherine took a thoughtful sip from her cup. The cause behind such an effect seemed obvious—something was bothering her on a level so deep that her very subconscious had been thrown into a state of terror. And she believed she knew what that something had to be.

She stared into the aquarium, looking past the angelfish as the image of his face gathered in the shining water— Eliot. Less than two weeks had passed since they became lovers; yet since then things seemed to have undergone a subtle change. The night after they returned from Kiawah, he showed up early for a date. Although she raced to get ready, she kept him waiting forty minutes. When she emerged from the bedroom, she found him parked at her desk, reading her manuscript. As she walked in, she replaced the pages, then shook his hand as though they'd scorched his fingers.

"I had no idea your work was so steamy," he said. "Any chance of your cooling it down before someone like my mother reads it?"

He finished the remark on a chuckling note, and Catherine swallowed down a sense of alarm, only to have it resurface a few hours later when they returned from dinner. They were having coffee in the kitchen when he began lapsing into silence, his gaze straying out the doorway toward her workstation.

"What's wrong?" she asked finally. He looked around as though startled. But she had the odd feeling that he really wasn't.

"Am I so obvious?" When she gave him a small smile, he reached across the table and took her hand. "Catherine," he began in a way that suggested he was choosing his words with care. "We're a couple now—a team, if you will. And as teammates, whatever *one* of us does reflects on the other. Understand?"

"I suppose."

He brushed a kiss across the back of her hand. "Then you can understand that a great many of my constituents would be shocked that *my* girl was writing of such private things in such graphic detail."

If the heat that flooded her face was any indication, it must have turned beet red. Eliot seemed not to notice.

"As you know," he went on, "I live in the spotlight. People are watching me *and* my girl. It wouldn't take much to tone down the love scenes. A word here. A phrase there. Think about it."

After that night Catherine started noticing little things—like the times Eliot swept her hand away if she happened to chew a nail; or smoothed her hair back in place if she tucked it behind her ears; or the way he seemed to examine her from head to toe every time they went out, as though making sure she was presentable. Granted, they were just little things, but after a while she'd begun to anticipate them with flashes of feelings she thought she'd left behind on Legare Street.

She'd told herself she was overreacting. Everyone admired Eliot. "A true gentleman," Ann Marie was fond of saying. Even Aunt Sybil had bestowed an uninvited blessing. The Reynolds were part of the Charleston old guard; for once, Catherine was living up to "the name of Winslow."

But in spite of her efforts to focus on Eliot's sterling

qualities, Catherine continued to feel an elusive darkness stealing into their relationship. Maybe the dreams proved to what degree.

The following week she became convinced there was a connection. She had nightmares about the clown twice in a row, and it seemed clear they were triggered by an unprecedented quarrel with Eliot. The night of the argument they were cuddled in her bed after having made love, when he shifted up and gazed down at her.

"How's the book coming?" he asked.

"I'm almost there," she replied with a sigh. "Of course, that's what I keep saying, and my deadline's just around the corner."

Eliot brushed a strand of hair from her cheek. "Have you thought about what I said?"

"I'm not sure what you mean."

"You know," he said in a cajoling sort of way. "The love scenes in your book—did you give any thought to toning them down?"

"Yes. I gave it some thought."

He flashed one of his whining politician smiles. "Good." Planting a quick kiss on her forehead, he climbed out of bed and reached for his clothes. Catherine rolled back on the pillow.

"I don't want to mislead you, Eliot. I decided not to change anything."

He halted in the midst of pulling up his underwear. "Really. When did you decide that?"

She took a steadying breath and plunged into the unknown territory of holding her own. "I examined the scenes with an objective eye. They're passionate, yes. But they're not dirty."

"The eye of the voting public isn't as objective as yours."

Holding the sheet over her breasts, she shifted to a sitting position. "I can't write to please your constituents, Eliot. I—"

"Fine," he barked. Hurriedly getting into his clothes, he strode to the doorway and turned with a parting glare. "I've got my sights on the state senate, Catherine. And one day, Washington. I like the picture of you beside me, but not if you insist on undermining the importance of my career."

That night Catherine dreamed Nicki was at a restaurant

with friends when the clown in the tuxedo appeared at the table. His true face was still hidden, but this time the heavy makeup was flesh-toned. At a fleeting glance the spectral countenance could pass for normal, and was all the more scary for it.

He delivered an orchid to Nicki's plateside with a bow and departed amid applause from her unknowing dinner companions. Once again the note read: *You're mine.* This time Nicki reacted with characteristic boldness. Springing to her feet, she hurled the flower at the clown's back. "Stay away from me!" she yelled.

Yet the clown managed to have the final say. Swiftly turning, he peered at Nicki with hard black eyes and smiled. The effect was so sinister, so wicked, that she broke out in a sweat.

And once again Catherine spent sleepless hours waiting for the sun to come up. Early that morning a dozen long-stemmed white roses arrived. They were exquisite, but she preferred flowers with color. *Love ya,* the card read. Never once had Eliot said, "I love you, Catherine." It was always "Love ya"—which, to her ears, carried about the same weight as "See ya around!" *Little things.*

Just as she was leaving to open the clinic, he called. "Am I forgiven?" he asked with a smile in his voice.

Catherine supplied the expected response. "Of course."

"It occurred to me that I was doing the exact thing of which I was accusing you—denying the importance of your career."

It was exactly the right thing for him to say. The heaviness in her chest momentarily lightened.

"Anyway," he went on, "after I thought about it, I realized there *is* a certain glamour associated with romance novelists. Maybe I've been looking a gift horse in the mouth."

The heaviness returned. Catherine put a hand to her brow. "I'm not sure I like being compared to a horse."

He laughed. "Even a thoroughbred? Because that's what you are, Miss Winslow. Otherwise, you couldn't have raced away so swiftly with my heart, could you?"

Sometimes he could be so smooth. "Have I really done that, Eliot?" she questioned.

"What do you think?"

"Sometimes I—"

"You've got a birthday coming up in couple of weeks," he interjected, summarily cutting her off. "I figure that's a good time to show you how serious I am about us."

That night was one of the rare ones she had to herself, when Eliot disappeared to one of his occasional "late appointments." Catherine fell asleep on the couch, and the forbidding clown made another appearance. The sun was low, and long shadows streaked across the manicured greens of a cemetery. Nicki was among the crowd at a flower-decked grave site.

"We commend the spirit of Ed Coleman . . ." the minister was saying. Nicki's thoughts wandered to the idea of how fast the terrible thing had happened—one minute he was driving along; the next he was plummeting over a cliff. Who was going to handle her finances now? Mr. Coleman had always taken care of—

The thought was blasted from Nicki's mind as she glanced toward the drive where the hearse and limousines were parked. There, leaning casually against the side of a black car, was the clown. Once again his face was flesh-colored. Except for the tuxedo, she might have taken him for just another mourner.

Time seemed to freeze, along with her capacity for movement. And then, as though he'd been waiting only to be sure she saw him, he climbed into the black car and motored quietly away, passing out of sight just as the graveside service came to an end.

Nicki walked woodenly between Melrose and Austin as they returned to the limo. Her uncle opened the door, and she started to climb in, then drew back as she spotted the orchid and slip of paper on the seat. "He was *here*," she announced with a gasp.

"*Who* was here?" Austin asked.

"The clown."

Melrose frowned. "You mean that chap from the festival?"

"Get the orchid out of the car, will you?" Nicki said. "I don't want to touch the damn thing." Melrose removed the flower and lifted the note. "What does it say?" she demanded.

He held it out so she could read it, not that there was much to read. Just two words: *You're next.*

"I say it's time to call the police," Melrose stated.

Austin put a supportive arm around Nicki's shoulders. "There's no need to scare the girl."

"Maybe she *should* be scared," Melrose replied in a hard voice. "Maybe we *all* should be."

Thursday, June 30

In a gallant effort to end the feud that had smoldered between them since Kimo left the ranch, Austin threw a poolside "Cast-Off Party" the evening after Nicki's cast was removed in Hilo.

It was a balmy night. Torches ringed the party area on the back lawn, lilies floated on the surface of the pool, and the percussive island music of a hired band issued from the terrace, where a refreshment tent offered hors d'oeuvres and drinks.

Several dozen of the elegant old crowd had responded to Austin's impromptu invitation and were gathered about the glimmering centerpiece of the flower-strewn pool. It was nearly eleven, champagne had been flowing since nine, and the level of talk and laughter had reached a lively pitch.

Nicki stood by the shallow end of the pool with statuesque, raven-haired Elena, whose ankle-length black sheath provided a striking contrast to her own saucy lemon-yellow frock with spaghetti straps and a swirling skirt that stopped at midthigh.

"I'm having a *marvelous* time," Elena commented, lifting her voice above the music. "But of course, the soiree can't *truly* be considered a success until someone gets thrown in the pool."

"The night is young," Nicki answered. "That's what I love about this crowd—it's never late until the sun comes up."

Excusing herself from Elena, Nicki stopped and chatted with several other guests on her way to the refreshment tent. The bartender had just handed her a fresh glass of champagne when Austin stepped up.

"Have I regained your good graces?" he asked.

Nicki gave him a squinting once-over. Handsome as ever in white slacks and a floral shirt, he endured it with smiling complacence. "I suppose," she said eventually. "Although I may reconsider and require that you jump in the pool in an hour or so."

"In an hour or so I might be up for that."

Nicki surrendered a smile and scanned the festive scene, her gaze halting on a tall stranger standing across the way with Melrose. Amid the formally clad guests gathered about the pool, he stood out as a rebel, the open front of a black leather jacket revealing a T-shirt tucked into jeans. Torchlight limned a broad-shouldered, long-legged silhouette and glinted off a mane of hair that jeered at the carefully styled heads of the other men. Although distance camouflaged further detail, Nicki imagined he might well be sporting biker's boots and tattoos, as well.

"Who is *that*?" she asked.

Austin turned to follow her gaze. "Jack something-or-other," he replied with a smirk. "Melrose hired him—get this—as the company's new *driver*. I swear, ever since Ed Coleman went over a cliff, the old man's gone completely paranoid."

"Driver, hmmm?"

"Driver, mechanic, whatever. Melrose mentioned the idea of cleaning up the garage apartment and hiring somebody. I just didn't know he meant so soon."

Nicki studied the stranger's cocky stance. Everything about him gave the impression of a loner, a renegade . . . a challenge. "He doesn't look married," she observed.

"If you must know, Melrose says he's a widower. I never would have thought the old man had such poor taste as to bring a hired hand to a private party."

"Careful, Uncle. That snobbish streak you've been denying the past few weeks is starting to show."

He met her sharp look with one of patience. "It isn't snobbish to see things as they are, Nicki. That guy isn't any more in your class than Kimo is. It's not *my* doing; it's just the way it is."

At that Nicki set her glass on the nearest surface and started to walk away. Austin caught her by the wrist.

"Stick with your own kind," he advised. "If you've got to play, do it with Paolo or one of your other boy toys."

"I've grown tired of *boys,* Uncle," Nicki flared. "From a distance this one actually looks like a real, live man."

With a toss of her head, she started to move away. When Austin held stubbornly onto her wrist, Nicki yanked free and whirled.

"What *exactly* is your problem?" she cried. "First Kimo. Now this. You've never been so stern about the men in my life before."

"You've never been in this position before," Austin retorted.

"*What* position?"

"That of being stalked by an anonymous maniac."

The hated memory of the clown vaulted to mind, accompanied by a hot rush that rocked Nicki's stomach and flashed to her face. Although she hadn't actually *seen* him since Ed Coleman's funeral, the bastard had sent a wild orchid eight days ago by mail. The blossom was crushed inside the envelope, its accompanying note reading: *You are like this flower, beautiful and dead.*

The Hilo County police had rushed admirably to the ranch and had taken the evidence for testing, but to no avail. The ordinary white paper and black ink could have come from any one of a thousand sources, and there were no fingerprints but her own. The postmark said Hilo, but Nicki sensed that the clown was much closer. Sometimes she felt as though he were crouched just outside her field of vision . . . watching.

Nicki lifted her chin. "You're beginning to sound like Melrose. Weren't you the one who said there's no reason to be scared of someone who's afraid to show his own face?"

"That was before we talked to the police and I found out what some of these so-called stalkers have done to their victims," Austin returned. "The authorities have no idea how to identify this guy, and neither do you. For all you know, that could be him standing over there in that black leather jacket."

"Nope," she lightly returned. "Our driver has too much hair."

"Ever hear of something called a wig? I understand clowns have been known to wear them from time to time."

Nicki's burgeoning grin crumbled beneath the weight of Austin's taunt. Despite her denials, a despised feeling of terror smoldered within her day in and out—waiting, it seemed, for no more than a mere reminder of the clown before bursting forth to scorch and shake her.

"You've been gracious enough to give me this party, Austin," she snapped. "Let me get back to enjoying it, okay?"

Spinning around with a twirl of her short skirt, Nicki started along the torchlit boundary of the pool deck. She'd taken only a few steps when a ruckus erupted as Malia emerged from the house with a cart bearing a huge white candlelit cake. A drumroll issued from the terrace, and the band broke into "For He's a Jolly Good Fellow." All eyes turned Nicki's way.

Producing a bright smile, she changed direction and moved up the terrace steps. As she drew near, she saw that the coconut-frosted cake was fashioned in the hooked shape of an arm in a cast. Malia's handiwork. Nicki circled the cart and gave her a hug as the band reached the end of the tune.

"Blow out the candles and make a wish, *keiki,*" Malia suggested.

Although her voice was characteristically soft, her words were picked up by a few nearby guests. "Yes!" someone cheered. "Blow out the candles and make a wish!" Within seconds, the crowd had taken up the chant: "Make a wish! . . . Make a wish! . . ."

Drawing a deep breath, Nicki blew as hard as she could while fanning the length of the cake. There was a resounding hurrah when she succeeded in snuffing every candle. "Did you make a wish?" someone called, and triggered an echoing chorus of the question.

"Yes, indeed," Nicki announced, her gaze locked on the spot where Melrose and the new driver were standing. Onlooking guests cleared a path as she descended the steps and moved to the deep end of the pool. When she stopped before the stranger, he looked down with surprise signaled by the high cocking of a heavy brow.

He was taller than she'd surmised from a distance. Nicki was five-six, on top of two-inch heels, and he towered over her by half a foot. Terrace backlight revealed his hair to be brown, though she couldn't tell what shade. Poolside torchlight flickered in his eyes and hid their true color. To a degree his looks remained a mystery, except for features so classically perfect, they put to shame the statues she'd viewed in many a museum.

"Well, hello," he said in a deep, stirring voice. "I'm—"

"Jack something-or-other," Nicki broke in. "And *I'm* the girl with the wish." She pulled him down and kissed him with openmouthed abandon. Passive for a stunned instant, he then put a pair of strong arms around her and pulled her close.

A roar of approval rose from the crowd, but as his tongue moved into Nicki's mouth, the noise receded. Everything was silent and dark, warm and wet. There was the seductive flavor of liquor—not champagne, but whiskey— and the dizzying abrasion of a day's growth of beard. . . .

"I said, wake up, sleepyhead."

The voice boomed through her head like a thunderclap. Waking with a start, Catherine sat up and blinked. Eliot was standing by the bed, straightening his tie. "It's five o'clock," he announced. "I've got to be at a meeting miles away in a few hours."

Leaning down, he sought her lips. Yet when he found them, Catherine continued to taste the mouth of another man. She watched through a kind of daze as Eliot reached for his jacket and strode to the door. "I'll call you tonight," he tossed, and was gone.

A moment passed as Catherine remained bolt upright— her cheek tingling with the illusory rub of the dream man's beard, her flesh electrified with his touch.

"This is ridiculous," she mumbled finally, and climbed out of bed. Coursing through darkness illuminated only by the aquarium, she pulled open the sliding door and stepped onto the balcony in time to note Eliot's BMW cruising away from the stop sign below. As Catherine watched the taillights proceed up the street, she thought back to his remarks of the preceding night.

"The campaign is entering a new phase, Catherine. My schedule is filling up with out-of-town appearances that have to be made."

He'd gone on, in a tone of apology, to outline the many times he was going to be away from Charleston in the upcoming weeks. Deftly concealing the abrupt relief she felt,

Catherine had allowed none of it to show as she listened with seeming disappointment.

But now, as she watched his car fade from sight and knew that she had an entire three days ahead of her before she had to climb back on Eliot's bandwagon, she was flooded with merciful peace. Maybe all she needed was a break from his unnerving spotlight. Maybe a few days to herself would chase away nagging feelings of bleakness and nightmares of sinister clowns.

The eastern sky was growing light, the seaside air possessing the inimitable quality of freshness that only existed just before dawn. Catherine rested her forearms on the railing, peered out to sea, and drew a deep contented breath.

Her thoughts drifted, gradually coming to rest on the sensational man her mind had fabricated. In the soft, dreamy light of not-yet-morning, she found it easy to reconstruct the image of *Jack*—tall, strong, excruciatingly masculine, his perfect features glowing with torchlight as he cocked a sexy brow. Now, *there* was a hero for you.

Spinning at the rail, Catherine turned suddenly alert eyes to the computer beyond the patio doors. It had sat dormant the past few days while she searched for the perfect ending to her manuscript. Now she had it.

Hurrying inside, she warmed up the machine, scrolled to the final page, and concluded her second novel with a kiss that tasted of whiskey and smacked with the manly roughness of a day's growth of beard.

Chapter Seven

Friday, July 1

The party went on until three. The last stragglers departed sometime after four. And contrary to her habit of popping up with the birds, Nicki slept until half past noon when a merciless bar of sunshine lodged across her face. Locating her dark glasses on the bedside table, she crawled from bed, shrugged into a turquoise Oriental silk wrapper, and left her chamber. It wasn't until she neared the kitchen that her nostrils flared and her eyes fully opened . . . *Banana bread!* Malia had made banana bread!

Nicki paused in the kitchen doorway, affection welling up as she studied the back of the woman at the stove. Cooks and maids had come and gone, but Malia had been an institution since her arrival at the ranch three decades ago. She'd known Nicki's grandparents and parents. She'd been there on the night of Nicki's birth, the same night of her newly widowed mother's death. It was through Malia that Nicki had learned all she knew of the lost generations, for Austin refused to speak of them.

Nicki scurried across the polished floor and gazed at the golden loaf on the stovetop. "You made banana bread. For me?"

"Of course, for you," Malia replied with a sweet smile. "The rest of the house is quiet as a tomb. I don't expect to see Melrose or your uncle until it's time for supper." Nicki chuckled, then put a hand to her throbbing temple. "Out to the lanai with you," Malia added. "Coffee's on the table, and I'll bring the bread when it's cool enough to cut."

Despite the aid of sunglasses, Nicki shielded her eyes as she meandered along the breezeway and broached the veranda. From an invisible spot on the grounds came the hum of a riding mower; from the gardens, the twitter of birds; from overhead, the lazy whir of the ceiling fan. The scene was otherwise silent, the ranch hands having long ago departed for a day on the range.

Nicki took a seat at the patio table and poured herself some coffee. It wasn't until she lifted the cup and started to take the first, sacred sip that her glance traveled across the drive and halted. *Him!* Her attention thoroughly diverted, she took an ill-conceived gulp and nearly scalded her gums. Swiftly replacing the cup in its saucer, Nicki coughed, grabbed a napkin, and pressed it to her lips.

In her initial passing glance, she'd failed to notice that the company limo Melrose typically used was parked by the garage. Jack was washing it, wearing nothing more than a pair of hip-slung jeans. Annihilating the distance of the present, Nicki's memory replayed the moments he'd held her.

"That was fairly nice," he'd said after his kiss seemed to move the earth. "Did you have something in mind for an encore?"

And then the reveling guests had parted them, denying Nicki the opportunity to put the upstart soundly in his place . . . or, perhaps, to call his bluff. She never would know what she might have said, or how he might have reacted. Minutes later he departed the poolside scene.

Nicki's eyes narrowed behind the shaded glasses as she took a cautious sip from her cup. Last night darkness had cloaked the details of Jack's handsomeness. Now it was the glaring sun. Beneath it his hair glimmered like burnished gold—although she knew it wasn't blond, and imagined that it must be the sun-streaked hue of chestnuts. His torso gleamed like molten copper. Once again Nicki attributed the effect to sunlight, although she couldn't blame the sun for the seeming perfection of his physique, which called to mind the fashioning of a sculptor.

"He is quite a specimen, eh?"

Nicki looked up with a start as Malia placed a couple of platters on the table. *"Quite,"* she answered testily.

"I watched you with him at the party last night," Malia went on. "It was *you* who put your arms around *him.* But through my eyes, it appeared that he gave back more than expected."

It was useless to try to hide anything from *those* eyes. Malia had been raised on the carefully handed down lore of her Hawaiian ancestry and had long been recognized across the island as a wisewoman versed in the traditions of the ancients. She knew the ways of nature, the cycles of history, the paths of the stars, and the secrets of the human heart.

With a noncommital grunt Nicki began loading her plate with banana bread and melon slices.

"There is a strength in that one." Malia added. "Without so much as a word of direction, he already has put the garage in a kind of order I have never seen."

"Really? How do you know?"

"I went to him. The man accepted coffee and a roll from my hand. No more. Yet his smile of thanks was bright and pure as the dawn. Yes, I would say there is great strength in that one, and an equal measure of honor. I suspect that he would protect those he cares for at the risk of his very life."

"Let's hope *that* won't be necessary," Nicki muttered as she selected a slice of melon, and unknowingly drew a sharp look.

Malia studied her as Nicki bit into the melon with the unselfconscious relish of a ten-year-old. In many ways she remained so like a child—lighthearted, free-spirited . . . vulnerable. The idea of the clown who'd been stalking her struck terror in Malia's heart and brought back an icy feeling of fear she'd locked away more years than she cared to count.

On that long-ago night of madness, a storm had raged, its din adding a howling accent to the frenzy within the house. And suddenly, amid the noise and chaos, it arose like a silencing phantom—a dark, heart-rending moment of choice, when forces of time and circumstance joined hands to carve a fork in the road. Both paths were unthinkable; yet one had to be followed.

After that night the saving grace that had enabled Malia to carry on was the belief that such a dark moment would never—*could* never—come again. But Nicki's sadistic clown had stirred the old fear, suffusing it with new life, imbuing it with the power to clamber at the walls of Malia's memory.

Her vision swerved to the man in the distance. And now Jack appeared—big, strong, beautiful . . . like a warrior sent to fight in a predestined battle. Malia sensed that he would protect Nicki; also, she sensed a different kind of threat.

"He is a man of honor," she stated. "But I warn you, *keiki,* I also see an aura of danger. Do not lose your heart to him."

Nicki sputtered around a mouthful of cantaloupe. "Who said I was going to lose my heart to him? You know as well as I that I've barely said two words to the man!"

Malia arched a knowing brow. "Words mean nothing. It is when the words stop that the heart falls."

"Well, *mine's* not going to fall! For heaven's sake, Malia, do you honestly think some rough-hewn maverick could walk in here—"

Malia stopped her with a silencing hand. "In one way you are like your uncle. The mountain peak no one has conquered is the one you must climb. Instead of being frightened away by that which cannot be done or cannot be had, the two of you rush after it like beasts gone mad. Take care that the unattainable does not seduce and break your heart for you."

With those parting words Malia retreated along the breezeway. Nicki's gaze returned to Jack. By the time he finished washing the sweeping white length of the car and began to wax it, her hunger was sated and her brain fully alert.

Pushing out of the chair, she secured the sash of the wrapper about her nakedness and stepped from the shelter of the lanai. The lawn was a cool cushion beneath the soles of her feet, the heat of the sun a torrid mantle settling on her bare head and silk-clad shoulders. Keeping to the grass, she followed the curve of the steaming asphalt drive toward the Lincoln limo. She drew within twenty feet. If Jack noticed her approach, he gave no sign of it.

"Good morning," she greeted as she arrived.

"Afternoon," he flippantly returned without a glance.

So! He *had* noticed, but simply had chosen to ignore her. Nicki's chin went up as she strode around the shining hood of the car. "I'm Nicki—"

"I know who you are," he interrupted and finally surrendered the courtesy of straightening from his task. "The name's Cantrell. You can call me Jack."

"I planned to," she retorted. A corner of his mouth lifted in a grin, which he all but hid as he turned to toss a rag into a nearby bucket. The action drew attention to well-honed biceps. And as he propped a casual elbow atop the roof of the car, she noted the ridged tension of his abdomen, like a sun-bronzed washboard a person could probably bounce a quarter off.

"You disappeared in quite a hurry last night," she added.

"Today is my first day on a new job. Some of us have to work for a living, you know."

Nicki folded her arms across the front of the silk wrapper. "Meaning?" she prodded.

"Meaning, I don't think you plan to put in a day's labor in bare feet and sunglasses and that . . ."—he flicked the hand of the arm resting on the car, the gesture encompassing the length of her—"whatever-it-is you're wearing."

As her temper flared, she forced a bland smile. "You don't approve of me, do you?"

"It's not up to me to approve or disapprove. I just work here."

"That's right . . . which means you work for *me*."

He shook his head. "I work for Mr. Melrose."

"It's the same thing."

"That wasn't my understanding when I took this job."

Unfolding her arms, Nicki spread her palms. "I own everything around here for as far as you can see. Do you understand *that*?"

With slow deliberation he scanned their surroundings. "Nice place," he said finally. As he met her eyes once more, he tendered a crooked grin that bore not the slightest resemblance to the "pure as dawn" smile Malia had described. In fact, it made Nicki want to smack his insolent face.

"I've decided to go shopping," she announced.

"Where does a lady like you go shopping in *this* neighborhood?"

"The town on the leeward coast. It's a thirty-minute drive."

Jack's gaze—and seemingly his interest—shifted to the nearby collection of cleaning supplies. "There are a half dozen vehicles in the bays of this garage. If I had to bet, I'd say the one with your name on it is the red Ferrari." With that he pivoted and stopped to gather a clean cloth and tin of wax.

"There's not enough room in the Ferrari for what I plan to buy," Nicki snapped.

"What are you planing to buy?" he tossed over his shoulder. "Major appliances?"

She took an incensed step in his direction. "You're missing the point, Jack. I'd like you to drive me."

He leisurely straightened and turned, cloth and wax in hand. "You know, I did some homework before I took this job, and I realize that you're an heiress who stands to inherit—as you say—everything for as far as I can see."

"Thank you very much," she remarked in a seething tone.

Jack walked up to her, his height seeming to gain monumental proportion as he gazed down, another smirking grin on his lips. "I'm also aware that until next summer, when you come into your inheritance, you have no acting power over anything. For now, Melrose runs things, and he's the man I work for."

Head tipped back, Nicki glared up at him from behind the dark glasses. "Are you saying you won't drive me?" she barked.

"I'm saying you're not my boss," he replied.

"We'll see about that!"

She high-stepped away toward Melrose's quarters. Jack Cantrell followed, and she had the impression he was silently laughing at her back with every step. He was no more than a few paces behind when she burst into Melrose's sanctum, where the old man looked up with a start from his easy chair.

"Melrose!" Nicki began emphatically. "This . . . *person* refuses to drive me into town!"

"What?" Melrose sputtered.

"I haven't refused anything," Jack put in mildly.

"You have, too!" she accused.

"What?" Melrose repeated. "You two kids want to go to town?"

"She's no kid," Jack stated. "And I've got plenty to do around here without taking *her* for a joy ride."

"Honestly!" Nicki exploded, at which point Melrose rose from his chair and stepped forward.

"There's nothing to be done around here that can't wait," he said. "Go ahead, Jack. Take the girl to town."

"All right, if you say so," Jack grudgingly mumbled, as though he'd just been condemned to the guillotine.

"For heaven's sake!" Nicki exclaimed. "I've never had to *bulldoze* a man to get him to take me somewhere before."

"I'll just bet," Jack returned. "I'll bet you've had all the guys jumping through *your* hoops since about the age of two."

At that Melrose had the bad manners to guffaw, and then try—with no success whatever—to cover it with a jag of coughing. Nicki stomped across the room and whirled at the doorway.

"You may pick me up in an hour," she announced when the grinning newcomer condescended to look her way. "And I've changed my mind. We'll be taking the Ferrari after all, *if* you think you can handle it." His reply was an impudent salute. Turning on her heel, Nicki stormed toward the main house like a tornado.

A scant hour later she fluffed her newly shampooed hair and stepped back to peruse her reflection. The sundress was sky-blue silk, splashed with a pattern of white feathers. Its halter neck flattered her sun-kissed shoulders; its short skirt showed off her legs; its color took the blue of her eyes a shade deeper. The volatile mood coursing through her veins flushed her cheeks to near scarlet. Exiting her chamber at an impatient pace, she swept into the hall and nearly collided with Austin, who was still in his dressing gown and apparently on his way to the kitchen.

"Good afternoon, Uncle," Nicki said as she moved past.

"You only call me that when you're mad as hell," he replied in a hoarse voice. "Where are you going?"

"Town," she tossed back.

"Town? Why the hell do you want to go there?"

Good point. She never went to *town*, which was divided in distinct halves—the east end, a bustling district of over-priced shops and tourist traps; and the west, a slumlike area where the unwary straggler was almost certain to be mugged. Casting a look over her shoulder, Nicki smiled at Austin's horrified expression.

"Why the hell not?" she replied, and was still smiling as she pushed through the door in a swirl of silk and saw Jack waiting in the drive. Resting a hip against the Ferrari, he was wearing black jeans and T-shirt, matching boots, and aviator glasses. His wet hair was combed back and gleaming. At her appearance he straightened from the car, an incredible figure of a man.

A sensual thrill washed over her, and Nicki put a deliberate swing in her walk as she strolled toward him. His response was to pull something from his back pocket. It wasn't until he plopped it on his head that she recognized it as a chauffeur's cap he must have found in the bowels of the garage. Without a word his gesture made the insulting statement that the only reason he was there was because he'd been ordered.

The pleasurable thrill abruptly vanished, along with her hip-swinging gait. As Nicki swiftly crossed the remaining distance between them, he opened the passenger door with a flourish.

"You made your point," she said. "Now take that thing off. It looks ridiculous." Giving her a short bow, he swept the cap from his head and tossed it to the back floorboard. Nicki didn't look at him again as she climbed into the car and he closed the door. Donning dark glasses, she followed his progress around the hood and watched peripherally as he climbed into the driver's seat.

"Turn right out of the ranch," she commanded, then peered wordlessly ahead as he scratched down the drive. He probably expected her to comment on the fact that he was obviously no novice behind the wheel of a sports car. She didn't, and silence became a cold war.

His window was open, and wind rushed through the cab, sweeping away any semblance of nearness. Typically, the drive to town took a half hour, but at the speed at which he was expertly negotiating the curvy cliffside road, she estimated it would take no more than twenty minutes. They reached the halfway mark, and as they rounded the point, Nicki saw that the hang gliders were out. She decided to end the war, if only briefly.

"Ever tried it?" she asked, lifting her voice.

With a show of manners that nearly made her drop her

teeth, he rolled up his window. "Sorry. I didn't hear. What did you say?"

"I asked if you've ever tried hang gliding."

"Nope. I'm a man with both feet planted on the ground."

"And I'm a woman who was born in the air."

"How'd you manage that?"

"I was born in a helicopter on the way to the hospital. Maybe that's why I like gliding so much. When you're up there, it's like you know what the wind is for—to lift and carry you, to take you up and let you soar like the birds. A hawk flew with me once."

When Jack gave her a doubting look, she went on insistingly. "He *did*. In Colorado. A red-tailed hawk flew with me around and around, looking me over, and I said: 'My wings are bigger, buddy.' But he had the last laugh. I lost the air and had to go to ground. When I looked up, I saw him circling above me, and I know he was laughing. Come to think of it, you remind me of that hawk."

The man's heavy brows rose. "Yeah?"

"Yeah," Nicki affirmed. "*He* unloaded all over my head, too."

Jack threw back his head and laughed. "You're something else."

"Considering the source, I'm sure that can't be a compliment."

He didn't agree, or disagree, and she said nothing more until they broached town.

"Park there," she directed when she saw a spot in front of a shamefully high-priced dress shop. Nicki waited for him to come around and open her door, then climbed out, stepped up on the curb, and turned an expectant look in his direction.

Jack closed the Ferrari door with an irreverent hip. "I brought you. I hope you don't expect me to shop with you, too."

"You could come inside, at least."

He gave a short laugh. "No, I don't think so. I'll wait here."

"What if I need help with my purchases?"

He leaned back against the car. "I'll be here."

Nicki pranced away and set the stage for the next two hours, during which she visited shop after shop and bought parcel after parcel only so she could reappear and order Jack to load her packages. He did so time after time with a know-it-all expression that pushed her temper to the limit. Exiting the last of the boutiques, she plunged thoughtlessly into the straw market that fed off the east-end tourists, but bordered the west-end slums.

Here, the locals hawked handmade crafts with the desperation of the poor. Here, the natives were not above grabbing an arm to slow down a potential buyer. Twice, without so much as a turn of her head, Nicki pulled free of grasping fingers as she made her way down the dirt path between booths, her mind firmly on Jack Cantrell and oblivious to everything else.

Perhaps that was why she—a native herself, who should have known better—was caught off guard when she felt a wrenching pull at her shoulder and realized someone was trying to grab her purse. Luckily, she still had a hand on the bag as the shoulder strap flopped to her elbow. Nicki spun around and confronted a dark-eyed local six feet tall and outweighing her by a hundred pounds.

"Let go," he commanded.

"No," she mumbled. He gave a nod over his shoulder, and two more just like him appeared from behind the last booth on the row. To her right was a wilderness area fronted with a stand of bamboo; to her left, the hulking bodies of three would-be assailants.

"Let go," the first repeated, and gave such a severe yank to the purse strap that Nicki lost her footing and fell to the dirt. She didn't have time to reconsider and relinquish the bag. She looked up, saw the guy whip out a switchblade, and . . . out of nowhere the avenger flew into the scene in a blur of black.

His body was airborne, his leg extended. She heard an "Oof!" as Jack's booted foot connected with the thug's diaphragm. The knife fell to the ground, along with the leader of the pack. The other two closed in, and Jack went airborne again—his body whirling in midair, his leg whipping around and . . . Bam! Bam! Two staccato thumps sounded out the attackers' stricken jaws, and they stumbled back. By this time the first had grabbed his knife and was back on his feet. Swiftly followed by his partners, he made for the trees and disappeared behind the screen of bamboo.

Looking up with her mouth hanging open, Nicki blinked as Jack dropped to one knee beside her. "This is my fault," he was saying. "I was playing around, and I should have been with you."

She tried to gather her wits as he helped her to her feet. "Where did you learn to fight like that?" she managed.

"The streets of Chicago."

"That didn't look like any street-fighting I've ever seen."

"I've had some training," he admitted.

"Training, huh? What are you, a black belt or something?"

"Something like that. Are you all right?"

She brushed a few streaks of dirt from her skirt. "I'm fine."

"You sure?" Jack added, his fingers stroking her arm as he set the purse strap back in place.

Nicki's gaze lifted to the dark shields of his aviator glasses. "I'd go through it again to get *this* kind of reaction."

Though Jack quickly withdrew his hand, he bestowed a fleeting grin. "Why didn't you just let them have your purse?"

"I don't know. It didn't occur to me."

He shook his head. "You're something else, Nicki. And in case you're wondering, that *is* a compliment."

The sweetest warming glow began stealing over her . . . until it was stopped cold by a patch of color that drew her eye to the dirt. A fuchsia orchid. There were no other flowers on the forsaken marketplace path—just a single wild orchid, as though it had been tossed at her feet.

"He was here," Nicki whispered. "The orchid. It's his calling card.

Jack went to pick up the flower and gave her a scowling look. "Are you talking about the clown?"

"Did you see him?" she shrilled. Jack shook his head as Nicki's eyes began to fill with stinging tears of fright. Turning away, she fished in her purse and swiftly put on her dark glasses.

"Melrose told you?" she inquired after a moment.

"Yeah," Jack's grim voice replied from behind her. "He told me you're an expert horsewoman who took a bad fall, too."

Nicki looked around. "But that's not part of this."

"How do you know?"

A numbing chill swept over her. Nicki hugged herself, and Jack responded by stepping over and placing a warm hand at her elbow.

"Let's head back," he suggested. "I think we've had enough shopping for one afternoon." Nicki remained in a daze as he walked her to the Ferrari and they drove away from the miserable coastal town. When they reached the comforting familiarity of the seaside road to the uplands, Jack removed his sunglasses and looked her way.

"Feeling okay?" he asked.

"Except for being scared out of my mind, I'm perfectly fine."

"Melrose says you won't consider leaving the island," he commented. "If you're so scared, I wonder why not."

"And let the bastard chase me away from my own home?" Nicki flashed. "In his dreams, buster."

Jack laughed, although when she looked at his profile a moment later, she found him staring ahead with menacing intensity. "Do me a favor," he said then. "Tell me everything you know about this damn clown."

He was strong and solid as a mountain, and it showed in his eyes. The irises were predominantly a cool gray-green, the shade of moss, but accented with other colors that streaked from the pupils like rays of a sunburst. There was the gold of shimmering sand, the auburn of glistening clay, the brown of sunlit earth.

The July sun wasn't the sole reason for Catherine's sense of warmth. Images of Jack from last night's dream had lingered through the day, as had a glow that was at once warm and sweet, hot and thrilling. It felt like falling in love.

Setting aside the daydream, Catherine strolled across the beach and rounded up the Saturday crowd of children for dismissal. Waterfront Clinic was considered a success by all. City officials touted it as a victory; beachside homeowners, as an enhancement to property value; and tourists and residents alike, as a haven where one could enjoy the waterfront with the security of a lifeguard in residence. As for Catherine, her feeling of success was rooted in the fifteen children from the wrong side of the tracks who showed up religiously for lessons.

As she donned a parka over her wet swimsuit, she kept an eye on the kids approaching the street. A smile rose to her face when they proceeded exactly as they'd been trained—forming two lines and catching hands, the first line heralded by thirteen-year-old Leon, the second by pretty, vivacious Angel, who both looked and acted in a manner more mature than her twelve years.

They were such a motley crew of characters, from tiny, towheaded Michele—the baby of the group at five—to lanky Leon, who was Kenny Black's second in command. Some were dark, some fair, some verging on adolescence, a few not long out of toddlerhood. Their common ground, and bond, was the dismal neighborhoods they managed to escape each day at the clinic.

In the past month Catherine had gleaned enough information to form a picture of the life into which these children had been born. Their environment was comprised of row upon row of run-down apartment buildings, where derelicts slept in the alleys and gangs ruled the streets. It was a place of fights, thefts, knifings, and shootings; of drug deals and black-market goods; of homes where some absentee parents worked their fingers to the bone trying to make ends meet, and others dozed their way through existence in an alcohol or drug-induced fog.

In short, the future bequeathed to these children was one without prospects or hope. She liked to think the clinic might be a small step in the right direction—a foothold they might use to climb out of the cycle that threatened to drag them down.

Catherine continued watching as they crossed the street, a happy, chattering band on their way back to the slums. It was hard to believe the clinic had come into being so recently. Her sense of purpose in working with the kids felt long-instilled. When they disappeared around the corner, she turned and surveyed the horizon. The afternoon was overcast and muggy, the inlet subdued and placid, disturbed only by the rhythmic splashes of the solitary swimmer doing laps between the ropes.

Kenny had developed the habit of staying behind and practicing while she closed up and policed the beach. The result was that, in barely four weeks, he'd shown amazing progress. The boy she'd pulled out of the surf two months ago bore no resemblance to the swimmer now executing a strong freestyle stroke from rope to rope.

Catherine believed only part of Kenny's progress stemmed from the natural athletic ability he possessed. Another part, she sensed, came from a drive to rise above the traditional pastime of hanging out on a street corner like most teens in his neighborhood. The past few weeks she'd developed a great deal of admiration for Kenny. All the kids looked up to him, and he was paving the way for *them* to rise above tradition, as well.

As she completed her rounds and returned to the lifeguard stand, Kenny waded out of the water to meet her. "I'd like to ask your opinion about something," he said. "I was thinking I might try the jock thing at school this year. You know . . . maybe go out for the swim team?"

"That sounds great, although you say it as though you're not quite sure whether you want to or not."

"I'm sure I *want* to," Kenny slowly replied. "I just don't know if I'll be good enough."

"If you keep going the way you *have* been, you'll be plenty good enough by end of summer," Catherine assured him. "I was watching you earlier. Your freestyle stroke is really coming along."

His brows drew together. "I like freestyle, but what I really want to learn is butterfly. It's cool."

"The fly, huh? You know, most people consider butterfly the toughest stroke of all."

"I'll bet you can do it."

"Well, yes . . . I can do it."

"Then if I work hard enough, I'll bet I can get it."

Catherine smiled as she unzipped her jacket. "I'll bet you can, too," she said. "Let's go."

After another hour in the water, Catherine walked home with her spirits flying. Eliot was coming back tomorrow night, but even the prospect of returning to his spotlight failed to bring her down. Letting herself into the penthouse, she looked around the quarters as if for the first time, and felt the blessing of her escape from Winslow House anew. So what if she was about to be pulled back onto Eliot's stage? That was okay. Everything was okay. In fact, all was right with the world.

The sun had been down for an hour. *It will be after supper,* Eliot had said. *Of course,* Marla had thought. He never came to her apartment in daylight, but only under cover of darkness—like a vampire feeding in the night.

Everyone thought he wasn't returning from the campaign trail until the next day. Only *she* knew he was coming back to Charleston tonight. He'd been playing the clean-cut senate nominee for nearly a week and was hungry to let his true self out, even if it meant driving long secretive miles to reach his prey.

Marla stepped back from the mirror and examined her reflection. She'd picked up the dress just yesterday, when she happened to see it in the front window of Carlotta's. Made of white, gauzelike cotton, it was gathered with a ruffle about the shoulders and fell from a demure empire waist to the ankle.

Although she'd never worn much white, she lately had developed a penchant for the color. The dress from Carlotta's was the fourth white garment she'd purchased in as many weeks, plus a selection of shoes and purses. Nowadays she could afford to go on shopping sprees if she liked. A hefty boost in salary had come along with the "Marla Sutton Gallery."

Marla's gaze lifted to the eyes that regarded her solemnly from the mirror. Too bad neither her fancy wardrobe nor other luxury items that had fallen into her lap brought the happiness she would have expected. A couple of weeks back she'd been late for an "appointment" with Eliot at Kiawah because her car broke down. The next day an effusively courteous salesman from Charles Towne BMW called. Her messenger had arrived with the cashier's check, he said. When could they expect her to select her new BMW?

Feeling like Cinderella, Marla had parked her cranky sports car for the last time and driven away in a shiny black sedan that purred over the pavement. A few nights later when she met Eliot at the Kiawah house, she ran in and threw her arms around his neck. "Thank you so much for the BMW," she said with a smile, which Eliot swiftly wiped from her face.

"I've got plenty of money, but my time is limited," he snapped. "I couldn't afford to waste it on that wreck you called a car."

Thus, fast as lightning, he'd struck down the fragile joy that had dared to glimmer within Marla for a few days. How stupid she'd been to rush in and thank him. There was no generosity in his gift. No care or feeling. The BMW was merely another silken bond to ensure his hold on both her body and her silence.

After all, it wouldn't do for the public to know what she knew. At first Marla had thought her lover's taste for rough sex was merely a streak. Now she knew the truth. Eliot was perverted. It was the acts of hurting and degrading that most stimulated him. Oh, how his black eyes gleamed when he made her cringe or wince or cry out, only to smother her cries with a cruel mouth.

And so day after day she drove around town in an immaculate car, wearing pristine white and thinking she'd never known it was possible to feel so dirty.

Eliot arrived at nine. As soon as she opened the door, he stepped in and kicked it closed. His reserved attire of suit and tie was typical. So was the paradoxically brutish way in which he grabbed her, his embrace landing crushingly about her rib cage.

"I thought about you while I was away," he muttered. Abruptly releasing her, he stepped back. "New dress?"

"Um-hmmm," Marla replied with attempted lightness. "Like it?"

"White," he muttered with glittering eyes "The color of virgins and sacrifices."

She turned away from that glittering, frightening look. "Does that mean you like the dress, or not?"

Eliot captured her chin and yanked her around. "It will do nicely for what I have in mind. I'm taking you somewhere special."

No one was out and about on the sultry summer night as Eliot escorted her to the silver BMW parked down the block. No one saw as he produced a strip of black cloth from the glove compartment.

"What's that for?" Marla demanded.

"An adventure," he muttered.

She couldn't help it. She couldn't submit as he started to blindfold her. When Eliot sought to tie the strands at the back of her head, she swatted his hands away.

"Don't do that again!" he bellowed in her face. "Everything has worked out so far, hasn't it? The 'Marla Sutton Gallery' publishes every week on schedule, doesn't it?"

His ear-splitting reminder quelled her rebellion. Despite a skyrocketing sense of anxiety, Marla sat still as stone as Eliot blindfolded her—then added insult to injury by binding her hands with something that felt so smooth and silky, she thought it might be the tie from around his neck. "Just so you won't be tempted to peek," he curtly tendered as he started up the BMW.

They rode for twenty minutes or so. Marla could sense the streetlights flashing by . . . then no light at all as they apparently reached the outskirts of the city.

"Why do I have to be blindfolded?" she ventured.

"Not knowing where you are is part of the thrill."

They turned onto a rough, bumpy road that jostled her against the car door. "Where are we?" Marla tried once more.

"I'll never tell." They proceeded along the rutted thoroughfare another ten minutes before Eliot stopped the car, grabbed her by the elbow, and pulled her roughly into the open. "Before I take off the blindfold, do you have any idea where you are?"

The night air was filled with the rowdy voices of crickets and the pungent scent of pine. "The woods somewhere?"

"That's good," Eliot pronounced, and stripped the blindfold from her eyes. They were standing in a clearing surrounded by the seemingly endless blackness of a forest. Directly ahead was a rustic cabin whose lines she could barely make out from the meager illumination of a single lamplit window. The setting was picturesque, the glow at the window serene, and Marla was shaken to the core by a contradictory premonition of danger.

"Would you untie me now, please?" she asked as Eliot propelled her toward the entrance.

"Not yet." Swiftly unlocking the massive wooden door, he ushered her inside, where the main room with a fireplace was furnished in an early American motif of rough-hewn furniture and gingham curtains.

"Very quaint," she said. "Untie me now, okay?"

Eliot arched a brow and pushed her toward another heavy wooden door in the corner. "You haven't seen the best part yet."

The door opened onto a flight of stone steps. "You want to show me the fruit cellar?" she questioned.

He laughed, and the sound bounced against the stones in sharp reverberation. "Yeah," he muttered as he urged her down and down, where flickering light played across an earthen floor.

Marla halted on the bottom step. Perhaps the hidden room had been a fruit cellar *once,* but no more. It had been transformed into a look-alike dungeon. Torches studded the walls, as well as a set of shackles and a collection of whips. There was a barred cell in the corner, and a long table in the center of the room adorned by an array of erotic devices.

"What *is* this place?" she breathed in a tone of horror. "Some kind of S and M chamber?"

"I prefer to think of it as a game room." Proceeding down the final step, Eliot turned and extended an inviting hand. The red glow of torchlight danced on his face and burned in his eyes.

"You've come a long way already, Marla," he said. "It's just one step down." His gaze captured hers, he smiled an evil smile, and Marla felt as though she'd locked eyes with Satan himself. How strong was his power; how weak her own will.

God, help me, a voice within her whispered, then shrieked in terror as Marla placed her bound hands in Eliot's waiting palm.

Chapter Eight

Paniolos Hale was a joint that lived up to its name. Pictures of rodeo riders adorned the walls, along with so much riding tack and hardware that the place had the leathery aroma of a stable. A trio of lamps suspended over the pool tables provided dingy light, which was further muted by a haze of tobacco smoke. The jukebox played island music, the bar stocked Hawaiian beer, the kitchen served native fare, and the tables were monopolized by locals who either were, or once had been, *paniolos*.

Peni ambled up to the bar, which was tended by the *hale* owner, fifty-year-old Luika, who was as wide as she was tall. As usual, they were the only two females in the place.

"I'd like to buy the champ another beer," Peni said.

"You got it," Luika returned, and waddled over to the taps, where she proceeded to draft a mug of Kimo's preferred brand.

He'd routed the competition and taken first place by storm at today's annual Kohala Invitational Rodeo. Of course, the invitational was nothing compared to the giant Fourth of July event day after tomorrow in Waimea, which was launched by a parade of flower-draped horses and riders, and attended by thousands. But each year, diehard fans made it a point to attend the preliminary Kohala rodeo, which previewed the field of competitors and gave an indication of whom to favor at Waimea. Once again, that was Kimo.

Luika returned with the beer. "Did you see him ride today?" When Peni nodded, she added, "How did he look?"

"Better than ever. Wiamea's in his pocket, and he'll be taking the prize to Parker's. It will be the first time in years the trophy hasn't gone to a Palmer Ranch *paniolo*."

"You say that as if you are glad," Luika commented with a puzzled look, "when you yourself are a Palmer Ranch *paniolo*."

"Maybe not for long. I've been thinking about making a change like Kimo did. After all, the Parker place is a lot bigger."

"But Palmer Ranch is so beautiful."

"Yeah, I guess . . . if you care about that kind of thing."

Peni glanced toward the front table where Kimo was waiting, and found him peering out the window overlooking the boardwalk. She was struck by the notion that he was thinking about Nicki—maybe because the only times Kimo lost his typical cocky contentment to a show of moodiness was when he was daydreaming about *her*.

Picking up the mug, Peni returned to the table with a lively step and the intention of turning his mind to other things.

"Mahalo," he said when she delivered the beer, and mustered a grin as she took her seat across the table. "This is the third one you've bought me, Peni. I'd say you've congratulated me enough."

"You deserve it," she earnestly replied. "You were great today." Kimo shrugged and took a gulp from the mug. "Any news on an opening out at Parker's?" she added.

"Not so far. I gave your name to the foreman like you asked. How come you're so anxious to leave Palmer Ranch all of a sudden?"

Peni balled up a fist and gave his arm a comradely jab. "We've been riding together for ten years, pardner. I miss ya."

God, yes, I miss you, she thought as he surrendered a smile. The days of riding with Kimo had been the most glorious of her life. Out on the range she could watch him and love him and have him all to herself, with only cattle and horses for competition.

Peni glanced aside as lights flashed across the window. A long white car pulled to a stop at the boardwalk.

"That's Melrose's limo," Kimo noted. The headlights went off. A man climbed out and headed for the saloon doors. "Who's the guy?"

"Jack Cantrell," she answered. "He showed up at the ranch a few days ago." The tall *haole* strode into the tavern and proceeded to the bar. Peni noted the way Kimo's attention zeroed in on him. Of course. Any man grazing on Nicki Palmer's range was of immediate interest. A bitter taste filled Peni's mouth, and before she knew it a caustic remark was spilling out.

"The new stud in Nicki's stable," she added.

Kimo met her eyes with a sharp look. "I'm sure he has some function other than that."

"He's *supposed* to be Melrose's driver," Peni retorted. "But so far I haven't seen him drive the old man anywhere. I've spotted Cantrell twice the past few days. Both times he was with the princess, and both times she was all over him like a rash."

After talking to Luika for a moment, the stranger approached their table. "Mind if I interrupt for a minute?" he greeted with a friendly smile. "Your name is Peni, right?"

"Yeah," she mumbled with surprise. There were a couple dozen riders at the ranch. Had he learned all their names in a few days?

"And Kimo?" he added, his gaze shifting across the table. "I'm Jack Cantrell." He offered a hand, and Kimo joined him in a shake. "I hear congratulations are in order. Can I buy you a drink?"

Kimo lifted his mug. "Already got one."

"In that case, I wonder if you could spare me a few minutes. I'd like to talk to you about Nicki Palmer." In a gesture Peni found revolting, Kimo straightened in his chair. "In private, if it's not inconvenient," the *haole* added.

Great, Peni thought as Kimo gave her a swift, meaningful look that said, *Get lost.* Noisily scraping her chair back from the table, she rose to her feet and, with a passing glare for Jack Cantrell, strolled off toward the bar.

"What's this about Nicki?" Kimo asked as Cantrell took a seat in Peni's newly vacated chair. "Is she all right?"

"Nicki's fine. I'm just trying to gather a few facts."

"About what?" Kimo questioned with a frown.

"About how an expert rider like Nicki managed to fall off the back of her horse a while back."

Kimo took a drink, his gaze leveled on the man across the table. "Why do *you* want to know? Is it like Peni said?"

"I have no idea what Peni said."

"That you and Nicki are lovers."

Cantrell shook his head. "Nicki's a beautiful woman. But we're just friends." Kimo eyed him in silence. "I care about her, okay?"

"That's easy to do."

"And I think she might be in danger."

"What kind of danger?" Kimo demanded.

"She's received a couple of threats. I'm not at liberty to say more, but it occurred to me that the chain of bizarre events seems to have started with her fall. I understand you were the one who brought her in from the range. Was there anything about the accident that struck you as—well—peculiar?"

Kimo leaned forward and rested his elbows on the table. "I take it you've already spoken to Austin Palmer?"

"The man wouldn't give me the time of day."

Kimo tendered a fleet grin. "Okay, I'll tell you what I told *him*. I examined Nicki's saddle, and what I saw made me wonder if it had been tampered with." He quietly related his findings about the rotted stitching on the saddle's billet strap, the high gloss on the surrounding leather, and the lingering scent of neat's-foot oil compound.

"There's no way to follow up on it now," Kimo said finally. "The saddle was destroyed. Everyone believed Nicki's fall was a freak accident, and after awhile I started believing it, too."

"Can you think of anyone who might want to hurt her?"

"No. But I can remember asking myself the same question when I took a good look at that saddle."

Cantrell gazed across the tabletop for a moment. "One last thing," he then said. "I understand you resigned from the ranch that very day after an argument with Austin Palmer."

"So?" Kimo guardedly returned.

"So, Melrose said it was about Nicki—that Palmer wanted you to keep your distance from her."

"And that's just what I'm doing, isn't it?" Kimo asked in a hard voice. Draining the last of his beer, he rose to his feet. "I've had a long day. I think I'll get going."

"I'll walk out with you," Cantrell chimed in, and followed his path through the saloon doors to the boardwalk. "Are you planning on sticking around awhile, or just passing through?" Kimo inquired as he stared aimlessly into the night.

"I'll be around long enough to make sure Nicki's safe."

Glancing aside, Kimo scrutinized the man beside him. "You look like you can take care of yourself. Just make sure you take care of *her,* as well."

"You can count on it." With a tug of his hat brim, Kimo started to walk away. "Hey, man. Can I give you a lift somewhere?"

Kimo turned with a faint smile. "No, thanks. My place is just down the block. You know, I used to daydream about riding around in that big white flashy car." The meager smile drained as his head began to fill with old fantasies of Nicki. "I got over it," he concluded, and, stepping down from the boardwalk, strode into the cloaking darkness of the deserted street.

After instructing Nicki not to leave the ranch or even take a horseback ride alone, Jack had been absent all day on the premise of "errands."

"You don't expect the clown to come *here,* do you?" she'd asked that morning as he prepared to depart in the limo.

"I don't know," he replied. "So far, the only times he's approached you, he's had the camouflage of a crowd on his side. Just stay close while I take care of a few things today, okay?"

The way Jack had taken on the cause of protecting her was heartwarming; the businesslike distance he invariably put between them, just the opposite. Nicki had never met such an infuriatingly elusive man. Having expected him back in time for supper, she'd dressed in a clinging electric-blue halter dress. When supper came and went, she visited with Melrose, her eyes peeled toward the window for signs of Jack, but to no avail.

Now she kept watch from the sheltering portico of the west wing. Malia had retired at a typically early hour. Austin was out for a night of gambling at a shipboard casino. All was dark and still, but for the whirring breeze from the ceiling fan and the bubbling sensation of Nicki's simmering irritation.

It was after ten when the limo cruised up the drive. Jack

stopped by Melrose's quarters, disappeared inside for a few minutes, then proceeded to the garage apartment—the blinking on of lights signaling his homecoming. Walking purposely to her quarters, Nicki picked up the bottle of Malia's homemade kahlúa—with a festive red ribbon tied about the neck—and made quick progress along the footlit path from house to garage.

Pausing outside, she peered through the screen door and could see pretty much the whole of the efficiency apartment. Couch, TV, and coffee table were just inside the entrance, kitchen table and appliances in the far corner, and, facing them, the bedroom area. Having removed his shirt, Jack was sprawled across the bed in a pair of jeans, perusing an array of paperwork.

"Knock, knock," she said, and walked straightforwardly inside.

Jack leaped from the bed as she continued toward him. "I come bearing a housewarming gift," she added. Shifting the bottle into his hands as she strolled past, Nicki took a seat on the edge of the mattress and demurely crossed her legs.

"Make yourself at home," Jack offered with a slight grin.

"Thanks. I will. Got any glasses? That's Malia's homemade kahlúa. You'll never taste better." Nicki glanced to the array of papers and folders at the foot of the bed. "What's all that?"

Sweeping up the material in his free hand, Jack moved off toward the kitchen. "Just a project I'm working on," he tossed back. Setting the papers aside, he reached up to produce a couple of glasses from the cabinet. The shifting muscles of his bare back captured Nicki's eye, and she ended up studying the length of him.

"So what have you been up to tonight?" he asked as he proceeded to uncork the bottle.

Wondering what the hell you've been up to, Nicki thought. "Not much," she replied. "I talked to my friend Elena for a while about the birthday party." Jack meandered back, handed her a glass, and offered his own for a toast.

"Thanks for the housewarming gift. Cheers."

"Down the hatch," Nicki responded as she clinked her glass against his. They took a sip, and Jack gave her a quizzical look. "Did you say birthday party? Whose?"

"Mine, of course. On July ninth. Elena has arranged a wonderful party at the Mainsail Yacht Club. In fact, that's one of the reasons I came over. I was hoping you'd agree to be my escort."

"No," Jack succinctly replied.

Staring up at him for a shocked moment, Nicki rose huffily from the bed. "Well, you don't have to be *rude* about it. Don't worry. There are any number of men who would *love* to be my date."

"I'm not turning you down for a date, Nicki. I'm saying there shouldn't *be* any party, not right now."

"Why the hell not?"

"The clown. It's too perfect an opportunity for him."

"I *want* my birthday party, Jack."

He gazed at her with grim steadiness. "Look, Nicki, if you won't evacuate to a safe location until something can be found out about this guy, then at least accept the fact that you're going to have change your lifestyle."

"I *will* change my lifestyle . . . except for the party."

Jack rubbed his forehead as though he were suddenly extremely weary. "You just *had* a party a few nights ago."

"At the pool? That was just a get-together. More than a hundred people are expected at the Mainsail for my birthday. The invitations went out weeks ago. It's to be a black-tie affair with a banquet, music, dancing—"

"No," Jack quietly reiterated.

"There's nothing I can say to persuade you to be my escort?"

"If you insist on exposing yourself in such a foolish way, you're on your own, baby. I won't be accomplice to a situation that makes no sense. So far the clown has contented himself with notes and flowers, but we don't know what he's planning. If he wanted to make another appearance, he couldn't ask for a better setup than a big fancy shindig with lots of guys in tuxedos coming and going."

Turning her back on him, Nicki set her glass on the bedside table and clasped her hands. After a moment she turned to face Jack with a determined look. "All right, then. I'll consider telling Elena to call off the party on one condition. *You* take me to the Mainsail for a birthday celebration. *Then,* if I expose myself, you'll be right there to cover me."

A grin tugged at the corner of Jack's mouth. "You put it in such a way that I don't see how I can refuse."

"Good," Nicki pronounced. "Then we have a date."

"Apparently so. . . .What are you doing?" he added as she matter-of-factly plucked the glass from his hand and deposited it next to hers. "I hadn't finished that, you know," he pointed out.

"You can do that later," Nicki replied, and leaned toward him.

"What's on your mind *now?*"

"I like you, Jack."

"I like you, too, Nicki," he warily returned.

Rising on tiptoe, she wrapped her arms around his neck and received an electrifying brush of manly hair across skin left bare by the halter bodice of her dress. She was about to kiss him when Jack stopped her by pressing a pair of fingertips against her lips.

"Whoa, lady," he murmured.

"Why? I thought you said you liked me."

"I do."

"Well, then . . ." She moved against his chest once more, only to have him stop her once more. Nicki looked up with annoyance. "What the hell is the matter, Jack? We're both grown-ups here."

"Me a little more than you."

"How old *are* you?" she demanded. "Thirty-two? Thirty-three?"

"Thirty-*seven*," he announced, as though confessing to the age of Methuselah.

"That's nothing. We're well within the same age bracket."

Jack disengaged her wrists and enfolded her hands in a warm grasp. "In years, maybe. I'm talking about experience."

"I've had my share of experience with men," Nicki snapped. "Enough to know when I'm being thoroughly kissed. Ever since the pool party, you've acted like that kiss never happened. Well, it *did.* And I couldn't help noticing you put your heart into it."

"You started it, remember?" he pointed out.

"And you joined in with great zest!"

"Yeah, I guess I did. But it's not gonna happen again."

Nicki snatched her hands from his and took a backward step. "Why not? Do you find me completely unattractive, or what?"

His sparkling gaze swept over her. "I'm sure you've turned enough heads in your time to know you're a knockout. The fact is that I'm a lone wolf, Nicki. Sure, we could have a sweet little affair, but that's all it could be. And right now I have a gut feeling you need a friend a hell of a lot more than a lover."

"You could be both. And you haven't *always* been a lone wolf. You're a widower, right. You were married once."

Jack's heavy brows furled. "That was a long time ago. Since then the only kind of lovin' I go in for is the no-strings, one-night kind. And you're no one-night stand."

Nicki planted a frustrated hand on her hip. "Maybe it could lead to more than one night if you gave me half a chance."

"Maybe so. That's why I'm not giving you half a chance."

"Fine," she returned with a smoldering look. "Be seeing you." Spinning on her heel, Nicki stalked away. Jack hurried after her and put a detaining hand on her shoulder.

"Where are you going?" he demanded.

She whirled to face him. "What do *you* care?"

"I *do* care. Why don't we do something fun together tomorrow?"

"What's that supposed to be? Some pitiful crumb of attention you feel free to throw my way? Let go of me, Jack." She attempted to brush his hand from her shoulder. His grip tightened.

"Be mad at me if you want," he said heatedly. "But don't throw a temper tantrum and do something foolish."

"Such as?"

"Such as flying out of here in the Ferrari to parts unknown, or some such bullshit."

"I believe I've had my quota of bullshit for one night, thank you. Let go of my shoulder."

"Promise me you're going to the house," Jack commanded. Nicki's gaze swerved to his. Her cheeks were red with anger, her blue eyes glittering like a pair of jewels. "Promise," he insisted.

"Oh, all right!" she exploded. "I'll go straight to my

room, okay? Now let go. You've given me a damn headache."

As soon as he released her, Nicki swept out like a stormy wind. Jack hovered at the doorway, watching as she dashed along the footlit path and darted safely into the house.

"Fireball," he muttered with a listless grin, and suddenly remembered how bone-tired he felt. Here in Hawaii it was half past ten, but back home in Chicago it was the wee hours. His body still wasn't used to the time change. Dousing the lights, he stripped off his jeans, stretched out on the bed, and closed his eyes.

Little by little his thoughts left the image of Nicki's incensed face and returned to the mystery man who was stalking her. Jack didn't have to retrieve his research from the kitchen to be able to picture each page. The dossier included notes from conversations with everyone he'd managed to interview, dates and descriptions of the clown's appearances, and photocopies of similar MOs—none of which had panned out—solicited from the Hilo County Police Department.

There were statistics on Nicki herself—parents, deceased; siblings, none, but for a stillborn twin lost in the same difficult childbirth that had claimed their mother. Nicki's sole living relative was Austin Palmer, and although Jack didn't like the man worth a damn, he had to admit that—if anything—Palmer seemed *overly* protective of his niece.

Despite the fact that Jack's usual result in an investigation was to ferret out a jealous family member or lover, this time circumstances pointed to the perpetrator being a psychotic stranger who unfortunately had fixated on Nicki Palmer.

Could be the stalker would back off once Nicki stopped being so readily available. Could be he'd played out his hand with a series of threatening notes. But Jack didn't think so. Neither did his client, who'd gone to great lengths to hire him from thousands of miles away with the instruction of leaving "no stone unturned."

Opening his eyes, Jack peered into the darkness. There might be a lot of threads he couldn't tie together in this case, but on one subject his instincts had never wavered— the clown in black would strike again. When he did, Jack intended to be ready.

Saturday, July 9

On Catherine's twenty-ninth birthday, Ann Marie treated her to Saturday brunch at the Mills House, which was as famous for its champagne Mimosas as for its buffet of croissants, crepes, and quiches. They adjourned to Catherine's kitchen, where she put on a pot of coffee and opened Ann Marie's present—a first-edition, leatherbound copy of one of her favorite childhood tales.

The sight of the book brought back memories of stolen hours at the Open Window . . . and a string of dismal birthdays at Winslow House—ignored by Aunt Sybil, forgotten by her father, observed by Catherine, alone, in the tower bedroom, and marked by resigned wonderings of why she'd ever been born at all.

Shaking off the desolate thoughts, she looked across the breakfast table. She'd always thought Ann Marie had the look of a Grecian statue come to life—slim and graceful with dark upswept hair, high cheekbones, arching brows. At the moment her classic features were aglow with affection.

"I love the book," Catherine murmured. "Thank you so much."

"You're so welcome, sugar."

"I've never had such a nice birthday."

"And it's just beginning," Ann Marie commented. "Where did you say Eliot's taking you tonight?"

Catherine smiled. "Poogan's Porch. It's always been one of my favorite places. Like I said, I've never had such a birthday."

"Enjoy it while you can, dear," Ann Marie advised with a light laugh. "You're twenty-nine. According to feminine tradition, this is supposed to be the last birthday you celebrate."

A half hour later the two of them were still lingering over coffee when the doorbell rang. It was a delivery from Carlotta's, one of the most exclusive salons in the city.

"Carlotta's, hmmm?" Ann Marie said as Catherine walked in with a dress box bearing the boldly scripted logo. "Somebody paid a pretty penny, and we know who." Catherine opened the attached card. *For tonight,* it read. She offered the note for Ann Marie to have a look. "Very nice, sugar. Now open the box and let's see what's inside before I die of curiosity."

Excitedly removing the lid and tissue, Catherine barely heard Ann Marie's exclamations of "It's gorgeous!" . . . "It's elegant!"

"It's *gray,*" she mumbled with a stricken look.

"It's not *gray,*" Ann Marie countered. With a swift hand she whisked the shimmering frock out of the box and held it up. "It's silver," she added. "Look how it catches the light."

With an elaborate cowled neck that draped over the shoulders, the sheath was concocted of some kind of woven mesh that did, indeed, shine with metallic highlights. But to Catherine's eye it was still gray—and upon leaving Winslow House, she'd promised herself she'd never again wear the hated, colorless color.

"Try it on," Ann Marie urged, and Catherine retired to the bedroom, secretly hoping to find some flaw with the thing. But Eliot was on the money. The dress fit perfectly.

"You look beautiful," Ann Marie pronounced.

"Don't you think it's too much for Poogan's Porch? I'd been planning on the red dress I wore to that charity benefit." *Red!* Eliot had exclaimed upon seeing her that night. *Is there something wrong with red?* she'd asked. *It doesn't photograph well. . . .*

"The red is lovely, too, but of course you must change your plan and wear Eliot's gift. Truly, it couldn't be more perfect."

"Right," Catherine murmured. "Just like everything he does."

"What was that?" Ann Marie queried.

She turned away from her reflection and mustered a smile. "Nothing. I think I'll hang it up now."

When Ann Marie took her leave, Catherine tried to ignore the air of gloom that had fallen over her birthday afternoon. But every time she went into the bedroom and noted the dress hanging in readiness by the closet door, her mood sank a little lower. That evening she derived no more pleasure in donning the garment than she had earlier in the day. Eliot, however, was enchanted.

"You're breathtaking," he said with a look of approval.

"So are you," Catherine returned, and meant it. Dressed

in a starched white shirt, dark suit, and tie, he would draw the eye of every woman they passed. "Thank you for the dress," she added.

"I knew it was you as soon as I saw it," he replied.

Catherine's mien of pleasantness flickered, but held. Never had such a lovely creation been *less* "her." She hated the damn gray dress; even worse, she felt neurotic for hating it.

It was nearly eight o'clock as they drove toward the destination of 72 Queen. Streetlamps glowed against the twilight, illuminating the District with picturesque charm. In order to be sure of getting into Poogan's Porch on a Saturday night, Eliot had booked their reservation weeks in advance. Turning onto Queen Street, they were confronted with a long line of parked cars, except for one vacancy precisely in front of the establishment, which seemed to have been left for their convenience.

"The luck of a birthday girl, I presume," Eliot said, and smilingly nosed the BMW into the space.

As he got out and came around, Catherine smoothed her skirt and shored herself up. *Begone, dark feelings,* she silently commanded. *It's my birthday, and I'm going to have a wonderful time.* The sentiment sparkled in her smile as Eliot ushered her out of the car and up the walk.

Built in the decade preceding the Civil War, the white peak-roofed building had been designed as an elegant Charleston home but, like many others, had found a new identity in the twentieth century. Fronted with live oak and two stories of porches from which it took its name, the popular restaurant was famous for its continental cuisine and impeccable service. As Catherine and Eliot stepped inside, they were greeted by the buzz of a capacity crowd.

The maître d' stepped swiftly to meet them. "Good evening, Councilman." Escorting them to the staircase, he flourished a hand. "Your table is above. Henri will seat you."

Following his direction, Catherine lifted her gaze and began to climb . . . toward a dark-haired man in a tuxedo. The sight of him stirred a tremor in some netherworld of consciousness, and the image of Nicki's clown traipsed across her mind's eye. A moment later the waiter's smiling face came into focus. He took the lead toward the enviable front veranda, Eliot commandeered her elbow, and Catherine was just beginning to savor the succulent aromas drifting through the dining salons when they broached the porch.

"Happy birthday!" The chamber erupted with the chorus, and Catherine leaped back as much as Eliot's corraling hand would allow. As he released a booming laugh, her stunned gaze swept the candlelit tables. Ann Marie was there, and Eliot's parents . . . Councilman and Mrs. Rudd, and . . . *Aunt Sybil*! The rest of the crowd of thirty or so was comprised of dignitaries she'd come to know through Eliot, as well as a sprinkling of news reporters.

Eliot held up silencing palms. As the commotion settled, he turned to Catherine. "Are you surprised?" he asked. When she silently nodded, the crowd broke into good-natured laughter.

"Do you think you can stand one more surprise?"

"I'm not sure," she mumbled to another round of chuckles.

"You'll have to do your best," Eliot replied. "Because I've asked these people here for more reasons than one." Stepping up to Catherine, he took her hand. "I've asked them here as witnesses."

There was a gasp from the crowd as Eliot went down on one knee. Flash bulbs began to pop, and Catherine's heart to pound.

"Catherine Winslow," he said in a ringing tone. "Will you do me the great honor of becoming my wife?"

Catherine had the feeling that the onlookers broke into excited chatter at that point. She failed to hear as she seemed to slip outside herself and view the scene from a floating distance. It was a picture straight out of a storybook: the handsome prince kneeling at the lady's feet, looking up with adoring eyes.

"A simple yes will do," Eliot prompted with a confident smile that brought Catherine spiraling back to reality. A suspended moment of silence befell the candlelit tables. She could feel the eyes of the crowd, could sense their bated breath.

"Yes," she surrendered, her whisper met with the jolting noise of a cheer. Eliot rose to his feet and produced a velvet box from his breast pocket. A moment later he was slipping an emerald-cut diamond onto her finger. It fit as perfectly as the gray dress.

As Catherine looked up from the jewel, her gaze chanced to turn toward the table where Aunt Sybil was preening before Councilman Rudd like a proud mother peacock. For a scary moment Catherine thought she was going to be sick, but then years of self-discipline came through. Swallowing down the lump in her throat, she pasted the expected smile on her face.

Champagne flowed, along with a number of toasts. After a spectacular meal that Catherine was barely able to touch, the waiter wheeled in a table with a cake inscribed not with "Happy Birthday," but "Congratulations." Eliot never would have considered anything other than a successful outcome to his plan.

The hours passed. The women exclaimed over her ring. The men clapped Eliot on the back.

"Any idea of a wedding date?" a reporter asked at one point.

"Yes, I have an idea," Eliot replied. "Catherine! Come here a minute. You, too, Ann Marie. I've a feeling you'll be matron of honor. We may as well get your approval here and now." As she and Ann Marie joined him, he stretched a welcoming arm around each of them and smiled as the reporter lifted his camera.

"I was thinking of September twenty-fourth," Eliot then said. "That would give my future wife a chance to complete her summer program at Waterfront Clinic. It's really quite remarkable the difference she's managing to make in the lives of those children."

Pressing a quick kiss to Catherine's cheek, Eliot added, "*Plus* it would give us time for a leisurely honeymoon before the elections." He turned to Ann Marie. "What do you think, Ann Marie? How does the twenty-fourth of September strike you?"

"It's a marvelous month for a wedding in Charleston," Ann Marie chimed. "The summer crowds are gone. September is perfect."

Perfect, Catherine silently repeated behind her frozen smile—like the gray dress, and the huge diamond, and the spectacle of a proposal to which she could hardly say "No," or "Maybe," or "I must think," or anything other than the answer Eliot willed.

"But it's so close!" Ann Marie quickly added. "Hardly more than two months. There are so many arrangements to be made."

"Mother is putting the finishing touches on the Reynolds portion of the list," Eliot responded, and turned to Catherine. "I hope you like big weddings. Our side is numbering close to three hundred. By the way, I happen to know St. Michael's is available on the twenty-fourth. Five o'clock? High formal? What do you think?"

Catherine could no more force a sound from her throat than she could fly. She found herself nodding assent, to which Ann Marie clapped her hands to her cheeks.

"St. Michael's! How beautiful! I can just see you, Catherine, walking down the aisle in a white gown with scads of train."

Catherine stood there, a picture of serenity, while her emotions tumbled like crazed acrobats. *That's it, then,* she thought. *I'll be married to Eliot at five o'clock, September twenty-fourth, in St. Michael's, with hundreds of people watching while I walk down the aisle in a dress with scads of train.*

Through the rest of the celebratory evening, she mingled . . . and smiled when it was required . . . and God, how she fought to capture any semblance of the bright spirits such an occasion should afford. But they dodged every effort—like pretty bubbles whisked away by her grasping hand . . . floating ever more elusively off the porch, beyond the peaked roof, and into the muffling darkness of the low-country summer night.

Chapter Nine

For the past week nearly every thought in Nicki's head had centered around Jack Cantrell. The morning after he flatly refused her kiss, she stayed in her quarters, seething, and avoided him for the entire day. By evening, however, the truth had smacked her in the face: *This* attitude wasn't going to get her anywhere.

If she'd given up the first time things got tough, she'd never have climbed her first mountain. So, on succeeding days when a moment of privacy arose and Jack stalwartly— if diplomatically—sidestepped the opportunity for an amorous advance, Nicki merely thought toward this night, her birthday. Tonight, she had him all to herself. Tonight, she hoped to work the magic of what Elena called "the notorious Nicki charm."

She dressed in the cheery splendor of a chamber that looked like a birthday garden. The past two days vans from all over the island had arrived at the ranch to deliver— under Jack's watchful eye—an array of packages and flowers. A dozen arrangements filled the room with fragrance and color, including a vase of tall red roses from Paolo, a huge basket of bird-of-paradise from Melrose, and from Elena—who knew all about the elusive Jack and Nicki's hopes for the approaching evening—a bottle of champagne accompanied by a bunch of balloons inscribed with the sentiment of "Good luck!"

Earlier in the day at a celebratory family luncheon, for which Malia prepared a smorgasbord of Nicki's favorites, Austin had presented her with a magnificent pair of three-quarter-karat diamond earrings, and Malia with a selection of shimmering evening nylons. Fixing the diamonds at her ears, Nicki pulled on a pair of translucent black nylons that cloaked her legs with the sheen of a starry night, then took further sensual pleasure in donning the almost indecently short, strapless, ruby-sequined sheath that hugged her figure with a sparkling splash of scarlet.

She considered it her fail-safe dress. Three times she'd worn it, and on each occasion had succeeded in drawing the ogling stare of every man who crossed her path.

Stepping into black *peau de soie* heels with tiny rhinestones across the toes, Nicki dabbed perfume in every erogenous zone she could think of, and was ready by a quarter to seven. Jack wasn't due for fifteen minutes, and although she liked the picture of him calling for her at the door, she decided to forgo that pleasure in favor of quelling her impatience for the night to begin.

Moving quietly into the hall, Nicki scanned its length for signs of Austin or Malia. When her uncle learned of her birthday night plans, he'd been vehemently against the idea of her spending the evening with "that damn surly driver." And although Malia had said nothing, her eyes had expressed volumes of apprehension.

Avoiding them both, Nicki left the house by means of the seldom-used portico and strolled to the garage beneath a clear sky aglow with the fire of the descending sun. When she looked through the screen door of the apartment and spotted Jack standing in the center of the room, she caught her breath.

Tonight, the renegade she was accustomed to seeing in jeans and T-shirt was wearing cream-colored trousers, a matching loose-fitting jacket, and a silky shirt about the shade of his golden green eyes. All decked out in fashion-magazine finery, his long sun-streaked hair settling rakishly about the shoulders of his jacket, Jack was as picture-perfect as any male model.

His attention was centered on something he was holding. Nicki's eyes widened when he lifted the thing to a telltale firing position, and she clearly saw the pistol. After a moment of peering down the barrel, he lowered the weapon, reached behind his back, and neatly tucked it in a holster hidden beneath his jacket.

"What's the gun for, Jack?" He spun around as Nicki opened the screen and stepped in. His gaze swept over her, and he whistled.

"Man," he said. "You are going to stop some traffic tonight."

Her preoccupation with the pistol stole her attention from the compliment. "What's the gun for, Jack?" she repeated.

He gave her a solemn look. "I've had it a long time, Nicki. Don't worry. It's licensed, and I know how to use it."

"Great, but why wear it tonight?"

"Just a precaution."

"Isn't a karate black belt enough precaution?" she pressed.

Jack walked up to her and lightly gripped her bare shoulders. "I just like to be prepared. Forget about it, okay?" he requested, and wiped the thought of the pistol from Nicki's mind as he put a strong arm around her waist and escorted her to the Ferrari.

As they drove along the seaside road toward the Mainsail, Nicki was deluged with echoes to which she turned a deaf ear. Mostly, they sounded like Malia's voice whispering about "the unattainable." Mostly, they cautioned against feelings that had already taken root. Nicki studied the masculine hand on the stick shift. It was sun-browned and masterful, and the thought of it on her body triggered an erotic image.

"My, my," she sighed.

Jack glanced her way. "Did you say something?"

"No, nothing," she answered, and retreated behind a blithe facade that was both old and practiced, new and untried. Many men had sat in that seat beside her. None had made her feel that she couldn't categorize them, dally for awhile, then continue without a backward glance. Until now.

Eventually Nicki directed Jack onto the palm-lined drive leading to the Mainsail Yacht Club. Glimmering shafts of light played across manicured greens and gardens as they drove past clusters of luxury bungalows tucked among screens of palmetto.

"Pretty, isn't it?" she said.

"Pretty ritzy," Jack replied.

"My grandparents were among the founding members of the place. Of course, it's grown a lot since their day."

Suddenly Nicki was showered by the strange sense of

radiance that had come over her from time to time since childhood. She had no idea what it was or meant, and had always thought of it simply as "the feeling," one of those inexplicable things like déjà vu. When it happened, she was flooded by an ethereal sense of warmth. She hugged herself as the shimmering sensation continued.

"I can roll up the window if you're cool," Jack said.

Looking aside, Nicki gave him a smile. "On the contrary. I'm very warm. Sometimes the strangest, nicest feeling comes over me. It's like I'm not alone, like someone's watching over me."

"Maybe your guardian angel," Jack suggested.

"I never knew my mother. I like to think that sometimes she looks in on me. Does that sound nutty?"

"Not at all," he responded with a conspiratorial grin. "And even if it did, it's your birthday, and you're entitled to think whatever you like—nutty or not."

Parking in the shelter of palms, they went inside where Nicki was effusively greeted by the maître d'. "I was devastated when I heard your birthday party was canceled."

"Yeah. Me, too," Nicki answered with a sly glance at Jack.

"How nice that you should visit us after all," the maître d' added, and showed them to a table overlooking the marina. Except for a few scattered couples who were dining, and a group of barflies watching baseball on the big-screen TV in the neighboring club room, they had the place to themselves.

"If my *party* were going on," Nicki murmured as the waiter approached, "the place would be *packed.*"

"Exactly," Jack responded with a contented look.

The waiter took their orders, returned with cocktails, and faded politely away. As Jack took a sip of his drink, he turned toward the window. It was a pretty sight—the last rosy rays of sunset glinting on dark blue water, the boats bobbing up and down at their moors in a dancing rainbow of colors.

"There are some nice-looking boats out there," he said. "I'll bet some of those yachts would go for—what?—a quarter of a million? Half a million?"

"I guess so."

"Which one is the *Nicki?*"

She looked across the table and found Jack watching her. "None of them. My grandparents docked a couple of vessels here. My father, too. But boats aren't my thing."

"Too tame?" Jack teased.

"Anything but," Nicki soberly replied. "My grandparents were avid sailors. They died on a voyage they'd made a hundred times—an explosion no one could explain. My father was an expert diver who drowned one day when his equipment failed. Again, no one could explain. As they say, the sea rarely gives up her secrets."

"I'm sorry," Jack said. "I didn't know."

Nicki shrugged as she glanced back to the window. "Water is pretty to look at, but it's treacherous, too. It seems to me that if we humans were meant for it, we'd have been born with gills."

"One could argue a similar point about the wind you're so wild for, you know."

She met Jack's eyes with a puzzled look. "What do you mean?"

"From what Melrose says, I gather you've scaled the most fearsome mountains in the world, defying gravity with nothing but ropes and pins to hold you up. And hang gliding is one of the most dangerous activities ever conceived. One might say that if we were meant to soar with the birds, we'd have been born with wings."

"Touché," Nicki returned with a dimpling smile, at which point Jack was the one to shrug and look away. "I guess it's each to his own particular poison," she went on. "What's yours, Jack? If it's fast cars and loose women, I'll be happy to supply both."

"You're too much," he muttered with a small grin.

Nicki set down her glass and cradled her chin in her palm. "Tell me. What's the thrill you can't resist, hmmm?"

"Well, it's not defying gravity, I can tell you that."

"Come on, Jack."

He sat back and eyed her. "The thrill I can't resist?"

"I'm sure you must have one. Everybody who isn't a total bore has a secret thrill. And you're far from boring."

"You'll be disappointed," he warned.

"I doubt it," Nicki replied with piqued curiosity.

"Okay, then. It's mysteries. I can't resist a good mystery, or even one that's not so good. It's like an obsession. I've read every author you can name. In fact, I used to belong to a club that mailed me a dozen titles a month."

She straightened from her propped position with a grimace. "You're telling me the thrill you can't resist is *books*?"

He chuckled. "I told you you'd be disappointed."

"Damn right," she confirmed.

Throughout a sumptuous meal of grilled swordfish with all the trimmings, for which the Mainsail chef was widely known, Jack remained a tolerant subject for the biographical questions Nicki fired. He talked easily about restaurants, museums, and landmarks of Chicago, which was one of the major mainland cities she'd never visited. He painted vivid pictures of the neighborhood where he grew up, the local college he attended, and the hankering to see the world that eventually led him to the Hawaiian islands.

Things were going so well Nicki didn't want to risk spoiling them with the bluntly personal inquiries that danced on the tip of her tongue. When, during this series of events, had Jack gotten married? And to whom? How long had it lasted? Had there really been nothing but one-night stands since she died? After the waiter cleared their dinner plates, he delivered a cake for two with a single burning candle, "Compliments of the gentleman."

Nicki's face lit up with delight. "Thanks, Jack."

"My pleasure. Make a wish."

"Indeed I shall," she replied, and conjured a memory of the last time she'd made a wish over a candlelit cake, which had ended in a delving kiss from the man across the table. Jack arched a brow as though silently scolding her for what she was thinking.

With slices of the exquisitely rich cake, they had demitasses of coffee with Kahlúa. And after that the maître d', waiter, and chef approached the table and insisted on opening a bottle of champagne and toasting her birthday. By the time she and Jack rose from the table, it was nearly midnight and they were the only souls but staff left in the place. Nicki felt as though she were floating as she proceeded down the quiet hall toward the entrance, her hand tucked intimately in the crook of Jack's arm.

Exiting the building, they stepped into a setting made for romance. A huge yellow moon hung over the deserted parking lot while a seaside breeze rustled the fronds of nearby palms . . . and played with the glistening hair of the tall man beside her.

"That was truly a lovely birthday dinner," Nicki said.

"I enjoyed it, too," Jack replied with a smile. "You didn't mind missing out on a big bash too much?"

"Not a bit. You didn't mind being manipulated into bringing me here too much?"

"Not a bit."

Running her hand along the sleeve of his jacket, Nicki stepped close and lifted her eyes. "Could I have my wish now?"

The smile slowly drained from Jack's face. "Are you implying what I think you're implying?"

Her dreamy sense of enchantment faltered. "Don't make a big deal out of it, Jack. Just kiss me." He responded by catching her chin in firm fingers and bending down until his nose was an inch away. Moonlight glimmered in his eyes as they bored into hers.

"Will you loan me a wish in these last few minutes of your birthday?" he asked.

"Sure," Nicki whispered.

"Then I wish you'd stop making me out to be the heavy, when all I'm trying to do is the right thing." With that Jack released her and strode off in the direction of the Ferrari. After a stunned instant of immobility, Nicki spun around and spread her arms.

"Who says it's the 'right thing'?" she called to his back, and started after him. But just as she spanned the distance his long legs had created, Jack flung out a barricading arm.

"Don't come any closer," he commanded. "Somebody's been here."

She peered around his side. "What?" she questioned . . . and then saw the orchid pinned beneath the windshield wiper. Suddenly the air of romance evaporated. Suddenly the night was cold and dark. She hung back as Jack moved forward, plucked the hated flower, and tossed it away from the Ferrari.

"I don't see a note," he said. "But there's a big jagged scratch on the hood. It could have been made with a screwdriver, maybe a knife. Stay where you are. I'm gonna check this out."

Fishing a penlight from some unseen pocket inside his jacket, Jack lifted the hood and examined the engine. Nicki paced a ten-foot length of the parking lot.

"Everything here seems okay," he pronounced.

"Good. Can we get out of here?"

"Just hold on, Nicki." Shrugging out of his jacket, Jack tossed it in her direction. As she caught it, he removed the pistol and holster, and carefully set them aside. "I'm gonna take a look underneath," he added. Sitting down in front of the Ferrari, he starting shimmying beneath it on his back.

"What the hell are you searching for?" Nicki called as she maintained the instructed, hovering distance.

"Nothing in particular," he called in return. "I just wanted to check— Hello."

"What?" she cried. "What is it?"

Jack crawled from beneath the car and swiftly closed the distance between them. Once again his eyes sparkled down at her, only this time their glimmering light seemed to signal a state of danger. "Looks like our friend, the clown, has taken a step beyond sending flowers. The son of a bitch cut the brake line."

She clutched the bulky warmth of the masculine jacket to her breast but was nonetheless swamped with a chilling sense of horror. The curving cliffside road back to the ranch, plus no brakes, added up to one thing. "He's gonna get me," she murmured.

Jack placed a pair of comforting hands on her shoulders. Nicki barely felt his touch. "Come on, now—" he started to say.

"He *is* going to get me!" she broke in. "At Ed Coleman's funeral he left me a note that said, *You're next*. He means it!"

Lifting his hands from her shoulders, Jack captured her face in warm palms. They were hard and forceful and wonderfully tender all at the same time. "Look at me, Nicki. And believe what I say. He is *not* gonna get you, okay? I won't let him."

She stared with burning eyes, longing to believe what Jack was saying, but terrified beyond believing in anything but the merciless intent of the clown.

"For now, we'll go back inside and call the police," Jack stated. "Our boy just graduated into a new category."

"What do you mean?" Nicki prodded from between stiff lips.

Jack's brows furled, his moonlit features taking on a stormy look. "This isn't just stalking anymore," he said. "This is attempted murder."

Murder! As quickly as the shocking word echoed in Catherine's mind, the image of Jack began to shrink and move away, gaining velocity until—like the headlight of a night train—it sped into blackness.

She turned her head with a start, her eyes flashing through darkness, as her brain scrambled to make the jump from the world of Jack and Nicki to her own. After a moment she became aware of Eliot's arm lying across her chest. Shifting out from under it, Catherine crawled from bed, went into the bathroom, and flipped on the lights. As she reached for the faucet, a sparkling ray flashed from her left hand.

Her gaze flew to the rock of a diamond, and it all came back—Poogan's Porch, the surprise party, plans for a September wedding. Eyes lifting, she stared into the mirror above the sink as her memory re-created the picture of Eliot on one knee. *Will you do me the great honor of becoming my wife?*

She'd hidden her misery through the crawling hours at Poogan's Porch . . . and later when her fiancé sealed the bargain by amorously claiming his bride-to-be. Now her feelings were free to come to the surface, and Catherine's eyes filled with hot tears.

It shouldn't feel this way, an inner voice whimpered. And the amazing dream bore out her secret doubts. It had been so clear, so sharp. She could even picture the shape of the scratch on the hood of the Ferrari.

She once had read that dreams were the subconscious's symbolic replay of conscious thought and emotion. And she could still feel the terror of the moment when Jack announced the clown had struck. As tears spilled over, Catherine closed her eyes and summoned the vision of Nicki's dynamic protector. But even as his features materialized, she faced the truth.

Jack existed only in the realm of dreams. In the real world there was no beautiful hero to come to the rescue.

And if her life were truly about to take a turn over a cliff, the only one who could stop it was herself.

It was half past six, the sun barely up. Marla rose with a feeling of contentment. Sunday mornings were her favorite times nowadays. If Eliot was in town on Saturday, he always passed the night with Catherine, so there were no fresh marks or memories to get past. And probably three or four days of freedom remained before Marla had to start thinking about seeing him again.

Pulling on a white robe, she toddled into the kitchen to start a pot of coffee and fetched the newspaper from the stoop. As she waited for the coffee to brew, she found intrusive thoughts of Eliot sneaking in to shadow her sunny morning.

Daring sex play and experiments with bondage had degenerated into thinly disguised beatings, and with each trip to the still-unknown location of the cabin in the woods, the differentiation between brutal lord and cringing subject became more painfully clear. Inch by degrading inch he was annihilating the person she used to be. Soon there would be nothing left, and the worst part was the sluggish powerlessness she felt to stop him.

Trying her best to shut down her dark train of thought, Marla opened the newspaper, turned to the local section, and was stopped by the front-page headline. COUNCILMAN TO WED MERMAID, it read. There was a three-column story, and a picture of Eliot bending to one knee before Catherine—just like in the storybooks.

Reaching across the counter for cigarettes, Marla lit up and looked at the photo once more. So . . . the Republican candidate for state senate had played things to the hilt, and had staged a proposal the voters would never forget.

Marla blew a column of smoke at the smiling likeness of the devil's face. In a way, she wasn't at all surprised.

Monday, July 11

A police squad headed by a sharp young lieutenant named Tanaka responded to Jack's call from the Mainsail. They confiscated the Ferrari and thoroughly examined it before returning it to the ranch two days later. Austin, Melrose, and Malia, as well as Nicki and Jack, gathered in the study to hear the findings.

"There were no fingerprints anywhere on the car except those of Miss Palmer and Mr. Cantrell," he said. "In fact, there's no indisputable evidence of tampering. The break point on the line was frayed. It's possible that it snapped on its own."

"Yeah, just like the stitching on Nicki's saddle a couple of months back," Jack commented with a morose look.

"Isn't there *something* you can do?" Austin barked.

"Yes," Melrose chimed in. "Protective surveillance, for instance. Can't you assign someone?"

"I understand how you must feel," Tanaka replied. "But I don't have the manpower. There are crimes going down in our jurisdiction every day—larceny, assault, homicide, crimes with hard evidence. In this case I know what the presence of an orchid *suggests*. But supposition carries no weight in court, and that's all we have—supposition."

He cast a sympathetic look in Nicki's direction. "I understand you're a world traveler, Miss Palmer. You might consider leaving the islands for a while, until this 'clown' has a chance to lose interest."

"But what if he *doesn't* lose interest? What if he follows? Here at home, at least I'm surrounded by friends."

"You have a point," Tanaka admitted. "Then, let's analyze home security. I noted your alarm system. Is it in good working order?"

"It's the top of the line," Austin put in. "I upgraded last year."

"Good," Tanaka pronounced. "What about security guards?"

"We've got twenty-four-hour patrols around the house and outbuildings," Austin replied.

"Provided by a trio of retired *paniolos,*" Melrose pointed out. "They're as old as I am, and about as slow."

Tanaka looked at Nicki once more. "Want a suggestion?"

"Sure," she replied with a shrug.

"You've got the money. Hire yourself some private talent."

"Private talent?" Austin echoed with a frown.

"Yes," Nicki thoughtfully murmured, her eyes widening as they turned to Jack. "And I know just where to get it."

Austin stepped forward and cut his eyes toward Jack. "If you want a professional, I'll find someone suitable. You don't know anything about this guy's credentials."

"You should see his karate moves," Nicki remarked.

"Tae kwon do," Jack corrected with a small grin.

"I had Jack checked out before I hired him," Melrose announced.

"You wouldn't mind loaning out the services of your driver?" Nicki asked, and, upon receiving a grandfatherly wink, looked swiftly to Jack. "Will you take the assignment? I'll make it worth your while."

"I'm already being paid well enough," Jack mumbled.

"You could provide around-the-clock surveillance?" Tanaka asked.

"As long as my employer cuts me loose," Jack answered, and glanced toward Melrose, who responded with: "Consider yourself loose."

"Tae kwon do, huh?" Tanaka mused with an assessing up-and-down look. "Black belt?"

Jack gave him a short nod. "If I'm going to do this, I need to be closer to Nicki. In the garage apartment, I'm too far removed."

"I'll make up the guest suite down the hall from hers," Malia quietly announced, and drew Austin's raging eye.

"Can no one *hear* me?" he bellowed, his glare swerving from Malia to Nicki. "I said *I'll* find someone suitable!"

Nicki strolled up to him, planted her feet, and confronted him with an unyielding look. "I'm perfectly capable of hiring *my* own 'talent,' Uncle. And I want Jack."

That night, after a stilted supper during which Austin relentlessly scowled and Malia—in typical fashion—maintained the serene facade that everything was as usual, Nicki helped Jack transport his belongings from the garage apartment to the quarters down the hall from her own. He didn't have much—the most cumbersome items being a couple of boxes full of paperwork and mystery novels. After dumping a box in the center of Jack's newly acquired bedroom floor, she curiously withdrew one of the paperbacks.

"The Headless Corpse?" she voiced with distaste.

Jack glanced over from the closet across the room. "That's a pretty good story, actually."

Nicki tossed the novel back into the box. "I guess there's no accounting for some people's taste."

"Yeah, well . . . at least I don't have to perform death-defying feats with mountain peaks and hang gliders to get my kicks."

"Don't knock it till you've tried it," she sang, and took a sweeping look about the guest chamber. Done up in cool shades of blue and green, the spacious suite offered a terrace view and featured all the appointments of a luxury hotel, including a wet bar and mini-fridge freshly stocked with snacks and drinks.

"Do you think you'll be comfortable here?" she asked.

Jack walked toward her, a grin playing about his lips. "I'll try to manage. How about you? Will you rest more comfortably with me nearby?"

Nicki gazed up at him and was showered with a flurry of resurfacing attraction. "I'll try to manage."

But despite the comfort of Jack's newly instituted residency, Nicki found it impossible to rest as images of the clown revolved through her mind.

Bit by bit the airy familiarity of her chamber seemed to close in. Each shadow suggested a face peering through the blinds, each sound a stealthy footstep. Sometime after midnight she gave in to the temptation to creep down the hall, where a strip of light showed beneath Jack's door. She lightly tapped, and within seconds Jack—who was wearing nothing more than a faded pair of gym shorts—was whipping open the door and pulling her inside.

"Is something wrong?" he demanded, his hands gripping her shoulders.

"No . . . yes . . . not really," Nicki stammered. "I'm just shaky, Jack. I hate to admit it, but this guy's getting to me."

Jack released her shoulders with a light squeeze. "If you ask me, you've been handling this thing like a champ. Want some water? A drink, maybe?"

"Whiskey," Nicki decisively replied. Leading her to a seat on the bed, where one of his notorious mystery novels was propped open, Jack poured her a shot and sat down beside her. He watched her consideringly as she did away with the contents of the shot glass.

"Better?" he asked. When she nodded, he said, "Would you like me to walk you back to your room and make sure everything's secure?"

"I'm not feeling *that* much better," Nicki objected. "I don't want to be alone."

"Want to spend the night here with me?"

Her brows lifted as a smile spread across her face. Stretching sexily on her side, she patted the spot beside her. Jack rose to his feet, his expression a mixture of amusement and disapproval.

"Platonically speaking, of course," he added. Turning off the bedside lamp, he took a pillow from the bed and headed for the couch across the room. Nicki watched him go with dismay.

"Couldn't we at least *sleep* in the same bed?" she complained.

"No, I don't think so. I'm a man with honorable intentions, but I'm not made of stone."

She gazed in his direction with surprise. "That sounds encouragingly as though you're tempted."

"Oh, I never said I wasn't *tempted*," Jack responded with a rumbling chuckle. Stretching out on the couch, he switched off the remaining light and plunged the chamber into darkness.

"Good *night*, Nicki," he concluded with staunch authority.

Snuggling beneath the covers, she breathed in the scent of Jack, forgot all about the sinister clown, and drifted to sleep with a smile on her face.

Chapter Ten

The engagement of state senate candidate Reynolds to the Charleston mermaid wasn't just announced by the media, it was seized upon. Film from the surprise party featuring Eliot's dramatic proposal was shown on TV, pictures appeared in the newspaper, and it was the hot gossip topic on local radio. The newly engaged couple were the darlings of the city.

After a deluge of congratulatory luncheons and cocktail parties, Eliot vanished once more to the campaign trail—not that the publicity flagged. One day while Catherine was grocery shopping, an elderly lady stopped her, asked for an autograph, and reached into her shoulder bag. Catherine thought she meant to produce a copy of *Passionate Bride*. But no. It was a local magazine with a picture from the engagement party on the cover.

If ever there had been an opportune moment to stem the tide, it must have passed while Catherine was in a state of shock. Now, with each passing day, the snowballing issue of the wedding became more mammoth, and the whispering notion of doing something to stop it more scandalous.

Ann Marie offered to help with the arrangements. Catherine dazedly relegated the duties. It was Ann Marie who reserved St. Michael's, spotted the one-of-a-kind satin gown "with a train a mile long," and collaborated with Eliot's mother and Aunt Sybil on the guest list, which topped out at five hundred and one.

As Ann Marie excitedly reported her progress, Catherine shrank behind the mask of old. On the outside she presented a placid mask; on the inside she felt as though she were constantly on the verge of screaming. Her life didn't seem her own anymore, but some wild thing rollicking beyond her control . . . like a runaway stagecoach in an old movie.

And all she could do was watch, frozen and speechless as the child in the tower bedroom. Much as Catherine hated the idea, she sensed the specter of browbeaten years with Aunt Sybil rising up to haunt her.

She carried on as in the old days, by blocking out reality. There were times when she performed as the fiancée, but in her private thoughts the wedding remained a mirage that would never come to pass. She filled her days with the clinic, the evenings that Eliot was away with visits to her father, and at night she dreamed.

The dreams came almost every night now, and rather than fading the next day the scenes remained vivid. Every nuance and intonation, every expression and emotion, seemed emblazoned on Catherine's heart—from the cold starkness of Nicki's fear to the radiance of her adoration for Jack.

Although a scary aura remained as the stalker seemingly bided his time, the tone of the dreams shifted. Technically, Jack remained on Melrose's payroll, but as far as Nicki was concerned, he was *hers* now. They toured the pastures on horseback and hiked the grounds. If she left the ranch, Jack drove her. If she attended a rarely permitted social function, he escorted her.

Nicki was head-over-heels in love with a man who, from the beginning, had rejected the idea of an affair, and continued to stick to his guns. Even the knowledge that Jack would risk his life for her didn't make up for the fact that he consistently resisted her as a woman.

"Why do you insist on treating me like a kid?" she demanded on one occasion. Jack reached out and tousled her hair.

"That's who you are to me—the kid sister I never had."

"I'm *not* a kid. I'm a full-grown, twenty-nine-year-old woman."

"Years don't tell the story, baby. It's the mileage."

Catherine remembered their exchanges gesture by gesture, word for word, and often dwelled on them intentionally to avoid facing her own rapidly unfolding story. The country club ballroom was reserved for the wedding reception. Invitations were selected and sent off for engraving.

Eliot popped in and out of Charleston, staying just long enough to whirl her through some social fete, before disappearing to his campaign duties once more.

Catherine witnessed the events as though separated from them by shifting clouds. When she was on the beach with the kids, her true self swelled to the surface. But when she left the mermaid and returned to the bride-to-be, it shriveled beneath a brilliant rain of good wishes.

Ironically, a telling blow came from the frail hand of her father. When she had an hour or so to herself, Catherine stopped by the house, and was consistently alarmed by the way his body seemed to be shrinking into the bedclothes. In contrast the power of his mind grew stronger, his delusionary periods fewer. One morning in early August, she drove by for a quick visit before time to open the clinic. Her father asked that she read the newspaper, and took interest in a story about Eliot. It was no surprise that early polls predicted him a winner in November.

"And you will be by his side," her father said.

Catherine folded the newspaper and lay it on the server by the bed. "Yes. I suppose I will."

"Your mother and I are extremely proud of you."

Leaning forward in her seat, Catherine placed her hand on his.

"Oh, I don't mean she dropped in today and told me so," her father went on. "I know she died many years ago, but my spirit grows nearer to hers day by day. Do you understand?"

"I think so, Father."

"Then understand that our greatest happiness comes from yours," he concluded, and it was all Catherine could do to keep from bursting into tears. Giving him a quick kiss, she made a hasty exit and nearly collided with her aunt, who apparently had been eavesdropping outside the door. Folding her hands across her stomach, Aunt Sybil proceeded to the stairs, her girth filling the staircase and forcing Catherine to follow slowly behind.

It was a maneuver she remembered in detail. *A lady walks with measured tread,* the instruction echoed in Catherine's mind, and sent a chill down her spine. Continuing to block her passage, Aunt Sybil meandered to the front door and turned.

"I must say the way you've turned out has surprised me in the most pleasant of ways," she then announced.

"That makes my day," Catherine returned, and was as shocked by the flip remark as her aunt, whose black eyes instantly narrowed.

"Was that sarcasm in your voice, young lady?"

Catching her lip between her teeth, Catherine glanced aside to the shadowed, heavy furnishings of the parlor. "No," she mumbled.

"I didn't hear you."

Catherine's head snapped around. "No, ma'am, I said."

"I should hope not when I spent the better part of my life trying to cleanse you of such disrespectful habits."

"If you'll excuse me, I promised Ann Marie I'd drop by the bookshop at nine-thirty."

After a long, silent, tortuous moment of scrutiny, her aunt stepped away from the door, and Catherine fled the house.

"I'm sure she'll be delighted," Ann Marie was saying into the phone when the subject of her conversation walked into the shop. With a bright smile she motioned for Catherine to join her at the counter. "Yes. I'll be sure to pass that along. It does, indeed, show a great vote of confidence. Thank you."

Ann Marie replaced the receiver and looked up excitedly. "What perfect timing! That was your editor. She loves the sequel, and that's not all. They want you to work up a proposal for a trilogy. A three-book contract, Catherine! Isn't that wonderful?"

"Wonderful," she affirmed with the ghost of a smile, and for a moment looked just like the sad little girl of years gone by.

Ann Marie's expression fell. "What is it? What's wrong?"

"Nothing," Catherine replied, and made a visible effort to cheer up. "I just thought I'd stop by."

Ann Marie studied her with doubting eyes. "Your father hasn't taken a turn for the worse, has he?"

"No. He's the same, although he continues to weaken."

"Is everything okay at the clinic?"

"Everything is *great* at the clinic. Kenny Black has a real gift. By end of summer he'll be swimming circles around me."

"Then there must be a problem with Eliot." Once again Ann Marie was reminded of the troubled child as Catherine mutely stared. "Tell me about it," Ann Marie urged, and cast a precautionary glance about the shop. "No one ever comes in this early but you, Catherine. We can talk, *if* you want to."

Finally, Catherine revealed the cause of the circles under her eyes—nightmares of Nicki being stalked by a sadistic clown. Ann Marie well remembered Nicki. As a child Catherine sometimes wrote stories stemming from "the dream," and Ann Marie had marveled at an imagination capable of producing such a free-spirited butterfly of an alter ego. Nicki had always been the fearless adventuress. Now she was afraid. It seemed logical Catherine was feeling a threat from somewhere, or some*one*.

"Do you think Eliot is responsible in some way?" Ann Marie gently asked. "Has he said or done something to frighten you?"

"No. It's just that . . ." The deep blue eyes took on an unmistakable sheen. "Sometimes he scares me to death," Catherine whispered. "Sometimes I get the feeling that, like Nicki's clown, Eliot is creeping up on me—that soon he'll be taking over, and I'll lose control of my life all over again."

"Oh, dear," Ann Marie murmured. Hurrying around the counter, she peered into Catherine's face. "First of all, sugar, you don't have to do a single thing you don't want to. If you don't want to marry Eliot, then don't. But also, don't let the past corrupt that lively imagination of yours. He is *not* Sybil Winslow."

Catherine nodded in agreement, though her eyes continued to glisten. Ann Marie cupped her cheeks in motherly palms. "All brides-to-be have nerves of one kind or another. Considering what you've been subjected to in your lifetime, I don't find it odd that you might be more sensitive than most."

"You think it's just nerves?"

"Yes, I do," Ann Marie replied. "And I'm certain Eliot doesn't have any idea you feel this way. Talk to him. I know it doesn't come easy for you to speak up, but you must remember that he can't read your mind. Now, when do you see him next?"

"Tonight. Finally, after months of parties and trips, we're going to do something we've never done before—stay home and watch TV. There's a documentary he wants to see."

"Sounds like a perfect opportunity to me," Ann Marie declared. "Will you talk to him?"

"I'll try," Catherine murmured.

"Just one piece of advice, okay?" Ann Marie concluded with a teasing wink. "Don't start out by telling him he's a clown."

They ordered pizza, opened a bottle of wine, and settled in front of the television. Eliot had sent her flowers two nights ago when he had "an unavoidable late appointment." White roses again. From their position on the dining table across the room, the fully opened blossoms filled the air with fragrance.

Instead of watching TV, Catherine found herself studying the flowers and remembering the card that came with them. *Love ya,* it said. When the documentary broke for a commercial, Eliot stretched and turned to her with a lazy smile. She gathered her courage and voiced the question in her mind.

"Eliot . . . do you realize you've never told me you love me?"

"Of course I have. I tell you all the time."

"Not really," she said quietly. "Not as though you mean it."

Rising to his feet, Eliot unexpectedly swept her up in his arms. "Shall I show you how much I mean it?" he asked, and started with her toward the bedroom.

"Don't you want to see the rest of the documentary?"

"Not as much as I want to see the rest of you."

And yet despite the lusty way he possessed her, Eliot never uttered the three words that might have chased some of the shadows from Catherine's mind. The next day Ann Marie called and asked if she'd had any luck talking things over with him.

"That was all it took," Catherine lied, and found herself, once again, hiding her doubts like dirty secrets.

*   *   *

Giving the door a light tap, Nicki sauntered into the guest suite. "Hey, Jack. How about some seafood tonight? I've had a taste for *mahi mahi* all day."

The spacious room was in the perfect order in which he always kept it, but empty. "Jack?" she called, and then caught the sound of running water. She proceeded to the bathroom. The door was cracked a few inches. Nicki pushed it fully open. The shower curtain was clear plastic. She could see the outline of his body as he reached up and swept the hair back from his face.

"Okay, big boy," she whispered as she stepped out of her sandals. "Let's see if you can resist *this.*" Peeling off her sundress and underwear, she left them in a pile at the bathroom entrance and walked noiselessly across the tile floor.

"What the hell?" Jack sputtered as she stepped into the shower. His eyes were wide, his face a portrait of shock, as he backed the length of the stall and bumped against the wall. Nicki laughed. Leaning into the streaming jets, she drenched herself, then stepped from the veil of water in his direction.

"What the hell?" she repeated airily. "It's a full-grown woman, Jack. Just like I've been trying to tell you. And you, my friend, are most *definitely* a full-grown man." His hands were propped against the sides of the shower stall as though he expected the floor to drop out from under him any second. The stance afforded Nicki a full frontal view.

"Glad to see you're not modest about it," she added, and moved toward him. Only then did he move a hand, and it was to clamp it on her shoulder and hold her at arm's length.

"Stop, Nicki."

Her blood was hot and racing . . . pounding between her thighs. "You can't mean that," she murmured.

"I *do* mean it," Nicki's eyes flashed to his. "You're beautiful," Jack added in a husky voice as water streamed down his face to drop in beads to his chest. "But I can't do this."

She cast a bold look at his aroused manhood. "Looks to me like you can," she retorted. "Yep, everything seems to be in good working order. *Superb,* in fact."

"It works, all right, but . . . we're *friends,* Nicki. I'm not in the market for anything long-term, and I refuse to let a brief affair destroy what we've got. I care about you too much."

Nicki wrenched out of his grasp. "Honestly, Jack!" she exploded. "Even with no clothes on, you're the biggest stuffed shirt I've ever met!"

Jack's arm fell to his side, but Catherine continued to feel his hand on her shoulder. His image grew cloudy, but she felt his mouth at her breast. The primeval ache bloomed at her core, but with a desperation she'd never known.

Her head twisted on the pillow. She moaned. And then he was inside her, filling the desperation. Catherine's legs went around his hips, clasping him to her, urging him deeper. And something unknown flared to life and began to pulse and build, sending flashes of heat through the whole of her body. By the time her impassioned mind wakened to the truth of things, she was in the clutches of orgasm . . . and so was Eliot.

Catherine gasped for breath as he went still and withdrew. Her breathing gradually calmed. After a few minutes she turned her head and opened her eyes. Having rolled to his side, Eliot was propped on an elbow, watching her. Moonlight silvered his hair and gleamed in his eyes.

"Well, *that* was different," he said in a pleased voice.

"Yeah," Catherine breathily responded. "Different."

"I'll have to wake you up that way more often." He reached over and traced a path along her cheek. "What's this? Tears?"

She lifted a hand and felt the wetness. "Guess so."

"I've never moved you to tears before," Eliot observed in the same cock-of-the-walk tone. Folding his arms behind his head, he lay back and, seemingly, basked in the glory of his macho aplomb.

Catherine sat up and swung her legs over the side of the bed.

"Where ya goin'?" he lazily inquired.

"Bathroom." She rose to her feet, her knees threatening to buckle before she could walk shakily into the next room. Pushing the door closed behind her, Catherine switched on the light, grabbed the sink, and peered into the mirror.

Her cheeks were streaked with tears, her eyes round as saucers.

Heretofore, she'd always faked it. Heretofore, she'd had no idea what the big deal was about. Now she knew. But was it her illustrious fiancé who had delivered her to that shimmering plateau? No. It was Jack—man of her dreams, figment of her mind, entity who didn't exist.

Catherine laughed, and the sound reverberated on a note of hysteria. "What's going on?" Eliot called from beyond the door.

She sidestepped and turned on the shower faucets. "Nothing!" she called back. "I'm going to take a quick shower!" When the water began to steam, she stepped into the tub and propped her hands against the sides of the stall, holding herself steady much as Jack had done. *Jack . . .* The whisper of his name in her mind lured her into closing her eyes, and she could see him standing before her as clearly as if he'd been there in the flesh.

A half hour later when Catherine came out of the bath wearing her robe, Eliot was serenely snoring away. She, on the other hand, had never been more alert in her life. Tiptoeing from the bedroom, she paced the living room, glanced at the angelfish, and walked to the sliding doors.

Moonlight danced invitingly on the rippling water, and she longed to go for a swim, but knew it wasn't feasible to be down there alone at one in the morning. Turning her back on the alluring nightscape, Catherine started back across the room, her gaze lighting on the computer as she passed her workstation.

She wished she could put this energy to use on the trilogy proposal she was supposed to be developing, but the imaginative mind that had always been so full of tales was void of all but one. The only story Catherine could feel was Nicki's. The only hero she could picture was Jack.

That epic was etched in her mind with all the graphic precision of a map—the carnival where Nicki first encountered the clown, the party where Jack showed up, the fracas with the thugs in the straw market, and on and on. Around and around the scenes had circled Catherine's brain. Over and over the lines had played, until she knew them all by heart.

Halting in midstride, Catherine whirled around, her gaze

targeting the long-idle workstation. Once the idea dawned, she couldn't get to the computer fast enough, and waited impatiently while the machine went through its whirring warm-up.

This is not at all what you're supposed to be writing, her conscience scolded, but did nothing to dampen Catherine's excitement. Although there was a hero and heroine, the story was nothing like a romance. She supposed it would be categorized a thriller. She'd never written a thriller before; plus, she had no idea how the story might end.

Regardless of the myriad objections raised by the logical side of her brain, as soon as the computer bleeped a signal of readiness, Catherine's fingers began to fly over the keyboard.

The Clown Wore Black

Someone was watching.
The lights of the carnival continued to glitter, the crowd to mill, but the bright scene grew dim as the feeling enveloped her like veiling fog. Someone was following—his eyes moving over her inch by inch, sending shivers scurrying in their wake. . . .

Friday, August 12

Peni spent most of the night at Paniolos Hale, getting blistered on beer while keeping a bleary eye peeled on the saloon doors. Kimo never showed.

"What the hell *else* is new?" Peni muttered to herself as she stumbled inside the empty house. Picking up a bottle of her father's vintage kahlúa from the kitchen, she threw off piece after piece of clothing on the way to the bath. God, it was hot.

Turning up the bottle, she lost her balance and grabbed for the doorjamb. Or maybe it was just her blood that was on fire. She turned on the shower and left the water cold. But even as it poured over her from head to toe, Peni continued to burn. She thought of Kimo's hands, touched herself, and came with bittersweetness beneath the discreet cascades of the showerhead.

But the gnawing fire only returned. Reaching outside the plastic curtain, she retrieved the liqueur from the back of the toilette. Sometime later Peni caught a glimpse of herself putting on lipstick and combing her hair. . . . Still later she had the impression of donning the white ruffled dress she'd worn to high school graduation and driving somewhere. . . .

And suddenly Kimo's face swam before her against the backdrop of his casually sloppy bachelor's apartment. "Kimo," she mumbled. Locking her arms about his neck, Peni was about to kiss him when he grabbed her wrists and stepped free. His look of horror wrenched her to instantaneous, excruciating sobriety.

"Are you drunk?" he asked as he corraled her errant limbs. Peni's mind reeled. Snatching free, she turned her back.

"Don't get all excited," she cautioned. Taking several blind steps toward the door to Kimo's lodgings, she dismally remembered standing outside and pounding at the portal until his lights came on. She squeezed her eyes tightly shut and tried with all her might to still the mortified shaking of her lips.

"It was just going to be an aloha kiss," she added.

"Is one of us going somewhere?" Kimo questioned from behind her. Taking a deep breath, Peni turned and faced him.

"Yes. *I* am," she announced. Suddenly she could see her course of action. Suddenly everything was clear. "Do you remember that my neighbor always wanted to buy the house?" she went on. "Well, I've decided to sell it to him, lock, stock, and barrel. It's time for me to get the hell off this piece of volcanic rock."

"What brought this on?" Kimo asked with a frown.

"Nothing sudden." Deep inside Peni felt as though everything were melting down, surrendering to a seething inevitability that had waited all along.

"Where will you go?"

"To visit my brothers, start a new life somewhere. There's nothing for me here, Kimo. I've known it for a long time."

"I'm sorry you feel that way, Peni. But if it'll make you

happy to strike out and see the world, then I wish you luck."

"Thanks." She started to turn. Kimo caught her by the arm.

"Aloha, then," he murmured. Stepping close, he pressed a kiss to her cheek and smiled. "Take care of yourself," he added.

"Yeah. You, too," Peni brusquely returned.

Backing abruptly away from his light touch, she strode to the open doorway. "I hope you find what you're looking for," Kimo called after her. Peni's eyes were hard as she turned for a final look at the man she'd loved all her life.

"I have a feeling a whole new world is opening up for me, Kimo," she said with deadly earnest. "Just as soon as I pay my final respects out at Palmer Ranch."

Nicki pivoted before the mirror. Fastening behind the neck, the swimsuit plunged in front and bared her back to the waist, its high-cut legs arching to the crest of her hips. Hot pink. She'd always liked the sound of that.

Jack was working out in the deserted riding ring. It was an ideal place to practice tae kwon do forms, he'd told her, and had adopted the habit of spending an hour or so there most evenings after supper. As soon as Nicki spotted him on this particular Saturday evening, she'd headed for her room and sought out the daring swimsuit she'd brought back from Paris.

The occasion for its debut was perfect: the night hot and sultry, Melrose retired to his quarters, Austin absent with Malia on a rare shopping trip to her home village markets. Nicki and Jack were virtually alone on the property. Throw something hot pink into the bargain, and who knew what might happen?

Giving her reflection a final, satisfied once-over, Nicki strolled out of the house and enjoyed watching Jack do a double-take as she approached the riding ring. He was wearing white loose-fitting pants and nothing more. Above the twilit glow of the garment, the dark shape of shoulders and chest were etched against the dusk. Her pulse quickened at the sight of him.

"That's a nice bathing suit you're almost wearing," he said.

"Glad you noticed."

She ambled close and pressed a fingertip to his glistening chest. "I was thinking that after such a hot workout, you might be in the mood for a cool swim. The pool was cleaned today, and the water looks awfully inviting."

She trolled the fingertip down his chest scant seconds before Jack captured her hand. "Careful, Nicki. One might think you're not quite the debutante you seem."

"One might think correctly, Jack, *if* one had any brains."

He shook his head as he digested that, but his gaze ended up traveling the length of her. "Yeah," he said eventually. "I think a swim would do me good about now."

While she waited for Jack to change clothes and join her, Nicki took a drink out to the darkening terrace and lowered herself into the cooling shallows of the pool. Extending her arms, she rested her neck against the side.

So far, so good. He was on his way, and the scene was even more perfect than she'd imagined—the air filled with the fragrance of flowers, the lantern light slinking across the water in seductive slivers.

She closed her eyes and sank into a daydream that turned sensual as she pictured Jack swimming toward her from the deep end while she lolled in the shallows. His hair was sleek and wet, his eyes fixed on hers as he reached the end of the pool and grasped the deck. The length of his body floated above her, gradually drifting down to settle flesh upon flesh. . . .

Nicki heard a muted footstep behind her, opened her eyes, and smiled. "If you think you can sneak up on me, you're wrong," she announced without looking around. "I have the ears of a fox."

Something sailed past her nose and landed with a *plink!* atop the water. Terror wiped the smile from Nicki's face as she recognized the fuchsia petals of a wild orchid. As quickly as the realization dawned, a gloved hand of steel grabbed her arm, and another pushed her head beneath the surface.

Nicki thrashed and clawed, and made no progress at budging the vise-like grip holding her down. She peered frantically into the shifting depths of water, and suddenly there was an explosion of bubbles through which Jack's form emerged. The gloved hands released, and an instant later Jack's fingers closed about her rib cage and jerked her into the air. Nicki came up sputtering.

"Take it easy," Jack commanded. "Take slow breaths."

She gasped and coughed, but little by little, second by endless second, her ability to breathe returned. Lifting her gaze, Nicki focused tearing eyes on Jack's anxious face.

"Better?" he demanded. As she nodded, they heard the sound of a car engine starting up nearby.

"Damn son of a bitch! He drove right up to the damn house!" With that Jack heaved himself out of the water.

"Where are you going?" Nicki cried in a rasping voice.

"Maybe I can catch the license number."

"No! Don't leave me!" Jack turned and stared down at her. "Please!" Nicki desperately added, at which point he climbed back down into the water and gathered her in his arms.

"Okay," he mumbled. "Don't worry. I'm not going anywhere."

Nicki clung to him and began to sob. "Did you see him?" she wailed after a moment.

"All I saw was a guy dressed in black holding you under. I didn't wait to see anything else." The horrifying image triggered a new round of racking sobs.

"Don't cry, baby," Jack urged. "We'll get the bastard."

But even Jack couldn't soothe the fear that continued to strangle Nicki like a pair of steely hands. She hadn't believed until now—not really. But after this a person would have to be blind not to see the truth.

Whatever his twisted reasoning might be, the clown in black didn't intend to stop until she was dead.

Chapter Eleven

Thursday, September 1

"Don't cry, baby," Jack urged. But even he couldn't soothe the fear that continued to strangle Nicki like a pair of steely hands. She hadn't believed until now—not really. But after this a person would have to be blind not to see the truth.

Whatever his twisted reasoning might be, the clown in black didn't intend to stop until she was dead.

Catherine shut down the computer, leaned back in her chair, and closed her eyes. It was three in the morning—again—but although she was tired, she was filled with satisfaction. *The Clown Wore Black* had caught up to the action of the dreams, and it was turning into the best work she'd ever done.

With Eliot out of town so much, it had been easy to let him abide with the misimpression that after full days at the clinic, she was devoting evenings to the trilogy proposal her publishers had requested. She instinctively knew he wouldn't approve of the project that had taken her over so completely that she now felt more a part of Jack and Nicki's world than her own.

She couldn't put the story on paper fast enough and now was hungry to divulge her secret work to Ann Marie and find out if she agreed it was worthy of publishing. Making the decision to drop the manuscript by the bookshop later that day, Catherine journeyed to her chamber, flopped across the bed, and grabbed a few hours' sleep before time to open the clinic.

That day she was weary and preoccupied and didn't take

much note of the fact that Kenny was absent. But the next morning when he failed to show, she was struck by the certainty that something was wrong. Maybe he was sick. She decided to check her records for his address and drive over that afternoon. As it happened, she didn't have to wait that long to catch a glimpse of the boy.

Finishing a lesson at eleven, Catherine walked over to the lifeguard stand for a towel and noticed a souped-up, gunmetal-gray car parked by the curb. The driver revved the engine. He had a cigarette hanging from his mouth, and . . . it was Kenny!

Catherine started toward the car, but when he saw her intent, he flicked the cigarette out the window, scratched off, and sped down the street. She strode toward the nearest cluster of children on the beach. "Okay, guys. What's going on with Kenny?"

The boys mumbled they didn't know and drifted toward the shoreline. All the girls but one followed. Saucy, ebony-skinned Angel sidled up to her. "He's drivin' for the Pirates now."

"The Pirates? Who are they?"

Angel rolled her eyes. "Lord, honey, don't you know nothin' but how to swim? They're a street gang," she added in a whisper before moving swiftly away to join the others.

After closing the clinic at four, Catherine drove to the street Kenny had listed on his registration form and tried not to be shocked by the slumlike neighborhood of delapidated apartment houses. Porches sagged, laundry fluttered at open windows, loiterers stared—their hooded eyes following her progress as she located the building and climbed a dank stairwell to 2B. There was no bell. She knocked repeatedly, but no one answered. Catherine cruised the depressing streets hoping to spot the gray car. She was about to give up when she spotted a dingy-looking bar with a sign announcing: PIRATES' DEN.

She cruised slowly past and tried to peer inside. But the shades were drawn. If she wanted to know whether or not Kenny was inside, she was going to have to go in and look. Making a resigned U-turn in the deserted street, she parked near the entrance, took a deep breath, and walked to the door.

Leaving the sunny sidewalk, Catherine stepped into com-

parative blackness and was stopped by the deafening noise
of heavy metal music, and the overpowering odors of beer
and smoke. As her eyes adjusted, she saw that there were
twenty or so people gathered throughout the place. A couple were women, the rest men. All of them looked like
cutthroats. All were staring directly at her.

She almost turned around and left. But then the image
of Kenny's face flashed through her mind. Hiding her
trembling hands in the pockets of her shorts, Catherine
made herself move around the bar toward a hefty, long-
haired bartender with a dish towel slung over his shoulder.
As she reached him, someone turned off the music, and
the dive was plunged into silence. All eyes and ears were
on her. Catherine cleared her throat.

"Would you happen to know the Pirates?" she asked.

Her query was met with a roar of laughter. She glanced
around and noted a man rising from a back table. In the
dim light he looked dark and foreboding as he swaggered
in her direction. He was, she guessed, in his mid-twenties
and about six feet tall, with an additional inch courtesy of
biker boots. He wore a red bandanna that tied back long
black hair, black sunglasses, a strong-man T-shirt, and tight
jeans with a gash across the knee.

As he drew near, Catherine noted the JOLLY ROGER tat-
tooed on his biceps. The overall effect was something of a
cross between Hell's Angel and buccaneer.

Stepping up beside her, he propped a hip against the bar.
"The name's Gino, honey. I run the Pirates. What can I
do for *you*?"

Catherine did her best to look directly into the opaque
shields of his dark glasses. "I'm looking for Kenny Black.
I was told I might find him with your . . . *group*."

"Yeah, Kenny. My man's running an errand at the
moment."

"You mean he's driving one of your cars?"

"Why do you want to know?" Gino warily returned.
"You're not a cop. I can spot a cop a mile away."

"No. I'm not with the police. I'm just concerned about
Kenny. After all, he's only fourteen."

"Turned fifteen last week."

"But he has no license. It's illegal for him to drive."

Gino threw back his head and laughed. "Hey, Bobby,"

he called then. "You didn't let Kenny drive without no license, did you?"

"No sir, Cap'n," his cohort called back. "Gave him one myself." There was a round of laughter. Gino's attention returned to Catherine, and he removed his sunglasses to reveal shocking blue eyes—so light against his olive skin that they gave his face an eerie, supernatural look.

"You come into the Pirates' Den and question how the captain runs his ship?" he challenged. "Who the hell *are* you, anyway?"

"My name is Catherine Winslow," she spilled out in a rush. "I'm in charge of Waterfront Clinic, and Kenny's been attending all summer long. But he missed the past couple of days, and—"

"Wait a minute," Gino broke in. "You mean *you're* the Charleston mermaid?" When she timidly nodded, he turned and called out to the others, "Hey, guys! This is the mermaid—you know, the one who pulled Kenny's ass outta the ocean!"

Catherine was astonished as the gang members gathered around, some of them clapping her on the back, others hooting their approval. "Hey, girl, that's cool," one of the women said, only as Catherine gave her a nervous smile, she realized the curvaceous black female in the skin-tight jeans and low-cut top was no woman, but a girl—sixteen at most.

The realization squarely reminded Catherine of the purpose that had brought her to the Pirates' lair. Kenny couldn't end up in a place like this with a life like this. He just couldn't. She met Gino's eyes with newfound conviction.

"Kenny has come a long way at the clinic," she stated quietly. The voice of the gang members died down, and once again the attention of the entire place seemed poised and waiting for what she would say next. "He's a talented swimmer with tremendous heart," she went on. "If Kenny keeps working the way he has this summer, there's no telling where it could lead—maybe to a college scholarship and a wonderful future."

"Some say his future lies with the Pirates," Gino remarked, and elicited a chorus of cheers. Catherine swallowed hard and called on every ounce of courage she possessed.

"Exactly my point," she countered. "Kenny can't have both. It's either the life of an athlete or the life of a Pirate. Which do *you* think would be best for him?"

Losing their easygoing aura of amusement, Gino's features took on a swift look of sharpness. "College scholarship," he muttered. "You people live in such a fairy tale. What about right now, this minute, when there's no money for food or rent? What good are your scholarship fantasies here and now, huh?"

Catherine blinked. "Is this about *money*?"

"*No*, it's not about *money!*" Gino boomed in response. "It's about tradition, and the code of the street, and looking out for our own because nobody else gives a damn."

"You tell her, brother," someone called out, and was joined by others who shouted similar sentiments.

"It's about the older ones taking care of the small ones until they can grow up and do the same," Gino went on. "It's about the Pirates watching out for my man Kenny since he was old enough to get caught stealing candy from the drugstore!"

This time his inspired followers broke into applause. "I find that extremely honorable," Catherine murmured.

Gino raised his hands for silence and craned his neck in her direction. "What was that again? I didn't quite catch it."

She drew a steadying breath. "I said, I think it's honorable of you to care for the small and weak."

"Yeah . . . well . . ." Gino grunted.

"But I still think my way is best for Kenny," she added.

Gino scrutinized her, his pale eyes narrowing. "When Kenny gets back, I'll pass along the message that he has a choice to make. What the man decides after that is up to *him*."

A buoying sense of relief rushed through Catherine. "That's very fair of you, Gino. Thanks."

His reply was a regal nod before replacing his sunglasses. The Pirates moved silently out of her way as Catherine turned and carved a path toward the exit. When she reached the doorway, the earthshaking music resumed. She hurried outside, was momentarily blinded by afternoon light, and thought the sweltering summer air of Charleston had never seemed so sweet.

That evening she savored another tranquil night of Eliot's being a hundred miles away. At half past eight she walked out on the balcony. The slow summer dusk was deepening, dressing the seascape in dreamy twilight. Her gaze traveled the beach and lit on a dark-haired figure sitting all alone. His back was to her as he looked out to sea, but she instantly recognized Kenny.

Catherine hurried downstairs and across the street, noting the presence of the gray Pirates' car parked halfway onto the curb by her building. She was quite close before Kenny caught the sound of her footsteps in the muffling sand. With no more than a passing glance, he peered ahead once more.

"Mind if I sit down?" she asked.

"Suit yourself," he answered with slurred *s*'s, and turned up a beer. Getting down on the sand beside him, Catherine said nothing until he crushed the empty can.

"Where did you get that?" she said then.

Kenny snorted. "There might not be any food in the house, but there's always booze."

"Booze isn't good for you. Neither is smoking, or driving a souped-up car for a street gang."

"Get off my case," he muttered.

"What the devil's wrong with you, Kenny?"

He glared her way with bloodshot eyes. "You're from a different world. You couldn't understand in a million years. Let's just say there are more places to drown than the ocean."

"Like where?"

"Like, why the hell should you care?" he fired.

Catherine tipped her head as she watched him. "If for no other reason, then how about the old Chinese proverb: Once you save someone's life, you're responsible for that person from then on."

"That's dumb. And we ain't in China."

"*Aren't* in China," she gently corrected, at which point Kenny erupted like a volcano.

"What the hell difference does it make how I talk? I'm going *one way*! I was born to go *one way*! And where I'm going, they don't care how you talk!"

Catherine took hold of his shoulder. He tried to jerk away, but she held on. "Listen to me, Kenny. Listen!" After a moment he turned. "It doesn't have to be that way. Maybe I can help if you talk to me. Why have you stopped coming to the clinic and started driving for the Pirates? What happened a few days ago that made everything suddenly wrong?"

The smoldering eyes so bereft of their usual laughter burned into her. "It didn't happen just a few days ago," he mumbled finally. "Ever since Ma died last year, my old man's been hittin' the bottle heavy. Last month the shipyard canned him, and he's been on a binge ever since. A few days ago he signed himself into detox, mostly to avoid the landlord. We can't make the rent."

"I see," Catherine murmured. "How much do you need?"

"Five hundred by the first of the month," he replied heavily. "Which was yesterday. I can get the money from the Pirates. I can't get it anyplace else."

"That's not necessarily true. Maybe there are avenues you haven't considered. We'll talk it through, but not out here. It's getting dark. Come on." Catherine hooked Kenny's arm about her shoulders. "Up we go. Just lean on me."

"Where we goin'?" he asked when she managed to pull him slippily to his feet.

"To get some food and coffee into you," she replied.

Heaving for breath and supporting Kenny with most of her body, Catherine struggled up the stairs to the penthouse, pried her key ring from the hook on her belt, fumbled with the lock, and finally managed to push the door open.

"Wow! Cool aquarium!" he cheerfully exclaimed.

"Keep those feet moving, Kenny. Let's not stop until we're in the kitchen." Propping him in a chair at the table, Catherine put on coffee and slapped together a fat sandwich of ham, cheese, lettuce, and tomato. While Kenny devoured the fare as though he hadn't seen so fine a meal in days, she slipped into the bedroom, wrote him a check, and tucked it in her T-shirt pocket.

When she returned to the kitchen, the sandwich plate shone as though it had been licked clean, Kenny was sipping from his coffee cup, and the eyes he turned on her were astonishingly clear. Catherine glanced at his empty plate.

"Would you like another?" she asked.

He leaned back in his chair and rubbed his stomach as though it were full to the brim. "That was aplenty. Thank you, ma'am."

"You're welcome. I have something else for you, too." Producing the check, Catherine smoothed it out on the table.

"What's that?" Kenny said, and leaned abruptly forward.

"A way to make rent until you can pay me back."

Lifting the check, he read it and looked up with shock. "A thousand bucks? I can't take it, Catherine."

"Yes, you can. Look at it as a business arrangement. In exchange for rent money until you and your father are on your feet, I expect certain things."

"What things?"

"That you'll stop driving for the Pirates. That when school convenes, you'll try out for the swim team. And finally, that when you get a job, you'll gradually pay me off."

Kenny stared at her, a look of hope flooding his face and promptly ebbing. "I'd like a job, but who'd hire a kid off the streets whose latest reference is the Pirates?"

"I have a friend who owns a bookshop on King Street. She's always complaining that she can't seem to find a reliable person to work in the stock room."

"You think she might hire *me*?" he breathlessly ventured.

Catherine smiled. "I think she very well might."

The doorbell rang. She jumped at the fleet thought that it might be Eliot—who had made it clear a number of times that she must always "preserve the line" between providing direction for the children at the clinic and becoming personally involved with them. Remembering that he was miles away, Catherine relaxed for the brief moments it took to walk to the door, then stiffened when she saw Gino and two of his hoods waiting on the stoop.

"I saw the GTO downstairs and the lights in the windows," Gino said. Having changed from the afternoon, he was wearing black jeans and bandanna, a billowy-sleeved white shirt, and a gold hoop in his right ear. Tonight there was nothing of the Hell's Angel about him, but only the rakish flair of a pirate.

"Mind if we come in?" he added.

"Please do," Catherine responded, her heart pounding as the three men strolled inside.

"I was going to bring your car back," Kenny piped up.

Gino offered a pearly smile. "I know, man. I wasn't worried. I was *curious*."

Catherine had the impression Kenny grew a couple of inches as he stepped up to the bigger, older man. "And—uh—I don't mean to seem ungrateful but I don't think I can drive for you anymore. It looks like I might be getting another job."

"Is that a fact?" Gino returned. "So, what you're telling me is that you've made your choice, and you've decided to go with the mermaid, here."

"Yeah," Kenny murmured. "That's what I'm telling you."

Catherine tried to read the gang leader's expression, but couldn't. Earlier in the day it had taken all her courage to face him in his den. Now she drew another shuddering breath, moved close, and spoke for his ears alone.

"You don't need Kenny, Gino." His unnerving eyes swerved to hers. "Do you?" she added timorously.

After an agonizing moment of scrutiny, he replied, "You're right. I don't need Kenny, but I need my wheels. Arturo! Bobby!" he continued, lifting his voice. "You want to get the keys from my man, here, and take care of the GTO?"

"Sure, Gino," the pair answered as Kenny handed over the keys.

"How about it, Kenny?" Gino added. "You want a ride back to the neighborhood?"

"Nah, man," Kenny answered, his gaze turning to Catherine as he moved to the threshold. "I think I'll walk. Stay in shape, ya know? After all, I'm going out for the swim team this fall."

As Kenny disappeared through the door, the brilliance of the smile that bloomed on Catherine's face started way down deep inside, as if a flickering glow had been fanned to flame. Arturo and Bobby followed Kenny out, and she was left alone with the powerful Gino. She steeled herself against jumping as he unexpectedly reached out and lifted a strand of her hair. His pale eyes settled on hers as he rubbed it between his fingers.

"Fine," he mumbled. "Like spun gold." Apparently noting her stricken look, he straightened and backed off.

"I checked out that clinic of yours, ya know," he said.

"Did you?" Catherine managed.

"It's cool. It gives the kids something to look forward to."

"That's what I was hoping for."

"Looks like your hopes panned out, then."

"Thank you, Gino. For everything." Catherine offered her hand for a shake. In continental fashion he lifted it to his lips and pressed a kiss to its back. He grinned when he looked up to see her expression of shock.

"Don't look so surprised. I *am* Italian, after all. Ya know," he went on, "maybe if *I'd* met a lady like you when *I* was Kenny's age, things would have turned out different. You're doing a good thing here, Miss Mermaid. Someday if the Pirates can do something for *you,* you let Gino know, eh?"

When he left, Catherine stepped out on the balcony and looked down, where she saw that a shiny black limo—fitting transport for the captain of the Pirates—had joined the souped-up GTO.

"Hey! What do you think?" Gino's voice bellowed from below. "You think I can ride in two cars at one time? Arturo! Take the GTO back to the club! Bobby! Open the door of the limo, will ya?"

A moment later the cars pulled out of view, and Catherine went back inside with a quizzical smile on her face. Life was so odd. Sometimes you found sunshine in the strangest corners.

Saturday, September 3

In Charleston, Labor Day weekend was the last big bash of the summer. Tourists filled hotels, beaches, and streets; locals who didn't leave town banded together in private parties behind garden walls.

In Catherine's case the holiday heralded the beginning

of prematrimonial fanfare that would pave her way to the altar, with a Saturday night of chamber music and hors d'oeuvres at the Battery mansion of Councilman and Mrs. Rudd. The affair was black tie, and more than seventy people were expected to attend the soiree in the often-photographed music room noted for its magnificent eighteenth-century Venetian chandelier.

Eliot was picking her up at seven-thirty. It was a quarter past the hour when Catherine donned the ankle-length black sheath with the cloud of an overskirt in midnight chiffon. Although she generally found black dresses depressing, she liked this one, and it was perfect for an evening of formal music. But only a small part of her mind was on the process of dressing; the rest was firmly entrenched in memories of Ann Marie's praise.

She'd shown up an hour ago, *The Clown Wore Black* in hand. "Once I read the first page, I was hooked."

"Really?" Catherine questioned with a surge of pride. "Do you think we can sell it?"

"You bet I do. It's absolutely riveting, and your publisher puts out a line of mysteries as well as romance. Print out a copy for me, sugar. There's plenty here to send to New York."

Various scenes from the manuscript monopolized Catherine's thoughts as she pinned her hair in a twist and fixed pearls at her ears. Even Eliot's tall, dark appearance in a tuxedo was most striking in its sharp reminder of the garb of the clown.

The short drive to South Battery was lengthened by holiday hordes, who nosily peered into Eliot's BMW at stop signs. Finally, they arrived at the prestigious house with blazing lights. Leaving the car with a valet at the courtyard gate, she and Eliot made the grand entrance, exchanged greetings with host and hostess, and were swept into the midst of the richly robed, well-wishing guests.

At half past eight the chamber orchestra started tuning up. And when the betrothed couple entered the music room to be seated in chairs of honor, the guests greeted them with a round of applause. Catherine barely heard. Her ears were still ringing with Ann Marie's raves.

A feeling of effervescence buoyed her through most of the night, lifting her above the actualities of expertly played stringed instruments and well-groomed chatter. It wasn't until a quartet of musicians began a somber selection late in the repertoire that she began to drift back to earth.

Perhaps it was the ominous notes of Schubert's "Death and the Maiden" that scraped her state of mind off the ceiling. Little by little her heightened senses settled to a mode of intake. Bit by bit, pieces of reality began to log in.

And suddenly it was as though she stepped from a fog.

Catherine looked around with a start, and for the first time that night truly saw the glittering assembly in the Rudds' music room, truly registered the reason they were there. While she'd submerged herself in fantasy, the reality of time had marched on. The distance was gone. The wedding was upon her.

She cast a sharp look at Eliot's profile. And it was wrong. Suddenly she saw everything so clearly. While she muffled whispers of "little things" in a blanket of Nicki and Jack, she'd become so wrapped up in the dream's story that she'd forgotten its message: *Marrying Eliot is wrong.*

As Catherine sat primly by his side, her feeling of panic mushroomed. She must *do* something. And yet, as the night wore on, all that she *did* was exactly what was expected. When the music ended, the bride-to-be applauded. When given a cue, she smiled like a doll whose string had been pulled. The inevitable had arrived, and she was no more prepared to handle it now than the night Eliot had put a ring on her finger.

The wretched party finally came to an end. The quiet ride home was the right time to say something, but she felt as though a boulder had lodged in her throat. Later, when Eliot stripped, got into bed, and rolled matter-of-factly on top of her, Catherine used the oldest excuse in the world for the first time.

"A headache?" he repeated with an irritated edge in his voice. "Well, take some aspirin and get rid of it. I'll wait."

Thankfully, he couldn't wait long enough. While she lingered on the balcony by reason of availing herself of fresh air, he fell asleep. As for Catherine, the birds had begun to chirp when she surrendered to exhaustion and curled up atop the covers, her back turned to the man who slept beneath them.

*　　*　　*

The September third wedding of Barbara Nakamura and Edward Post was one of the premiere social events of the year. Nicki had known both bride and groom for years, and when Jack announced that she simply could *not* attend the grand festivities—which would take place in a spectacular resort on the Kona Coast—Nicki's temper had boiled over with all the frustration and fury that had been stewing inside her for weeks.

"If I let the damn clown scare me out of going *everywhere,* then I might as well be in prison!" she'd railed. "Think about it, Jack. Don't make me more of a victim than I already am."

Eventually he'd given in and escorted her to the affair. Set against the outdoor splendor of exquisite gardens, the late afternoon ceremony was beautiful, the clubhouse reception the height of elegance, and by early evening Elena had consumed far too much champagne. Nicki stayed with her in the ladies' room, forgetting about time until a sharp rap sounded at the door.

"Nicki?" Jack's voice boomed. "Are you in there?"

After that he'd insisted on an abrupt exit, and had inspected every inch of the Ferrari before allowing her within twenty feet. The trip along the Kona Coast had passed in silence. Now, as they cruised the seaside road of the upcountry, Nicki studied him. In the phosphorescent light from the dashboard, his white shirt glowed like foxfire while his profile appeared dark and grim.

"I didn't mean to scare you, Jack," she said finally.

"I know. Your friend had too much to drink, and you helped her. It was the right thing to do."

"I was only gone fifteen minutes or so."

"Fifteen *long* minutes when I had no idea where you were."

"I'm sorry," Nicki offered.

Jack gave her clasped hands a light squeeze. "It's okay. I'll get over it. I've just had a bad feeling all night."

Indeed, Nicki thought. He'd had a "bad feeling" ever since the incident at the pool two weeks ago. Since then she'd seen a new side of Jack. The teasing moments of before were few and far between. His eyes seemed to be constantly watching, his ears continually pricked. Lately he reminded her of the lone wolf he claimed to be—his fur standing on end as he sniffed danger.

He downshifted and turned through the gates to the ranch. Porchlight beamed at the crest of the drive, where a police car was parked by the front steps. A solitary officer was leaning against the side of the vehicle, smoking a cigarette. Jack snorted as they drove past. "A lot of help *he* is. What does he think the clown's gonna do? Walk in the front door? Look at the car. It's not even pointed in the right direction to give chase."

"Lieutenant Tanaka said the mere presence of the police—"

"Lieutenant Tanaka ought to have this place under covert surveillance *right now*," Jack barked.

"This isn't Chicago, Jack. This is the boonies. The police don't have the manpower to do what you're suggesting."

He shook his head. "I understand the limitations, but I sure as hell don't like the deal." Executing a smart U-turn, he pulled onto the shoulder by the lanai and killed the engine, the Ferrari's nose pointing neatly down the drive.

It was after eleven, and the moon was high, bathing the night with a luminous blush. The setting was beautiful and romantic, but as usual Jack showed no inclination toward romance as he briskly ushered her out of the darkness and into the porchlight.

"Evenin'," the officer greeted. "Everything's been quiet."

"That's reassuring," Jack muttered. Unlocking the door, he held it open for Nicki to pass.

The house was quiet—Malia presumably long abed, and Austin away for the weekend on a climbing trip that had been planned for months. After the clown's harrowing attack at the pool, he'd nearly canceled, but Nicki had forbidden it.

"We can't let this madman ruin *all* our lives," she'd insisted.

And so, for all practical purposes, she and her handsome escort had the place to themselves. In the old days Nicki would have plumbed such an opportunity with drinking and dancing and, possibly, lovemaking till dawn. Those old, lighthearted pre-Jack days seemed long ago. Now her days were heavy with bittersweetness. She knew she had one kind of Jack's love; it just wasn't the kind she wanted.

Putting a hand to her back, he propelled her along the hall to her chamber and instructed her to wait while he turned on lamps and looked around. After a moment Nicki strolled inside.

"Everything's just as I left it, Jack."

"Um-hmmm," he grunted, and, after checking the window latches, crossed to the closet, where he shoved aside hangersful of clothes and peered within.

"Would you care to look under the bed?"

Turning from the closet, Jack ambled over and gazed down with those warily watchful, wolflike eyes. "This isn't funny, Nicki."

"I know," she replied. "I'm just tired. I don't think I'm up to being properly terrified at the moment."

Jack surrendered the smallest of grins. "Get some rest, huh?" he said, and planted a brotherly kiss on her forehead.

He closed the door softly behind him, and Nicki pictured him settling his long frame in the overstuffed chair he'd parked outside her room. Since the pool, he'd spent every night there. Unzipping her dress, she left it in a silky pile on the floor, pulled on a T-shirt, and went to bed. But she didn't sleep.

The night waxed on as she lay in the dark and stared at the ceiling, beset by a numbing fear—not of the stalker, but of what was to come with Jack. She didn't know what else to do to make him fall in love with her, and sensed that when the clown crisis was over, he was going to leave the ranch—that he was merely passing through her life and one day would be gone.

The one that got away, she thought, her spirits sinking to a new low as the phrase seemed to fit Jack to a tee.

There was a stir of air by her face. Nicki listlessly turned, and a noiseless shadow loomed before her eyes—the rounded shape of a head, the whites of eyes shining from a dark mask, and the white V of a shirt glaring between black lapels. Before she could release a terrified scream, he covered her mouth with a block of tape and grabbed her hands.

She kicked at the covers while he tightly wrapped her wrists in more tape. When he snatched back the sheet, she landed a kick to his ribs. He whirled and slapped her so hard with a leather-gloved hand that she nearly fell off the bed. Momentarily stunned, she failed to fight as he taped her ankles, hoisted her up, and landed her like a sack of potatoes over his shoulder.

By the time she regained her wits, he'd unlatched the window facing the pool and was on his way out with her. Nicki threw out her constricted arms, grabbing for anything. Her fingers closed on the cord to the blinds. She clasped it for dear life. Just as the madman's progress ripped it searingly from her grip, she heard the clatter of the blinds flying up to the cornice.

The clown heard it, too. Despite the weight of the body over his shoulder, he loped across the terrace and plunged into the covering darkness of the rear grounds.

All Nicki could hear was the thud of his footsteps and the intermittent gush of breath that exploded from her nostrils with every jolt. She tried to pummel his back, but could force no strength into the attack as she jostled upside down atop his rock-hard shoulder.

Blood was rushing to her head. It felt twice its normal size. Nicki fought to lift it long enough to cast a desperate, jerking look in their wake. The moon threw the line of redtip hedge in dark relief. It marked the boundary of the rear grounds. There was nothing ahead but a hundred yards of grassland sweeping to the . . . Oh, God! He was going to throw her off the cliff!

At low tide the boulder-strewn beach was a thirty-foot drop. At high tide, towering waves crashed against the craggy seawall. Either way she'd be dead in seconds.

Nicki began to struggle with everything she had. She thrashed her hobbled legs. She flailed her arms. A gunshot rang out from somewhere behind them. She stiffened, paralyzed with hope. Two more rapid shots split the night. They sounded closer.

Thank God, Nicki thought before the clown's cruel shoulder knocked the prayer from her mind. With a burst of determination, she wrenched her body in a violent twist that made her captor stumble . . . and afforded a split-second glimpse of an approaching blur of white—Jack's shirt!—before Jack smashed into them and sent her tumbling raucously to the ground.

Nicki pushed to her hands and knees, and shook her

head. The ringing in her ears dissipated, and she clearly heard the roar of ocean waves. Her eyes turned sharply toward the sound. She was only ten feet from the cliff.

Shifting onto her backside, Nicki looked frantically around. The two men were circling mere yards away, like partners in a deadly dance. Then Jack struck, the white of his shirt seeming to soar through the air as he went for a kick to the clown's chest. But, no! The damnable phantom blocked the kick, pulled Jack off his feet, and fell upon him.

Nicki ripped the tape from her mouth. "Jack!" she shrieked as the struggling men rolled dangerously close to the precipice. She strained to see through the darkness as her shaking fingers tore at the layers of tape binding her ankles.

"Dammit, dammit, dammit, dammit!" Nicki swore, her voice rising with every curse. When her panicked gaze lifted, the men were on their feet once more . . . right at the edge.

"Move back!" she cried, her words cut short by the overwhelming *crack!* of a gunshot.

She jumped and stared, her wide eyes frozen on the scene. Time seemed to hang as the men's silhouettes were branded against the moonlit horizon—locked in a fierce embrace, poised in an instant of shocked stillness that seemed to quell the beat of Nicki's heart.

A horrified scream tore from her throat as both hero and villain toppled over the ledge.

Chapter Twelve

Catherine woke with a scream ringing in her ears and tears streaming down her cheeks. She got up, went into the bathroom, and splashed her face with cold water. Still, she couldn't stop shaking or crying.

How real it all seemed—the terrifying attack of the clown, the heart-stopping sight of Jack falling over the cliff, presumably to his doom. She fought to push the image from her mind and gain a grip on reality. Minutes passed as she focused on the soothing water she continued to ladle over her face. *It was just a dream,* she told herself. *Just a dream.* Her tears slowly ebbed. Her breathing gradually calmed.

Patting her face with a towel, Catherine walked disorientedly out of the bathroom—noting, first, that the sun was up, and second, that Eliot was standing at the foot of the bed, fully dressed and glaring at her. He tossed a stack of papers onto the tousled covers. The manuscript! She lifted burning eyes to his.

"Where did you get that?"

"From your desk."

"I don't appreciate your going through my desk, Eliot. *Or* reading my work without my knowledge."

"Work?" he questioned in a way that reminded her dismally of Aunt Sybil. "Surely you don't mean to publish this."

"I've put a lot of effort and hours into—"

"You mean *this* is how you've been spending your time these past weeks? Producing this trash about a psychotic clown?"

"It's not trash. It's a thriller, and there are plenty of authors out there producing thrillers."

"Listen to me," Eliot said, his black eyes hard with rage.

"I bent about the romance novels. Now it's your turn to bend. I will *not* have my wife's name on this garbage."

Catherine gazed at his angry, self-righteous countenance, and a shocking sense of strength began to rise within her, filling her veins, bursting to fruition in an explosion of defiance.

"Well, then, I suppose that means the name on it won't belong to your wife." She stared levelly into his eyes, noting as the glint of rage changed to a show of incredulity.

"What are you saying, Catherine?"

Once uncaged, the will to rebel grew stronger by the second. Walking over to the bed, Catherine removed the diamond ring from her left hand and set it atop the disheveled pile of pages.

"This isn't going to work out, Eliot."

He barked a harsh laugh. "You must be joking."

"I think you can see that I'm not joking, and I'm heartily sorry for having misled you these past few months."

"Misled?" he shrilled.

"You don't really want me, Eliot. Not the real me. And I now know that I don't want you."

His reddened face took on a look of absolute fury. "Are you hinting there's someone else?"

Catherine thought of the dream man who had captured her own heart along with Nicki's. "No," she replied with a small smile. "Not in the way you mean."

"This is insane. We're getting married in three weeks. Five hundred people are invited."

"They'll have to be notified. I'll see to it."

Eliot stared at her in a moment of stupefied silence. "I can't believe this," he then uttered. "In fact, I *won't* believe it. And I'm certainly not going to stand for it."

"I'm afraid you'll have to stand for it. I'm not marrying you in three weeks, or ever."

"What the hell's come over you, Catherine? Are you sick?"

She stifled the startling impulse to laugh. "Look on the bright side, Eliot. You can probably parlay this breakup into a publicity sweep that will plant public sympathy firmly behind you just in time for the elections."

He snatched the ring off the bed. "The next time I give

this to someone," he bellowed while brandishing the diamond, "I'll make damn sure she's worthy to wear it!"

"I understand. As I said, I'm truly sorry—"

Catherine broke off as Eliot whirled out of the room. A sense of freedom poured through her, pure and cleansing, like a draught of springwater. She absently followed in his path and was watching through a kind of euphoric daze when he whipped open the door, marched out, and slammed it behind him.

An hour later Catherine donned a tank suit emblazoned with a Red Cross emblem, settled in the sunny breakfast nook, and savored the best cup of coffee she'd ever tasted. She'd had a mere two hours' sleep, but felt completely energized.

What a beautiful day lay ahead. Sunday was play time at Waterfront Clinic. She gave no formal lessons, but responded to the kids individually if any of them wanted one-on-one instruction. They usually preferred simply to cavort in the water as she kept lifeguard watch until four.

The school year started Tuesday after the Labor Day holiday, and the clinic would move to a weekend schedule. Autumn was creeping up on summer. Today was one of the last two days of vacation. The kids would probably be feeling their oats, she thought with a smile that ebbed as she considered the idea of how much she was going to miss seeing them on a daily basis.

After returning from the beach, maybe she'd take Ann Marie to supper and tell her the news about the canceled wedding. She'd be disappointed at first, Catherine knew. But the bottom line was that Ann Marie wanted her happiness. And—heavens above—Catherine had never felt so happy, so content, so free to embrace the life she'd longed for throughout the years at Winslow House.

The doorbell rang. Catherine glanced at the clock with a start. It was mere minutes past eight. Who would come calling at eight o'clock on a Sunday morning? Surely Eliot hadn't returned.

She warily approached the portal. "Who is it?"

"Open up and find out," answered a muffled female voice. Catherine opened the door an inch's worth and peeped out.

"Are you alone?" Marla demanded.

"Marla!" Catherine exclaimed, and drew the door wide. "Yes, I'm alone. Come in." As the redhead strode into the room, Catherine was taken aback by the change in her. She was wearing a dark kerchief around her hair and a stark black pantsuit with a long, concealing jacket. The saucy walk was gone. So was the air of laughter and mischief that had always surrounded her. Something was wrong. Something had been wrong for a long time.

"It's good to see you, Marla. I've thought of you often these past few months. Would you like a cup of coffee?"

She lifted her eyes, and Catherine was chilled by the haunted look within them, the dark circles beneath them. It was as though Marla had aged a dozen years in as many weeks.

"This isn't a social call, Catherine. I've got something to say, but first I must insist on complete confidence. What I'm about to tell you must remain between us. Agreed?"

"Okay," Catherine acquiesced. "I agree."

"Whatever you may think of me after this, I want you to know that my motives in coming here are strictly aboveboard. Frankly, I'm here because I believe you're in danger."

Without further preface Marla shrugged out of the sleeves of her jacket so that it hung at her elbows, revealing a halter-necked black top that bared her shoulders. She turned, and Catherine gasped. The fair skin of Marla's back was blotted with bruises, marred with long red welts. Whip marks!

"Who *did* this to you?" Catherine whispered, at which point Marla swiftly replaced the concealing jacket and spun around.

"He dangled the 'Marla Sutton Gallery' in front of my nose, and I took the bait," she replied woodenly. "The affair started the very first night he took you out. We used to meet at the Kiawah Island house. But for the past month or so, he's been taking me to a secret cabin stocked with every sadistic device you can think of, and some you couldn't imagine. You know all those 'late-night appointments' he had? They were with me."

Catherine stared as she tried to grasp the revelation. "You mean *Eliot*?" she squeaked. Marla nodded. "You mean that while he's been playing fiancé with *me,* he's been doing *this* to *you*?"

When Marla nodded once again, Catherine bolted to the bathroom and knelt at the toilet just in time. Marla slowly followed.

"Are you crying or throwing up?" she asked from the doorway.

"Both," Catherine answered with a rasping cough.

Marla stepped calmly to the sink, dampened a washcloth, and handed it over. Catherine covered her face with it and tried to block out the sordid pictures that were flooding her brain.

"I made up my mind to do what was necessary to get what I wanted," Marla went on. "Now I can only pray Eliot gets elected and moves miles away to Columbia. But not with you, Catherine. For now he's keeping his dark side a secret from you. But he can't hide it forever. It will come out, and God help his poor wife once it does. Don't let that woman be you."

Removing the cloth, Catherine flushed the toilet and climbed to her feet. "That's right. You don't know. I broke up with him." Marla's mouth gaped open. "Just now, in fact," Catherine added. "Hardly more than an hour ago."

"You're kidding." Catherine flourished a left hand bereft of the flashy diamond. "You mean I went through this for *nothing*?"

"Hardly for nothing, Marla. It means a lot that you came and tried to warn me."

"A day late and a dollar short, I guess."

"Better late than never," Catherine countered.

"You're not taking this the way I expected."

"What did you expect?"

Marla shrugged and couldn't quite hide the wince that crossed her face. "If you despised me, I wouldn't blame you."

Catherine gave her a searching look. "I could say the same. Watching Eliot parade around town with *me* couldn't have been much fun. So *that's* why you dropped out of touch so suddenly."

"In the beginning, when I thought I cared for him, I was jealous," Marla admitted. "That was a long time ago."

"Boy, was I stupid," Catherine mused. "It's all so clear

to me now, the way Eliot swept into my empty little life right after I made headlines as 'the Charleston mermaid.' If not for that, he never would have looked twice at Catherine Winslow. He used us both—me as a ticket into the spotlight, and you as . . ."

"His whore?" Marla callously supplied. "You can say it. There's nothing you can call me I haven't already called myself."

"I was thinking more along the lines of *victim*," Catherine returned. "The villain in all of this is Eliot. I always knew he had a tendency to be domineering. I just never suspected to what extreme. Marla . . . have you considered pressing charges?"

She emitted a short laugh. "Against Eliot? Now, *there's* a short course to disaster. Do you have any idea how well connected he is? It would be like a mouse squaring off against a lion."

"Women do it," Catherine pointed out.

"Not with a man like Eliot Reynolds," Marla fired back. "He'd have the whole thing turned against me in a heartbeat. First he'd see to it that my column was killed. Then, who knows? In the end he'd come out smelling like a rose, and I'd come out with my life in a shambles. No. I've come this far. I can ride it out."

"Your back doesn't look as though it can stand much more riding," Catherine remarked. "Have you seen a doctor?"

"Eliot takes care of me personally. After all, the better I hold up, the harder he can play."

A spine-chilling shiver raced over Catherine. "Let me help. I'll go with you to the authorities and tell them about all the times he disappeared for his 'late appointments.' "

Marla looked away, but not before Catherine saw the sheen that sprang to her eyes. "I'll stand by you, Marla, and maybe between the two of us we can put together a good enough case—"

"Case?" she interrupted, and lifted her glistening gaze. "Thanks for the thought, Catherine, but there's no such thing as a 'case' against Eliot Reynolds. I can't even supply the location of his little 'game room.' Every time he's taken me, I've been blindfolded. In the end it all would boil down to his word against mine, and I have no doubt of how *that* would turn out."

Catherine lifted a shaky hand to her brow. She tried to think of something, *anything,* to suggest that could possibly help, but her shocked mind had gone blank.

Sniffing back her tears, Marla lifted her chin. "You want to help me?" she questioned. "Then just leave me alone while I get through this. I've got a date with the devil at eight, and I don't need you undermining my resolve." Walking out of the bathroom, Marla headed for the door at a fast clip. Catherine hurried after her.

"You're supposed to see him at eight?"

"Um-hmmm. And now that you've given him the ax, I'm sure he'll be in a delightful mood."

"Don't, Marla. Don't go."

Pulling open the door, Marla turned and expelled a heavy breath. "What the hell am I supposed to do, Catherine?"

"Disappear. Stay here if you want to. Just *don't go.*"

"Then what? Get it twice as bad tomorrow night?"

"No. Don't get it *at all* tomorrow night, or ever again."

"You've made your choice, Catherine. And I've made mine."

When she started to walk out, Catherine blocked her path. "Don't let him do this to you, Marla."

"I'm well past the age of twenty-one, girl," she returned without meeting Catherine's eyes. "You've got to give me room to make my own decisions."

"Please," Catherine pressed. "There's got to be a way out of this. All we need is a little time—"

"I'll think about it, okay?" Marla snapped, and, pushing roughly past, hurried down the stairwell.

The brilliant first day of Catherine's newfound freedom was suddenly cast in shadow. Even after she opened the beach, which was bustling with touristing families as well as clinic regulars, she found the back of her mind dwelling on the image of her once-vibrant friend's haunted eyes and desecrated flesh.

And all at the hand of Eliot Reynolds. He'd baited her, caught her, and corrupted her. He'd gutted Marla's very soul with all the mercy of a steely blade. And every time

Catherine remembered his hands on her own body, she shuddered with revulsion.

At two o'clock she looked up to see him striding toward her, his impeccable attire suggesting he'd just come from church and a traditional luncheon at the country club. Beyond him at curbside his distinguished parents stood by their vintage Rolls-Royce and looked on. *Hypocrite!* Catherine longed to scream as Eliot stepped up with a supercilious expression. Oh, but she wished she hadn't given Marla a promise of confidentiality. How she longed to slap Eliot down and grind his well-groomed face into the sand.

"I just stopped by to see if you've come to your senses," he said with the arch of a brow.

"Indeed I have." The politician's smile spread across his face. How empty it looked to her now. He lifted a hand as though planning to place it on her shoulder.

"Don't touch me," Catherine commanded. His hand halted in midair. "Ever again," she added.

As his arm dropped to his side, Eliot's smile disappeared. "So you're still entertaining the crazed notion of calling everything off?"

"It's not a notion, it's a fact. Everything *is* off—absolutely, irrevocably *off.*"

His eyes narrowed to glittering black slits. "One day you'll be extremely sorry about this, Catherine."

"The only thing I'm sorry about is the code of honor that prevents me from saying what I think of you."

"Goodness," Eliot said with a sneer. "I wouldn't have guessed the little virgin had such fire. Why did you keep it hidden all this time? A little flare-up now and then would have been fun."

Catherine was so choked with disgust she couldn't speak. Nor could she bear to look at him. Turning her back, she brought the abysmal encounter to an end and walked across the beach to join the children. A short while later, when she glanced toward the street, the Rolls-Royce was gone.

She spent the next two hours feeling as though an anvil had materialized in the pit of her stomach. Although she kept diligent watch over the waterfront, the back of Catherine's mind hovered between the revolting idea of what Eliot had done to Marla in the past, and the realization that

time was running out before he would commit another such
travesty tonight.

There had to be a way to stop him. He wasn't
invincible . . . or was he? She pictured the civic leaders
with whom Eliot was bosom buddies. One was the commis-
sioner of police. She imagined the old guard of Charleston,
stirred to outrage by Eliot's parents, who would close ranks
and turn all the power of society against any "fallen
woman" who sought to topple their fair-haired boy.

The more Catherine thought about it, the more defeated
she began to feel. Marla was right. In the event of an open
challenge, all the upstanding, upright dominions of the city
would unite behind Eliot.

It was almost time to close the park when Catherine was
struck by an idea so revolutionary that it was like a bolt
from the blue. What, then, of the dominions that were *not*
so upstanding?

At four o'clock she swiftly made her rounds, sent the
beach crowds on their way, and chased Kenny out of the
water. Despite her efforts to hurry, it was five by the time
she walked into the Pirates' Den, only to be told by
Bobby—or Arturo, she wasn't sure which—that she would
have to wait. Gino was in the back room "with associates."

A quarter of an hour passed. Catherine hardly noticed
the ogles of the half dozen gang members in leather and
jeans who kept their distance as she perched at the bar in
her incongruent getup of sneakers, shorts, and jacket over
a wet bathing suit. Her mind was rooted on the idea of
time slipping through her fingers like sifting sand. Less than
three hours remained before Eliot would be stopping by
for Marla. He was never late.

As Catherine kept her eyes trained on the Budweiser
clock over the bar, she reflected on the night Gino had
showed up at her door, and his offer to let him know if
the Pirates could ever do her a favor. Maybe he hadn't
meant it. Maybe he'd want no part of a stand against one
of Charleston's most prominent men.

It was nearly half past five when Gino emerged from
the backroom with his "associates"—three tough-looking men
who gave meaning to the word *unsavory*. The men strolled
out with curious glances in her direction, and Gino joined
her at the otherwise deserted bar. He looked much as he

had the first time she saw him—red bandanna, shades, white T-shirt, tight jeans.

"Well, hello," he said, giving the greeting a lyrical lilt.

"Hello, Gino."

"What brings *you* to this neck of the woods?"

"Do you remember saying I could come to you if I needed help?" Catherine sensed the sudden alertness behind his dark glasses.

"I remember," he replied. "Are you in trouble?"

"A friend of mine is."

"And you think I can help."

"I hope you can . . . if it's not too much to ask."

Gino propped an elbow on the bar. "Why don't we find out? Tell me about this friend of yours."

"She was lured into a relationship with a powerful man, and now he's beating her and degrading her in all sorts of ways. She thinks that if she goes to the police, they'll end up taking *his* side. I think she's probably right. He has a lot of connections."

"I don't like freaks who beat up on girls," Gino remarked. "It gives the rest of us a bad name."

"He takes her to a cabin in the woods someplace outside Charleston. She doesn't know where. He blindfolds her, and he's coming for her again tonight at eight o'clock."

"Tonight, huh?"

"Are you busy this evening?" Catherine blurted, and felt excruciatingly foolish as a sexy smile curved Gino's lips.

"Another time and place, and I might think you were asking me for a date." When Catherine only stared, red-faced and tongue-tied, he chuckled. "Relax, honey. As it happens, me and the boys were just talking about having nothin' to do tonight. I think they'd get into this. They don't like freaks, either."

"You mean you'll help us?"

"I'll figure something out," he said, and Catherine felt such relief that she almost threw her arms around him.

"Thank you," she mumbled instead.

Gino considered her from behind the shades. "So what do you want to happen to this guy? You want him to disappear?"

"Not in the *mortal* sense," Catherine carefully replied. "I don't want anyone hurt, not even him, but—"

"But you want him out of the picture so he's not around to beat up on your girlfriend."

"Oh, yes. Out of the picture would be great."

"Maybe we can scare him out of town. Who's the guy?"

"Councilman Eliot Reynolds."

"I know him—tall, dark hair, drives a silver Beamer."

"He's powerful," she reiterated. "He won't scare easily."

Gino gave her a complacent smile before calling over the bartender. "Hey, Jimmy. Hand me something to write on, will ya?" When the bartender complied, Gino shoved the pad and pen in her direction. "Write down your girlfriend's address for me."

When Catherine finished, he tucked the note in the pocket of his jeans. "You might want to give it until nine-thirty or so and then stop by your friend's place to welcome her home. For now, get going. And don't come around the Den for a while."

Now that she'd successfully enlisted the aid of Gino and his Pirates, Catherine suddenly felt as though she'd started a wildfire without any idea of where it might turn. She climbed slowly down from the stool. "And no one will get hurt, right?"

"Hey," Gino muttered in a scolding tone. "Either you trust me, or you don't. Which is it?"

"I trust you," she replied with a hesitant smile. "But I can't help wondering what you're going to do."

"The less you know, the better. Let's just say the councilman is in for a life-changing experience."

Briskly propelling her forward, Gino escorted her to the door. Catherine stepped into the Sunday afternoon light while he remained in the shadow of the dingy threshold. The distance between their two worlds seemed to crystallize in that moment, and yet somehow they'd bridged the gap. She searched the tinted lenses that concealed his eyes.

"Thank you, Gino."

"Get lost, Miss Mermaid," he returned, and, backing away from the entrance, was quickly swallowed in the murky darkness of Pirates' Den.

Until that morning with Catherine, Marla had discussed Eliot with no one. Tonight she'd found that talking had made it all more real—the agonizing anticipation of the moment his BMW would appear, the degradation of being bound and blindfolded. All of it seemed to fall on heightened senses. Now she descended the stone steps of the hated cabin with more than usual dread.

It will be over soon, she valiantly told herself. *Don't let him do this to you,* Catherine's remembered words echoed.

Annihilating Marla's reverie, Eliot pushed her to the wall and fixed the shackles about her wrists. He was impatient tonight, and she knew why. He was furious about Catherine.

"Women are bitches," he growled in seeming affirmation of Marla's thoughts.

She was wearing a new white dress with a sailor collar that closed down the front with a series of gold buttons shaped like tiny anchors. Eliot blithely took hold of the neckline and ripped open the front so that the buttons went flying.

"This is a brand-new dress," she mumbled.

"Buy yourself another. You can afford it these days."

Hastily unsnapping her bra, he folded back each lacy cup so that Marla stood before him with her garments hanging off her shoulders, frontally nude but for a flimsy pair of bikini underwear. Gathering her breasts in firm hands, Eliot squeezed her nipples until she released a whimper.

Only then did he back away. Hungrily eyeing her, he stripped off his shirt and threw it to the earthen floor. *No,* Marla thought with rising panic. She couldn't stand it. Not anymore.

"Eliot," she began in a shaky voice, "I'm not feeling well. You're going to have to undo me."

"You look perfectly well to me."

"No, really," she insisted. "I'm not up to this."

He came near and pressed the front of his body against hers. His chest hair nuzzled her abraded nipples, his hardness ground against her stomach. "Then I suppose you'll have to put some effort into rising to the occasion," he muttered.

Prying a hand between their bodies, he reached inside her panties. Marla caught her breath and tried with all her might to keep her thighs tightly closed. He chuckled, his breath hot on her face as he worked a cruel finger inside her. Marla was pierced by the feeling that she was unraveling, coming apart in shreds. She had no more strength. She couldn't endure. She would lose her mind if she had to bear his touch for one more instant.

"No-o-o!" she exploded, the protest emerging in a hysterical wail. "I can't do this anymore! Please, let me go! Please!"

Yanking his hand from her underwear, Eliot grabbed her by the chin. Marla heaved for breath as she stared into his black eyes.

"You want to give up your fancy column, bitch?" he demanded. "And the car? How about that? You want to give that up, too?"

"Yes! Yes!" she cried as tears ran over. "I'll give it all up! I'll give up everything!"

Brusquely releasing her, Eliot stepped back and drilled her with an evil smile. "Too late. We made a deal." He crossed to the wall with the collection of whips and selected a long coil.

"No!" Marla shrieked as he started toward her. "No!" the word burst forth again, and rang with all the mindless terror she felt as Eliot mercilessly lifted the whip.

There was a commotion on the stairs. Eliot's arm halted in midswing. Marla turned wild eyes toward the stone steps as a troop of five masked men with guns invaded the cellar.

"I believe the lady said no," one of them remarked.

Eliot started toward him. The marauder lifted his weapon.

"Come on, man," he invited. "I'd just as soon end this with one shot here and now."

Eliot froze in his tracks. "This is private property," he announced, at which point the man in the ski mask—the obvious leader of the group—heartily laughed.

"Man," he uttered in an amused tone. "The *least* of your worries is that we're *trespassing*." Every vestige of amusement vanished as he added, "Now, where's the key to those nifty-looking shackles over there?" After a moment's hesitation, Eliot jerked his head in the direction of the table behind him.

"Somebody let the lady loose and give her a jacket," the intruder commanded.

"You don't know who you're messing with," Eliot snapped.

"You're wrong. I know exactly who I'm messing with, Councilman. But you know what? To me you look just like any run-of-the-mill sick bastard. Let's check out that theory, huh?"

Striking swiftly as a snake, he grabbed the coil from Eliot, brandished it with practiced skill, and zinged it across Eliot's bare flesh.

"Dammit!" Eliot bellowed as he grabbed at his chest.

"Yep," the gun-wielding stranger affirmed. "You bleed just like any run-of-the-mill sick bastard." Throwing the whip aside with a show of disgust, he added, "What's the matter, Councilman? Isn't it the turn-on you expected?"

As soon as Marla's wrists were freed, she pulled the ravaged front of her dress together, then jumped as her masked savior draped a denim jacket about her shoulders.

"What the hell do you want?" Eliot boomed as she looked on with wide, bewildered eyes. "Money?"

The leader shook his head. "Money ain't gonna buy you out of this one. You stepped on the wrong toes, buddy. You're a marked man. If I had *my* way, I'd shoot you down right now. However, I *do* have orders, which are to give you a chance to clear out on your own, not just out of town but out of the country. Of course, if you *don't* . . . then your ass belongs to *me.*"

"You're crazy," Eliot spat. "Who the hell sent you?"

"I guess you'll have time to try to figure that one out in South America, or wherever you light after leaving the States."

Eliot drew himself up and glared at his challenger. "I am not leaving the States. I'm a state senate candidate in the November elections, for God's sake!"

"Not anymore," the stranger placidly returned.

"I'll have you in court for this!" Eliot boomed. "No matter what it takes! I'll find you and have you locked away for life!"

Once again the leader of the masked men laughed. "I admire your spunk, man, but you don't get it. We ain't talkin' 'bout courts, here. We're talkin' 'bout *justice.* We're talkin' 'bout you getting in that pretty little Beamer of yours one day and having it blow up in your face."

"You can't be serious," Eliot muttered.

"Bobby, it seems the man needs convincing. Get the

place rigged and meet us out front. Everybody else, clear out."

The marauder who'd given her his jacket prodded Marla toward the steps. Moving on shaking limbs, she looked over in time to see the gang leader jam the barrel of his gun in Eliot's ribs.

"This is quite a little nest you've fixed up for yourself here, Councilman," he said. "Take a last look, and get movin'."

Minutes later Marla sat in the back of a white van, peering through a tinted window as the despicable cabin exploded in a burst of fire. Two masked men climbed into the front of the van.

"Sit back and relax, lady," the driver said. "It's over. We're taking you home." Her last glimpse of Eliot was of him standing with his arms raised, under threat of the mysterious leader's gun, with the hellish light of flames dancing over his form.

The drive to Charleston passed in a shocked blur. When the van pulled over in front of her apartment building, Marla climbed out on legs that felt as though they were made of rubber, and took wobbling steps to the sidewalk. The van sped away, and she looked up with surprise to see Catherine hurrying toward her.

"Are you all right?" she asked anxiously. And suddenly Marla knew—somehow, some way, Catherine was behind this whole miraculous thing!

Her raw eyes filled with quick new tears. Wordlessly wrapping her arms around Catherine's neck, Marla buried her face against the solid shoulder of the mermaid and wept.

Chapter Thirteen

Tuesday, September 6

Leaving her car with a valet blocks away, Nicki took a cab to Hilo Medical Center. The red Ferrari would have drawn immediate attention, which was exactly what she *didn't* want. She could picture the sensationalistic headlines if the media caught scent of the fantastic tale that reached a climax three nights ago.

SOCIALITE STALKED BY SADISTIC CLOWN . . . and so on. As it was, a relative handful of people entrusted to silence knew the story, and Nicki planned to keep it that way.

She felt sufficiently disguised in the white blouson pantsuit fashioned on the lines of a harem outfit. Billowing cuffs covered the red marks on wrists and ankles, legacies of the binding duct tape. Makeup camouflaged the bruise on her cheek, testament to the clown's ringing blow. Her hair was hidden beneath a white silk turban, her face behind giant dark glasses.

She walked through the bustling hospital lobby and boarded the elevator, drawing no more notice than her exotic ensemble was due. As she rode to the third floor, she flashed on images that had circled her mind relentlessly since that fateful night—the two men falling over the cliff . . . the frantic moments when she crawled along the edge, screaming and searching the moonlit waves for sign of Jack. It had seemed like years before she saw his dark figure separate from the rollicking sea and climb onto a rock a hundred yards from the spot where he fell.

The doctor said such a fall easily could have snapped his neck. Jack had escaped with three cracked ribs and considered himself lucky. The current, he said, had snatched the stalker down and away as soon as they hit the water. His body hadn't been found. The theory was that the single bullet Jack managed to fire had struck home, the fall had finished the job, and the anonymous assailant had been washed out to sea.

Nicki still had phantasmic feelings about the clown, and the way he seemed capable of appearing and vanishing at will. On the surface she accepted the theory endorsed by Jack and the police. Deep down she retained the eerie feeling that, someday, she and the clown were destined to meet again.

The elevator stopped, and Nicki started down the corridor toward Jack's room, beset by a different fear. Now she knew the truth about Jack. Far from being a vagabond chauffeur, he was a private investigator from Chicago, hired by Melrose to come on the scene undercover and safeguard her from the stalker. Now that the danger had passed, Jack would be leaving. That was what big brothers did with kid sisters, wasn't it? Leave them behind?

"Well!" he exclaimed as she walked in. "Who do we have here?"

Nicki took off the glasses and twirled them as she strolled to his bedside. "I'm incognito. Did you recognize me?"

"Not at all!" Jack replied with mock sincerity. "I thought Lana Turner had come calling. You just missed Lieutenant Tanaka."

"What did he have to say?"

"That my instincts are brilliant."

"He's right. If you hadn't been like a watchdog perched at my door, you never would have heard the blinds, and—" Nicki broke off with a shudder. "Never mind. I don't want to think about it."

She gingerly perched on the side of his bed. Above the white bandages encircling his rib cage, Jack's shoulders appeared dark and massive. She was reminded of that first day when he was washing the Lincoln, his shirtless body gleaming like bronze.

Nicki looked down and flicked an imaginary speck off the sheet. "Melrose told me all about you."

"Melrose doesn't *know* all about me."

"A private investigator hired all the way from Chicago. No wonder you like mysteries so much. You're a damn detective. You could have told me, Jack."

"Melrose didn't know how you'd react to the idea. As it happened, you and I got along, and I was able to do the job without blowing my cover. Covers work best on a need-to-know basis. The only one who knew was the man who hired me."

"I'll have to remember to take this up with Melrose, then."

"He was worried about you, Nicki. So was I."

Her eyes lifted. "And we'll never know who the clown was, or why he was after me, will we?"

Jack started to shrug, and cringed at the effort. "I don't know," he then replied. "The police combed the grounds, and no vehicle was found. It was like the guy dropped out of the sky into your bedroom. Right now the case reads: 'Identity and motive unknown.' But you never can tell. When he turns up missing, somebody could check his residence, find evidence linking him to you, and the answer could come to light. It's happened before."

"Are you going to stick around and see if it happens this time?" He looked uncomfortably aside. "I didn't think so," Nicki quietly added. "You're going home, aren't you? To Chicago."

His glimmering eyes met hers once more. "When I can travel in a week or so, yeah. It's where my life is, Nicki."

"Your real life, you mean. Not this make-believe one you've been playing at with me."

He reached over and squeezed her hand. "One thing hasn't been make-believe. I care about you, Nicki. I always will."

She mustered a smile. "I feel the need to get away for a while myself. How would it be if I tagged along to Chicago and took a look at this 'real life' of yours?"

"You wouldn't last a day in my real life."

"No?" she lightly queried as her heart crashed to her feet.

"No. It's far too crude for a high-flying bird like you. Not a yacht club in sight." Nicki's eyes began to burn as she recalled Malia's words: *Take care that the unattainable does not seduce and break your heart for you.* Being forewarned had done nothing to keep it from happening. Pulling her hand from beneath Jack's, Nicki replaced her dark glasses and rose to her feet.

"I thought your answer would go something like that. So I made other plans." Bending over, she pressed a kiss to Jack's unshaven cheek and backed away before he could see the sheen in her eyes. "I leave for Europe in the morning," she added.

Though he tried to cover it by glancing aside, a pained look came over him. "Europe, huh? What are you gonna do there?"

"Defy a lot of gravity—first in Italy, then Austria. After that I may visit a friend in Paris for a while. I don't plan on coming back to the States for quite some time."

Jack gave her a long, searching perusal. "Take care of yourself, baby."

"You'll miss me," Nicki brightly returned.

"I know," he responded without the slightest hint of humor.

"I love you, Jack," she added, and brought a slow, seemingly regretful smile to his face.

"You love everybody, Nicki. And everybody loves you back."

Having retreated across the small room, she opened the door, stood in the threshold, and took a last look—soaking up the lines of his form and face, committing each detail to memory.

"There's just one problem with being so widely loved," she said. "When you finally narrow the field to one, you can't seem to make the guy take you seriously. Be seeing you, Jack."

Her head was high, and no one would have suspected the tearful pools behind the dark glasses as Nicki walked away from the hospital and out of Jack's life.

On September eighth, in a moving TV speech during which Councilman Reynolds declared his "abiding love for Charleston and her people," he cited "personal problems" as the reason for his resignation from both the city council and the state senate race.

Shocked rumors began to fly that he was leaving the country, and everyone was certain that the demise of Charleston's brightest star was due to his being jilted by "that crazy Winslow girl." No longer the darling mermaid, Catherine was a pariah.

But despite the looks and whispers that followed her about town, she was filled with a peace she'd never known. She'd faced the tiger, slain the dragon, and she'd never be the same again. The ghost of Catherine of Legare was banished.

A few afternoons after Eliot's farewell address, she was picking up behind a Saturday crowd on the waterfront when she glanced toward the street and spotted the black limo. As the car moved slowly past, the back window went down, and a muscular arm with a tattoo emerged to raise a fist in a silent signal of triumph. Catherine had time only to break into a smile before the arm withdrew, the window went up, and the Pirate's limo cruised away.

On the final Saturday of September, she received a poison pen note from Mrs. Reynolds. *You've destroyed my boy, and if I weren't a lady, I'd* . . . Catherine didn't bother to read further before dropping the embossed sheet of stationery in the trash.

It didn't surprise her that Eliot had used her once again, this time as a scapegoat to an outraged public and family. Catherine didn't mind. Her sense of victory overshadowed any pesky sting of gossip. Eliot would never know of her part in the true catalyst of his hasty departure. It gave her a certain perverse satisfaction to think that, this time, it was *he* who was in the dark.

That night Catherine put the finishing touches on *The Clown Wore Black,* and two days later expressed the final chapters to New York. Although the story wasn't *"at all"* what her publishers had expected, they'd decided to accept it for their mystery line. It was due to publish at the beginning of next summer.

October faded into November, and Catherine took joy from spending her days exactly as she pleased. For the first time in months, she had the leisure to read, and constantly had a book under way. She hung around the Open Window with Ann Marie, visited with her father, and developed the habit of stopping by the high school to watch Kenny's swim team practices. He'd been selected to anchor the freestyle relay and swam butterfly on the medley.

The boy was shining like a star. His father was back at work at the shipyard, and with Kenny's part-time job at Ann Marie's shop, the two of them were well on their way toward paying off her loan. As usual, Catherine was terribly proud of Kenny.

Quite often she stopped by the newspaper to have lunch with Marla, who was beginning to show signs of her old self. There were still occasions when the haunted look came over her, and Catherine knew she was thinking of the bad times. They never spoke of Eliot, or that harrowing night when Marla collapsed in Catherine's arms. But the bond between them was solid as granite.

December dawned, autumn turned to winter, and most nights Catherine read herself to sleep, which was bereft of any memorable dreams. They'd stopped when Jack and Nicki parted. Apparently she had no more need of the dream saga that had swept her up like a tornado, terrifying her, wrenching her, but also inspiring her to action against the biggest mistake of her life.

The crisis with Eliot was past, and Jack and Nicki were gone. Catherine knew they were nothing more than figments of her imagination, but that didn't stop her from feeling their absence. She missed Nicki as keenly as a lost friend. And there was a hole in her heart where Jack used to be.

On Christmas Eve she returned from tea with her father, feeling particularly lonely. The day was overcast and cold, the briny wind biting as Catherine walked onto the deserted beach and stared out to sea. A gust of wind blustered past. Catherine pulled her coat collar snug about her throat.

She couldn't count the times she'd longed for just one more dream, one more memory. She'd have thought the details would fade, but they remained clear—the look of Jack's face, the sound of his voice, the sensation of his touch. Sometimes she caught herself staring into the distance where a haloed vision burned a hole in reality. *The name's Cantrell. Call me Jack . . .*

Sometimes in the shower she could close her eyes and feel the weight of his hand on her naked shoulder. On occasion he seemed so close, Catherine felt that a mere veil kept him from her sight—that if only she knew how to rip away the curtain, Jack would be there.

Tears sprang to Catherine's eyes. She obviously had gone quite "round the bend," and had no doubt every psychiatrist in the city would concur.

"Hey! Merry Christmas!" She turned as the familiar voice rang against the wind. Bundled up in a big ski jacket, Kenny looked tall and grown-up as he strode toward her with a beaming smile.

"And a very merry Christmas to *you*," Catherine greeted.

"I stopped by your place. Then I spotted you down here." His smile vanished as he looked into her tearing eyes. "What are you doing out here, anyway? Is something wrong?"

She passed a gloved hand beneath her eyes. "No. Nothing's wrong. I just feel a little bluesy today. It can happen sometimes at Christmas. You miss people."

"He's not worth it, Catherine," Kenny returned with a grimace. "I never thought Reynolds was good enough for you."

"Oh, I wasn't referring to *him*," she replied with a laugh.

"Are you sure? Because you've been different ever since the two of you split up."

"Do you think so, Kenny? Different in what way?"

His dark eyes searched hers. "Calmer somehow. Smooth like a lake, but a little sad, too."

"That's very perceptive. It's exactly how I feel. But don't worry. I'll get past the sad part."

Kenny cast a sweeping look up the beach. "Suddenly this reminds of that time last summer—you and me out here on the beach. I was about as low as anybody can get. Remember?"

"Of course I remember."

He opened the great, bearlike arms of his ski jacket. "How about you lean on me this time?"

A loving smile spread across Catherine's face as she stepped into the circle of Kenny's arm. And together they gazed across the frothing whitecaps of the winter sea.

PART TWO

The dream is the small hidden door in the deepest and most intimate sanctum of the soul, which opens into that primeval cosmic night that was soul long before there was a conscious ego and will be soul far beyond what a conscious ego could ever reach.

—Carl Jung

Chapter Fourteen

Monday, June 26

The Windy City was living up to its name. The sky was heavy with clouds threatening a summer storm, but those that hung lowest were scuttling across the skyline on a southbound draft that picked up a chill as it crossed the lake, then whipped in howling currents along alleyways and around corners.

Jack huddled in his windbreaker as he strode along the street toward the bookshop. When he arrived, he glanced in the front window and spotted the topknot of Matilda's gray hair. Peering diligently through spectacles, she was poring over some book or other. The grandmotherly shopkeeper was the most avid reader he'd ever known, and the two of them shared a taste for mysteries, although hers ran more to the gruesome than he could tolerate.

"Hello, gorgeous," Jack greeted as he swept through the door.

"Sweet-talker," she accused. "Well, will you look at that? Jack Casey got himself a respectable haircut."

Jack ran a palm over his shorn locks. The military buzz that had been necessary for the undercover job he'd just completed had grown out to a length of close to an inch and a half—just long enough so that when he combed it, the short layers folded together like the feathers on a duck's wing, except for the front, which continually bugged him by falling forward.

"It'll grow," he mumbled. "What do you have for me?"

"They're wrapped up and waiting and already charged to your account." Reaching beneath the counter, she produced a bundle in brown paper. "You've got a couple of whodunnits by people you're familiar with, plus a thriller by a new author, Cat Winslow. It's a pretty good read in a macabre sort of way."

"Macabre, huh? I like the sound of that. Thanks, Matilda. Call me when you get something new, huh?"

"Don't I always? . . . Hey, Jack," she added as he started to leave. Jack turned with a questioning look. "A parting word of advice: Keep the haircut."

"Will it get me a date with you?" he asked.

Matilda slipped him a wink. "Anytime, sonny boy. Anytime."

Jack stepped out of the shop to find that spattering raindrops were beginning to fall. Luckily, home was a short distance of three blocks up and one over. He had the city sidewalks to himself—everyone else presumably having taken cover from the impending deluge. Tucking the package inside his jacket, he traversed the three blocks at a loping gait and turned onto McCreedy Street.

As he approached, he studied the circa 1940 apartment building on the corner. Last night, when he returned from a ten-week trip, he hadn't noticed how dingy the place was beginning to look. The neighborhood had run down since he and Ellen had rented the ground-floor apartment seven years ago. Since then he'd made a success of his business and could afford bigger and better.

Jack unlocked the door, walked in, and looked around. But this place was all he had left of her, and he wasn't going anywhere. The curtains and wallpaper and painted kitchen cabinets were Ellen's, as were the potted plants on the back stoop and the buttercups that came up every spring to line the cement. When he went away on an assignment, as he had the past couple of months, he paid a service to take care of them.

Moving into his office, Jack set the package of books on the corner of his desk. He'd just returned from an assignment for the military at a base in California, where he'd infiltrated a drug trafficking ring. The pay was good; the tension, high. It was good to be home. But as usual when he traveled, the stack of correspondence awaiting his return seemed mountainous.

Taking a resigned seat behind the desk, he cleared a pile of mail from atop his calendar, which had been left open in the middle of April. Turning an indiscriminate chunk of pages, he flipped to the first week of July, and the significance of the approaching date dawned on him. July third. A week from today.

Reaching swiftly for the phone, he dialed the number of Grace's flower shop. The old chant—*Grace and Bobby, Ellen and Jack*—ran through his mind as he waited for her to pick up.

"Hi, sweetie," Grace affectionately greeted. "I was expecting your call. Did you just get back from California?"

"Last night. Listen, Grace, I just realized—"

"Don't you think I know what you realized? Long-stemmed American Beauties on the third."

"Six this year," Jack instructed.

"I know, sweetie."

There was a momentary lull before she added, "J-a-c-k," drawing out his name in a singsong way that made him picture her gazing up at him while she twirled a curl of red hair—just as she'd done since she was eight years old.

"W-h-a-t?" Jack mimicked with a smile.

"I don't care if you make fun of me or not," she poutily returned. "Bobby and I are worried about you."

"What have I done now?"

"It's what you *haven't* done, Jack. You haven't truly *lived* in six years."

Jack's smile faded. "Don't get started on this again."

"I only do it because I love you. *And* Ellen. We were best friends from the time we could walk, Jack. If anybody knew her better than you, it was me. And I know she wouldn't have wanted you to shut yourself off like this."

"I do *not* shut myself off, Grace."

"You never see any women."

"I *do* see women."

"Wrong," she returned. "Every now and then you have an affair. For sex. I'm talking about companionship. I'm talking about caring for a woman, loving a woman—"

"Grace!" he cut in sharply.

"What?" she meekly replied after a moment of silence.

"I don't *want* to care for another woman," Jack stated. "I don't want to *love* another woman. And I don't want you to keep trying to fix me up with every nice girl who crosses your path. There will never be another Ellen. Okay?"

"Okay." Grace surrendered, her tone sad and hopeless.

Jack expelled a heavy breath. "Just pick out some pretty roses, will you?" As he hung up the phone, his eyes cut to the wedding portrait on the bookshelves. The familiar form of the brunette in the white gown met his burning gaze, but as so often happened, the image soon began to blur and shift. He covered his eyes with balled fists, but they failed to block a cruel replay of those final seconds when Ellen smiled and waved from the car window, then vanished in a blinding explosion of flame.

Springing from the chair, Jack stalked into the kitchen, ripped open a pack of cigarettes, and lit up. He'd quit years ago, but had picked up the habit again in California, where everyone under investigation had smoked like a chimney. Taking a hard drag, Jack peered out the window over the sink.

The clouds had let go; the rain was coming down in torrents to the accompaniment of booming thunder. But the power of the storm without, paled beside the inner flood of six-year-old anguish that swept once more through the caverns of Jack's heart.

From the time they were kids, it had been "Jack and Ellen"—childhood sweethearts who lasted from junior high to high school, through city college and the police academy, all the way to the altar. She became a teacher, and he a cop.

She'd always been against his joining the force, especially after he made detective and started going undercover. "It's too dangerous," she'd always said. "I can take care of myself," he'd always replied. Nevertheless, she'd pleaded with him to leave.

God, if only he'd listened to her. It was his fault she was dead, and nothing was ever going to change it.

"Damn the storm," Jack muttered. Smashing the cigarette into the nearest excuse for an ashtray, he grabbed a parka and immersed his guilt in a grueling run along the rainswept city streets. When he returned, he was drenched and exhausted, but the memory had ebbed once again to a murky depth of consciousness.

After a hot shower and light supper he put in a few hours on paperwork. It was nearly ten when Jack sprawled across the bed and unwrapped Matilda's package. As soon as he saw the title, *The Clown Wore Black,* he was intrigued. And after reading the first few pages, he thumbed through the rest with rising astonishment.

Damn! It was Nicki's story. Nicki's and his. It was set in California instead of on the Big Island. And the heroine's last name had been changed from Palmer to Summers. But everything else was on the money, right down to the use of his alias, Cantrell.

Jack closed the paperback and looked again at the cover. A pair of black eyes peered from a white mask. The title and author's name were in red. Cat Winslow. He scoured the back and inside covers looking for the customary paragraph about the author, but there was none. Reopening the book, he went through it at the pace of a speed reader.

Long before he finished, Jack was certain that either Nicki had a writing talent about which he'd never known or, more likely, she'd collaborated with this Cat Winslow, who happened to be a damn good writer. Either way, Nicki was behind the novel. There was too much in it that the two of them, alone, had shared for there to be any other explanation—incidents described in vivid detail, conversations reported word for word.

It surprised him that she'd decided to go public after everyone went to such pains to keep heiress Nicki Palmer's name out of the scandal sheets. It annoyed him that Nicki would broadcast a story of which he was such an integral part without even telling him. Especially since she'd used his name so freely.

Jack was frowning as he checked his watch. Nearly eight o'clock in Hawaii. Vaulting off the bed, he went into the office, flipped through the Rolodex, and located the private home number of Palmer Ranch.

"I want everything to be perfect," Austin stated.

Malia looked up from clearing the table. In the glow of candles, he appeared young, golden, and beautiful—just as he was years ago. The day she first saw Austin, a flame had burst to life inside her, and it had burned like a fever ever since.

For the moment Malia was alone with her love, and she allowed the light of passion to spill from her eyes as she gazed at him.

"Everything *will* be perfect," she said. "For you have

seen to it. The Volcano Lodge has always been one of her favorite places, and you have arranged such a wonderful birthday ball—music, catering, all of her friends invited. But I believe the part Nicki looks forward to most is the time you and she will have together before everyone arrives—climbing the Pali once more."

"It had to be the Pali," Austin thoughtfully returned. "We were celebrating her tenth birthday when I first took her up to the lookout. I can still remember the excitement on her face when we reached the top. She turned leeward just as the waves crashed into the point and the Aloha Blow-Hole roared like a typhoon as it spewed water a hundred feet into the air."

"Next weekend will make our *keiki* very happy."

Austin looked up with electric blue eyes. "Nicki's not a baby. In less than two weeks, she'll observe her thirtieth birthday by opening a trust worth millions."

"She will always be our *keiki* to me," Malia returned with a soft smile. "No matter how many birthdays she may have."

The phone rang. Malia proceeded to the kitchen as Austin rose from the table and crossed into the neighboring study.

"Austin Palmer here."

"Good evening, Mr. Palmer. It's Jack Casey."

Austin scowled into space. "I understand from Melrose that you were well paid for your services. What the hell do you want?"

"I want to talk to Nicki," came the straightforward reply.

"That isn't possible. My niece is in Europe. In fact, she's been out of the country since that mess last summer."

"That 'mess' is what I wanted to talk to her about."

"I'm glad I can interrupt you, then. We don't talk about those particular few months of last year."

"I just wanted to ask her—"

"Are you hearing me?" Austin shouted into the mouthpiece. "We've done our utmost to forget the matter, and I insist that you refrain from dredging it up! Don't call here again!"

Slamming down the phone, he stomped to the liquor cabinet and poured himself a Scotch.

"Who was that?" Austin concealed a start of surprise as Nicki's voice sounded out from behind him.

"Nobody," he casually answered. "Just a guy trying to sell me something I don't want. Care for a drink?"

"No, thanks. I don't need it."

Turning with a full glass in hand, Austin took a sizable gulp and grinned. "I don't think you've ever *needed* it. Still, from time to time you've been known to drink me under the table and come up bright-eyed and bushy-tailed the next dawn."

Casting him a benign smile, Nicki wandered to the French doors that opened onto the patio and gazed through the screens at the gathering dusk. "It's a beautiful evening."

Austin strolled to her side. "It's good to have you back. I was beginning to think you might never come home. After the rugged challenges of the Alps, it should be a pleasant change for you to hike the Pali."

"It's always pleasant going up the Pali," Nicki said.

"Then the day after we return, you go to Pacific B and T, claim your inheritance, and become one of the richest women on the islands. How does that make you feel?"

Nicki turned to Austin with a solemn look. "No different than I've always felt. Or you. Allowances have always given us more money than we could spend, haven't they?"

"I don't know. I could have spent a little more if I'd put my mind to it," he quipped, and turned up his glass.

"Money's nice," Nicki commented. "But I've come to realize in the past year that there are things it can't buy. Do I really have to go to Oahu?"

Austin regarded her with surprise. "Of course. Your mother's will stipulates that you must appear at the bank on your thirtieth birthday. Why? What do you have against Oahu?"

Nicki folded her arms and shrugged. "Nothing, really. It's just that, except for flying in and out of the airport, the last time I was on Oahu was for Ed Coleman's funeral. The clown was there, too. Remember?"

Austin frowned. When he frowned that way, it threw his boyish face into sinister lines.

"The clown is dead, Nicki. Dead and gone."

"They never found his body, or any clue as to who he was. How can you be so sure?"

"His body washed out to sea. Take a look over the cliff at high tide sometime. It's not so tough to accept."

"Perhaps. But sometimes I still feel the hovering of something evil, like a darkness just beyond my line of vision."

Austin emitted a short laugh. "What are you saying? The clown has been resurrected as some evil specter who roams the sea cliffs? Come on, Nicki. You're being morbid. Maybe you should reconsider the idea of a drink." She shook her head. "Well, if you'll excuse me, I think *I'll* have another."

As her uncle returned to the liquor cabinet, Nicki strolled onto the patio and gazed toward the glowing lights of the pool. Malia's carefully tended plumeria scented the night with the inimitable fragrance of the islands and turned Nicki's thoughts once more toward the past.

That night a year ago, plumeria had been in the air, along with torchlight and music and laughter. The "Cast-Off Party" guests had numbered several dozen; Jack had stood out among them like a renegade knight. After blowing out the candles on the cake, she'd carved her way through the chattering crowd.

"Well, hello," he'd said. "I'm—"

"Jack something-or-other," she'd broken in, and, locking her arms around his neck, had pulled him down to her mouth.

Nicki relished the memory. The great healer of time had done that for her; the first few months after she and Jack had parted, she'd hardly been able to suffer the memories, much less enjoy them. Now things were different. Now her perceptions seemed to be coming from a very new, very wise point of view.

The past eight months she'd returned to the old Nicki with her jet-set clique of European friends. She'd rekindled old flames with Carlo in Italy, Heinrich in Austria, and Jacques in Paris. But the man who had haunted her thoughts was Jack. Because of him, she knew what she could feel for a man, and flings were cheap imitations. Because of him, she looked at herself through new eyes.

It was time to stop drifting through life on an aimless social stream. It was time to get serious about the ranch, and the company, and the heritage passing into her hands from those of her mother and father. In short, it was time to stop being a party girl and become a Palmer.

And maybe if she started doing something worthwhile with her life—maybe somewhere along the line—she'd end up deserving more than a cheap imitation.

Nicki turned to go back inside, an absent smile curving her lips. Wouldn't Jack be surprised? His kid sister may have done precious little of it in twenty-nine years, but now it seemed that, somehow, she'd grown up overnight.

Friday, June 30

"Can I get you anything else, Mr. Casey?" the stewardess asked as he handed her the supper tray.

Jack looked up and gave the petite brunette a smile. She'd been notably attentive throughout the flight, and he had the impression that if he asked for her number, he'd get it. But his mind was on other things.

"No thanks, Susan. How much longer before we land?"

"We'll be starting the descent in about twenty minutes. Are you visiting friends in Charleston, Mr. Casey?"

"More like business associates."

"Ever been to the city before?" she asked, taking her time as she cleared his supper tray and stowed it in her serving cart.

"Nope. Never been south of the Mason-Dixon line, actually."

"There's a lot to see and do in Charleston," she remarked. "Are your associates going to show you around?"

"I don't know," Jack replied. "I hadn't thought about it."

"When I have time, I'll jot down a few notes on attractions you shouldn't miss. What would you say to that?"

"I'd say, thanks. That's nice of you."

"That's how we are down here south of the Mason-Dixon line," Susan returned with a saucy smile, and proceeded along the narrow aisle with her cart. He watched as she departed, appreciating the swing of her hips until he became aware that the silver-haired lady next to him was glaring in admonishment.

Clearing his throat, Jack turned to gaze out the west-facing window of the jet. The horizon was a masterpiece of color—the fire of the setting sun painting the sky with splashes of red. The old rhyme came to mind: *Red sky at morning, sailor take warning; red sky at night, sailor's delight.*

Well, at least this spur-of-the moment, what-the-hell adventure was under way with an omen of good weather. Curiosity had landed him on this southbound jet—pure, bristling curiosity. Four nights ago he'd opened a paperback novel, and now the man who'd made a career of solving other people's enigmas was keenly caught up in one of his own.

After Austin Palmer hung up on him, Jack had spent the majority of the next day rereading the novel with a sharp eye, seeing things he hadn't noticed the first time and becoming increasingly intrigued by the author who had portrayed him in such intimate detail. The mystery of *The Clown Wore Black* had taken on broader lines at that point. It wasn't about just Nicki anymore, but about Cat Winslow as well.

Someday Jack would ask Nicki for an explanation, regardless of what her uncle had to say. But for the foreseeable future, the blond bombshell was "defying gravity" somewhere in Europe. Chances were that Cat Winslow was more immediately within reach.

Yesterday morning Jack had called the New York publishing house listed in the front of the novel, had been put through to a fast-talking editor, and had been given the nonyielding spiel. If he was interested in communicating with the author, he was welcome to write her in care of . . . and so on.

He'd waited until the lunch hour and called again. This time he was put through to a youthful-sounding assistant, who refused to relinquish information about the author, but eventually divulged the name and number of her agent, a Mrs. Duvall of the Open Window bookshop in Charleston, South Carolina.

Jack had reflected on the situation before he made the call. Charleston was far removed from the New York publishing world. Why would an author have an agent there unless she lived nearby? As he dialed the South Carolina number, he'd slipped into the persona of a guileless Cat Winslow fan seeking an autograph.

He was glad he'd adopted such a tack when Ann Marie Duvall answered his call. She spoke with a genteel Southern accent, and a great deal of unabashed pride in Cat Winslow.

"I'm an avid reader of mysteries," he said. "And *The Clown Wore Black* is one of the most unique I've seen in quite a while."

"Yes, it *is* well done, isn't it? Particularly since it's her first attempt at writing a thriller."

"I was wondering about the source of the novel. Is it based on a true story?"

"Oh, no," the Duvall woman assured him with a lilting laugh. "It's pure fiction, straight from the author's imagination."

"I see," Jack murmured, his curiosity taking on a new edge. "As it happens, Mrs. Duvall, I'm going to be in Charleston this weekend. I wonder if the author might agree to sign my copy."

"Of course, Mr. Casey. I'm sure she'd be delighted. Just stop by my shop when you get to town. Do you have the address?"

So the bluff had paid off, and he was on his way to Charleston to meet Cat Winslow. Pure fiction, huh? Straight from the author's imagination? Right.

It was nearly eight o'clock when the plane came to a halt at the gate. Shouldering his carry-on bag, Jack got in line behind the silver-haired lady and moved gradually toward the exit, where a quartet of airline personnel were bidding passengers good-bye. Susan was among them, and when Jack reached her, she pressed a folded note in his hand.

"The attractions I was mentioning to you, Mr. Casey."

"Thank you, Susan."

"My pleasure, sir."

As he proceeded along the ramp, Jack flipped open the note and wasn't surprised to see that she'd written her name and phone number. But as he entered the airport, his train of thought bypassed Susan and sped toward the objectives of acquiring a car and a map, and finding his way to King Street. Tucking the note in his wallet, Jack headed for the line of car rental counters.

By the time he rented a fancy Buick sedan, drove from the airport to the city, and cruised into the area announced

by a marker as HISTORIC DISTRICT, the lingering twilight was
fast turning into night—a very mild night compared to what
he'd left behind in Chicago.

Shrugging out of the jacket with the copy of *The Clown
Wore Black* in the pocket, Jack checked his watch: 8:40.
He had no idea how late the bookshop stayed open. Still,
he carried on toward that destination along narrow lanes
lit by streetlamps and lined with a pattern of antiquated
shopfronts, restaurants, and privacy walls forbidding passersby anything more than distant looks at the tall, Civil
War–vintage town houses behind them.

The walks were teeming with pedestrians coming and
going from various establishments. There were even horse-
drawn carriages carting people along the quaint thorough-
fares. Apparently the nightlife of Historic Charleston was
one of its attractions. One thing was sure: It kept traffic to
a crawl. Another ten minutes elapsed as Jack methodically
followed the map to King Street.

He traveled three blocks before his searching gaze lit on
a sign heralding THE OPEN WINDOW. The lights were still on.
Lucking into a space near the corner, Jack parked the
Buick, grabbed the novel, and hurried back to the shop.
An attractive dark-haired woman moved to greet him as
he walked in.

"Mrs. Duvall?"

"Yes," she affirmed.

"Hi. I'm Jack Casey. We spoke on the phone yesterday."
He held up the copy of *The Clown Wore Black*. "I just got
into town and was hoping to get this signed sometime."

"Is tonight too soon?"

"Hell, no!" Jack responded with such eagerness that he
drew one of the musical laughs he remembered from the
phone.

"I enjoy seeing a reader's enthusiasm toward a book,"
she then said. "Especially one by Cat Winslow. As it happens, she's due here at any moment. She's visiting her father, who's in failing health, and she'll be stopping here on
her way home. When I told her of your phone call yesterday, she said she'd be happy to sign your novel. Would you
care to browse until she arrives?"

Jack was several minutes into browsing the mystery section as the back of the shop when the tinkling bell of the

front door sounded out. He meandered alongside the bookshelves, discreetly watching as Ann Marie Duvall went to meet a slim blonde wearing white shorts and sneakers, and a sleeveless denim shirt. Her limbs were shapely and suntanned, her chin-length hair smooth and golden and sparkling with lights from the sun.

"How is he, sugar?" Jack heard Mrs. Duvall ask.

The blonde—presumably Cat Winslow—tucked her hands in her pockets and shrugged. "He's had three ministrokes in twelve days, Ann Marie. The doctors say it's just a matter of time. All we can do is keep him comfortable."

"I'm so sorry, dear."

"Me, too," the blonde replied, then looked around as Jack moved into the perimeter of her vision.

"Oh, sugar," Ann Marie said. "This is the gentleman, Mr. Casey, who wants you to sign his copy. . . ."

Jack tuned out the rest of what Ann Marie Duvall said as familiarity struck. He moved forward, his gaze zooming over the blonde. The height and form, the shape of the face. Beneath a wisp of bangs, her features were frozen in a look of shock, as though she were seeing a ghost.

"Jack?" she questioned on a note of disbelief.

"Nicki?" he returned in a matching tone. Scrutinizing the familiar features, he noticed she wasn't wearing her usual lipstick and makeup. In fact her complexion was clean-scrubbed to a peaches-and-cream kind of glow. As he was digesting the observation, she took a slight step forward and lifted a hesitant hand to his face—her fingertips meeting his cheek tentatively, haltingly, as though she expected the touch to go clear through.

Jack's searching gaze narrowed on her eyes, which were wide as the sky. And it was then that he beheld the telling difference. Nicki's eyes sparkled with teasing; these held none of that shifting light, but instead were an unwavering deep blue. Fathomless. He shook himself against the notion that he was falling into them. Hair and makeup could change. But not eyes.

"Who *are* you?" she breathed, seemingly in horror.

"I'm Jack Casey, alias Jack Cantrell," he replied with perplexed curtness. "Who the hell are *you*?"

The light touch on his cheek fell away as her knees buckled and she started sinking. Dropping his copy of *The

Clown Wore Black, Jack quickly reached out and caught
her under the arms. Her eyelids fluttered, then flew wide
once more as she started scrambling for her footing. Once
she regained it, she backed out of his grasp and kept on
backing away until she bumped against a counter. The Duvall woman flew to her side.

"Oh, my goodness," she twittered. "You mean, this is
the Jack? My goodness, Catherine! What can it mean?"

With a scowl of confusion, Jack stooped to pick up the
paperback novel and walked toward them. "Catherine?"
he questioned, and lifted the book. "As in Cat Winslow?"

She nodded, her eyes still big and deep as the sea. Jack
peered as he struggled to make sense of the face before
him—Nicki's face . . . rather, *almost* Nicki's face. *Almost*
Nicki's exact double. His thinking veered as a memory
flashed forward. Before taking the job in Hawaii, he'd com-
piled the routine stats on Nicki. His mind's eye homed in
on the remembered page of facts: *Parents: deceased. Siblings: none, but for a stillborn twin.*

Unless you believed in doppelgängers, this wide-eyed
woman had to be Nicki's erroneously reported "stillborn"
twin.

"Nicki's your sister, right?" he ventured.

"No," she whispered. "Nicki's not real."

Perplexity tumbled into irritation, and Jack promptly lost
patience. "What?" he boomed. "What do you mean,
Nicki's not real? What the hell's going on here?"

Ann Marie Duvall hurried up to him as the blonde continued to stare. "You can't possibly know how shocking
this is, Mr. Casey."

"Oh, I don't know," he flippantly returned. "I'm feeling
fairly shocked at present. Actually, I've been feeling pretty
damn well shocked ever since I opened *The Clown Wore
Black*. How come no one bothered to let me know such a
book was being written, much less published?"

Ann Marie Duvall straightened at that point and confronted him with a feral look. "There are a great many
questions to be explored, young man," she announced.
"For the moment, I suggest the three of us adjourn to my
apartment and have a stiff drink."

Chapter Fifteen

Untasted glass of sherry in hand, Catherine perched on the seat of the stiff-backed Chippendale. A thousand questions were spinning through her mind, but she couldn't force a word past her dammed lips as she stared, in stunned silence, at Jack.

He was standing by the bar where Ann Marie had poured the two of them a whiskey, and now was hurriedly murmuring an explanation about "the dream." Catherine paid no heed to their muted dialogue. Her attention was riveted on Jack, her eyes following his every move, seizing on the familiarity of the way he stood . . . and held his head . . . and took a drink. Even the black jeans and boots and white, open-throated shirt were familiar.

This couldn't be. It just couldn't be.

Depositing his shot glass on the bar, he started toward her chair. Catherine's heart began to pound as he sought her eyes and captured them. He peered down for a moment before sinking to a crouch before her and offering a small smile.

"Judging from what Ann Marie just told me, I guess you were pretty surprised when I showed up," he said. The voice of her dreams sent shivers up her spine. Catherine nodded.

"This is turning into quite a mystery," he added.

"You cut your hair," she mumbled.

Jack's smile broadened as he ran a palm over the top of his head. "So I did." However inanely the dam had been broken, once Catherine spoke, she emerged from her dazed state, and a stream of questions spilled forth.

"Are you telling me Nicki is real, too? Who is she? Where is she? How can this be happening?"

Jack raised a cautioning hand. "Take it easy, okay? I

have a theory about all this, but let's get some facts straight first."

"What kind of facts?"

"We could start with your dreams. Can you remember when you first started dreaming about the clown?"

Setting her glass on the neighboring tea table, Catherine put a shaky hand to her brow. "I don't know. I can't think."

"Just give yourself a minute," he suggested. "Then try to think back. It was last summer, wasn't it?"

"Yes," she answered eventually. "I remember now. The children were out of school, but it wasn't yet officially summer. The first time the clown appeared, Nicki was at a carnival. It was June. Does she look the way I described?"

"She looks *exactly* as you described. Everything does."

"Well, if she looks exactly as I described her, then— except for her hair—she looks exactly like me. You thought I was Nicki when you first saw me downstairs. Didn't you?"

"For a minute," Jack replied, his gaze roaming her face before returning to her eyes. "But there are differences. The longer I look at you, the more I see."

Circling behind Jack, Ann Marie came to stand by Catherine's chair. "There's an old saying about everyone in the world having a look-alike. I never imagined it might be true. If Nicki isn't the dream side of Catherine I've assumed her to be all these years, then who in the world is she?"

Jack settled back on his haunches. "Does the name Palmer mean anything to you, Catherine?"

"Nicki Palmer," Catherine voiced in a tone of amazement. "Now that I say the name, it seems I've heard it before."

Jack nodded with a slow smile. "Nicki Palmer—socialite, heiress, daredevil . . . Why am I telling *you*? It occurs to me that, in a way, you've known her a lot longer than I have."

"So all these years I've been dreaming about an heiress who looks just like me?" Catherine blurted.

"Technically speaking, I'm not sure your experiences are actually *dreams.*"

"What, then? Visions?"

"No." Glancing briefly aside, Jack rubbed his forehead as though trying to force some kind of answer into his head before meeting her eyes once more. "Think back to last summer again, back to the time when *I* was in the dreams. Can you remember waking from any of them and noticing what time it was?"

"The time? I don't know. I can't recall—" Catherine broke off as a memory leaped to mind. *It's five o'clock,* Eliot had said. *I've got to be at a meeting miles away in a few hours.* And then he'd kissed her, but she'd continued to feel the thrill of Jack's mouth.

"I remember the pool party," she continued, forcing her eyes to remain on his, though every second they seemed drawn to slip to his lips. "The first time you and Nicki met. When I woke up, it was five o'clock in the morning."

"What was happening in the dream just before you woke?"

"Nicki had blown out the candles on the cake, and . . ."

"And she kissed me. Just as you wrote in the novel."

"Yes," Catherine affirmed. "What does that tell you?"

"It tells me that the action of your dreams, and the actual events that took place, unfolded simultaneously."

"How do you arrive at that?" Ann Marie inquired.

"Like I said," Jack replied, his gaze remaining on Catherine. "My theory is that you haven't been dreaming at all. I believe your subconscious has been connecting with Nicki's actual life. Why the episodes have come to you as dreams, I don't know—maybe because you were most receptive when your conscious mind was asleep. But all along, from the time you were kids, I believe that Nicki has been sending, and you receiving."

"But that's impossible."

"Unusual, maybe, but not impossible. A minute ago, when you told me about waking from the dream of Nicki's party, I became certain that it was no dream. Somehow, you were picking up the actual occurrence during the actual minutes it was happening. You see, that night when Nicki kissed me, it was midnight in Hawaii, which would have made it five in the morning here in Charleston."

"Hawaii?" Catherine repeated with a new jolt of astonishment.

"Despite the fact that you set your novel in California, you described the ranch so accurately," Jack commented. "I assumed you knew. Palmer Ranch is located on the Big Island of Hawaii."

"*I* was born in the Hawaiian islands," Catherine whispered.

Ann Marie bent close. "Were you, sugar? I never knew that."

"My mother was having a difficult pregnancy," Catherine went on in the same whispering tone. "Father took her away, to a resort home owned by a friend in the islands. They brought me back when I was a month old."

"What do you know about that," Jack murmured. "Well, that clinches it as far as I'm concerned."

"Clinches what?" Ann Marie piped up.

"Last year, when I was doing research before taking the case in Hawaii, I came across something—a matter of public record that I assumed to be of no significance. Now I wonder."

"What did you come across?" Ann Marie demanded as Catherine stared, once again rendered silent by the feeling that something monumental was about to come to light.

"You know, Catherine," Jack went on in a gentle tone, "under certain circumstances people have been known to connect in uncanny ways. Science doesn't have all the answers yet, not when it comes to people who are genetically linked."

"You mean like twins?" Ann Marie voiced on a shocked note. "My goodness! I've got a book downstairs on that very subject!"

"I don't know how this happened," Jack continued, his eyes boring into Catherine. "But according to the records, Nicki had a twin who died at birth. Now that I've met you, I think the baby survived, after all. I think that somehow, some way, the twins were separated. One remained in Hawaii, the other came here."

Catherine stared as the implication sank in. "Nicki's my . . . *sister*?" she haltingly questioned. With contrasting speed she shot to her feet. Jack abruptly did the same and took her shoulders in steadying hands. Catherine looked up, felt the shock of him anew, and then the larger shock overwhelmed her once more.

"Nicki's my sister," she said again, the questioning note having vanished. "It's true. I know it. I have to see my father."

"I'll drive you," Jack declared.

"Heavens above! I'll go, too!" Ann Marie joined in.

*   *   *

Jack found Winslow House to be as depressing as it was aristocratic. There was a darkness about the place that had nothing to do with night . . . an air of gloom that hung like fog. He tried to picture the sun-kissed girl from the bookshop growing up in such a mausoleum, and couldn't.

Ann Marie's hurried words about Catherine's tyrannical aunt had done little to prepare him for the austere woman wearing a stark black bathrobe and an expression to match. The moment they entered the house, she'd come swooping down the stairs, the sleeves of her robe flapping like the wings of a raven.

When she found out they meant to see her brother, she'd taken a firm stance at the staircase and had forbidden any of them to pass. Jack had interceded at that point. "Surely you're not implying that you have the authority to keep a daughter from her ailing father," he'd said.

As "Aunt Sybil" stepped forward to give him a tongue-lashing, Catherine had slipped swiftly past her, followed by Ann Marie, and then Jack himself—with the woman in black hot on his heels. Now she stood guard by the chrome-appointed hospital bed in the second-floor chamber, her beady eyes trained on her niece as though she expected Catherine to try to snatch the stricken man from under the sheet and make away with him out the window.

The frail man had lost most of his motor capabilities, except for the right hand, which occasionally lifted enough to allow him to fan his fingers. His speech was slurred to the point that Jack couldn't understand a word he said, Catherine, who was kneeling by his side, obviously did.

She spoke in murmuring tones, and her father replied. Jack couldn't remember ever having seen a picture like it— the dying man, the golden girl . . . like an angel come down to collect a spirit. After a few moments she turned to the bedside table and opened a drawer, apparently at her father's instruction.

"His private papers are in there!" Sybil squawked.

"I know," Catherine placidly replied, and continued probing through the drawer's contents. "He said there's a letter for me."

Eventually she produced an envelope. "This has my name on it, Father." His fingers fluttered approval. Cather-

ine withdrew a letter and held it to the light of the lamp.
"It's dated 1973, just after Mother . . . before your first
stroke," she concluded.

The man's hand lifted, signaling her to read on. "Dearest
Catherine," she began in the accented voice that grew more
musical to Jack's ear with every word. "If I have found the
courage, I am delivering this letter by hand. If not, I have
gone to join your mother. Either way, I ask your forgiveness for not having told you the story before now, the story
of how you came to be our miracle child. We have loved
you as our own, but the fact is that you are not our biologi-
cal daughter. *That* child was lost to us a week before you
arrived."

Jack was following Catherine's every gesture so intently
that he noticed immediately when the paper she was holding began to shake. She stopped reading, and his heart went
out to her.

"Ann Marie?" she said ultimately. "Would you mind
finishing this for me?"

"Of course, sugar," Ann Marie replied, and hurried over
to take the letter. "Where are you? All right. I see . . . As
we told you, your mother's pregnancy was a difficult one.
Doctors warned that it was doubtful she could carry a full
term. We took a house in Hawaii, hoping the change of
scene and climate might help.

"The breezes of the Kona Coast were, indeed, uplifting.
And we were well looked after by a Hawaiian girl, Kila,
who wouldn't allow your mother to lift a finger. But I suppose some things are not meant to be. Your mother miscar-
ried and lapsed into a severe depression. I feared for her
life.

"Then, on July tenth, Kila came to our house with a
newborn girl. You weren't even a day old. The baby's life
was in danger, Kila said, and would reveal nothing more,
but only urged us to take you far away as soon as possible.
We looked on you as a gift from God, and from that moment you became our Catherine. The next day we sailed
from the Big Island to Oahu and took lodging under a
different name. A month later we returned to Charleston.

"Your mother reclaimed life through you, my dear. It
was inconceivable to me to bring out the truth while she
lived. But now that she's gone, and I don't know how I

shall survive without her, I realize you should not be left
unknowing. Of your true origins I know nothing more than
this letter states. Of one thing, however, I can assure you
forever—no daughter was ever more loved than 'our
Catherine.'"

By the time Ann Marie finished reading, there was a
lump in Jack's throat the size of Nebraska.

"Thank you, Father," Catherine whispered. The man's
eyelids closed, and Jack fancied a look of peace about him
that hadn't been there before.

"You've got what you came for," Sybil's harsh voice rang
out. "Maybe now you'll leave us in peace."

Jack glared at the woman by the bed. Her eyes were
leveled on Catherine—spewing volumes of wordless hatred.
Catherine seemed not to notice as she rose to her feet and
glided around the bed, holding the letter to her breast. Ann
Marie fell in behind her as she left the room. Jack brought
up the rear, bestowing a full-fledged scowl on Aunt Sybil
as he passed.

"I'll be back to check on you, Terrence," she announced.

"I'll bet he can't wait for *that*," Jack muttered.

"Did you address me, young man?" the woman in black
inquired from behind him. Denying her the courtesy of
looking around, Jack quickened his pace, bypassed Catherine and Ann Marie on the stairs, and proceeded to the
front door ahead of them.

"It's no surprise to *me* that you haven't a drop of Winslow blood in your veins!" This time the hateful voice managed to make an impact on Catherine. Halting in the foyer,
she turned. Ann Marie stopped with her, and they waited
as Sybil Winslow descended the last few steps of the
staircase.

"There's no need for ugly talk," Ann Marie chided.

"Not ugly, just plain," came the cutting retort. "She's
never had the character to carry the Winslow name, and
she knows it."

Jack's ire began to boil as he snatched open the door.

"And now we find out she was picked up like a sack of
shells off some beach," Sybil concluded, and pushed Jack
over the edge.

"What witch farm did you hatch out of, lady?" he demanded as he stalked up to the women.

"I beg your pardon!" Sybil blustered.

"It's not *my* pardon you should beg," Jack replied as he placed a hand on Catherine's shoulder. "It's *hers.*"

"It doesn't matter," Catherine murmured.

"It would matter to anyone with even the most common sense of decency," he declared. "Obviously, your aunt hasn't got a shred."

"You . . . you upstart Yankee!" she stammered, her beady eyes wide for once. "You get out of my house this instant!"

"With pleasure," Jack returned, and, planting a firm arm around Catherine, swept her out of the witch's den.

The night air was notably sweet and fresh, a welcome relief from the atmosphere of the house. Keeping a guiding hand at Catherine's waist, Jack ushered her to the Buick parked at the curb and opened the passenger door. Ann Marie got in the back, and the exodus from Winslow House began in the kind of stupefied silence that follows a hurricane.

Turning off Legare Street, Jack headed back the way they'd come. It was after eleven, and the bustling traffic had thinned to a stream. The late hour had wrought a change in the Historic District, which now appeared soft and dreamy with antiquity.

Jack looked toward Catherine. She was peering ahead, still clutching her father's letter. Was it only a couple of hours since they met? It seemed they'd traveled a million miles together since then. He glanced in the rearview mirror and managed to catch Ann Marie's eye.

"I'll drive her home if you'll tell me how to get there," he quietly suggested.

"Thank you, Jack. I'll check on her first thing tomorrow." Dropping Ann Marie at the bookshop, he proceeded according to her directions toward a condo off East Bay. Catherine remained still as they cruised along the lamplit streets.

"Wow." The word was so faint, Jack wasn't sure if he'd heard it. He glanced Catherine's way. She continued to peer ahead as she went on in the same meager voice. "I've always had this feeling, like part of me was somewhere else and I was supposed to be there, too. Now I know why. Do you think Nicki has any idea?"

"I have no reason to suspect that she does."

"I must see her. I'm going to Hawaii."

"Nicki's not there," Jack confided. "I talked to Austin Palmer a few days ago. According to him, Nicki's in Europe. She's been out of the country since last September."

"That's when the dreams stopped. . . . Oh, my gosh," Catherine added in a rush. "It just struck me that the clown was no dream. He was real. You almost died. Nicki almost died. I nearly lost her before I even knew— Where exactly in Europe *is* she?"

"I don't know. And judging from Austin Palmer's attitude, I don't think he's about to give me any further information regarding Nicki's whereabouts. He hung up on me."

"Well, then," Catherine softly concluded, "it all comes back to the fact that I'm going to Hawaii. From there I'll get in touch with Nicki. I must."

"I guess that follows," Jack responded. "But you ought to let the dust settle before you make any decisions. There were things in your father's letter that bear some thinking."

"Like what?"

"Like the fact that the woman who brought you to the Winslows said your life was in danger."

"I don't care about that. I'd go tomorrow if my father weren't so gravely ill."

Jack came to a stop at a red light and gave Catherine an assessing once-over. She meant what she said, all right. But she had no idea what she was getting into. Neither did he, really, except for a gut feeling that there was a hell of a lot more going on than met the eye. The Palmer estate was worth millions, and when money was involved, there was no telling what people might do. The light turned green, and Jack looked ahead once more.

"You shouldn't go alone, Catherine. A lot of questions have been raised, and it wouldn't be wise to walk into Palmer Ranch without any answers. When the time is right, I'll go with you."

"You *will*?" she said, her voice full of wonder.

"Sure. Why not?" Jack carelessly returned. When he glanced her way, he saw that she was regarding him with a marveling look. "I feel I have a part in this, too, you know," he added. "Besides, I never could resist a good mystery."

"Wow," Catherine murmured again.

"Yeah," Jack agreed with a chuckle. "Wow."

A moment later she pointed to the building on the corner just ahead. "That's it right there," she announced. "You can park in that space by the palm tree." Pulling over where she indicated, Jack took note of an elegant town house trimmed with wrought iron and balconies. Killing the engine, he turned Catherine's way and stretched an arm along the back of the car seat.

"Thank you for driving me home," she said.

"No problem." The beam of the street lamp on the corner drifted into the car, lighting up the whites of her eyes so that they seemed to glow. Jack was abruptly aware of their closeness . . . and a sharp sense of attraction.

"I don't know where my manners are," Catherine commented with a slight smile. "Would you like to come in for a cup of coffee?"

"Actually, what I'd like is to use your phone. Can you recommend a place to stay around here?"

"You don't have a place to stay?"

Jack shook his head. "I drove straight from the airport to the bookshop."

"Oh, no. It's a summer weekend. Everything near the District is bound to be booked. I know. You'll stay at my place tonight."

"No, really—"

"Yes, really," Catherine insisted.

"I don't want to impose."

"You won't be imposing. I have a couch that opens to a bed, and you've come all this way. The least I can do is give you a place to spend the night. Now, where are your bags?"

"I have one in the trunk. Are you sure about this?"

"Completely sure."

"Well, I've heard of Southern hospitality," Jack said with a grin. "I guess this is it."

"That's right," Catherine replied, her eyes meeting his with a look of tenderness that wiped the grin off his face. "Welcome to Charleston, Jack. It's awfully good to see you."

Catherine led the way through the recessed entrance and started up the steps to the penthouse. Sometime during the brief walk from the street to the courtyard, the buffering entrancement of her father's revelation had evaporated. With each passing instant she became more keenly cognizant of the here and now—the tinkling spiral of the fountain in the garden, the shifting shadows on the footlit stairwell, and, most acutely, the presence of the man behind her.

With the thud of his every footstep, his name sounded in her mind's ear. *Jack . . . Jack . . .* over and over. By the time Catherine unlocked the door and stepped inside, the name seemed to throb with her blood through the whole of her body.

"Nice place," he complimented as he followed her in.

"Thanks," she replied with a fleet smile. "Just put your bag down anywhere, and I'll show you around."

"Okay," he casually returned. But now his every casual word and gesture seemed to yank at Catherine's memory, startling her with trills of déjà vu. Unloading his shoulder bag near the aquarium, he gazed at her expectantly.

"Um, *this,*" she said with a flourish of her hand, "is the sofa bed. It's queen-size. I hope you'll be comfortable."

"I'm sure it'll be fine."

With a brisk nod Catherine proceeded through the living area. "And *this,*" she continued as she drew open the sliding door, "is the reason I bought the place."

Following her onto the balcony, Jack rested his hands on the rail and drew a deep breath of the ocean air. "I can understand why," he commented, and looked her way. "This is quite a treat, particularly for an inland, big-city boy."

A breeze ruffled his hair, moonlight sparkled in his eyes, and a rush that started in the pit of Catherine's stomach bolted to her throat. With a mute smile she stepped inside and scarcely waited for him to join her before skirting into the dining room.

"This, of course, is the dining room," she remarked, moving swiftly on. "And the kitchen." Putting the breadth of the room between them, she opened the adjoining door. "There's access to the bathroom here. I'll just lay out some fresh towels for you."

As she withdrew a set from the linen cupboard, Jack gave her a start by strolling into the bath and through the other open door to her bedroom. Catherine trailed to the threshold. His back was to her as he directed a sweeping look about her chamber. She took the opportunity to devour the sight of him.

She'd been in love with the man for a year, and he hadn't a clue. What would he think if he knew the way she'd longed for him? What would he say if he knew the way he'd changed her life? There was nothing he *could* say; he could only squirm and look embarrassed, and at the thought of such a spectacle, Catherine recoiled in self-consciousness.

Jack turned and spread his palms. "And *this*," he announced with the slightly crooked grin she well remembered, "is *your* room."

"You're teasing me," she objected as he walked toward her.

"Just a little." When he reached the doorway, he took hold of the sill above his head and gazed down. Catherine was struck by how tall he was. "Thanks for putting me up," he said. "I owe you one."

"You've already given me more than I can ever repay," she murmured. Hastily laying down the towels, Catherine escaped into the openness of the kitchen. "Would you like me to put on some coffee?" she asked as Jack wandered in.

"No, thanks. But I'll take a beer if you've got it."

"I'm sorry. I don't drink beer, but I have white wine."

"Wine is good."

Catherine turned, opened the cabinet, and started to rise on tiptoe to reach the wineglasses. Jack ambled up behind her.

"Allow me," he said, and stretched a long arm over her shoulder to the top shelf. The action caused his chest to brush against her back, and she thought she might jump out of her skin.

"Here you go," he added, and innocently handed her two goblets. Once in her grasp the glasses began to shake, and before Catherine could transfer them to the counter, they knocked together with a telltale clink.

"Are you okay?" Jack asked. "You seem a little nervous."

Sidestepping away from his nearness, Catherine turned and braved the challenge of looking him in the eye. "I'm *terribly* nervous. I wonder if your realize how strange it is for me to see you standing here in my kitchen like a regular person."

Jack propped a hip against the counter and folded his arms as he studied her. The breadth of his shoulders was outlined in white, the length of his legs etched in black. The way he was standing struck her as excruciatingly sexy, as did the look in his eyes.

"I *am* a regular person, Catherine," he stated in a deep voice that enhanced the effect. "Just a regular guy, ya know? But I can understand why the sight of me still shocks you a little."

"A little?" Arching a brow, she moved swiftly to the fridge. "Wine is a great idea." Jack laughed at that, and received the glass she offered him a moment later with an amused expression.

"Thank you, ma'am," he said, and extended his goblet. "I have the perfect toast. How about, to dreams come true?"

"Very appropriate." After taking a sip that was more of a gulp, Catherine glanced up and found that Jack was studying her over the rim of his glass. She helplessly looked away.

"It's moving on toward midnight," he observed. "Maybe I should line up a reservation for tomorrow. Any suggestions?"

"The Indigo Inn is nearby," she answered without meeting his eyes. "I'll get the number for you."

While Jack made the call, Catherine bustled the cushions off the couch, unfolded the mattress, and set about making the bed. She was moving at fidgety high speed, and by the time he got off the phone, she'd done the sheets with hospital precision and was tucking in the final corner of the blanket.

"I was going to offer to help," Jack said as he walked over.

"That's okay. What did the Indigo Inn have to say?"

"They had a cancellation. I can check in at noon."

"Good." Straightening from the bed, Catherine cast a quick smile in his direction. "You see? Everything's working out."

"It sure is," he returned in a way that seemed laced with a provocative undertone.

But then maybe she was reading into the way Jack sounded, and looked, and seemed prone toward searching out her eyes. Tipping his head, he consumed the last of his wine and set the glass aside.

"Would you like to wash up?" she asked.

"That would be great. Unless you want the bathroom first."

"No, no," Catherine assured him. "I think I'll wait and take a long, hot soak in the tub—" She broke off as the image bloomed with the very implications that had her so on edge.

"Sounds nice," Jack offered, his voice rumbling in the quiet room, stroking her nerves with a masculine touch.

"Make yourself at home," Catherine chirped before making a quick exit to the privacy of her bedroom.

Closing the door behind her she hurried to the bathroom door and shut it, as well. She leaned back against its solidity, closed her eyes, and started taking rhythmic breaths. Scarcely a minute had passed when she heard Jack enter the room from the other side.

Sprinting away, Catherine sank to a seat on the bed. "Calm down," she told herself. But when the shower came on, the image of Jack standing naked beneath the water came so sharply to mind that it sliced through any such resolve.

Her cheeks caught fire as the memory of the dream expanded. She recalled every detail of his body—tall and long-limbed and solid as rock. His sun-bronzed skin gleamed with a sheen of water, the tan line around his hips calling attention to the breath-arresting display of his manhood.

Covering her face with her hands, Catherine flopped back on the bed. She was still there sometime later when a rapping noise shattered her reverie. She bolted to a sitting position.

"It's all yours, Catherine. Sleep well, huh?"

"You, too," she called with fabricated lightness.

Sleep well, Catherine repeated to herself as she watched the strip of light at the base of the door disappear. It was entirely possible she might never sleep again.

Chapter Sixteen

A crowd of more than sixty attended the grand opening of the Mainsail Yacht Club's elegant new dining hall. Christened the "Founders Room," the expansive salon featured tall sea-facing windows, a landscaped entryway of palm and anthurium, and a gallery wall of ornately framed photographs of the club founders.

The fiery light of sunset streamed through the windows to glimmer on the sterling service of an exquisite buffet and the crystal appointments of satellite carts tended by waiters offering liquor and champagne. The room was filled with the fragrances of culinary delicacies, expensive perfumes, and the floral leis draping the necks of the chic attendants. Among them was a sampling of the islands' most influential citizenry.

From her position near one of the floating bars, Nicki spotted Melrose at a table in the far corner. She was on her way in his direction when she was waylaid by Paolo.

He lifted her hand and pressed a warm kiss to its back. "You're looking more beautiful than ever, Nicki. Would you grant me the honor of escorting you from supper?"

Nicki looked into his dark eyes and found them sparkling with provocative promise. In the old days an escort from Paolo would have led to a private party at his oceanside hacienda. Funny how the prospect no longer held any appeal.

"Sorry. I have a previous commitment," she lied.

Paolo scowled. "Since you returned from Europe, you've been hiding away. The crowd is anxious to see you."

"The *crowd* will see me at my birthday party next weekend. I believe I noticed your name among the acceptances." She kissed his cheek and picked up the nostalgic scent of his custom-made cologne. "See you there," she added, and moved on.

Confirming that Melrose was still alone at the table in the far corner, Nicki skirted the periphery of the crowd. There was a deserted corridor of space along the gallery wall featuring the ten portraits of the Mainsail founders. Each photograph was carefully tinted, framed in antique gold, and illumined by a small lamp at the top of the frame.

Nicki continued in Melrose's direction, her attention passing from one picture to the next as she strolled along. The final portrait was of her grandparents. She'd seen the likeness before. Melrose had a small copy of it among the photographs in his office. Her study narrowed on their sun-struck hair and laughing eyes—so like her father's and her own. And Austin's.

She'd made a point of asking Austin to attend the dedication supper. But he refused, as he always refused to be part of anything done in his parents' name. Nicki sighed as she turned and took the last few steps to Melrose's table.

"I'd been with the company ten years when that picture was taken," he said as she arrived. "It's hard to believe it's all coming to an end."

"That sounds gloomy," she returned, and slipped into the chair across the table from him. "What are you talking about?"

"I'm talking about the fact that I'm retiring, Nicki."

"Retiring?" she echoed in a shocked tone. "But you can't, Melrose. 'The company' is you, and you're 'the company.' "

He emitted a soft laugh. "I'm seventy-one years old, and I've had two mild heart attacks. I should have retired long ago."

Nicki stared at the grandfatherly face framed by snowy hair. "But how will everyone manage without you?" she sputtered.

"They'll manage. I've spent the past months lining up the transition. Tomorrow morning I leave for San Francisco—mainland headquarters, my last stop. After next week's ledger of meetings, everything will be set. I would have told you sooner. We just haven't had much chance to talk since you returned from Europe."

"Does Austin know?"

"Yes. He's been aware of it for some time."

Nicki's gaze settled on the twinkling eyes beneath the bushy, silver brows. "I don't suppose he's expressed any interest . . . in becoming involved at the company, I mean."

"Austin?" Melrose queried with a laugh. "You know your uncle. Everything he likes is fast—fast cars, fast friends, fast money. The kind of long-term diligence it takes to run a corporate conglomerate isn't in his makeup."

"Maybe it's in mine," Nicki said.

Melrose looked at her with surprise. In a strapless red dress, she was bright and lovely as always. But there was something different about Nicki. He'd noticed it on several occasions since she returned from the continent, and he saw it now as she looked at him with marked concentration.

"I've been meaning to ask you about the company," she added. "How does it work?"

Melrose chuckled. "What kind of question is that?"

"A week from Sunday I gain a seat on the board, and I'm absolutely ignorant. I probably couldn't even follow the proceedings of a meeting."

"Nor do you have to. Nothing is changing. Technically, you've always had a seat on the board, and I've exercised your proxy. I assumed you'd want the incumbent CEO to continue doing so."

Nicki shook her head. "What I *want* is to learn. I want to be more than a pampered figurehead living off the company, Melrose. Someday I'd like to take a part in running things. I was going to ask you to teach me, and now you tell me you're retiring."

He arched a brow. "So you had it in mind to be my protégée?"

"Yes, I did. I do. We could still do it, couldn't we? We could still use your office at the ranch. I mean, you're not planning to take off on a world tour or something, are you?"

"That's not part of the plan, no."

"Then will you do it?"

Suddenly her eyes reminded him of her grandfather's, steel-blue and steady. Strong. Melrose had always loved Nicki for her wit, charm, and spirit. Never before had he detected the strength he now saw in her eyes. It was part of the new air about her.

"Ask me after you come into your inheritance," he replied. "If you haven't changed your mind, we'll set something up."

"I won't change my mind," she stated.

"I hope not. You make me proud, Nicki."

"Then maybe there's hope for me yet," she said. "Will you be back from San Francisco in time for my birthday party?"

"Have I ever missed one of your birthday parties?"

Nicki showered him with a smile as she rose to her feet. "So, I'll be seeing you at the Volcano Lodge on Saturday."

An hour passed. In between conversational exchanges with acquaintances, Melrose kept across-the-room tabs on the popular heiress. It was nearly ten when the crowd began to dwindle, and he noticed Nicki once again trying to extricate herself from Paolo's wandering hands. Melrose walked up to them with a smile.

"Hello, Paolo," he greeted. "Sorry to interrupt, but I'm afraid I have to steal Nicki away. Business, you know." Taking charge of Nicki's elbow, he steered her out of the elegant room.

"That was pretty smooth," Nicki commented.

Melrose slipped her a wink. "I was considered rather dashing in my day. I've still got a move or two left."

Exiting the clubhouse, they stepped into the moonlit night and the gust of a leeward breeze. Many of the luxury cars that had filled the lot had already departed. The familiar white Lincoln was parked nearby. The sight of it still startled Nicki with the memory of Jack. Maybe it always would. Melrose hailed the new driver—a burly, rather stern and silent Hawaiian—and the limo moved obediently toward them.

"Can I offer you a ride?" Melrose asked.

"No, thanks. The Ferrari is there by the terraced gardens."

"I'll walk you over." Motioning for his driver to follow, Melrose offered an arm, and the two of them started across the parking lot. As they drew near the Ferrari, Nicki glanced ahead and came to an abrupt halt.

"What the hell is that?" she demanded.

"A damn wild orchid," Melrose returned, and stepped briskly over to pick the thing from her windshield. "I think you can relax, Nicki. There's no note in sight." He directed a searching gaze to the flanking embankment. Above the flowering gardens was a natural forest of palm, banyan, and underbrush.

"It's a breezy night," he offered. "I suppose it could have blown down here from one of those orchid plants."

It was a logical explanation, but as Nicki's scalp prickled and flesh crawled, she knew it was the wrong one. The intuitive explanation she *felt* was right. The orchid hadn't been blown onto her windshield, it had been placed there . . . by the clown.

"I have a request," she said. "Would you ask your driver to check my brake line?"

The bulky Hawaiian found it tough going to slide under the low-slung Ferrari. But he did as he was bade, and when he finished checking things out, Nicki felt secure enough to climb into the car and start it up. The motor roared in precision fashion. "Everything's fine," she pronounced.

"Okay," Melrose acknowledged as he backed away. "Then we'll see each other Saturday." With a wave of farewell, he got into the back of the limo, and the Lincoln rolled away.

Nicki revved the engine, her unsmiling gaze swerving to the flower-banked slope, climbing to the veil of trees. The moon was high, the silvery silence of the parking lot seeming to seal her in a private forum with her invisible tormenter. Shifting into first, she lifted her voice above the noise of the Ferrari.

"Come and get me, you son of a bitch!" she yelled, and sealed the challenge with a spray of flying gravel as she sped toward the long drive leading to the seaside road.

Atop the forested hill she left behind, the foliage of parted branches fanned together with a swish as the leather-gloved hand withdrew. Now there was no Jack Cantrell to intervene. Now there was no one to stand in the way. The stalker in black chuckled so softly that the fronds of a camouflaging fern barely stirred.

"All in good time, Nicki," came the threatening whisper. "All in good time."

Over the course of a steaming bath and the space of several ensuing hours, Catherine's thinking had evolved through countless childhood memories of Nicki, had moved on to the traumatic dreams of last summer, and finally had come to focus sharply on the miracle of the flesh-and-blood man asleep in her living room.

Donning a robe over her nightgown, Catherine stole into the neighboring room illumined by the aquarium and crept to the sofa bed. Jack was bare to the waist where the sheet covered him, one arm tucked behind his head, the other flung in her direction. She traced the lines of his shoulders, arms, and chest. Against the pale bedsheets, his skin appeared the color of caramel, smooth and glossy.

She knelt quietly by the bed. The feathered layers of his tawny-streaked hair made him look younger than a year ago. Emotion welled up. Tears stung her eyes.

God, how she loved him, and longed to spend the rest of her life with him. But even as Catherine felt the longing, she sensed its blasphemy. Her quota of miracles was filled by the simple fact of Jack lying there before her blurring eyes. She could ask for nothing more.

On the cool plane of slumber, Jack felt a sudden warmth pouring over him. He woke with a start, his gaze sweeping the area as his hand reached for the pistol under his pillow. There was no pistol. And the satiny cushion wasn't his pillow.

The facts registered just as his vision collided with the blonde by the bed. The events of the past hours whirled through his mind—the flight from Chicago, the appearance of Cat Winslow at the bookshop, the emotion-packed visit to the house on Legare . . . and the hard time he'd had falling asleep because he couldn't stop thinking about the woman who was now at his bedside.

"I'm sorry," she said. "I didn't mean to wake you. I'll go."

Jack sat up. "No, don't," he objected.

Catherine gazed at him questioningly. Man, she was pretty, the glow of the aquarium lighting up her white robe and golden hair. *Like an angel,* he thought again. Keeping his naked lower half covered, Jack shifted back against the sofa cushions.

"I mean, what's the matter?" he added. "Can't you sleep?"

She settled back on folded knees. "Not really."

Her eyes were glistening like starlit pools. She almost looked like she'd been crying. "You all right, Catherine?"

"Yes," she replied with a faint smile. "There are just so many questions."

"Feel like talking?"

"Only if you do."

"Sure," Jack returned, and stifled a yawn. "What time is it?"

She offered an apologetic grimace. "About three-thirty, I'm afraid. Would you like to change your mind?"

"Nah. I'm a night owl at heart." He glanced to the table by the sofa, where he'd emptied the contents of his pockets, including a pack of cigarettes. "Mind if I smoke?"

Catherine raised a brow. "I didn't realize you smoke."

"I quit years ago, then picked it up again on my last job."

"I think there's an ashtray around here somewhere," she said.

As she walked off toward the kitchen, Jack lit up and reflected on the odd circumstances between him and this woman. Before tonight he'd never laid eyes on her, and yet after all that had happened, he felt that he knew her—*really* knew her. For instance, Catherine would never knowingly cheat or abuse anybody. It wasn't in her. He knew that now. He'd come to Charleston with the idea of unmasking a slick, mercenary writer who'd taken advantage of himself, and possibly Nicki. What he'd found instead was a woman who'd reached inside his heart as innocently and easily as a child reaching into a cookie jar.

Returning with a cut-glass ashtray that looked more like a candy dish, she set it on the table and sat down in cross-legged fashion by the bed, keeping her lap covered with the folds of the terrycloth robe except for an errant, shapely calf. Jack couldn't help wondering what she was wearing underneath.

"So, what kind of questions are running through that mind of yours?" he prompted.

"How are your ribs?"

"My *what*?"

"You know," she said, tipping her head. "Your cracked ribs?"

"Oh," Jack muttered as another odd angle of their rela-

tionship jutted onto the scene. They'd never met before
tonight, but Catherine knew him from Hawaii, knew him
from countless hours and exchanges she'd witnessed
through Nicki. It was mind-boggling. He ran an absent
palm over his rib cage.

"They're good as new, thanks," he answered.

"I saw that fall, you know."

"So I gathered from your novel."

"You're lucky to be alive. Are you really a detective?"

He took a drag and smiled through the smoke. "Yeah.
I'm really a detective."

"That's quite a dangerous profession, isn't it?"

"It can be on occasion."

"Why do you do it?"

Jack lifted his brows as he tapped a column of ash into
the tray. "It's what I'm trained for. I used to be a cop."

"Really? In Chicago?"

"Yeah, in Chicago. Hey," he added with a grin. "Are all
your questions about me?"

"Some of them. Do you mind?"

"No, except that I'm at a disadvantage. What about
you?"

She shrugged. "My life has been uneventful compared to
yours. You've been to the house on Legare. I grew up
there, moved here when I could afford it. There's not much
more to tell."

Jack glanced around the pleasant room filled with plants
and an air of the tropics. "You live here by yourself,
right?" When she nodded, he took another puff and put a
cloud of smoke between them before adding, "Ever been
married?"

"Almost," she replied with a mildly surprised look. "I
was supposed to have been married last September."

He cocked a brow. "Any regrets?"

"None at all," she answered in that soft voice of hers.
"Is there anything else you'd like to know?"

"How about boyfriends? Got any who might not take
kindly to the idea of me staying the night?"

"No. You're safe," she replied with a teasing look.

Am I? Jack wondered as his eyes settled on Catherine's.
Their vivid depths were sparkling with the gleam of the
aquarium, where angelfish silently sailed. As before, when

he found his gaze locked with hers, he felt a powerful draw that she exuded seemingly without effort or design.

The atmosphere at the bedside turned suddenly intimate. Seconds ticked by, and Catherine's smile faded. Jack held stubbornly onto her eyes as the sultry heat of desire invaded his body, limb by limb. After a few more tantalizing instants, she glanced aside and broke the heated look.

Jack scrutinized the small amount of profile afforded by the frame of her hair. Her eyes were downcast, her lashes dusting her cheek. *Catherine* . . . all wrapped up in airs of charm and mystery, and a hint of unattainability that seduced him to the core.

"I wish you wouldn't stare at me that way," she said. "Like I'm some very unusual specimen you've stumbled across."

"That wasn't what I was thinking, Catherine."

She looked around. "What *were* you thinking, then?"

Jack took a long drag. At that particular moment, the way she was looking at him gave him the feeling that if he reached out and embraced her, she'd melt in his arms. The impulse was strong; a stronger feeling he couldn't put a name to held him back.

"Nothing ominous," he answered. Reaching over, he crushed the cigarette in the ashtray, and his gaze shifted to the copy of *The Clown Wore Black* he'd put on the bedside table. "I understand *The Clown Wore Black* is your first thriller."

"First and only."

"It's extremely good, Catherine. And I consider myself a fairly tough critic. Mysteries are a hobby of mine. I've read all the popular authors. In fact, I used to belong to—"

"A book club that mailed you a dozen titles a month."

The bewildering realization of her link with Nicki struck anew. Jack regarded Catherine speechlessly as she took on a look of mortification. "I'm sorry," she added. "Suddenly I feel like some horribly perverse eavesdropper or something."

"I don't sense much perversity about you," he commented with a light laugh that quickly passed as he surveyed the intriguing woman before him. What kind of intellect did it take—what kind of power—to do what she had done? If he hadn't pieced together the conclusion for himself, he never would have believed it.

"All those times," he added quietly. "The yacht club when the clown sabotaged the Ferrari, the pool when he held Nicki under, and that last night when he snatched her. You wrote about it all with such incredible detail—as if you were there."

"That's what it's like," Catherine replied, her vision shifting into the distance. "I've thought of this experience for so many years as *'the dream.'* I can barely grasp the idea that it's something else. When it happens, I guess I somehow tap into Nicki. What she sees, I see. What she feels, I feel."

"Wild," Jack murmured, and brought her eyes back to his.

"Now that I know the truth, I want so desperately to talk to Nicki," she said. "What can I do? How can I reach her?"

"We'll figure something out," he promised. "Maybe I can get my landlord to go into my office and look up Melrose's private number for me. I'll bet if the old man doesn't already know how to contact Nicki, he can find out."

"Thank you," she responded with a heart-stopping smile. Her face glowed with it. Her eyes shone. And Jack's simmering attraction boiled irretrievably to the surface.

"Did you put everything in the book?" he asked.

"I'm not sure what you mean."

"I mean, were there times you tapped into Nicki that you *didn't* write about?"

"A few, I suppose. Did you have something specific in mind?"

"Yeah, I did. Were you there that afternoon in the shower?"

Catherine's smile dissolved. "Which afternoon?"

"If you have to ask, then you weren't there," Jack countered. She continued to stare in obvious embarrassment. "But from the look of those blushing cheeks, I'd say you probably know the afternoon I'm talking about."

"I was only there for a little while," she meekly admitted.

"A little while, huh? Well, I guess it didn't take long to see what there was to see."

"You're teasing me again."

"You're right," Jack responded with a grin. "That was a juicy scene. How come you didn't put *that* in the book?"

"I felt it was a bit . . . personal."

"Good instincts." Jack's gaze moved boldly over her robed form. By the time it returned to her face, the pink of her cheeks had deepened to a scarlet that shone like fire in the muted light.

"I guess you and Nicki are pretty close to identical, huh?" he couldn't resist adding, at which point Catherine pushed hurriedly to her feet.

"I guess I'd better be going—"

"No, wait," Jack commanded. Reaching out, he caught the flap of her robe. She looked down at his hand and back to his eyes, her face still flaming. "Don't go," he added. "I'm sorry I embarrassed you. Come here. Sit down for a minute."

He tugged at the robe. She moved a wooden step forward. "Come on," he cajoled. Inch by inch Catherine followed his lead and gingerly settled on the edge of the mattress. Once again she looked at his hand. He'd allowed it to rest by her leg, and could feel the warmth of her thigh through the terry cloth. His fingers itched to touch her. Instead, Jack withdrew his hand.

"Slide back a little, or you're gonna fall off," he pointed out with a small smile. She did as he said, but her straight-as-an-arrow posture reminded him of a child who'd been sent to the corner to await some impending punishment. "Relax," Jack added.

"I'll try," she returned.

"This is an unusual set of circumstances, Catherine. In a way you and I met only a few hours ago; in another way we've known each other rather . . . intimately."

"I've known *you*," she corrected. "*You've* known Nicki. Don't make the mistake of thinking we're the same. I'm not at all like her."

"I started realizing that the first time I looked in your eyes," Jack stated. "I've never see eyes quite like yours, Catherine. They're unique. In fact, *you're* unique."

Catching her lip between her teeth, she glanced away. "Why? Because Cat Winslow turned out to be a freakish phenomenon of mental telepathy?"

Shifting forward, Jack caught her chin and turned her to

face him. "There's nothing freakish about it," he said, and let his hand settle comfortingly on her shoulder. "This ability you've got is a gift. It's amazing, all right, but in a good way."

"Can you imagine what a field day the doctors would have with such a gift? And the media? I know how it would be. My former fiancé was a political figure with a high profile. For a while it seemed that everything we did showed up in the newspapers, and when we broke up, well . . . suffice it to say I've been in the public eye before, and I hate it. Everyone stares. Everyone whispers. If this thing got out, Nicki and I would never have our lives to ourselves again. You won't talk to anyone, will you?"

Once again, with only a searching look from those deep blue eyes, Catherine summoned forth a storybook spirit of gallantry that made him feel like her knight in shining armor. "I'll keep the secret forever if you want me to," Jack vowed.

She reached up and closed cool fingers over the hand he'd placed on her shoulder. "Wanna know something?"

"What?" he supplied.

"You're even better in person than you were in my dreams."

A spectrum of feelings burst to life within Jack—the array vivid as the colors of a rainbow. There was the drive to enfold and protect Catherine, the urge to gather her up in passion, and a strange sensation of reverence that rendered his throat dry and his tongue tied. He leaned forward and planted a kiss on her forehead, then knew he should back off but didn't. He stayed there, his mouth a fraction of an inch above her skin, his breath stirring the wisps of hair across her brow as he breathed in a clean, electrifying fragrance of scented soap.

"You used to kiss Nicki like that," Catherine murmured.

"Did I?" Jack replied, his voice unmanageably thick and husky. "I can't remember just now."

He was so close she could feel his breath on her skin. It caressed like a summer's night breeze, warm and erotic.

This couldn't be happening . . . could it? Surely she'd misconstrued those occasions tonight when their eyes met and it seemed a lightning bolt passed between them. This was the man who'd fended off the alluring Nicki at every turn. Any second now he'd back away with a teasing grin . . . wouldn't he?

And still Jack remained poised above her, the implication of his nearness building like a cresting wave. Finally he moved inches back, his glinting gaze touching her eyes before dropping to her mouth. One hand still rested on her shoulder. He lifted the other and ran a fingertip over her lips.

"Your lips are shaking," he quietly stated. "If you don't want me to kiss you, just say, 'No, thanks.' "

"It's not that. It's just . . ." She trailed off as he pressed a kiss to the bridge of her nose.

"Just what?" he whispered as his mouth slipped to her cheek.

"I didn't expect this," she managed.

"Me neither." Jack's fingertip moved over her lips once more, this time gently pressing between them until they parted.

And then his mouth covered hers, his tongue moved inside, and a sensation of flying sparks showered Catherine. It was as though his unknown kiss was long known, his taste familiarly sweet. When he moved an arm to cradle her, she turned smoothly with his embrace, like a dancer following a lifelong partner's lead.

Lifting an arm about Jack's neck, she ran her fingers through his hair as he held her close against his chest. On and on his mouth made love to hers, and she'd never known such mounting desire. It was hot, liquid, racing through her veins.

Jack's hand moved down her throat and along her collarbone, traveling beneath the terry-cloth robe and confronting the spaghetti strap of her nightgown. Slipping a warm palm beneath that as well, he maneuvered slowly downward beneath the thin fabric. Catherine arched into his touch, catching her breath as he cupped her bare breast.

Jack caught his breath as well, and their mouths hovered over each other for a mind-blowing moment as he rubbed a caressing thumb over her nipple. A guttural moan escaped him as his mouth claimed hers once more. Swiftly removing his hand from her breast, he began blindly searching for the tie of her robe.

Every part of her body seemed to be pulsing. Catherine

had the sensation of sinking into the most deliciously warm, dark sphere where there was no sound but their mingled breathing, no reality but the meeting of their flesh. There was no one in the world but her and Jack . . . *and Nicki!*

Her eyes flying open, Catherine broke away. "We have to stop," she whispered breathlessly.

"What?" he mumbled.

"We have to stop now," she repeated.

His hand went still on the loosened sash of her robe. Lifting his head, Jack met her eyes. "You're kidding."

"No. I'm not." Firmly closing the neck of her robe, she slipped away and rose nimbly from the bed, where she proceeded to gaze down at him, her cheeks as bright as glowing coals.

Jack shifted back against the couch, wincing as his hardness stirred the covers. "Sorry," he said, his narrowed gaze sweeping the length of her. "I thought you wanted—I thought we *both* wanted . . . Hell, we *did* want it. So what the hell happened?"

"You're angry," she observed.

He held up a quick palm. "No, not angry, just . . . give me a minute to catch my breath." She stood there silently staring, seemingly mortified. Jack reached to the bedside table. "Mind if I smoke? I always enjoy a cigarette after I've just *not* had sex."

As he lit up, Catherine pivoted and walked stiffly toward her bedroom. He was about to call her back when she turned. Holding his tongue, Jack kept his eyes leveled on her slim form and took a hard drag off the cigarette.

"I've been in love with you since you first showed up in my dreams, Jack."

Gagging on the inhaled smoke that halted halfway down his throat, he peered at her through tearing eyes.

"But so has Nicki," Catherine added, then stepped inside her chamber and closed the door between them.

Jack stared unseeingly after her as the frustrated passion singing through his veins took a twist all on its own—changing, transforming, mushrooming into something bigger, hotter, all-consuming. . . . No. It couldn't be.

He became aware that minutes had passed when a column of cigarette ash dropped onto the snowy whiteness of Catherine's blanket. Cramming the spent cigarette in her cut-glass bowl, Jack leaped from the sofa bed, pulled on his clothes, and escaped to the private outdoors of the balcony. Planting a firm grip on the balcony railing, he peered into the starry darkness.

The strange feeling that came over him when he saw Catherine kneeling at her father's bedside . . . the fury that swept through him when her witch of an aunt attacked . . . the longing that swamped him in a mind-numbing flood as soon as he touched her . . . Damn. It was true. He was in love.

A while later he came in and plopped down in the chair facing the sofa bed. Not since Ellen had he experienced anything close to the emotion. In fact, this was different from Ellen. Part of the impact of *this* thing was how fast it struck. Zap! Like a bolt of lightning. Boom! And he'd fallen like a ton of bricks.

Jack's gaze narrowed on the touseled bedclothes where he'd held her. The fiery rush of desire returned, along with a blazing protective instinct. God, if anybody ever tried to hurt her . . .

The old nightmare blasted into his brain; only this time it was Catherine who turned with a smile before the car exploded in flames. Clapping his hands over his ears, Jack shuddered as the furies of hell seemed to shriek with laughter at his folly.

Chapter Seventeen

Jack woke to the aromas of coffee and something sweet baking in an oven. His mouth watered. Cracking an eyelid, he met the unblinking study of an angelfish, its round black eyes peering through the glass and seemingly down its nose.

He shifted up and came to grips with the stiff-jointed reality of the chair where he'd spent the night—or, rather, the morning. What the hell time was it? His watch was on the table by the bed. Squinting in that direction, he discovered the bed was no longer a bed but a sofa, the trappings of a passionate scene having been efficiently tucked away. Just as the thought formed, Catherine breezed into the room. She was wearing blue shorts and a matching top. And his stomach did a flip.

"Good morning," she greeted.

"Mornin'," Jack rumbled. "What time is it?"

"Nearly eleven."

"God, I haven't slept this late in years."

She came to stand before him. "I was wondering about this chair-sleeping thing," she remarked with a tentative smile. "Is it something y'all do up north, or just a personal preference?"

He gazed up at her, and the raging emotion possessed him anew. It was no passing effect, no mirage of closeness that faded like afterglow. He was in love with her. Putting a hand to his brow, Jack rubbed his forehead.

"You're still angry with me," she theorized.

"I wasn't angry, Catherine. A little frustrated, maybe." Mustering a grin, he lifted his eyes. "All dressed up and no place to go, ya know what I mean?"

She glanced away, her cheeks flooding with color.

"I'd kill for a cup of coffee about now," he added, and

it took no more than that to send her sprinting out of the room.

"Come on into the kitchen," she tossed over her shoulder.

"Be there in a minute," he called, and rose stiffly to his feet. Stopping by the bathroom, he washed up, berated his reflection in the mirror, and walked into the kitchen tucking his shirttail into his jeans. Catherine was pulling a pan out of the oven. Leaning over her shoulder, he took a sniff of the half dozen apple turnovers on the cookie sheet.

"Your coffee's on the breakfast table. Would you like cream and sugar?"

"No, thanks." He ambled to the table, picked up the designated mug, and took a swallow of the hot brew.

"I spoke to Ann Marie this morning," Catherine offered.

"What did she have to say?"

"She stayed up all night reading a volume of studies on twins who were separated at birth and reunited as adults. There was nothing like *my* experience, but there were some amazing reports. I guess I'm not a complete oddity, after all."

"You see? I told you."

"Yes," Catherine agreed with a smile. "You told me."

Jack silently watched as she began transferring the pastries from pan to platter. There was a nostalgic homeyness about the scene—a woman at the stove, conversation over coffee . . . For six years all the morning afters he'd known had been marked with expedient departure. But this wasn't a typical morning after, and Catherine wasn't just any woman. Jack took a hasty gulp as she strolled over to join him, coffee cup in hand.

"Have a seat," she invited, and sat down by the bay window.

"I spent the past few hours in a chair. I think I'll stand."

The summer morning was filled with sun, its beams pouring through the window and gilding her with light.

"That was quite a bomb you dropped before you walked out last night," he stated. When she gave him a puzzled look, he delivered a blunt reminder. "You said, and I quote: 'I've been in love with you since you first showed up in my dreams.' Remember?"

"But so has Nicki," she answered. "Yes, I remember."

"And that's why you broke things off? Because of what you think *Nicki* feels?"

"What I'm *certain* she feels."

Jack rested a hand on the back of the chair across from Catherine's. "Just think for a minute, okay? You know Nicki, maybe better than anyone. She falls in and out of love all the time. She loves everybody, and everybody—"

"Loves her back. I know. I recall what you said that day in the hospital word for word, Jack. But you were wrong. What Nicki felt for you was special."

He peered into Catherine's eyes. "And *you*? Did you mean what you said about the way *you* feel?"

He might have expected her to be shy. Instead, she smiled with radiant warmth. "Yes. I meant it."

A powerful rush swept over him, leaving his heart racing and his knees weak. "Maybe I'll sit down after all." Taking a seat, Jack warily eyed her. Bit by bit the radiant smile receded.

"There's no need to look worried," she said. "I'm not sorry you know how I feel, but neither am I trying to stake a claim."

Her eyes were glistening, but serene as the mirrorlike surfaces of frozen lakes. God, she was a mix—one minute fragile as a teacup, the next strong as steel. Jack reached across the tabletop and covered the hand by her cup.

"I care a lot about you, too, Catherine. It's just that . . ."

Pulling free of his grasp, she hid her hands in her lap. "I understand. You care for me the way you care for Nicki."

"I think you know that's not true. I never made love to Nicki—or *almost* made love, as the case may be."

"I can't help wondering . . . why me, then?"

"Why do you think?" he parried with a faint grin.

"Because the opportunity fell in your lap," she suggested.

Jack surrendered a quick laugh. "No, it had nothing to do with convenience." His expression settled to one of seriousness. "It was *you*, Catherine. To put it plainly, I couldn't seem to keep my hands off you." She didn't quite hide the pleased look that crossed her face. "The problem is that I just don't get involved," he added. "Not the way it would be with you."

She regarded him with those frozen eyes for a tense few

seconds before saying, "I put your lone wolf speech in the novel, remember? I'm aware of where you draw the line."

"Is that right," Jack muttered as mixed feelings roiled.

"Discussing reasons is a bit off the point, isn't it? In effect, it seems to me we're saying we want the same thing."

"Which is?" Jack stiffly prodded.

"To be platonic friends. Allies. To focus on tracking down my sister and finding out what happened thirty years ago."

Yep. That's what he'd meant to establish when he stated his position. But looking at Catherine now, and anticipating the times to come when they'd be thrown together, he figured it was going to be damn near impossible not to make a move *sometime*.

"I hope you haven't changed your mind about going to Hawaii with me," Catherine added.

"Now, more than ever, I *insist* on going," he stated.

"Then we're in agreement." Moving to the stove, she adroitly turned her back to him and started frosting the apple turnovers.

Jack took a halfhearted swallow of coffee while his eyes scanned the length of her. "I guess I should get ready to head over to the Indigo Inn," he said, and pushed to his feet.

"Would you like to stay long enough to eat?" she asked without looking around.

"Maybe you could wrap up a couple of turnovers for me," he answered, and retreated from the kitchen. Scarce minutes later he was zipping up his bag when she came in and handed him a covered plate.

"Do you mind if I ask how long you plan to stay in town?"

"I don't know, Catherine. This whole thing has been so damn surprising. I don't have a plan yet."

She nodded in seeming thoughtfulness. "If there are no other cases in front of this one, I was thinking that perhaps the proper course would be for me to hire you like Nicki did."

"I don't want your money," he gruffly returned. "I told you last night I have a personal interest in this. After I check in at the hotel, I'll try to get through to my landlord. Then maybe I can reach Melrose and start rounding up some answers."

"Thank you, Jack."

"Don't thank me. Like I told you, I'm in." He looked at

her. She looked at him. And he almost reached for her. "Give me your number," he commanded. "I'll be in touch."

Catherine returned from her desk, offered a slip of paper, and proceeded toward the entrance. Tucking the number in his shirt pocket, Jack shouldered his bag and followed her to the threshold, where she opened the door and drew it wide.

"Don't be a stranger," she tendered with a friendly smile.

"You'll hear from me." Her smile faltered as he took a step closer. "I meant it when I said I care about you, Catherine." She said nothing, although her cheeks went rosy in a mannerism he was beginning to find familiar.

"And I want you," Jack huskily added. "Even though I know I shouldn't." The covered plate had his left hand occupied. He lifted his right and threaded his fingers into her hair.

"What are you doing?" she whispered.

"Damned if I know," he mumbled as he bent to her lips.

He'd been lying to himself when he thought he might give her an innocent parting kiss. As soon as Catherine's mouth opened to his, the whole torrid thing came to life all over again. Pushing forward until she was pinned against the door, Jack pressed his body against hers and toyed with the idea of kicking the door closed, dropping the plate of turnovers to the floor, and . . .

His brain flickered to life. Breaking away, he gripped her jaw and peered into her eyes. "I'm sorry," he muttered.

One instant his mouth was on hers, and Catherine began to melt as she had the night before. The next heartbeat Jack was disappearing down the stairwell. She closed the door and sagged against it. Her legs felt like spaghetti, and her head seemed to weigh a ton, all two thousand pounds of it teetering between the elation of being held by Jack, and the desolation of how empty home seemed now that he was gone.

I want you, his voice echoed above the pounding in her ears. The mere fact that he'd even *appeared* was a miracle, but to think that he might actually feel some kind of desire . . . The sudden thought of Nicki straightened Catherine's spine and wrenched her mind off Jack. Striding to the phone, she dialed Marla's number.

"Hey, girl," Marla greeted. "What are you up to?"

"Can you spare me a few hours, Marla? The sooner the better."

"Okay," she responded on a curious note. "What's going on?"

"I need to get into the newspaper archives. There's someone I'd like to check out, someone with a fairly high profile. It occurred to me there might be photos of her in your files."

"Sure. We can check her out. Who is it?"

"I'll fill you in. But Marla, we have to be discreet about this, *extremely* discreet. I don't want anyone else at the newspaper to know what we're up to. Can you do that for me?"

"After what you did for me, do you really think you need to ask that question? I'll pick you up in thirty minutes."

They spent an hour and a half at the newspaper, which yielded two blurry wire photos of Nicki Palmer. Marla suggested a change of tack. They went to the public library and started researching periodicals. That was when Catherine struck gold. In a year-old issue of *Town and Country,* there was a four-page spread on the ranch estate of the Hawaiian heiress, complete with pictures of the house and grounds, and a full-page portrait of Nicki.

Catherine looked into the face she knew so well. Their features were alike, no doubt of that. But the spirit in the eyes, the mischief in the smile, even the flirty way she tipped her head—all those things were uniquely Nicki.

"Except for the hair, the two of you are *identical!*"

"Do you really think so?" Catherine mumbled.

Marla emitted a short laugh. "I don't know about *you,* girl," she said, "but *I* need a drink." After photocopying the magazine pages, they drove the short distance to East Bay Trading Company. The downstairs bar area was bustling with a Saturday crowd. They took a table on the quieter upper level.

"This is one of the most amazing stories I've ever heard," Marla commented after taking a swig of her margarita. "You don't suppose Nicki has been having these 'dreams,' too, do you?"

"I don't think so. Something Jack said rings true to me.

He called Nicki the sender and me the receiver. That's the way I think it must have been all these years."

"So what are you going to do?"

Catherine sighed. "What I'd *love* to do is get Nicki on the phone and spill the news. But I can't. This is the sort of thing one handles in person. For now I must be patient. As soon as it's feasible, I plan to travel to Hawaii. Jack's going with me."

Marla arched a brow. "Oh?"

A smile flitted across Catherine's face. "You needn't say it *that* way. Jack can't resist a good mystery. That's all."

"And yet he stayed at your place last night."

"He had no reservation. Besides, nothing happened . . . much."

"Much?" Marla repeated in the manner of a pouncing cat. "How *much,* exactly, *did* happen?" Heat rose to Catherine's face as the thought of Jack filled her mind. "Honestly, Catherine! If you don't tell me the juicy stuff, I'm going to kill you. Is Jack as attractive in person as he was in *The Clown Wore Black*?"

"More so."

"Did he kiss you?" Catherine glanced into the glimmering depths of her chardonnay. "Did he make love to you?" Marla excitedly trilled, at which point Catherine looked up.

"You read the book. You know how Nicki feels about Jack. I had to stop."

"In the middle of . . . Oh, my gosh," Marla said, her green eyes wide. "What happened then?"

"*Nothing* happened then. He left this morning for the Indigo Inn. That's it."

"That's *it*? You are so infuriatingly tight-lipped, Catherine! For heaven's sake, how do you *feel* about him?"

She returned Marla's wide-eyed look with a steady gaze. "I'm in love up to my neck, okay? But there's no good in dwelling on it. Jack has his own reasons for not becoming involved. When you add his reasons to mine, you get a stalemate."

"But you *are* going to see him again."

"He said he'll 'be in touch,' whatever that means."

"I gotta hand it to you, girl. You're a better woman than I am. If I were in *your* shoes, I'd be sitting by the phone."

"That's exactly what I want to avoid."

Marla considered her for a scrutinizing moment. "I wish you wouldn't be a martyr about this, Catherine. If you're in love with the man, go after him."

She shook her head. "I just found out I've got a sister, Marla. I'm not going to take the man she loves as *my* lover before I even have the chance to meet her. I'm just not."

"No," Marla replied. "You're too good for that. Unlike me. I took *your* man as *my* lover, remember?"

Catherine gave her a startled look. "I never would have made that correlation in a million years. *Eliot* is the one who engineered that whole thing, not you."

"Maybe. But I wasn't a complete innocent, or I never would have gotten involved." When Catherine started to object, Marla raised a silencing palm and leaned forward. "You deserve the real thing, girl. And it sounds like Jack is the guy who can give it to you. Don't end things before they can even begin."

"I have to be content with just knowing him, Marla. That's the way it's going to be. Now, can we talk about something else?"

The supper hour was dawning when they left the Trading Company and walked out to Marla's BMW. "Would you mind dropping me at Winslow House?" Catherine asked.

"Sure, but why the hell would you want to go *there*?"

Catherine chuckled at her horrified tone. "To look in on my father, of course."

Marla shook her head as she nosed the BMW into the streaming summer traffic of the Historic District. "I've said it before, and I'll say it again—Catherine, honey, you're a far better woman than I am."

The Indigo Inn was built around a courtyard with a fountain, furnished with antebellum period pieces, and rich with the aura of Charleston tradition and hospitality. After checking in, Jack had spent most of the afternoon intermittently trying to get in touch with the resident manager of his apartment building. He finally got through sometime around five, whereupon it took another half hour of waiting and the promise of a fifty-buck tip to prod the guy into opening his apartment and searching out Melrose's unpublished number.

It was the lunch hour in Hawaii when Jack called, got

the machine, and hung up without leaving a message. He
wanted to talk to Melrose in person. The mystery just now
coming to light was rooted in the past. Maybe the man
who'd been an integral part of the Palmer empire for forty
years had a few answers. Deciding to try later, Jack showered, dressed, and checked his watch. Six-thirty. He had
the whole night ahead of him.

The thought of Catherine crowded in, as it had been
prone to do all afternoon. Leaving the solitude of his
room—which tempted his attention toward the number by
the phone—he strode down the stairs, through the courtyard, and on to the front of the inn. Joining the throng of
pedestrians on Meeting Street, he followed the flow into
the heart of the Historic District.

The evening was balmy, the air humming with the music
of sidewalk cafés. He stopped into Café 99, where a jazz
band was playing, and had a few drinks—which turned out
to be his first mistake, because when he pulled out his wallet to pay the tab, he spotted Susan's number and ended
up calling her.

A scant thirty minutes later, the attractive stewardess arrived at his table, wearing a sexy black dress and an alluring
smile. And as soon as he saw her, Jack knew how wrong
it was. Carelessly, thoughtlessly, he'd created a situation in
which he was using one woman to try to forget another. It
wasn't fair to either one of them.

Plus, it didn't work anyway. He and Susan dined under
the stars. Music played. Drink flowed. And the intoxicating
air of Charleston spiced the night with a sense of romance.
But the more Jack made the effort to smile and flirt, the
more deeply the thought of Catherine entrenched itself in
the back of his mind.

After dinner it was guilt more than anything else that
made him agree to Susan's suggestion of taking a ride in
one of the horse-drawn carriages parked up the street. Jack
settled beside her on the leather seat, stretched the expected arm around her, and the carriage set off on a leisurely tour—making its way along lamplit streets, turning
along lanes with historic markers. Susan occasionally
pointed out a landmark of some sort.

Somewhere along the way Jack's attention left her as his

mind's eye filled with the vision of Catherine, her fair hair shining like a halo, her eyes shimmering like sunlit pools.

"Jack!"

"What?" he exclaimed with a start. The image in his head disintegrated, and he was confronted with Susan's face, her dark eyes snapping with anger.

"Where *are* you?" she demanded. "It certainly isn't with *me!*"

Jack emitted a heavy breath. "I'm sorry, Susan," he began.

At that moment the blaring horn of a passing car full of teenagers made him glance up. And suddenly Jack realized where he was. King Street. Ann Marie Duvall's bookshop was dead ahead. He cast a sharp look toward the shopfront. It was nearly eleven, and the crowds had diminished. There were but two women standing on the sidewalk—a blonde and a brunette. Catherine and Ann Marie.

God couldn't have brought him to his knees more efficiently with a lightning bolt. Jack was struck motionless as the plodding horse took him mercilessly into Catherine's line of vision—separated from her by a distance of no more than the width of a parked car. The clatter of the carriage drew her eye. She looked their way, her passing gaze halting and returning, her eyes growing wide as they locked on Jack.

The vehicle proceeded languidly past. But even when Catherine was no longer in sight, Jack found it impossible to move as he felt the shock and hurt of her eyes following him down the street. It was Susan who broke the breathless stillness of the carriage. Plucking his arm from around her shoulders, she instructed the driver—in a tone that pierced Jack's daze—to take her to the corner of Meeting and Water streets. *Immediately!*

Plopping back in the seat, she gave Jack a murderous glare. "That's where I had to park, and I *still* made it to Café 99 in a half hour."

Jack looked stoically into her accusing eyes. "I owe you an apology, Susan. I don't know what to say except—"

"Save it," she cut in, and the final minutes of the carriage ride elapsed in stilted silence. At the designated corner Susan climbed down from the carriage without a word. By the time Jack paid the driver and hurried after her, she'd already started her car. He knocked on the window. Finally she lowered the glass.

"This is Saturday night, Jack. I could have done better than to spend it with a man whose mind is so obviously on someone else."

"I didn't mean for things to turn out this way, Susan."

"If I weren't so pissed off, I'd say she's a lucky girl." With that Susan pulled smartly away from the curb and left him staring at her fast-retreating taillights.

Jack trudged the long blocks back to the Indigo Inn and entered his plush quarters feeling like the biggest jerk who ever lived. Dropping his key in a sterling tray on the dresser, he lay down on the poster bed and covered his eyes with a forearm. Minutes later he sat up, checked the slip of paper by the phone, and dialed Catherine's number.

"Hello, there," her recorded voice greeted. "Sorry I can't take your call. Leave a message, and I'll speak with you soon."

He cleared his throat as the mechanical tone sounded. "It's Jack. Pick up if you're there." Silence. "Okay. I guess you're not home. Listen, I really want to talk to you. I'm in Room 230. Call when you get in. It doesn't matter how late. Just call me."

Jack lay back on the bed. The hour grew late. And he fell asleep, fully dressed atop the covers, while listening for the phone to ring. The next morning he tried again. The machine picked up once more.

"Catherine," he pronounced with an irritated edge in his voice. "It's eight-thirty Sunday morning. Call me." At ten, when he'd still heard nothing, Jack stomped out of the room, devoured a full Southern breakfast at a restaurant down the street, and emerged with the plan of walking the relatively short distance to Catherine's condo off East Bay.

Scaling the stairwell, he knocked at the door and pressed his ear against the wood. There were no footsteps. No sound of any kind. She wasn't in there. He returned to the Indigo Inn, stopped by the office, and checked for messages. No calls.

The desk clerk gave him a hospitable smile. "Might I inquire how long you'll be staying with us, Mr. Casey?"

"Who the hell knows?" Jack barked, and brought a startled look to the clerk's face. "Sorry," he added. "I haven't decided yet."

As the day wore on, his frustration grew more keen.

He placed calls to Melrose, Catherine, the Open Window bookshop, and even the phone book listing for A. Duvall. Machines responded every time. Seeking to channel his energy, Jack grabbed the stationery pad and pen from the dresser, settled in the overstuffed chair by the reading lamp in the corner, and put his mind on considering Catherine in the stark light of a case.

Mystery twin surfaces after nearly thirty years, he wrote. *Just in time to claim half of an inheritance worth millions,* his mind continued. If he didn't know the amazing truth about Catherine, he'd think it was a scam.

Beginning with her father's letter, he wrote down the meager clues he had to go on in the decades-old mystery. The Winslows' cleaning girl, Kila, had brought them the infant when the baby was barely a day old. Who was Kila, and how was she connected to the Palmers? What did she mean when she said the baby's life was in danger? In danger from whom?

The few facts at Jack's disposal triggered a snowballing list of questions. Was a death certificate on record? If so, what physician had signed it? What the hell happened that night thirty years ago? Of one thing Jack was dead certain: If Catherine was in fact who she *must* be, foul play had been involved.

Throughout the afternoon and early evening, the phone remained dismally silent. When darkness fell, Jack left the room, had a sandwich and beer at a District pub, and walked to King Street. A CLOSED sign was on the bookshop door, and the windows of Ann Marie's upstairs apartment were dark.

Jack turned away from the deserted shop and ambled in the direction of the Ashley River. The streets of the District were noticeably quieter on this Sunday eve. Presumably, the weekend tourists had departed and natives were enjoying the tranquillity of a Sunday night at home behind garden walls.

When he broached the College of Charleston at St. Philip and George streets, he was lured onto campus by the lights of the library building. A cute, freckle-faced coed was staffing the front desk. After filling out an ID card, he was given blushing permission to use the research area, which was empty except for a few summer session students.

Jack passed the next hour researching the subject of telepathy. The available volumes ranged from the rumina-
tions of a self-proclaimed psychic to an austere journal of
studies by a panel of doctors in Wisconsin. The two sources
presented opposing corners. On one extreme you had zeal-
ots who touted the existence of UFOs and Atlantis as well
as ESP; on the other you had scientists staunchly dedicated
to the dissection of telepathic incidents in search of "logical" explanation.

Throughout his scanning of materials, Jack didn't spot a
single report that came close to the extraordinary feat Catherine had been accomplishing, effortlessly, since she was a
mere girl. She was right. If news of her experience leaked
out, both she and Nicki would be hounded for the rest of
their lives.

Church bells rang the hour of nine as he left campus.
Once again he trod the lamplit streets to East Bay. Like
before, Catherine's condo was deserted, its emptiness seep-
ing through the door with cold silence. Jack could picture
the angelfish peering haughtily toward the portal at his repeated knocks.

He tucked a business card in the crack of the door before
leaving. Maybe she'd gone out of town. Obviously she was
staying somewhere else, probably with a friend—but if not
with Ann Marie, he had no idea with whom. As he walked
back to the inn, Jack reflected on the irony. In a matter of
hours he'd come to know Catherine Winslow on a pro-
found level that was, at present, of no help. He knew her
heart, mind, and soul; not her habits.

The night waxed on, long, quiet, and lonely. Was it only
twenty-four hours since he had paraded past her with another woman? It felt like a week or two had gone by.

Jack stalked the confines of his room, eventually becoming so exasperated that he nearly called the airlines to book
the next flight back to Chicago. But he didn't call. He
couldn't leave, not with the memory of Catherine's look of
hurt burning into his brain like a branding iron. Sometime
around two a.m. he dialed the number he now knew by
heart, and wasn't surprised when he heard the excruciatingly familiar "Hello, there" of her machine.

"Catherine," he murmured. "I wish like hell I had some
idea of where you are. I want to talk—no, I *need* to talk

to you. When you check your messages, please call me at the Indigo Inn."

But his telephonic pleading yielded no results. Turning on the TV against the swelling silence of the richly appointed room, Jack fell asleep with the black-and-white images of an old movie flickering across his face.

The last vestiges of twilight were fading as Sister Ann hurried across the abbey grounds. She was almost late for vespers . . . again. Still, as she neared the main hall and noted the lights in the kitchen, she stopped to peep in the screen door. Just as she suspected, it was Jane—down on her hands and knees scrubbing the floor. Risking yet another scolding from Mother Superior for being late, the young sister stepped quickly inside.

"You don't have to do that, Jane," she gently chided. "Our Lady of Mercy is a shelter for those in need. We don't ask to be repaid. Besides, the work you've already done these past two months has more than made up for your bed and board. Mother Superior says so."

The dark-haired woman rose to her feet. "I enjoy earning my keep, Sister. Besides, it's good exercise." As she dropped her scrub brush into her pail and wiped her hands across her apron, Sister Ann took on a look of mischief.

"Are you still planning to attend the Waimea Rodeo day after tomorrow?" she whispered.

"Oh, yes. But it's our secret. No one else must know."

"Don't worry. You can trust me. I am a *nun,* for goodness' sake. It's just so exciting! Seeing your boyfriend for the first time in a year. Tell me again, Jane. How handsome is he?"

"*Extremely* handsome," she smilingly answered. "With hair as black as night and eyes blue as the sea."

Sister Ann noted that the smile quickly passed. "What's the matter? Is something wrong?"

She shrugged. "I just hope he's glad to see me. After all, I've changed a lot since the accident."

"Well, I'm certain you couldn't have been any prettier *then* than you are now."

A searching look issued from the woman's big dark eyes. "Do you really think that?"

"Think what?"

"That I'm pretty."

The sister gave her a smiling look of encouragement. "You're a knockout. Now I must go before Mother Superior has my hide."

A half hour later Peni closed up the kitchen and stepped into the breezy summer night. All was quiet but for the rustling fronds of palms and the distant angelic song of the sisters' evening prayers. As she walked along the path to the dormitory, she reflected on the chain of events that had brought her to this haven on the windward side of the island.

After visiting Palmer Ranch that night, she'd driven recklessly away from all that was familiar—away from all she knew and all who knew her. Somewhere along the way she stopped for beer and had downed a six-pack before reaching the windward shore and a series of bluffs overlooking the sea.

Perhaps it was the frustration of having failed in her deadly mission, perhaps the horror that she'd actually attempted it. Peni didn't think she'd ever be able to isolate the motive that had pressed the accelerator to the floor as she pointed the truck straight toward the bluffs and zoomed over the edge.

Later, she was told the truck crashed down on the beach of a popular surfing spot and she'd been found immediately by a couple of night surfers. Otherwise she would have died.

When she woke up, she was in a small local hospital with a broken femur, collarbone, and jaw. For six weeks her mouth was wired shut. The silver lining to the cloud was that, since she couldn't communicate, she gained the benefit of learning some startling circumstances without being expected to reply.

She'd had no identification on her person, and shortly after the surfers pulled her from the truck, it had exploded. There had been no way to trace her identity, and she'd been admitted to the hospital as Jane Doe. When she recovered enough to start writing simple replies to questions, the local police showed up.

"What's your name?" they demanded.

As an officer pressed a pen into her hand, Peni did some quick thinking. For all she knew, Nicki had recognized her and pressed charges. For all she knew, there was a warrant out for Peni Kahala's arrest. *I don't know,* she laboriously wrote, and through succeeding grueling months had maintained the masquerade of amnesia.

It took weeks of slipping discreet inquiries into countless conversations with countless nurses to find out that heiress Nicki Palmer was once again jet-setting about Europe, and had departed the islands at the end of last summer. There was no gossip about an attempt on her life. No rumor of a police search for her assailant . . . or for a missing person named Peni Kahala.

Apparently the charade had paid off. Everyone who knew her believed she'd quit her job, sold her house, and gone to the mainland to visit her brothers.

With great relief Peni had turned all her energy toward recovery. She was in casts for four months, intense physical therapy for another four, and since coming to live as a charity case at the abbey had continued with private workouts. Her efforts had rewarded her, finally, with total fitness.

Entering the dormitory, she proceeded down the quiet hall and entered the small room barely large enough to hold the sparse furnishings of a single bed, dressing table, and bent-wood rocker. Closing the door, she glanced toward the mirror hanging on the back and met the still-startling sight of her reflection.

For some reason God had allowed her to survive "the accident." And Peni thought she knew why. Eleven months later—and forty-two pounds lighter—she was a different woman.

Despite weight-lifting therapy that had made her muscles strong as ever, her limbs were lithe and shapely . . . her figure no longer masculine in any way, but purely, voluptuously female. Within the thinner framework of her face, her cheekbones had emerged in two sculpted planes, and her eyes appeared huge. Months of seclusion from the sun had turned her complexion lighter and her hair darker—the glossy tresses having grown to a length that curved flatteringly at chin level.

Unless someone looked really hard, it would be impossible to recognize the old Peni. And there was only one person she wanted to look that hard.

Crossing to the tiny closet, she carefully withdrew the red dress. Upon arriving at the abbey, she'd become fast

friends with Sister Ann. It was impossible *not* to like the
young nun. There was a spirit of light about her that was
infectious, and Peni had found herself reaching for it the
way a flower turns to the sun.

Three weeks ago she'd become doubly appreciative of
their comradeship. A rich *haole* dropped off a carton of
clothes to be distributed among the needy. Shortly thereaf-
ter, Sister Ann had burst into her cell bearing the designer
dress with matching sandals trimmed in tiny red stones.

"This will be wonderful on you, Jane!" she'd exclaimed.

And she was right. Never had Peni been so shocked as
when she put on the dress and looked at herself. Its ruby
hue brought her coloring to vibrant life. Its halter neck,
cinched waist, and flaring skirt sculpted her figure to hour-
glass perfection. She looked like a damn movie star . . .
and *the plan* had been born.

Returning the dress to its waiting place, Peni stretched
out on the bed, turned off the lamp, and peered into the
darkness. She'd planned everything to the last detail. Day
after tomorrow at noon, she would catch the bus to Waimea. She'd arrive long after the preliminary festivities of
the Fourth of July event, but that didn't matter. All she
wanted was to see Kimo ride.

He'd win again. And after he defended his championship,
he'd hang around the rodeo tent with the other riders for
a while. People would stop by to extend congratulations.
The attractive brunette in the sensational red dress would
be among them.

Closing her eyes, Peni imagined his face upon seeing her.
First he would look bewildered as he tried to place where
and when he'd met this siren. Then his eyes would light up
with surprise . . . then slowly fill with a hot look of desire.

If he didn't ask her out for a drink, she'd offer to buy
him one. They'd stop into a bar—not like Paniolos Hale,
but a nice place with soft lights and music. Afterward Kimo
would take her to his place. In forty-eight hours she'd be
lying in his arms instead of on a hard lonely cot.

Peni sighed as the fantasy enfolded her in a warm embrace. God had plucked her from the jaws of hell and given
her another life. This had to be why.

Chapter Eighteen

Monday, July 3

Monday morning was hot and sunny, the temperature registering eighty degrees by nine o'clock. After a brisk shower and shave, Jack dressed in jeans and a light shirt—the last clean one he had with him—and faced the day with grim determination. It was the third of July, the anniversary of Ellen's death. Today he was going to find Catherine, say good-bye, and get the hell out of this seductive Southern town.

After packing his bag, he made a perfunctory call to Catherine's condo. When her machine came on, he hung up, dialed the airlines, and secured one of the last seats on a red-eye to Atlanta the next morning. His flight schedule called for a six-hour layover before he connected to Chicago, but he was lucky to get even *that* on the Fourth of July holiday.

Walking downstairs past the sparkling fountain in the courtyard, he checked out of the Indigo Inn and stashed his bag in the Buick. Could be he'd end up spending his last hours in Charleston strolling around the airport with no place else to go. Jack didn't care. All he knew was that he wasn't going to waste any more hours cooped up in a hotel room hoping for a phone call that never came.

He felt more like himself than he had the past couple of frustrated days. Today he had a plan, and if Ann Marie continued to be absent from her shop, he was damn well going to brave the depressing prospect of Winslow House. Somehow he was going to get a lead on Catherine and track her down. Today.

Stopping for lunch at the cozy restaurant from the day before, Jack then drove to the Open Window. As it turned

out, the first destination on his agenda paid off. The CLOSED
sign had been flipped over; the message on the door now
read OPEN.

"Yes!" Jack muttered, and pulled into the first available
spot down the street. Three days had passed since he first
walked into the bookshop on King Street. This time as he
entered, Ann Marie looked up from the counter with the
remembered smile. But her expression turned noticeably
hostile as she saw him.

Jack strode toward her, scanning the scene by habit and
determining that—except for a young mother with a toddler
on her hip in the children's section—he and Ann Marie
had the shop to themselves.

"My goodness," she said as he drew near. "I imagined
you to be on your way back to Chicago by now." Her
Southern voice dripped sweetness. But as Jack rested his
forearms on the counter and met her gleaming eyes, he
could see that she was mad as hell.

"I'm not leaving until I talk to Catherine," he stated.
"Where is she?" A single brow arched high as the back of
an incensed cat. "Come on, Ann Marie. I've called her a
dozen times. She doesn't answer. She doesn't return my
calls. Where is she?"

The high arch slipped from one brow to the other. "That
was quite a stunt you pulled—staying with Catherine one
night, painting the town with another woman the next."

"I did *not* paint the town."

"You hurt her, Jack." He suffered the dark-haired woman's scrutiny as guilty heat crept up his neck. "I must have
misjudged you Friday night," she continued. "The way you
rallied to her cause, it appeared you actually cared for
Catherine."

"I did . . . I do."

Ann Marie folded forbidding arms across her chest.
"That's somewhat difficult to accept when the picture of
you with your arms wrapped around another woman re-
mains so vividly clear."

Jack frowned. "Her name is Susan, and it's as simple as
this: I made a mistake. I knew it, Susan knew it, and I want
Catherine to know it, too. The only reason I came here is
to find out where she is. Are you going to tell me, or not?"

Ann Marie regarded him in cold silence.

"I have to see her, dammit!" Jack bellowed, and drew a startled look from mother and child across the way. But at least he managed to crack the stony veneer of Ann Marie's face. She gazed at him now with searching, seemingly reassessing eyes.

"Tell me, please," Jack demanded in a low, measured tone. "Where has Catherine been the past two days?"

"Perhaps you *do* care, after all," Ann Marie mused. He glared at her with obvious frustration. "All right," she surrendered after a moment. "Catherine has been at the hospital. Her father suffered a major stroke Saturday night. She'd stopped by to tell me when you rode past in the carriage. After it happened, I don't think she left the hospital except for one time to shower and change. She knew her father was dying, and every minute of the past forty-eight hours she's been expecting to hear the news. Finally it came. He passed away an hour ago."

"God, I'm sorry. Something like that never occurred to me. Is Catherine all right?"

"It's been sad and exhausting. She's very tired, but she's a strong girl in ways you may not have had a chance to see."

"I've seen a few," Jack commented. "Where is she now?"

"She's probably left the hospital by now. A friend was going to take her home."

Preoccupied with the sudden news, he turned and started to leave. He was several steps away when he came to his senses and looked around. "Thanks for telling me," Jack said.

"You're welcome."

"I noticed a florist down the street. Does she like flowers?"

"Anything but white," Ann Marie replied with a small smile.

Stopping into the flower shop, Jack selected a dozen yellow roses, which the florist arranged in green paper and tied with a yellow ribbon. As he drove across the District and drew near East Bay, church bells chimed the hour of two.

He peered ahead to the stylish town house on the waterfront lane. The bordering beach—with a sign announcing WATERFRONT CLINIC—was filled with kids, the street lined with cars. His spot from Friday night was taken by a BMW, and there were other vehicles parked behind it. Turning around at the end of the block, Jack pulled over behind the fourth car, killed the engine, and looked up just as

Catherine appeared at the corner, accompanied by a shorter woman with flaming red hair.

The "friend," he fleetingly surmised as his focus zoomed in on Catherine. She was wearing a white jacket that scarcely covered her behind. Her legs were bare, her golden hair shining in the sun. Jack's throat went dry. A moment later the two women embraced, and the redhead got into the BMW. After she drove away, Catherine crossed the lane to the beach.

Picking up the yellow roses, Jack got out of the Buick, leaned against the door, and continued to watch. The lifeguard—a dark-haired guy wearing nothing more than shades, a skimpy Speedo suit, and a whistle around his neck—strode to meet Catherine. When he took her familiarly in his arms, a distinctly unpleasant sensation washed over Jack. Straightening from the side of the car, he took a swift step, then halted as the crowd of kids closed in on the pair and separated them.

The lifeguard backed off, and Catherine sank to one knee to receive the hugs of the children, who presumably were expressing their condolences on the death of her father. Jack forced a swallow down his parched throat as he watched.

After several minutes Catherine rose to her feet, stepped out of sandals, and discarded the jacket to reveal a one-piece swimsuit that hugged her slim curves. She crossed the beach, walked out on the dock, and executed an arching swan dive into the deep blue channel waters.

"What the hell?" Jack muttered as she proceeded to swim with amazing speed in the direction of a distant buoy. Man, she was full of surprises. Mesmerized by the sight of her flashing through the water, he stared for a minute or so before striding to the beach and making a beeline across the sand toward the lifeguard. It wasn't until he closed the distance between them and the guy looked around that Jack realized he was just a kid.

"You must be a friend of Catherine's," he greeted, and offered a hand. From behind the dark glasses, the kid looked from the flowers to his face before joining him in a shake.

"I'm Kenny Black. Who are you?"

"Jack Casey."

The kid swiftly ended the handshake. "So *you're* Jack," he remarked in a scathing manner.

Jack gave Kenny Black a sharp look. He was about six feet tall and sixteen years old. The dark glasses did nothing to camouflage the antagonism on his tense young face. "You say that as though you've heard of me."

"Ann Marie told me a couple of things. You know, that move with the carriage Saturday night? Very uncool."

With that, Kenny turned dismissingly and gazed toward the sea. Jack followed his line of vision beyond the shore-lapping waves, where Catherine's arms made hardly a splash as she raced across the water's surface.

"I'm going to run the risk of asking you a question," Jack said. "What the hell is Catherine doing?"

"Her father just died. She's working it out."

"By taking a swim?"

The kid's head snapped around. "Man," he pronounced with a sneer, "you don't know the woman at all, do you?"

"I know some things. Obviously there's more to learn."

"Obviously."

"Why don't you fill me in?"

Kenny barked a short laugh and directed a sweeping look up the shoreline. "It's time for me to give the kids a lesson, and I'd appreciate it if you cleared off the beach."

"Hold on," Jack demanded as Kenny started to move away. Kenny pushed the shades to the bridge of his nose and drilled him with coal black eyes. "Look, kid," he added. "I care about Catherine."

"You've got a real funny way of showing it."

"And I'm not clearing out until I talk to her." They glared at each other for a few seconds before Jack cast an anxious look toward the sea. "Are you sure she's all right out there?"

Once again the kid uttered a mocking laugh. "Man, you don't know nothin'. That's the Charleston mermaid you're looking at. Up until a couple of years back, this beach was a total hazard. Catherine saved me from drowning out there by the dock, which used to be so broken down that one day a plank gave way and I fell through. If she hadn't come after me, I wouldn't be standing here. After that, she got the city to clean up the place and started a clinic for kids." Kenny paused long enough to give Jack another sneering once-over. "When Catherine's in the water, magic happens. *That's* why she's out there."

Feelings of pride and awe welled up in Jack. "Did you say 'the Charleston mermaid'?"

"That's what the newspapers called her."

Jack glanced toward the sea. Catherine's pace hadn't slowed. The way she moved was uncanny.

"You say you need to talk, so talk," Kenny snapped. "But I'm warning you, man. Don't hurt her again. You might be older than me, and bigger than me, but I'd be taking you down."

Kenny spun away, his feet kicking up sprays of sand as his lanky legs carried him swiftly toward the group of kids. Jack looked back to sea, his heart skipping a beat as, for a moment, he failed to locate Catherine. Then he saw the sleek head moving smoothly with the rippling waves toward shore. She stood at waist-high depth, moved out of the sunstruck water, and time seemed to shift into slow motion.

Her swimsuit was the same royal blue color as the sea from which she emerged, her skin glistening in the sunlight as though it had been brushed with a glaze of diamonds. Like an ocean goddess materializing on shore, she walked across the beach in his direction. *The Charleston mermaid.* Jack knew he'd carry the image forever.

When Catherine spotted Jack on the beach with Kenny, her heart began hammering so that the soothing influence of the water came to an abrupt end. As she swam to shore, she noted that Jack was now alone, holding a bouquet of flowers. Stepping out of the tide, she walked slowly toward him.

Throughout the dismal hours at the hospital, thoughts of him had remained coiled in the back of her mind, springing to the forefront whenever she took a break from her father's bedside. The pain of watching her father slip away was an old ache; the injury of seeing Jack with another woman, a fresh wound.

When Marla brought her home from the hospital, she'd seized on the business card tucked in the door. "Jack Casey!" she announced as Catherine proceeded through the living area, noting and ignoring the flashing red light on the answering machine as she walked past.

If Jack had left an awkward message after the abysmal way they'd crossed paths Saturday night, she didn't want to know. If he'd called to say he thought it best to fly back to Chicago, she didn't want to know.

But now here he was on her beach, roguishly breathtaking in jeans, boots, and a white shirt. As Catherine bridged the distance between them, she called on the old skills and forced a mask of calm to her face. "Hello, Jack."

"Hi." Retrieving her jacket from the beach a few feet away, Catherine slipped it on and stepped into her sandals. "You're something else in the water," Jack added. "The Charleston mermaid, huh?"

"How did you—? Oh, of course. Kenny. He loves that story."

"So do I," Jack replied in a deep tone. Catherine looked into his sparkling eyes—green, brown, gold . . . the colors of a sun-streaked forest. "I'm really sorry about your father," he added, and held forth the yellow roses wrapped in green tissue.

She cradled the long-stemmed flowers and breathed in their fragrance. "They're beautiful. Thank you, Jack."

"I only met him once, of course. But if it's any consolation, it was easy to see you gave him a feeling of peace."

Tears rushed to Catherine's eyes in a stinging tide. She kept her eyelids steadfastly lowered, her blurring gaze fixed on the yellow buds tinged with pink along the petals' edges.

"Are you holding up okay?" Jack asked.

"There's no denying I could use a shower and some sleep," she answered. Fighting the tears, she managed to chase them down the back of her throat as Jack took a step closer, his boots moving into the line of her downcast vision.

"Your father isn't the only thing I'm sorry about, Catherine. Saturday night you must have gotten the impression that—"

"You don't owe me any explanations," she announced to the roses. "That's the deal, isn't it? No explanations? No strings?"

"I was trying to forget about *you*," he said in a soft, irresistible voice that made her look up. Their eyes met and held. The sound of lapping waves accented the air, along with a salty breeze and the shimmering brilliance of the sun.

"It didn't work," Jack added, and Catherine couldn't hide the shiver that raced over her. He put a quick hand to her back. "Come on. You're getting straight into a hot shower."

They walked across the sunny street in silence. When they reached her door, Jack took her key and led the way inside. "I'll stay with you awhile," he declared. Catherine continued into the kitchen and took a vase from the pantry shelf. Jack meandered in and silently watched as she filled the vase with water and unwrapped the yellow roses.

"How about if I make you a sandwich or something while you're in the shower?" he suggested.

"That's very sweet, but you don't have to—"

"I'm trying to make things up to you, Catherine. Let me."

Her eyes burned from seawater and lack of sleep, grief and fiery love. Catherine trained her vision on her hands as she arranged the long green stems.

"Do you really want to make things up to me?" she asked.

"Absolutely. Tell me. What can I do?"

"Go home and pack for Hawaii."

"What? *Now?*"

Picking up the vase, she breezed past him on the way to the table and placed the roses in the center, where they were like bright pieces of sunshine against the backdrop of the sea-facing window. "Do you still want to go with me?" she questioned.

"Well, yes . . . *someday.*"

Catherine turned and confronted his look of stunned surprise. "Someday is here, Jack. My father's funeral is being arranged for the day after tomorrow. After that I'd like to go as soon as possible. If your schedule prevents your going, I understand."

"It's not my schedule that's standing in the way." She walked past him once more, this time on her way to the bath. Jack followed to the threshold. "It's my common sense. According to what Austin Palmer said, Nicki isn't even *in* Hawaii right now."

Catherine glanced his way as she retrieved fresh towels

from the cupboard. "Sunday is her thirtieth birthday. I have a feeling she'll be home for that, and I want to be there. After all, it's my birthday, too. Kenny has agreed to handle the clinic for a couple of weeks, and—"

"A couple of *weeks*?" Jack interrupted.

Placing the towels on the vanity, Catherine moved to the shower. "I imagine I'll want to stay at least a couple of weeks."

"You're being extremely hasty about this."

"I've lived nearly thirty years without meeting my sister. I don't call that being hasty." Turning on the hot water, Catherine stepped out of her sandals.

"You just found out the truth about Nicki a few days ago," Jack countered. "There are questions to be answered about her *and* about you. Plus, I haven't been able to reach Melrose, or—"

"Jack," she interrupted, and turned to face him. "I'm afraid there's nothing you can say that will change my mind."

"Even if I say that the more I think about this situation, the more dangerous I think it could be?" Catherine shook her head. "You absolutely should *not* rush into this," he went on in the manner of a scolding father. "There are too many unknowns. All I'm suggesting is a delay, a few weeks to ascertain the answers to a few questions."

The bathroom began to fill with steam. Countermanding the signal that it was time to vacate, Jack propped his tall frame in the doorway, folded his arms over his chest, and scowled at her. Catherine walked to the door and met his frowning eyes.

"I wish you could see how this chain of events appears to me, Jack. Everything has fallen so remarkably into place—you show up, we uncover an amazing link between Nicki and me, my father supplies a letter that is virtual proof of it. And now he's gone. And there's nothing to keep me from leaving Charleston anymore. Don't you see? It's as though it's meant to be. It's—well, it's a miracle."

"I never believed in miracles," Jack grumbled. "Not until I came *here*."

A secret smile tugged at Catherine's lips. She fought it down. "I feel as though I'm supposed to go. Please don't try to talk me out of it. Now, if you *really* wanted to make

things up to me like you said, you could try to line up some
travel arrangements while I'm in the shower."

Jack glared at her several long, punishing instants. Finally, with a dramatic exhale of breath, he straightened
from the doorjamb. "Dammit," he muttered. "I'll see what
I can do."

Catherine watched for a moment as he retreated grudgingly through the kitchen, the secret smile surfacing as she
quietly closed the bathroom door.

It was after five when Jack hung up the phone, replaced
his credit card in his wallet, and reviewed the itinerary he'd
listed on the pad by Catherine's computer. She would
spend Friday night in San Francisco, take off for Honolulu
Saturday morning, then make the hop to Hilo in the afternoon. He wasn't going to mention that his own flight plans
put him on the island a day and a half earlier. At least he'd
have thirty-six hours to gauge the lay of the land before
Catherine dropped in like a bomb from the blue.

Slumping back in the padded chair, Jack reached to the
corner of the desk and picked up the photocopied likeness
of Nicki's face. The picture was credited to a year-old issue
of *Town and Country*. Apparently Catherine had been busy
in the library before the emergency with her father struck.

Staring at the black and white page, Jack mentally added
color to the portrait and faced Nicki once more—zany,
flirty, indomitable Nicki. There had been times the past
year when the thought of her crossed his mind, always
nudging a smile to his face. Little had he suspected that
she would smash into his life again, this time as half of the
mystery of the Palmer *twins*.

When he put an end to Nicki's fiendish clown, he thought
he'd put an end to the intrigue of the Palmer family as
well. Now it appeared he'd only scratched the surface . . .
and the woman he'd fallen confoundingly in love with was
smack in the middle of it.

Jack ambled to her bedroom door. The shades were
drawn, the chamber in shadow, and Catherine was sitting
on the edge of the bed in the remembered white robe. Her
head was bowed, her wet hair slicked back, a forgotten
comb dangling from her fingers. As he walked in, she
turned aside and rubbed at her eyes.

"Everything's set," Jack ventured. "You stay Friday night in Frisco, and I'll meet your flight in Hilo Saturday afternoon. I made reservations at a hotel called the Hawaiian Sun. It's supposed to be nice. Okay?"

She looked around, her wet eyes glistening. "Thank you, Jack. Once again."

"Sure. You say that *now,* after manipulating me into doing exactly what you wanted. I've heard about you Southern belles."

She surrendered a flickering smile. "When do you leave for Chicago?"

"I have to be at the airport in eleven hours," Jack replied, at which point a tear spilled over and Catherine quickly reached up to wipe it away. "Are you all right?" he added.

She looked away on the pretext of placing the comb on the bedside table. "I've been thinking about my father. It's just so sad, you know? Most of his life was so terribly sad."

Jack sat down on the bed, stretched a sympathetic arm around her, and guided her head to his shoulder. Catherine released a long, shuddering breath. "Are your parents living?" she murmured.

"No. My mom died when I was a kid; Dad, right after I graduated from the police academy."

"I'm sorry."

"Yeah. Me, too."

"I can hardly remember the time before my father was bedridden. When someone has been sick that many years, you think you're prepared for the day he'll be gone. But I guess you never really are. Every time I remember he's dead, I'm still shocked."

"I guess that's a pretty natural reaction."

"Aunt Sybil says I'm the one who caused it."

"What?" Jack barked, so loudly that Catherine jumped.

"She says he never recovered after we showed up Friday night and the truth came out about me."

"That is such *bullshit*! I hope you don't believe her."

Catherine sighed. "Not really."

"For God's sake, Catherine, don't let that bitter old woman brainwash you. Your father was *glad* the truth came out. He was *happy* when you read his letter. Even a total stranger like me could see it. I swear, I never knew a woman could be so mean."

"You don't like her much, do you?"

"*Like* her? What I'd *like* is to *throttle* her." A moment of quiet followed his volatile remark before Catherine softly chuckled. "What's so funny?" Jack demanded.

She tipped her head and looked up to meet his eyes. "You."

Without thinking, Jack reached up and caressed her cheek. The texture of her skin was smooth and fine, the curve of her face delicate as a porcelain doll. A pounding rush of attraction propelled him to his feet. "You need to sleep," he announced.

"I'm not sure I can, but I'll try. What are *you* going to do?"

"I thought I'd stick around here until time to go to the airport, unless I'd be imposing."

"You wouldn't be imposing, Jack. I think you know that."

"Where's your hair dryer?" he demanded.

After coaxing Catherine to sit back against the pillows, he removed his boots, took a cross-legged seat beside her, and proceeded to dry her hair, his fingers fanning through the tresses along with the warming air. Like her skin, the silkiness of her hair seduced him, and what began as a project to get his mind off the idea of ravaging her produced the opposite result.

"You're awfully good at this," Catherine said after a while, her eyes closed and lips parted, begging him to kiss her.

With a final stroke of her hair, Jack turned off the dryer and set it on the table. Something made him say, "I used to do it for my wife." He glanced back to Catherine. Despite the fading light in the sequestered room, her eyes shimmered with the effect of sunbeams on water.

"What was her name?" she asked.

"Ellen. And today is the sixth anniversary of her death." He forced a small smile. "I don't know why I told you that. I haven't talked to anyone about her in years."

"If you feel like talking," Catherine said in quiet, careful fashion, "I'm a good listener."

"Yeah," he responded after a considering moment. "I

guess you're the one person I *should* tell about Ellen. Where's that glass dish of yours?"

Retrieving cigarettes and ashtray from the next room, Jack returned to sit on the edge of Catherine's bed. It was after six, and the light of the shaded bedroom was all but gone. He left it that way. Memories such as these were best resurrected in a dulling shroud of shadow. Tapping a cigarette from the pack, he lit up a smoke.

"I don't remember a time before there was Ellen," he began. "We grew up together, went to city college, and got married after freshman year. She became a teacher; I went into the police academy. She was against me being a cop from the start, but I was determined, and it wasn't enough just to be on the force. I took special training, ended up the youngest officer in the precinct to make detective, and started working undercover. I can't tell you how many times Ellen begged me to stop."

"She was afraid for you," Catherine offered.

"I know. And I used to tease her and laugh off her fears. Back then I felt like I was invincible or something—like I was living a charmed life and nothing could touch me. Believe me, I found out how wrong I was." He took a drag and punctuated the statement with an ominous pause as smoke furled in the air.

"What happened?" Catherine prompted.

"I went undercover in one of the smoothest rings in Chicago. They ran weapons, cars, drugs, the works, and they got away clean because the top guy, Tommy Simone, was smart. Ruthless, too. If you crossed Tommy, there was a good chance something was going to blow up in your face. He was an expert with explosives.

"It took me months to work my way inside. Finally, one night I caught the boss's eye when one of his goons picked a fight with me. Tommy liked my style. I became his bodyguard, and I was in so tight that the captain and the rest of the operation team couldn't believe it. Nobody had ever managed to get so close to Tommy before. Everything was going great. We planned to bust him in a couple of weeks. And then somebody rolled over on me."

"I'm not sure what that means," Catherine said.

"It means somebody blew my cover to Tommy. I never found out who. One day I went to the warehouse as usual, and the place was cleaned out. Empty. The next morning was July third. I went out back to wave good-bye to Ellen. She was taking my car to summer school. When she started it up, the car exploded."

Catherine gasped. "I'm so sorry," she whispered. Jack nodded as he reached over to crush the cigarette in the ashtray. "Did they arrest Tommy Simone?" she added.

"He had an alibi. There was nothing the police could do."

"You mean he got off scot-free?"

"Not exactly." Jack's gaze lifted to Catherine's shining eyes. "I quit the force, tracked him down, and provoked a fight. Tommy pulled a gun on me, and I killed him with it. They called it self-defense. The truth is, it was murder."

"No, it wasn't," she remarked on a defensive note.

"Maybe not according to the law, but I had murder in my heart. I went there with one purpose, to end the life of Tommy Simone. And that's what I did. But it didn't help. Nothing did. Ellen was dead, and my charmed life blown to smithereens."

"It was a terrible tragedy, Jack, but . . . you can't hold yourself responsible."

"I *can't*?" he questioned sharply. "If not for me, she'd still be alive." Shifting up from the pillows, Catherine gathered her knees beneath her and peered at him eye-to-eye.

"What happened to Ellen was one of those tragic things without rhyme or reason, Jack—like a plane crash or a car accident. Loved ones could torment themselves with questions like, why didn't I stop him from taking that flight? Or, why did I let her drive that night? The fact is that sometimes things happen that are beyond our control."

"That's a nice theory," Jack returned. "But it doesn't change the truth. If I'd listened to Ellen, she wouldn't be dead. Nothing's ever going to change that." His eyes began to fill with burning moisture. "Damn," he muttered, and scrubbed at his brow. "Maybe it wasn't such a good idea to talk about this, after all."

Leaning forward, Catherine stretched her arms around his neck in what Jack was sure she meant as a consoling embrace. But no sooner did she touch him than he found himself pulling her onto his lap, burying his hand in her hair, and turning her face to his. He kissed her with a driving mix of need and want, and she opened to his mouth in the same kind of driven way.

When she reached beneath his shirttail to rub his back, he ended the kiss long enough to snatch the garment over his head and toss it aside. Then he gathered her up once more and shifted her to her back on the center of the bed. As his tongue filled her mouth, he pried a knee between hers and stretched out on top of her, his hardness pressing through his jeans and her robe, asserting an erotic rhythm between her thighs.

Catherine moaned as he moved a hand inside the front of her robe, his fingers creating trails of shivers. Moments later he pulled away from her lips, and his mouth followed his hand, sliding warm and wet down the side of her neck, along her shoulder, moving on to bathe first one breast, then the other.

She felt as though she'd departed the temporal realm and drifted into a dimension where time was like molasses, thick and sweet and slow to the point that each sensation stretched out and luxuriated in fruition. It wasn't her first experience with a man, but it seemed so. Never before had she experienced the reactions Jack provoked with a touch that was both tender and masterful, languid and driving, lulling and arousing.

She held him close as he suckled her breasts, then took panting breaths as he kissed his way down the length of her body, evoking the feeling that she was being worshiped and devoured all at once. She had the sensation that she wasn't Catherine anymore, but some mythological siren breathed to life by the power of passion. There was no inhibition, no holding back, no cause for being but to possess as she was being possessed.

As Jack claimed her with his mouth in the most intimate way possible, Catherine feverishly ran furrows through his hair. As he shifted up to kiss her lips, she moved frenzied hands over his back. By the time he peeled off his jeans and moved against her, she was aching in a way she'd known only once—in a long-ago dream of the man who now held her. Clasping her legs around him, Catherine thrust her hips upward.

Jack twisted out of the kiss. "Damn!" he exploded as her sleekness enveloped him, clung to him. It was as though she molded to him. He moved cautiously; still, the sensation drove him out of his mind. When Catherine climaxed, his own came with such force that it seemed to rock the world.

Sometime later he woke from a kind of trance to find his arm still locked about her hips and his mouth planted on her neck. Jack drew a steadying breath and lifted his head. "Catherine?"

Her eyelids lifted a hair's-breadth for about two seconds. "Wow. Now I know why everybody makes such a big deal about sex."

"*Do* ya, now?" Jack responded with a soft laugh.

"I've only been with one other man. He was nothing like you."

His smile fading, Jack reached up and brushed a lock of hair from her cheek. His gaze roamed her features in the deepening darkness, settling on the fringe of lashes lining her closed eyes just as they flew open. "Oh, my gosh," she mumbled.

"What?" he said, his palm absently drifting along the crest of her shoulder.

"Oh, my gosh," she repeated, and, with no further warning, shimmied swiftly out from under him.

"What the hell?" Jack muttered as she grabbed the white robe, flew into the bathroom, and closed the door with a bang—the sound followed almost immediately by that of the shower. With a lift of his brows, he reached for his cigarettes and lit a smoke.

When the water stopped a short while later, he expected Catherine to return. Instead, after a quiet few minutes, he heard her in the kitchen. By the time he pulled on his jeans and meandered through the empty washroom, she was hard at work by the stove, beating the hell out of a bowlful of eggs. He walked up behind her and placed gentle hands on her shoulders. She jumped.

"I hope you like omelettes," she piped up. "I just remembered I haven't eaten since morning."

"Stop stirring for a minute, will you?" Jack said.

When she slowly complied, he turned her around to face him. "What is it, Catherine? What's wrong?" She caught her lip and leveled her gaze somewhere in the vicinity of his Adam's apple. "Tell me," he pressed.

"I've never felt anything like that before. It was . . ."

"Intense?" Jack suggested. "Yeah, it was. Extremely."

"Having said that, I hope it doesn't come as too much of a surprise for me to add that we must pretend it never happened."

A sinking feeling rocked his stomach. "We must? Why?"

"I've never even met my sister," she returned. "And I've already betrayed her."

Taking Catherine's face in his hands, Jack tipped her chin until she looked him in the eye. "I wish you wouldn't continue to blow that idea out of proportion. There's a special bond between me and Nicki; that's true. But it's not *this* kind. It never was."

"Maybe not to you, Jack, but I *know* how Nicki feels. I've known for a long time, and yet I . . ." Trailing off, Catherine retreated from his touch and walked to the end of the counter. "I just hope you agree we can put this behind us. When we see Nicki in Hawaii, things must be as though it never happened."

"I'm not sure I can pull that off," Jack said to her back.

She folded her arms across the front of the white robe. "So what are you telling me, Jack? That you're ready to leave your lone wolf ways and settle down with me?"

A hot flash of fear bolted through him. The more he loved her, the more it scared the hell out of him. Maybe someday something would happen to Catherine. Maybe it would be his fault.

"After I watched Ellen die, I swore I'd never love again," Jack stated grimly. "For six years being alone is all I've wanted. It's still all I can handle."

A look of hurt flitted across Catherine's face. She ended it with a tender smile as she strolled up to him and lifted a hand to his cheek. "You see? For different reasons we want the same thing. This is our one night, Jack—the night of my father's death, the anniversary of Ellen's. There's a symmetry to that. You and I needed each other. We'll never forget it, but . . ."

He cocked a brow. "But you expect me to pretend that I *have*?" Taking her hand, Jack pressed a kiss to her palm before looking up to meet her eyes. "I'll be honest, baby. I just don't know. If I'm not around you, that's one thing. But if we're together, I don't think I can hide what I feel . . . or want."

She pulled her hand from his grasp. When her voice came, it was characteristically soft, though somehow ringing with a paradoxical timbre that suggested the solidity of rock.

"Then you can't come with me," she declared.

"You mean to Hawaii?" Jack asked after a nonplussed moment. She nodded. "Well, that's just great, Catherine!" Striding to the breakfast table, he flopped down in a chair and gave her a condemning look. "*You're* still going, of course."

Her chin lifted. "You know I am."

"But I'm not invited if I don't keep hands off? Is that it?"

"I'm just saying that we must go back to behaving like friends," Catherine insisted.

Jack grunted a short laugh. "What they say is true— eventually your words come back to haunt you. I wonder how many times I've been on the *other* end of that 'friends' remark."

She held her tongue as he glaringly studied her. Standing there with tousled hair and bare feet, she was as lovely a creature as he'd ever seen. "Okay, I'll try," Jack said finally. "That's all I can promise. But I'll tell you one damn thing right now, Catherine. You're *not* going without me, and that's final."

"Is that right," she commented with a dawning smile.

"Yes. That is *right,*" he affirmed with a contradicting scowl.

She spread her palms with all innocence. "Okay . . . how do you like your eggs?"

Jack pitched in making western omelettes. After feasting on eggs and toast, and finishing off the bottle of wine from Friday night, he was in better spirits. As Catherine rinsed the dishes, he came up behind her and wrapped his arms around her waist.

"I've still got seven hours before I have to leave," he murmured at her ear. "Got any idea how we can pass the time?"

"Jack!" she exclaimed in the most scolding of tones.

"Okay. Just kidding," he said, and backed off with a grin. "Sort of," he added when she looked around. As it turned out, they flipped on the TV and settled on the couch. Catherine was sound asleep, her head resting on his thigh, by nine-thirty.

Jack dozed for a couple of hours, but mostly he watched her sleep . . . and experienced another onslaught of anxious thoughts. He had an eerie feeling about returning to Hawaii, especially with Catherine thrown into the equation. He'd nearly lost his life on that sultry volcanic isle. Now he was on his way back, and his sixth sense said the danger was even greater than before.

After a delayed flight and extended layover in Atlanta, Jack arrived in Chicago in late afternoon. It was nearly six by the time the cab pulled into the cemetery.

Turning up his jacket collar against a chilly drizzle, he made his way along the paved path to the grave site. Six long-stemmed American Beauties stood in the upturned vase—scarlet strokes against a background of manicured green, and the gray of hewn stone. His mind filled with contrasts. Red roses, yellow roses. Rainy cold, sunny warmth. Ellen . . . Catherine . . .

He focused on the chiseled name on the granite marker. Ellen Casey. Just reading her name on the gravestone wrenched him like always. But it wasn't the same. Part of his heart was still buried here with Ellen, but there was no denying that a fledgling part of it was reaching for the sun somewhere else.

God, Charleston seemed far away. In retrospect Jack recalled it as being filled with flowers, warm sea breezes, and the sound of church bells. "Be seeing you," Catherine had mumbled as he tried to slip noiselessly from the couch.

Now, as he remembered Nicki's trademark phrase issuing from Catherine's lips, he smiled. But then the Chicago wind whipped by and struck the warm illusion of a Charleston night from his face.

This was reality—this bone-chilling, rainy day with someone you loved lying in endless sleep at your feet.

Jack closed his eyes. For six years every prayer he'd sent from this spot had beseeched forgiveness—from Ellen, from God, from the universe. Today his entreaty was different. Today, with every fiber of his being, he prayed for the strength and wisdom to guide Catherine through the storm he sensed on the horizon.

Chapter Nineteen

The sun was going down on the Fourth of July. Fiery light flooded the rodeo grounds, which were strewn with flowers shed from hundreds of leis that had decked horses and riders in the Waimea celebration. As Nicki, Austin, and Malia approached the tent where riders were assembled, a breeze swept flower petals into swirling clouds along their path.

A young *paniolo* named Leke, who'd been with Palmer Ranch several years, had demonstrated superb skill and won second place in the prestigious rodeo. Despite his finest efforts, however, he hadn't come close to matching the superlative performance given by the defending Waimea champion. Once again Kimo had taken top honors, and deserved them.

Nicki, Austin, and Malia stepped inside one of the three entrances to the cavernous tent filled with horses, riders, and milling spectators. Leke was standing with his pony straight ahead, surrounded by his family and wearing a happy smile. After congratulating him, Nicki stepped aside and looked nonchalantly down the way, where Kimo was still mounted on his pinto, posing for photographers as a crowd of well-wishers looked on.

He was wearing buckskin chaps over his jeans, a royal blue shirt with an embroidered yoke, and—like the other riders—was sporting a *haku* lei headband around the crown of his hat. As she watched, he removed the flower-trimmed cowboy hat, leaned down, and planted it on the head of a young Hawaiian boy.

Nicki felt a rising warmth as she studied Kimo. She hadn't seen him in a year. His black hair was longer. Curling at his shirt collar, it glistened beneath the suspended lights of the tent. He seemed taller, his shoulders broader, legs longer . . . and suddenly his masterful seat on the pinto struck her as provocative. She blinked in surprise. Had he always been so sexy?

Images whirled through her mind—Kimo flashing a grin as he raced by on horseback, gazing down anxiously as he wiped dirt from her cheek, holding her close as they rode double. Nicki's inner warmth flared into unmistakable heat as the memories took on new meaning.

"Nicki!" Austin called. "Come here! Leke wants a picture!"

The revelational moment was shattered, but as she took a place beside Leke, the hot rush of Nicki's newborn awareness smoldered beneath her smiling surface.

When the photographers departed, Kimo dismounted and began obliging the surrounding crowd with autographs. After twenty minutes or so, the last of them departed. The rodeo tent was starting to empty, the dozen or so other riders now busy with unsaddling their ponies and rubbing them down.

Kimo turned to the pinto. "You were great today, boy," he said with a stroke of the animal's neck. The pinto leaned into him with a nickering nuzzle just as a chorus of wolf whistles erupted from the *paniolos* down the way.

Kimo glanced around to see a tall brunette walking toward him. Gathering the pinto's reins in an absent hand, he turned to give her his full attention. A scarlet dress showed off the knockout figure that had the riders staring after her. As she drew near, Kimo's study shifted to a pretty face with big brown eyes and full red lips.

"Well, *hello*," he greeted in a warm tone.

"Hello, pardner," she replied with a sultry smile.

The sound of her voice struck him with familiarity. Kimo stared as the realization dawned. "*Peni?* Is that you?"

She laughed—the sound airy, lilting, feminine. "Yes, it's me. Are you surprised?"

His gaze raced down the length of her, then zoomed back to her face. She was regarding him with dark, heavy-lidded eyes. Bedroom eyes. He could see Peni in there somewhere, but . . . damn! She was a different woman. "You look sensational," he managed.

"Thanks. I was hoping you'd notice."

"Any man with eyes would notice." She smiled again. "I haven't seen you in months," Kimo added. "Where have you been?"

She shrugged a golden brown shoulder. "After I sold the house, I—well, suffice it to say, I've been away for a while."

"Wherever you've been, it's obvious the climate agreed with you. You really do look great. Beautiful, in fact."

"I watched you ride today. *That's* what *I* call beautiful." She took a slow, hip-rolling step closer. "Would the champion permit me to buy him a drink?" she added.

"The champion would be honored," Kimo replied with a grin. "It will take me a few minutes to rub down the pinto and load him in the van. Wanna wait for me by the entrance?"

As she covertly watched Kimo with the curvy brunette, Nicki grew so edgy she felt her hair must be standing on end. She thought of last year, when she and Melrose saw him ride at the Upcountry Festival. He was with a lady in red *that* night, *too*.

"What are you looking at so hard?" She glanced around with a start. "Not *him* again," Austin added, his eyes leveled on Kimo.

Nicki tendered a stony look. "I would have thought you might have softened over the course of a year, Uncle."

"Why? Nothing's changed in the course of a year."

"You're wrong. *I've* changed, and I intend to take an active interest in the ranch from now on. Last summer you got rid of the best *paniolo* on the whole damn island. That was *not* a good move."

"I thought we put that matter behind us," Austin retorted.

"Not really. I shouldn't have let it slide then, and I'm not going to let it slide any longer. One day I picture Kimo taking his father's place and running things. His future is at Palmer Ranch. I perceive it clearly even if you can't."

"What *I* can't perceive is why we're wasting our time arguing about some half-breed cowboy!"

"If that's all you see in Kimo, it's *your* loss!" she fired into her uncle's flushed face, then noticed from the corner of her eye that the woman in red was moving away from Kimo.

"What makes a damn *paniolo* so special?" Austin challenged, and recaptured her attention. "Or is that the appeal, hmmm? Did you acquire a taste for slumming while you were away?"

Anger swept Nicki like an icy shower, chilling her flesh, freezing the look in her eyes to shiny hardness. "In my book there's nothing about Kimo and slumming that go together," she stated coldly. "Let's not fight about him again, Uncle. *This* time you won't win."

She spun on her heel and fleetingly noted that Malia caught Austin's arm and held him back when he would have followed. Nicki peered ahead to the spot where Kimo was rubbing down the pinto. As she drew within a few yards, he glanced up. A startled look crossed his face as he straightened from his task.

Kimo's heart began to pound in the old aching way. She was wearing a denim shirt and jeans, understated for Nicki, but somehow setting off the beauty of her face, which at the moment had a concentrated look that was a turnaround from her usual mischievous grin. It had been a year. He'd hoped the taboo feelings had dulled with time, but if anything they were sharper.

"I didn't expect to see you here," he said.

She offered a small smile. "If I'm home on the Fourth of July, I always turn out for the Waimea Rodeo."

"You didn't turn out last year. I remember seeing your uncle show up solo."

"You're right," Nicki answered. "Last summer, after you left the ranch . . . well, my life was a little crazy for a while."

Kimo arched a brow as he turned to rub the cloth along the pinto's neck. "That's not exactly unusual for you, is it?"

She stepped up to the pony and eyed him from the side. "I *did* see you ride at the Upcountry Festival, though. Remember?"

"Yep," he concisely answered as he moved to the pinto's back with long, practiced strokes.

"I sent you a note asking you to meet me that night. Why didn't you?"

Kimo's arm went still as he looked over. "Note? What note?"

"You didn't get it?"

"I have *never* gotten a note from you. What did it say?"

"That my uncle had no right to provoke you into leaving us. That you belong at Palmer Ranch, and we want you back."

Draping the cloth across the pony's haunches, Kimo turned to face her. "Your uncle and I don't like each other much, but on one thing we agree: It's no good for me at the ranch anymore."

Nicki stared up at him, a look of hurt filling her eyes. "Why do you say that?"

Kimo's gaze melded with hers, and his surroundings faded away. There was no sound but the thunder of his heart, no space but that in which he was corraled with Nicki. How many times had he looked into her eyes and held back? How many damn times?

"Why?" he repeated in a thick voice. "I'll show you why."

He took her face in firm hands, holding her steady as he bent to her lips with a forceful kiss. She was still for a stunned instant. Then Kimo's blood caught fire as she opened her mouth to his tongue. His arms went around her, desperately pulling her against him as his face slanted across hers.

An eerie shriek pierced the air, long and ringing like the wail of a banshee. Nicki tore out of the kiss and leaped back. Kimo looked around in a kind of daze, his vision lighting on Peni. She stood mere feet away, her bosom heaving, her eyes glaring from a face nearly as bright as her dress.

"Peni?" he mumbled. "Was that you?"

"Peni?" Nicki repeated in a tone of astonishment as the raven-haired woman threw back her head and laughed. The shrill, mindless sound was even more frightening than her scream. It stopped as abruptly as it began.

"None of it matters," she then announced with a sweep of her arm. "None of the pain or planning or hoping. No matter what I do, you're never going to get over her, are you, Kimo?"

"What are you talking about?" he rumbled as Peni's dark glare swerved to Nicki.

"And *you*," she uttered scathingly. "Why couldn't you just have drowned that night in the pool?"

Nicki lifted a hand to the base of her throat. *"You?"* she piped on a horrified note. *"You* were the one?"

"What's going on?" Kimo questioned, his frowning gaze darting between the tall brunette and the slighter blonde.

Peni targeted Nicki with a hard smile. No sooner had she done so than Nicki stepped forward and slapped her soundly across the cheek. Before Kimo could move, Peni drew back and landed a blow to Nicki's jaw that knocked her to the ground. Lunging forward, he caught Peni around the waist as she started to fall on Nicki, apparently with the notion of beating the hell out of her.

"What the devil's going on over there?" Austin Palmer yelled, and started running in their direction with Malia close behind.

Nicki cradled her offended jaw as she looked around, her eyes brilliant with tears. "She's the one, Austin! Last summer she tried to kill me! It was Peni!"

Peni squirmed in Kimo's arms and, with a burst of strength, broke free of his grasp. "What the hell is she saying?" Kimo demanded as Peni backed away with a panicked look.

"Somebody call the police!" Austin bellowed.

When Nicki attempted to climb to her feet, Kimo bent to help her, and that was all the break Peni needed. Grabbing the pinto's reins, she vaulted onto his bare back, kicked him in the sides, and galloped toward the nearest exit.

"Stop her!" Kimo thundered. But of course no one could. Peni was too good and too fast. She was out of reach in a matter of seconds. Returning his attention to Nicki with a bewildered scowl, Kimo succeeded in helping her gain her footing just as Austin smashed onto the scene and gave him a violent push.

"Get your hands off her," he growled as Kimo stumbled back.

"No, Austin!" Malia objected.

He whirled, his voice booming for all to hear as he went on. "You said it yourself a year ago, Malia! You said no good was going to come of it—Peni lusting after Kimo, *him* lusting after Nicki. That's what caused this whole thing, and now we find out it was *Peni* who was behind that villainy last summer." He turned and took a menacing step toward Kimo. "Is this clear enough for you, boy? Do you see what your rutting urges have spawned?"

"Stop it, Uncle!" Nicki commanded. "It isn't his fault!"

She looked around and met Kimo's gaze. "It *isn't*," she insisted as a trio of rodeo security officers ran up to them. Nicki had never seen such fierce emotion on Kimo's face. God, he was angry . . . and hurt. He peered into her eyes for a tense moment before lifting his hands as if in silent surrender and backing off.

"Were you hurt, Miss Palmer?" an officer demanded.

"I'm okay," she mumbled, and was drawn into the group gathering about Austin as he heatedly related the details of Peni's attack. When Nicki looked over her shoulder, she saw Kimo striding briskly away, back turned, shoulders squared.

By the time the local police arrived a short while later, it was impossible to tell which way Peni had ridden. She was long gone into the countryside, a curtain of descending darkness veiling her getaway. After Nicki finished giving a statement, she strolled into the starlit night and spotted Kimo standing by one of the police cars clustered outside the tent. As he noted her approach, he straightened and met her with a grim look.

"You don't have to look so mad at *me*," she greeted with a passing smile. "I'm on *your* side, remember?"

"What's all this about last summer?"

Nicki's gaze fell to the ground as she broached the dreaded subject. "I was stalked last summer, Kimo . . . by someone who eventually tried to kill me. The county police are on their way to talk to me right now. I always assumed the stalker was a man, but from what Peni said tonight, it sounds like *she* was the one."

"Your uncle was right, then," Kimo tightly declared. "I *am* at the root of this."

She looked up with swift indignance. "You are *not*. You can't hold yourself accountable for something *Peni* did."

A police officer strode up to the driver's side of the car. "Are you ready, Kimo?"

"Yeah. Be right with you."

"Where are you going?" Nicki asked.

Kimo's eyes sparkled like diamonds in the flashing light of the police car. "Peni can't travel on the pinto indefinitely. He's too conspicuous. She'll have to ditch him somewhere. I want to be there when they find him."

"Can we continue our discussion another time, then?"

"What discussion?"

"The one about you coming back to the ranch."

Kimo released a weighty breath. "I thought I made myself clear about that, Nicki. I've got no business being there."

"But couldn't we—"

"No! We *couldn't*! I'm in love with you, Nicki. I have been for years, and I'm sick of trying to hide it, trying to pretend I don't care when you take off for Europe, or off to a party with some other man. I don't want to be around it anymore."

"Things change, Kimo," she murmured after a shocked moment. "*I've* changed."

"Not *that* much," he countered. "You're still the princess of Palmer Ranch, and I'm still a *paniolo*. Nothing's going to change that. Ever."

Nicki stared as she searched for a way to say none of that amounted to a hill of beans . . . to say all that mattered were the astonishing feelings that had come to light this very night. Her whirling thoughts halted as Kimo snatched open the car door.

"Good-bye, Nicki," he said, the words ringing with finality as he climbed inside the police vehicle and it rolled away.

It was nearly midnight when the police located Kimo's prized pinto grazing in a field some miles south of Waimea. Early the next morning a pair of children on a neighboring farm discovered a fancy red dress and sandals lying on the ground by their clothesline. Some of the family's clothes were missing. Beyond that, no trace of Peni Kahala was found.

Friday, July 7

Exiting the coastal highway, Jack pointed the shiny black Cadillac toward the lights of Hilo. Cadillacs weren't his style, but with a flight thrown late by "technical difficulties," he'd had no time to be picky when he rented it. Turning onto Kilauea Avenue, he broached the downtown area where evening strollers meandered alongside wooden storefronts and historic buildings. Although Hilo was the commercial center of the Big Island, it retained a low-key charm from the plantation era of the 1800s.

It was also the county seat, which was the reason he chose to fly into Hilo International rather than Kona Airport on the opposite side of the island. Kona would have afforded closer proximity to the upcountry where Palmer Ranch was located, but the records he'd needed to check were here.

As Jack proceeded toward the strip of hotels overlooking Hilo Bay, he reflected on the information he'd managed to glean since landing on the island six hours ago. After speedily checking into the Hawaiian Sun, he'd made it to the County Building minutes before closing time and had found it necessary to get downright insistent with the sour-faced clerk in Vital Records before she granted him admission to the catalogs.

But insistence paid off. Not only did he locate the death certificate of Nicki's mother, Marie, but also that of Nicki's twin, who reportedly died of fetal asphyxiation and was interred at Palmer Ranch. Before the clerk kicked him out at five on the dot, he'd jotted down all the basic information on the certificates, including a lead: Dr. J. B. Whitmore of Hilo Hospital had certified both deaths.

Returning to his hotel room, Jack had called the hospital's main number with meager expectations. Hilo Hospital was now Hilo Medical Center, and thirty years was a long time. Chances were the doctor had moved on one way or another. He perked up when he was put through to a chatty maternity nurse who knew Whitmore personally. Relaying the information that the "highly respected" obstetrician had delivered half the residents of Hilo County before retiring two years ago, she added that although Whitmore had no phone, he now resided an hour's drive away on the Hamakua Coast, where he raised orchids.

Picking up a sandwich and drink on the way out of the hotel, Jack had wasted no time setting off for the Hamakua Coast. The nurse spoke of Whitmore as though he were a saint, but in Jack's mind a cold question remained. Nicki's twin had lived; so how come the "highly respected" doctor attested to her death?

He remained cynical as he drove toward Whitmore Nursery—that is, until he reached the farmhouse surrounded by flowers, and a plump snowy-haired man, with a tail-wagging collie by this side, met him in the drive. He was wearing a red shirt and overalls, and a pair of spectacles perched on the end of his nose. If he'd had a beard, he would have looked like Santa Claus.

"Dr. Whitmore?" Jack ventured.

"Nowadays it's just Jim. What can I do for you? A lei of Ms. Joaquim for a special lady, perhaps?"

"There's no special—well, actually there *is,* but I was hoping to talk to you about something other than orchids."

"Really? What might that be?"

"A case of yours from thirty years ago."

"*Thirty,* you say" Whitmore cheerily returned. "Lucky for you my memory hasn't gone the way of my figure. But you must bear with us. Sheba and I were just getting ready to make the rounds and turn off the sprinklers, weren't we, girl?"

Sunset turned to twilight as they toured the orchid fields. By the time they returned to the farmhouse and settled on the lanai, Jack's opinion of Whitmore had taken form. Goodness radiated from the man like warmth from a stove, and the idea of him taking part in something sinister just didn't fit. Whitmore fortified the impression when he responded frankly and openly to Jack's lead question about Marie Palmer.

"I've brought hundreds of human beings into the world," he said on a solemn note. "But in the process a few were lost. I remember every one of them, and I would have remembered Marie Palmer in any case. What do you want to know?"

"Anything you can tell me about the way she died."

"It happened on a stormy night that ended in a tsunami the next day," Whitmore mused. "The tidal wave demolished buildings, washed out roads, and made travel impossible for days. I'd been worried about Marie. She was fiercely devoted to her husband, and when she was six months pregnant, he died in a diving accident. She took it hard. In fact, she refused to accept his death as an accident. I'll always believe it was Marie's emotional turmoil that triggered her into early labor."

Whitmore's gaze shifted to the darkening field of flowers beyond the lanai. "I'd made arrangements to have her admitted to the hospital for the duration of her pregnancy so I could check her on a daily basis. She was scheduled for admission the following week. Obviously, it wasn't soon enough. Marie went into labor three weeks early out at Palmer Ranch. The emergency team airlifted her to the hospital, where I met the helicopter. Her daughter had been born on the way, and, although an undeniably small child, was perfectly hale and hearty."

I'm a woman who was born in the air, Nicki's voice echoed in Jack's memory.

"Marie, however, was hemorrhaging at a rate that outstripped transfusion," the doctor continued. "We rushed her into OR, and a team of us tried everything we knew. But we couldn't bring her back. She died without regaining consciousness."

"You were with her when she died?"

"Yes," Whitmore confirmed. "I was."

"What of the other?" Jack asked after a respectful moment.

The old man looked his way. "Other?"

"The other baby. Nicki's twin."

Whitmore regarded him over the rims of his spectacles. "You know, thirty years ago the medical profession didn't have the equipment we now take for granted. There were no sonograms, no electronic monitors. If I'd had such means, I'd have been able to detect that Marie was carrying twins."

"You didn't know?"

The doctor shook his head. "Their heartbeats must have been identical, and the position of one fetus obscuring the presence of the other. Until that night no one knew there were two, not even their mother. Apparently the first twin was stillborn shortly before the helicopter arrived at the ranch."

"Apparently," Jack repeated.

"Well, yes. The housekeeper, Malia, reported that the ill-fated birth occurred minutes before the emergency team got there. Both she and Austin Palmer witnessed the event."

"So . . . when did you actually examine the stillborn infant?"

A few seconds elapsed as Whitmore's gaze turned searching. "Thirty years ago the upcountry wasn't as accessible as it is today, Jack. Back then a great deal of the Big Island was covered with stretches of wilderness that were virgin to anything but native paths. When a tsunami struck, nothing moved across the island for days. As I recall, nearly a week passed before we could transport Marie's body to the ranch. By that time the infant had been buried next to her father in the family plot. You're not suggesting something was amiss, are you?"

Yes, indeed, Jack thought. "Not at all," he said aloud, and rose to his feet. "Thank you for your time, Doctor."

Popping out of his chair, the old man proceeded to a potted plant on a nearby table. "Before you go, let me give you something." Clipping a huge purple and yellow blossom—one of his favored cattleya orchids—Whitmore secured the stem in a vial and returned to offer it to Jack. "For that special lady friend of yours," he said with a wink.

Glancing now to the elegant flower on the neighboring seat, Jack thought of Catherine. She was arriving in less than twenty-four hours, and the first place she was going to demand to go was Palmer Ranch. Everything was funneling down to the ranch. Catherine was born there, somehow stolen away from there, and the two witnesses who falsified her death were there.

He was disappointed to find that Malia was involved. He'd always like the pretty Hawaiian woman with the quiet ways. As for Austin Palmer, when the man smiled, you got the feeling he'd prefer to be sticking a knife between your ribs, and Jack had a gut feeling Palmer was at the bottom of the scheme. Now all he had to do was figure out details like why, and whether or not Catherine was still in danger.

Pulling into the circular drive of the Hawaiian Sun, Jack turned the Caddie over to a valet and walked through the bustling lobby to the elevator. Proceeding to his room with a weary step, he slipped the security card in the lock and glanced one door down the hall—Catherine's door as of tomorrow afternoon.

The Hawaiian Sun was known for beautiful surroundings, gracious service, and excellent food in luau tradition. Furnished with the tropical grandeur of a Hawaiian plantation house, the softly lit bedroom was airy and spacious, with Polynesian art on the walls, leafy plants in the corners, and a soft breeze from a ceiling fan that gently stirred the sheer curtains at two opposing sets of patio doors.

The patios were the real selling point of the place. One overlooked the bay; the other opened onto a ten-story atrium that formed a cylindrical center in the hotel. Emulating a tropical forest, it offered a mountain landscaped with banyan trees and ferns, a cascading waterfall that fed a pond on the lobby level, and the bright colors and calls of tropical birds.

Catherine was going to like it, he decided. Emptying his pockets on a side table, Jack found a place for Whitmore's orchid in a glass on the wet bar and procured a beer from the fridge. Pulling off socks and shoes, he unbuttoned his shirt as he strolled across the room and stepped onto the outdoor balcony.

Down below torchlight ringed a patch of sand where a band was playing percussive island music. Beyond the beach the waters of Hilo Bay shone with moonlight. Man, it was pretty. Jack took a swig of beer, his thoughts drifting to his plans for morning.

He didn't have to consult his map to know there was but one route from Hilo to Palmer Ranch—back along Highway 19 and the Hamakua Coast from which he'd just returned, and on to the fiercely winding mountain road of the upcountry. He was looking at about a three-hour drive and would have to get an early start to make it to the ranch, find out what he could, and hustle back to Hilo in time to meet Catherine's flight at five-thirty.

He hadn't wanted to tip his hand with a phone call, and so had no idea who might be at Palmer Ranch when he crashed the gates. Maybe Catherine's intuition would prove to be on target, and he'd arrive to find that Nicki had come home for her birthday. Maybe Melrose, who had remained unreachable for days, would surface. Maybe Austin Palmer would provoke a fight, and Jack would finally get the chance to square off with him.

It seemed the variables tumbling through Jack's mind were endless, but one thing remained constant. Whether Catherine agreed or not, if he didn't like the lay of the land out at the ranch tomorrow, she wasn't going there. Period.

After a *"bon voyage"* supper, for which Malia prepared a smorgasbord of Austin's and Nicki's favorites, Nicki retired to her room to pack for the next day's trip to the

Volcano Lodge. In spite of the delicious fare, a pall had hung over the dinner table. All three of them were thinking about Peni Kahala and trying to pretend they weren't.

The police had been in constant touch the past few days. Peni's whereabouts remained unknown. A patrol was still combing the island for her, and Lieutenant Tanaka had furnished every possible port of exit with photos—though, in Nicki's opinions, the pictures wouldn't do any good. They'd been taken before Peni's remarkable transformation to a beauty.

At one point, when Tanaka heard of the upcoming celebratory weekend at the Volcano Lodge, he started to suggest that Nicki postpone the affair. "Don't even think about it," she vehemently interrupted. "I canceled my *last* birthday party because of this, and I'm not *about* to do it again this year."

Austin backed her up. "She's right, Tanaka. Hasn't Nicki lost enough to the threat of this damnable clown?"

Tanaka pacified himself with assigning an undercover detail to tomorrow night's gala. The officers would arrive at six, long before the onslaught of guests at eight. Nicki was secretly relieved protecting eyes would be trained her way. Although she did her best to persuade everyone, including herself, she wasn't afraid, inside she was shaking with the premonition that sometime soon her final reckoning with the clown was going to plant itself in her path, and there was nothing she could do to get around it.

Nicki's thoughts returned to the violent scene in the rodeo tent. She'd seen the hatred on Peni's face; she'd felt the strength in the blow to her jaw. Still, it was difficult to reconcile the idea of Peni Kahala, childhood pal, with that of the evil stalker. At least now Nicki had an answer to the question that had tormented her last summer: *Why?*

"Obsession makes people do mad things," Malia had said during one of countless conversations, the past few days, and the statement rang true. Peni had gone mad with obsession for a man . . . tall, dark, dashingly handsome Kimo . . . with eyes blue as mountain lakes and a mouth that—

Nicki brought herself up short as she started to slip once more into the daydream of reliving their kiss. Damn. For three days all she'd thought about was Peni and Kimo, Kimo and Peni. She was sick of it. Stomping to the stereo, she flipped on the radio and turned her mind staunchly to the task of packing.

Music livened the atmosphere as Nicki laid out a hanging bag and began selecting hiking clothes for the climb up the Pali. The cream-colored shirt and khaki shorts were years old and had been washed so often they were soft as a second skin; the wool socks and leather boots with Vibram soles were new imports from her recent sojourn in Switzerland. Adding a hooded windbreaker to the pile, she stepped over to the dresser and retrieved the hiker's belt from the bottom drawer.

Custom-made from the finest Italian leather, it featured a canteen engraved with her initials and a hunter's knife in a brass-tipped leather sheath. Austin had commissioned it for her nineteenth birthday, and although most hikers wore fanny packs these days, she wouldn't think of climbing the Pali without it.

Tucking her boots into the bottom of the bag, Nicki crossed to the closet and pulled open the double doors. With elaborate catering and music, tomorrow night's party—though staged in the rustic splendor of the lodge—was a formal affair.

Strolling inside the spacious wardrobe, she began looking through the numerous cellophane-shrouded cocktail dresses and evening gowns. Her gaze lit on the royal blue silk she'd brought back from the continent. Selecting it from the rack, Nicki stripped off the protective cover, held it up in front of her, and strolled to the cheval mirror. With spaghetti straps of rhinestones and a spray of sparkling stones across the bodice, the silk was cut in simple, clinging lines to the ankle, with a split on one side that reached halfway up the thigh.

A ringing whistle interrupted her thoughts. Nicki looked around to see her uncle standing in the doorway. "Now, *there's* an encouraging reaction," she said with a grin.

"Is *that* what you're planning on wearing to the party?"

"It's in the running," she answered, and looked back to the mirror. "What's your opinion?"

"My opinion is that none of the men will be able to take their eyes off you."

"That settles it, then. This baby goes."

As Austin laughed and started to move on, Nicki folded

the gown over her arm and moved to the door. "Thanks for the party, Austin." Pausing in the hallway, he turned to look at her.

"But most of all, thanks for thinking of the Pali," she added. "It's been a long time since we climbed together."

"Yes, I thought the idea fitting. Are you bringing along your hiker's belt?"

"What do you think?"

Austin smiled as he backed away. "I think I'd better get started packing, myself. We need to leave bright and early in the morning in order to take our time on the mountain."

Hanging the dress on a louvered door, Nicki returned to the depths of the closet. A half hour later she was zipping up her carryall when Malia stopped by.

"Can I do anything for you?" she asked.

"No, thanks." Stretching out on the bed, Nicki propped on an elbow and gave her a solemn look. "Unless you want to change your mind about coming to the lodge with us."

"*That* I will not do. Tomorrow is your day with your uncle."

"But at least you could come to the party," Nicki objected. "Everyone I care about will be there to celebrate *except* you."

Sitting down on the edge of the bed, Malia reached over and covered Nicki's hand. "We will have our own celebration when you return. I'm making you a present. It will be finished by then."

"A present?" Nicki piped up, her cloudy expression turning suddenly bright. "What is it?"

"I'm not going to tell you that!" Malia replied with a laugh.

"Come on. Just a hint."

"None whatever. It would spoil the surprise." She gazed at Nicki, her expression turning serious. "I won't belabor the subject, but I must say this: Take care tomorrow night. I feel pity for Peni, but also I fear her."

"It will be all right, Malia. The police are going to be there, and of course Austin and Melrose and a horde of friends." Nicki paused as her thoughts switched track. "You know, in spite of all the talk about Peni these past few days, there's something else that has been on my mind just as constantly."

"Kimo," Malia stated.

No matter how long she knew Malia, Nicki supposed she'd always be amazed by the woman's insight. "Were you aware that Kimo has feelings for me? Did you know that he . . ."

"Loves you? Yes. I've been aware of it for many years."

"Why didn't I see it?" Nicki murmured.

Malia smiled. "I have sometimes thought you conduct life like a parade, *keiki*—dashing past in a whirl of fanfare while the rest of us stand by and watch. The answer to your question is that you simply weren't looking."

"Well, I'm looking *now*, although it appears to be too late."

"Did Kimo say that to you?"

Nicki shrugged. "He said he'd always be a *paniolo*, and I'd always be a Palmer, or something to that effect."

"He's right. There are great differences between you."

"If you're talking about the Hawaiian/*haole* thing," Nicki flared, "I hate to point out the obvious, but you and Austin have been happy together for years."

"Yes," Malia admitted. "I never had a choice about what I feel for your uncle, or about the fact that I must be with him, regardless of all the differences between us, regardless of everything. If *that* is how you feel for Kimo, then you will know. There will be no questioning, no thinking, no choice. You will simply go to him."

"Simple as that, huh?" Nicki queried with wide eyes.

"Simple as that."

"Tell me something. How'd you get to be so smart?"

Malia chuckled and reached over to tousle the platinum locks. "To bed with you. If you're going to be climbing a volcano tomorrow, you'll be needing plenty of rest." Rising from the bed, she crossed the room on swift bare feet.

"Oh, Malia!" Malia turned at the doorway to find Nicki seated cross-legged atop the covers and wearing the inimitable, impish grin that transformed her appearance to that of a child. "Be seeing you," Nicki added.

"Aloha, *keiki*," Malia replied, and gently closed the door.

Chapter Twenty

Saturday, July 8

Thanks to a stalled livestock truck on the mountain road, it was after one when Jack turned onto the drive to the ranch. The sun was high and golden, the landscape green and rolling. His mind filled with memories of the last time he was here.

He slowed the car as he broached the formal grounds, which were deserted and still but for the sweeping arcs of mist from the sprinklers in the gardens. Cruising up to the house, he spotted Malia seated at the table on the lanai. He pulled to the side of the drive and parked.

"Aloha," she greeted as he scaled the steps.

Jack stepped into the shade of the porch. "Hello, Malia." Wearing a light floral muumuu, she was as he remembered her—black hair pinned up above a pretty face with a placid smile. On this occasion she was sewing a quilt that was draped across her lap, and presented as sweet a portrait of domestic womanhood as he'd ever seen.

He did *not* want her to be involved in the treachery of thirty years ago, and looking at her now, he couldn't believe that she was. Maybe some remarkable fact had yet to surface, something that would sweep the dirt away from Malia's door.

"I'm afraid I'm the only one here at the moment," she said. "But please have a seat. I just need to complete one more row."

Crossing to the table, Jack took the chair across from hers. "Where is Melrose these days?" he casually inquired. "I've tried to reach him by phone a couple of times."

"Melrose returns today after a week of business on the mainland. He's retiring from the company, you know."

"No, I *didn't* know. He struck me as the type who would sit in the director's chair until the bitter end. He's not sick, is he?"

"Melrose is simply growing old," Malia softly returned.

Jack watched as she completed a few rapid stitches. "What's that you're working on?"

"There. It's finished." Tacking the needle in the quilt, she held it up. "Nicki's birthday gift. I've embroidered thirty squares with scenes of the ranch. Do you think she will like it?"

"I'm sure she will. It's really nice." A pleased look covered Malia's face as she surveyed her handiwork. "You don't seem very surprised to see me after all this time," Jack added.

"When you left, I sensed that our paths would cross again. However, I didn't expect you on this particular day. I'm sure Nicki would have said something if she knew you were coming. Are you planning to surprise her at the party tonight?"

"The party," Jack repeated.

"Her uncle has reserved the whole of the Volcano Lodge."

"Nicki's *here*? I was *told* she's traveling in Europe."

"She returned home some weeks ago."

"Well, what do you know. Where is she now?"

"Nicki and Austin are climbing the Pali this afternoon." Malia frowned as she folded the quilt across her lap. "If you didn't come for the party, then what brings you here?"

"An unusual coincidence," Jack answered as he scrutinized the face across the table. She had the gentle eyes of a doe, and he felt like a wolf closing in for the kill. "Let me ask you something, Malia. Have you ever had a friend named Kila?"

"Yes," she replied on a curious note. "Kila and I grew up in the same village and remained close until she died last year."

"Did she ever work as a housekeeper on the Kona coast?"

Malia hesitated. "That was many years ago. Why are you asking questions about Kila?"

"Because her name has come up in an investigation."

A startled look came into the doe eyes. "Kila was one of the kindest, finest people I've ever known. I'm certain she couldn't have done anything wrong. What kind of investigation?"

"Kidnapping," Jack stated, and watched the color drain from Malia's cheeks. "Was Kila at the ranch the night Nicki was born?"

"No!"

"That's a pretty quick answer about something that happened thirty years ago."

"I remember every detail about that night," she insisted. "There was a terrible storm. The hospital sent a helicopter. Nicki was born on the way to Hilo."

"But before the chopper arrived, the first twin was born," he pressed. "*Stillborn,* according to county records. Only the recorded fact is false, isn't it? Otherwise, the baby couldn't have turned up the next day with your friend, Kila, at a resort home on the Kona coast."

Malia peered at him. The startled look gradually went out of her face as the old aura of tranquillity spun itself about her. "Old fires are licking my feet," she murmured. "I often wondered when the lost thread would be found, how it would work its way back into the tapestry. When *you* showed up last year, I knew you were an agent of destiny. I just never imagined to what degree."

Jack slumped back in his chair. "That's very poetic, but I don't know what you're talking about."

"You have found the child, have you not? Through some uncanny twist of fate, it is *you* who has been led to the child."

"The woman I've found is no child. She'll be thirty tomorrow, and *only now* is beginning to discover who she truly is."

Malia produced a small smile. "Ah . . . and I see you are intent on protecting her."

"If I can," he curtly replied. "My ability to do so would be greatly enhanced if I had some idea of what the hell happened the night she was born."

"It had nothing to do with my friend," Malia relinquished after a moment. "I went to Kila's house late that night, and she merely did as I asked. She had told me about a couple staying at a home where she served. They were good people, she said, and had just lost their baby girl."

"So you decided to give them a new one?" Jack sputtered.

She may have been initially ruffled by his questions, but now Malia was back in full, serene stride. With no more than the chiding arch of a brow, she regarded him in silence.

"In my business it pays to regard people as suspects," Jack sharply continued. "Their motives usually turn out to be pretty crass. But knowing you, I can't figure this. Why did you do it?"

She studied him for a moment before saying, "For reasons that are long past and healed, it was best for the baby to go away that night."

"Will you tell me those reasons?"

"No. I will not."

Jack set his jaw. "Why was it best for the baby to go away that night?" he tried again. "Was she in some sort of danger?"

"As I said, reasons for past deeds belong with the past."

Shifting forward, he gave her a piercing look. "You can't dismiss this blithely, Malia. A federal crime was committed."

"I believe there are greater forces in the world than man-made laws. *And* higher allegiances."

"You *stole* a baby," Jack challenged. "And in doing that, you stole her identity, her birthright, her whole life."

Malia steadily returned his accusing gaze. "In my heart I know that it was the other way around. I saved her."

"From whom?" he fired. "Austin Palmer?"

She rose briskly from her chair. "No more questions, Jack."

"Would you prefer that the authorities ask them?"

"Is that your plan?" Malia returned as she gathered the birthday quilt in her arms. "To bring in the authorities?"

Morosely perusing her, Jack rose to his feet. "I don't want to," he answered in a hollow tone.

"But you will do what you must do. Just as I did thirty years ago. And now, unless you have a warrant, I'd like you to go."

Without waiting for a response, Malia headed for the breezeway. Jack stared after her, and it struck him that her soft voice masked a will tough as iron. She'd confessed to taking part in the crime, but absolutely was *not* going to

elaborate—even to the police, even to save her own
skin . . . not if it meant pointing a finger at Austin Palmer.
Jack turned toward the lanai steps, his feeling of regret
about Malia being swiftly overtaken by a predatory urge to
nail Palmer's hide to the wall.

On the southerly outskirts of Hawaii Volcanoes National
Park, Pali Waipi'o, "Cliff of Arching Water," rose six thousand feet above the coast to overlook a horseshoe-shaped
inlet featuring the famed Aloha Blow-Hole. When the tide
was out, the inlet was calm. But when the Pacific rushed
to bite into the volcano's craggy coastal foot, waves tossed
tempestuously, and the blow-hole spewed hundred-foot
fountains into the air.

The Pali's last eruption, in the late eighteenth century,
had left the mountain riddled with lava tubes, a network
of corridors carved by molten streams on their way to the
sea. The blow-hole was linked to the mouth of such a tunnel, and its position on the peninsula that formed one of
the curving arms of the horseshoe inlet made it a popular
draw for guests of the Volcano Lodge.

Most of them, however, preferred to view the blow-hole
from the luxurious distance of the lodge's white sand beach.
Few made the arduous climb to the crater to do it.

Taking a final swig from her canteen, Nicki hooked it on
her belt. The wind at this altitude was fierce. Her hair was
blowing, her jacket billowing, as she took in the spectacular
mountaintop views.

Far to the west was the clouded peak of towering Mauna
Loa; closer in, the green foothills with a tiny red square
representing the terra-cotta roofline of the lodge. Directly
below, the mountain wall sheered away in a stark cliff that
had given the Pali its name.

As Nicki looked to sea, the blow-hole propelled a cas-
cade high into the air. At this distance the shape of the
flume resembled a giant white feather. She loved watching
the blow-hole, and had ever since Austin first showed it to
her twenty years ago. Lifting a hand to shield her eyes, she
was still watching when her uncle moved up beside her.

"I was just remembering the first time you brought me
here," she said, lifting her voice above the wind. "You told
me a story about Pele, the goddess of volcanic fire. You

said she had put the Pali to sleep, and that the roaring sounds of the blow-hole were actually the snores of the mountain."

"Did you believe me?"

"Of course I did. You mean, it's not true?"

With a quick laugh he looked to the west. "It's after three. We should start down. Why don't we take the short trail back?"

"Trail?" Nicki shrilled. "You call that obstacle course straight down a mountainside of fissures a *trail*?"

Austin gave her a teasing look. "You're right, of course. I wasn't thinking of the fact that you're turning thirty tomorrow. I guess you're getting too old to handle the rough stuff."

"Shut up, Austin. Lead the way."

Nearly an hour later, after a series of sheer descents and narrow, winding ledges pockmarked with fissures opening into the dark heart of the volcano, they'd made it halfway down. Nicki had removed her windbreaker and tied it around her waist; still, her blood pumped warmly through her body. Twenty feet ahead her uncle continued to negotiate the challenging terrain at the stalwart pace of an experienced climber.

Although Austin was past fifty and shouldering the burden of a backpack, he hiked at the speed of a young man. He moved smoothly around a jagged outcrop that momentarily blocked him from view. A minute later Nicki rounded the barrier and was surprised to find him seated on a boulder-strewn ledge that was ten feet wide at its broadest and bordered by a fissure nearly half its breadth.

"Let's take a break, shall we?"

"Here?" Nicki questioned.

"Why not? I like it here, don't you? Listen," he suggested, cupping a hand to his ear. "You can hear the blow-hole." With that he proceeded to remove his pack and set it aside.

"All right," Nicki mumbled with a shrug. Casting a wary look at the gaping fissure that dropped into blackness, she stepped carefully around and perched on a rock a few feet from the edge.

"There, now. Isn't that nice?"

Nicki looked over her shoulder. More than a thousand

feet straight down, the green treetops of the Volcano Lodge grounds hugged the base of the mountain. "Just peachy," she replied.

"You're perfectly comfortable?"

"Comfortable enough. What's with you?"

"I want you to do me a favor. Give me your hiking belt."

"My belt? Why?"

"No questions. It's part of a birthday surprise." Extending a hand, Austin beckoned. "Come on. The jacket, too. Give."

With a shake of her head, Nicki untied the arms of her jacket, unbuckled the belt, and handed them over. "Thank you," he said, and deposited the things with his pack. "Now your boots."

"You can't have my boots. I'm just now breaking them in."

"I must insist, Nicki."

"But I just got these—"

"Ahem!" he interrupted. "No questions, I said. Give me your boots. Socks, too." Although Nicki grumbled, she did his bidding. Tossing the requested items in Austin's direction, she twitched her bare toes and gave him a suspicious look.

"Have you gotten me some brand-new, super-deluxe hiking gear?" she asked. "Is *that* what's in that backpack of yours?"

"I'm not telling until I get the rest."

"The rest of what?"

"Your clothes. Not the underwear, just the shorts and shirt."

"In a pig's eye!" Nicki exclaimed with a laugh. "What's the matter with you, Austin? Are you getting weird in your old age?"

"Don't spoil this, Nicki. I want everything to be perfect."

"Well, everything's just going to have to be perfect with my clothes *on*!"

"It can't be. I need your shorts and shirt. For God's sake, every bathing suit you own bares more than a bra and panties. Come on. Indulge me this once."

She peered at him in indecision. Eventually, as Austin sternly stared, she found herself unzipping her shorts. What she began slowly, Nicki finished in a rush by pulling the shirt over her head, throwing the clothes in his direction, and covering herself with her bare arms to the best of her ability.

"If you tell anyone I stripped for you, I'll kill you," she threatened. Austin chuckled at that. Picking up the clothes, he put the shorts with her other things atop his backpack. The cream-colored shirt he continued to hold as he faced her once more.

"And now I'll tell you a story," he said.

"A *story*? Couldn't you give me the new outfit first?"

"This won't take long. It started with your grandparents."

"Oh, brother," she muttered under her breath.

"Everyone idolized them," Austin continued, his expression taking on a faraway look. "The great and glorious Palmers. It seems that only I could see them for the narrow-minded, sanctimonious people that they were."

Nicki caught her breath as she was swept by a sudden chill.

"You see, there was this incident when I was seventeen. I was waiting to pay my tab at the restaurant, and this guy broke in line—I mean, *right* in front of me, Nicki. He shouldn't have done that. *He* was in the wrong. Anyway, he died, and they called it manslaughter, and the glorious Palmers hushed it up. But secretly they started having me studied and evaluated and mentally dissected."

The chill graduated into freezing, numbing cold. "Give me my clothes back, will you?" Nicki said through stiff lips. Austin went on as though he hadn't heard.

"Psychopathic personality, they said. And so my illustrious sire and dam conspired to ship me off to an institution in Austria. Can you imagine? *Me,* institutionalized? I had no choice. I couldn't let it happen." Reaching into his pack, he withdrew a pair of leather gloves and started pulling them on. "They left everything to their darling Philip, of course."

She couldn't move. She could barely breathe. "Stop it," Nicki whispered. His eyes lifted to hers, and for a second she thought she was looking at the old Austin. For an instant she felt the dizzying hope that he was going to break into laughter at the obscene joke he'd managed to pull. But then, as he secured the second glove and flexed his leather-covered fingers, a look as hard and blank as stone came over him.

"Somehow Philip knew," he announced. "He never actually accused me of staging the explosion on their yacht, but I could tell by the way he looked at me that he knew. It wasn't enough that he'd inherited everything, including my rightful share. I endured his condemning looks for eleven long months."

You killed my father? My grandparents? You killed them? Anger shot through Nicki like a rocket, shattering the shell of shock. "You *beast!*" she shrieked.

Springing away from the rock, she lunged at Austin with the blind aim of pummeling his complacent face. But he was too fast. Catching her by upraised wrists, he twisted her in a raucous twirl that landed the back of her body against his front. He imprisoned her in iron arms.

"You're an agile girl, Nicki," he murmured at her ear. "But when it comes to brute strength, you're no match for me."

Shifting his grip, he grabbed her around the middle, whirled around and around until Nicki's legs were flying, then threw her. Off balance and disoriented, she landed on the hard ground. While she lay in stunned stillness, fighting to start breathing again, Austin plucked her hunter's knife from her belt, grasped her by the wrist, and slashed her open palm.

A scream tore from Nicki's throat. She tried to yank free of his hold, but couldn't as he wiped the bleeding gash with her shirt. When he finally let go, she scrambled away on her backside, forcing harsh breaths while her wide eyes took in the fact that Austin carefully folded the blood-stained shirt and set it aside before coming after her once more—the hunter's knife still menacingly in hand.

"Why are you doing this to me?" she managed.

"I didn't want to, Nicki. Really, I didn't. That's why I hired the clown. That son of a bitch Jack Casey is the one who made this necessary. If not for him, all of this would have been over with last year."

Crawling mindlessly backward, Nicki was unaware that she was drawing perilously close to the edge of the fissure. "You *hired* the clown? But what about Peni?"

"An unlucky girl. Now the police will blame her for *all* the actions of the stalker, when in fact Peni is responsible only for that clumsy attempt at the pool. Oh, and the rodeo, of course. I couldn't have staged a more timely appearance if I'd planned it."

"But *why?*" Nicki cried as tears sprang to her eyes.

"All these years what's rightfully mine has been sitting

in a trust with your name on it," Austin flatly replied. "I simply can't give you any more time. In two days you would have come into your inheritance, and an audit would have taken place. It would have revealed that someone's been dipping into the trust."

"I don't *care* about the trust!"

"You say that *now*!" he blazed. "I wager you'd be singing a different tune come Monday afternoon! But now . . . now there *is* no Monday afternoon. This way, seven years must pass before the case of Nicki Palmer's disappearance is closed, she's declared legally dead, and the trust is unfrozen. I can put things right in seven years, Nicki. And nobody will ever be the wiser."

He smiled, and his face became an eerie mask. Shrinking from the phantasmic sight, Nicki backed away, reached behind herself, and connected with nothing but air. Her wrist crashed against the rocky rim of the fissure, the same damn wrist that supported the wounded hand. Cradling the injured limb, she glared up at her uncle in tearful defiance. "You'll never get away with it!"

"I believe I will. From all appearances, it will look as though you returned from the hike to your room at the lodge, which I'll verify, and that the clown paid you a final visit. I believe a vanda orchid positioned strategically with your bloodied shirt should do the trick. Did you notice how rampant vanda is about the lodge grounds?"

"Don't do this!" she wailed as unheeded tears spilled over.

"There's no other way. Life is a journey of obstacles to be overcome, Nicki. And while all this has been somewhat cathartic, the time has come for you to get the hell out of my way."

With no further warning, Austin lunged and kicked her in the side. Nicki groaned as her body spun in the dirt, and then the ground fell from beneath her hips and she started going over the side of the fissure. She grabbed for a handhold and managed to catch the ledge. Her body hung suspended; her legs flailed and hit nothing. The opening was like a rabbit hole—straight down.

Stepping to the edge above her, Austin blocked the sun and created an ebony silhouette. "I must admit," he said in a tone of utmost casualness, "*you,* I'm going to miss."

Nicki's fingers began to slip. She clawed at the dirt.

*   *   *

There was a sloppy moment of screaming and struggling, but then her hands disappeared, and the noise came to an end in a silencing thud. Austin peered into the darkness. He couldn't see the bottom, but knew it was a twenty-five-foot drop. He'd measured it.

He tossed in the knife. After a few seconds there was a metallic clink as the blade hit rock on the invisible bottom of the crevasse. There was no other sound.

All was still, and a feeling of peace engulfed him as he stowed Nicki's belongings in his pack and continued down the steep wall of the volcano. It was always peaceful when he eliminated a problem that had come to be like a deafening buzz inside his head. Once the problem was gone, the noise stopped—first with his parents, then Philip, then Ed Coleman. Now Nicki.

The future was quietly clear now, except for a faint whir issuing from Melrose. Hell, the man was old and had a heart condition. Maybe he'd kick the bucket before he got too noisy.

The sun was low, the volcano throwing a mountainous shadow as Austin made his way through the foothills bordering the lodge. The staff was busy in the kitchen and Terrace Room, where a hundred guests would soon assemble to celebrate heiress Nicki Palmer's birthday. The police weren't due for a half hour, and there was no one to see as he stole across the shadowed grounds.

Pausing momentarily to snap a fuchsia bloom from an orchid plant along the way, Austin scaled the stairs to the unobtrusive back entrance of the suite he'd reserved for himself and the birthday girl. Leaving the door ajar, he proceeded directly into his own bedroom and discarded his hiking boots. Only then did he cross the receiving area in stockinged feet to Nicki's rooms.

It took less than three minutes to set the stage. Her boots, socks, and shorts he left in a casual pile on the floor of the dressing area. Looking through the closet, he withdrew the royal blue dress she'd brought for the party and spread it across the bed. Finally, he dropped the bloodied shirt on the bathroom floor and let the orchid flutter down to rest upon it. As a final touch he turned on the shower and left it running.

Before leaving her quarters, he paused for a last, scrutinizing survey. Satisfied that everything was as it should be, Austin returned to his rooms, stripped off his gloves and hiking gear, and got into the shower with a whistle on his lips.

Regardless of his efforts to make it from the upcountry to Hilo in record time, it was a quarter to six when Jack reached the airport. Leaving the Cadillac in a fifteen-minute zone, he raced down the terminal corridor just as arriving passengers were filing through the gate. Catherine was behind a group of a dozen or so. She spotted him, smiled, and emotion rose inside Jack so fast and hard that he ached with it.

She was wearing a slim pink dress and had a lei of white orchids around her neck. When she walked up to him, he took her in his arms and held her close. "Aloha," he mumbled, then came to his senses and backed away.

"Aloha to *you*," she returned with perceptible breathlessness, a rare slip for always-in-control Catherine.

A grin tugged at Jack's lips. "Baggage claim is this way," he said, and they joined the column of people streaming along the hall. After a moment Catherine glanced his way.

"So, tell me," she said. "What have you been up to?"

"Not much," he countered. "Everything okay at home?"

"Fine, thanks."

"Your father's funeral went well?"

"Yes. It was sad, of course. But considering the many years he'd been an invalid, I considered the turnout quite a tribute."

"Aunt Sybil didn't find some way to spoil everything?"

"My, she made quite an impression on you, didn't she?"

"I wouldn't call it an impression. It was more like a dent."

"Well," Catherine began with a laugh, "I admit she made a scene at the reading of the will. Father provided generously for her, but he left the bulk of his estate to me, including Winslow House. That was what set her off, so . . . I gave it to her."

"No kidding. You gave her the whole house just like that?"

"Just like that."

Jack perused Catherine's profile. "Did it feel good?"

"Pretty damn good," she forthrightly returned.

With a hearty laugh he planted an arm around her shoulders, and they walked in cozy closeness to the baggage area. After flagging a valet, Jack collected the Caddie and circled around to pick her up. After a few minutes peering out the window like an excited child, Catherine turned to concentrate on him.

Settling back in her seat, she folded her arms. "You managed to arrange things so you'd get here a full day ahead of me, and I'm sure you've been a busy bee. I hope you've managed to find out about Nicki. Is she at the ranch?"

"No," Jack answered without hesitation. "Nicki is not currently at the ranch." He glanced aside and beheld the epitome of crestfallen disappointment. "But she's due to return there before long."

Catherine perked up at that. "Before long? How long?"

"Look, Catherine. I'll tell you everything I've managed to find out, okay? But the hotel is just ahead, it's half past six, and I've been running around all day. Why don't we check you in, get cleaned up, and discuss things over dinner?"

She gave him a skeptical look, but her effervescence returned as they arrived at the Hawaiian Sun and she took a look at her quarters, which she enthusiastically toured as Jack took care of the bellhop. When he closed the door and walked into the room, he spotted Catherine on the atrium patio. Framed against the backdrop of a tropical waterfall, she made a lovely picture.

"Isn't this the most beautiful thing you've ever seen?" she asked, spreading her arms wide.

"I'd have to give that an affirmative," he replied. Jack stepped onto the balcony and was struck once more by the steamy atmosphere of the lush, fern-covered mountain, the cacophony of splashing water and squawking birds.

"Look at the colors of the birds," Catherine said. "They're the brightest reds and blues and yellows I've ever seen. And the flowers. I recognize hibiscus and a couple of the others, but which of them is making that delicious fragrance?"

Moving up behind her, Jack rested a hand on her left shoulder and pointed over her right. "You're probably talking about plumeria. See those clusters of cream-colored flowers? They have a particularly sweet smell. They're used a lot in leis."

As he finished speaking, it was the most natural thing in the world for Jack to run his palm along the bare length of her arm. Her skin was smooth and warm. He caught himself about the time he reached her wrist, but by then Catherine was pulling away.

"I'm very glad to see you, Jack," she said as he stared at her back. "But I wish you wouldn't . . ."

"Keep touching you?" he supplied with ungovernable sharpness. Yet when she turned to face him, there was such beauty and warmth in her face that he couldn't hold on to his sharp tongue.

"I promised I'd try," he added with a tight grin. "Guess I'll have to try harder."

With downcast eyes Catherine reached out, gave his hand a fleeting caress, then withdrew her fingers. "So will I," she murmured so quietly that he barely heard. When she looked up, her eyes were glistening with feeling. "Don't make me wait until dinner to hear about Nicki. Please."

His gaze darted between the haunting blue eyes. "All right," he surrendered. "I'll tell you what I've learned, as long as you swear not to go off like a half-cocked pistol."

"Is there a reason you think I will?"

"I think you're anxious to see the ranch and everything you've dreamed about." The exotic backdrop of rushing water and lively birds couldn't have been more contrary to Jack's grim state of mind as he considered embroiling Catherine in the mysteries of Palmer Ranch. "I think you're giving no thought to the way these people could react when you show up."

"You mean, they might not be altogether glad to see me."

"Some of them might not be. That's exactly right."

"Still, I need to know what you know. Tell me, Jack."

He peered at her another stalling instant before saying, "Wait here. I've got something for you." Striding next door to his room, Jack swiftly returned with Whitmore's cattleya orchid. Catherine gasped with pleasure as he handed it over.

"It's exquisite," she exclaimed.

"It's from the doctor who pronounced you dead thirty years ago," Jack bluntly returned. Beginning with the information he'd discovered on the death certificates and how it led him to the retired doctor-turned-orchid-farmer, he continued with his trip to the ranch and the story Malia had divulged about the night the twins were born.

"She *gave* me to her friend Kila?" Catherine chimed in a disbelieving voice. "Why?"

"All she would say was that it was in your best interest. Then she shut up tight. I suspect she's protecting someone."

"The man she loves," Catherine supplied. "Austin Palmer."

"Very good," Jack pronounced with a passing smile.

The tropical sounds of the atrium closed in as she continued to peruse him with obvious expectation. "Go on."

He gave his shoulders a light shrug. "That's it."

"You still haven't told me about Nicki," Catherine pointedly returned. "Where is she? When is she coming back?"

"Okay, okay," Jack said, his brows furling in scowling lines. "Here it is. Nicki's on the island."

"Now?" Catherine whispered, her eyes flying wide. He nodded. "Where?" she added.

"Palmer's throwing a birthday bash for her at the Volcano Lodge tonight."

"The Volcano Lodge? Where is that?"

"About an hour's drive from here, I'd say. But if you're thinking of going there tonight, you can forget it."

Catherine gazed at him. "You know I can't forget it."

Jack lifted an exasperated palm in her direction. "You see? This is why I didn't want to tell you. I knew you'd want to go, and it absolutely is not the thing to do, for several reasons."

"Such as?"

"Such as, I thought you wanted to keep a lid on this thing about you and Nicki."

"I do."

"Well, I'd like to know how you expect to crash her birthday party without blowing the whole thing sky-high."

Catherine gave him a look of infinite patience. "I'm not suggesting that we *burst* in, but that we *blend* in. There will be a lot of people there."

"Yeah, but you and Nicki will be the only two with the same *face*!" Jack objected. "Is this how you want to meet her after all this time? With a bunch of noisy party guests in the background?"

"No," Catherine softly answered. "I just want to see her, Jack. That's all I want from tonight—just to see my sister, for the first time, with my eyes wide open."

He stared at her, and the will to say no gradually slipped out of him, like air from a deflating balloon. Jack drew and released a heavy breath. "We're having dinner first," he then announced. "I'm starving, and we've got reservations downstairs for an hour from now."

A brilliant smile broke across Catherine's face. "Okay."

"Sure, it's okay," he grumbled. "Now that you've got what you want. I swear, Catherine. You play me like a damn violin."

Her smile faltered. "Don't say that."

"I *will* say that. Every time we're together you talk me into doing things I know damn well are wrong."

"Don't be mad," she murmured. Stepping forward, she lifted a hand as though to caress his cheek. "Please try to understand—" Jack captured her hand before it could make a connection.

"Let's just drop it, okay?" Releasing her hand, he stepped curtly away. "Can you be ready in forty-five minutes?"

When he left, Catherine wandered inside, executed a twirling pirouette, and fell back on the bed. He was angry . . . but he would be back. In less than an hour, Jack would be back. The miracle of his presence still stunned her, as did the fireworks that erupted each time they were close.

And Nicki was on the island. Here. Now. As the thought registered once more, Catherine received such a heady rush of closeness, she almost felt as though she could cry out her name, and Nicki somehow would hear.

Nicki . . . Jack . . . how she loved them both—the sister of her blood, the man of her dreams. There were shadows hanging over the three of them—Catherine couldn't deny that—but at this moment, with the sound of a waterfall in her ears and the fragrance of flowers in her head, she wondered if maybe the magic of this sunny isle could dispel any shadow.

The first sensation that burst onto the plane of consciousness was the throb in her head. Bang! . . . Bang! . . . Bang! . . . Nicki's skull reverberated with each boom like the cavity of a bass drum.

Fragments of information flitted into her brain, spinning and whirling like windswept leaves before settling on a barren landscape. It was cold. A million tiny, pointy rocks were biting into the flesh of her back and legs. And there was a smell of sulfur. She forced her eyelids to part and saw only darkness, except for a gray sheet of daylight sifting halfway down the stone wall overlooking her as she lay on her back . . . in a hole?

Seizing on the light, Nicki strained to focus. The wall wasn't made of stone, but of porous rock. Lava rock. Spreading the fingers of her left hand, she felt the roughened surface on which she was lying and confirmed what her eyes implied. Lava rock. She was inside a volcano.

Was she sleeping? Was this a nightmare?

Planting her palm firmly on the floor beside her, Nicki pushed up to a sitting position. Her head felt as though it might split open, the pain more sharp than she'd ever experienced in any dream. Supporting herself with her left arm, she lifted her right hand to her temple and became aware of a searing sting across her palm, which was wet and sticky. Blood. The realization panicked her to action.

Regardless of aches and pains that seemed to shoot through the whole of her body, Nicki shifted onto hands and knees and crawled to the wall. Grabbing hold of the rock, she determinedly hauled herself to her feet—which were bare—and clung to the precipice as it seemed to take on life and shrink away from her.

God, she was wearing nothing but her underwear. She *must* be dreaming.

And yet the longer she managed to keep herself vertical, the more certain Nicki became that she was fully awake. Having done their job, the five senses made room for the sixth. And suddenly she was struck by the certainty that this was no nightmare. Someone had put her here to die.

A nauseating chill swept over her. The clown. Looking

sharply to the opening some twenty feet above, Nicki half
expected to see his monstrous face peering down at her.
But the strip of daylight remained mercifully empty.

Allowing her eyes to close, Nicki rested her cheek against
the rock. Why the hell couldn't she remember anything?
What had the son of a bitch done? Drugged her, stripped
her, tossed her down a hole, and abandoned her for dead?

Though she'd allowed herself only moments of rest, when
she looked once more toward the light, she saw that it had
grown noticeably dim. Night was falling, and the illuminated strip reaching down the wall of rock was shorter by
half. Soon there would be no light at all in the subterra-
nean channel.

Nicki turned all her energy toward scaling the ninety-
degree incline. Plastering herself against the rocky wall, she
found holds with bare toes as well as fingers, and pulled her
body upward over juts and edges that scraped and jabbed.

A good climber never looked down, and Nicki felt no
compunction to do so as she inched her way up the sheer
face. Looking down never did anybody any good. The crevasse below was an inky black prison. She concentrated on
the escape hatch of dwindling light above. If only she could
reach it, the clown could be damned.

"Son of a bitch," she muttered, and had made valiant
progress halfway up the incline when a foothold crumbled
beneath her weight. She dug into the remaining points of
contact, only to have the second precarious foothold give
way. She hung by her hands, sought to better her grip, and
inflicted a new rip on the wound in her right palm.

Involuntarily recoiling from the pain, Nicki spent frenzied seconds trying to correct the mistake before the gravity
she'd defied for so long finally claimed her. Tumbling painfully down to her starting point, she landed with a jarring
thud.

The banging at her temples reached a new crescendo.
Locked in deafening isolation with the pulsing sound of it,
Nicki looked above, where the light was receding up the
rocky wall like an outgoing tide deserting a beach.

As she watched, it crawled relentlessly away—six
inches . . . three inches . . . two . . . one. . . .

When she was plunged into blackness, Nicki threw back
her ringing head and screamed.

Chapter Twenty-one

Standing before the bathroom vanity, Catherine fixed a dangling earring at her ear, then whirled as a scream split the air. She hurried into the bedroom, where the chatter of birds spilled through the open doors to the atrium. As she listened, she heard a high-pitched squawk that resembled a shriek.

Relax, she told her herself, but knew it would do no good. Tonight her nerves were strung so tightly that every sensation seemed to carry a double impact. The island colors were doubly bright, the sounds twice as vivid.

Moving to the dresser, she took an assessing look in the mirror. The royal blue silk was from the Eliot days, which in retrospect were so hazy they seemed a mirage. Reminiscent of a sarong, the bodice crossed in front and fastened behind the neck. From there the silk followed the contours of her body to the ankle, with a split to the knee on one side. It was a simple but elegant dress, and the dangling, burnished gold earrings set with mock sapphires added a nice touch of flash.

Sitting down on the bed long enough to put on evening sandals, Catherine walked to the atrium doors. The feeling of having stepped into a magical place continued. The intense beauty of the tropics was new, yet somehow familiar. She'd come into the world here, surrounded by miles of ocean. Maybe that was why she'd always had such a love of water. Maybe something inside had always related it to her birthplace.

A few minutes later Jack arrived, and was heart-stoppingly handsome in the splendor of a white double-breasted suit, black shirt, and silk tie. "Wow," he said as he looked her over.

"That's what *I* say," she returned. "You're wearing a suit."

Jack glanced down the front of himself. "Yep. That's what it is. You seem surprised."

"I just never pictured you all dressed up."

"I'm not entirely uncouth, you know. Are you ready?" he concluded, offering her his arm. And once again the spellbinding magic closed in.

Hawaiian music welcomed them as they entered the Polynesian Luau, the hotel's bayside dining room and nightclub. One wall was open to the beach, where torches ringed a stage of sand. The interior was arranged in a tiered semicircle facing the performing area, with sheltering palmettos and ferns creating nooks where wicker peacock chairs presided at candlelit tables.

As the maître d' led the way to the table Jack had reserved, Catherine noted that most of the nooks were full. Still, there was an air of privacy and romance. From their central position on the primary tier of tables, they had an orchestra view of the performing stage. She glanced in the direction of the darkening beach. The purplish rose streaks of sundown sifted across the sand, mixing with the flickering orange of torchlight.

"This is quite a place," she commented, looking back to Jack.

"The food is supposed to be good, too," he replied. "*And* there's a Polynesian review."

"It was nice of you to think of it."

Candlelight danced in his eyes. "My pleasure."

"In fact, *everything* you've arranged for this trip has been wonderful—the travel, the hotel, everything."

Jack cradled his chin in his palm and gazed across the table. "Guess I'm just that kind of wonderful guy."

Mimicking his posture, Catherine propped her chin and looked into his eyes. "Guess so," she smilingly agreed.

A bright light flashed across the table. They turned to see a young Japanese man with a camera standing nearby. "*Aloha,*" he greeted with a friendly grin, and strolled up to their table. "That was a nice shot. I'll stop by later and let you have a look at the print."

After the photographer moved on, a smiling waitress with long black hair to her waist appeared, and the evening progressed with a "luau feast for two." So big that it had to be delivered by a pair of waiters, the flower-trimmed platter was as long as the table was wide, and was brimming with a buffet of Hawaiian favorites. There were delicacies of pork and an array of seafoods, exotic fruits and breads, and a delicious glaze made from macadamia nuts.

As Catherine and Jack explored their way through unfamiliar dishes, the meal became an adventure of jokes and laughter. Catherine had never known such a night, nor such a feeling. Now and then she caught herself staring at Jack—amazed by the simple act of being with him, and at the way her hidden love continued to grow.

The smiling waitress brought a dessert topped with flaming Kahlúa just before the house lights went down and the entertainment began. A quartet of musicians ran onto the torchlit beach and started playing a variety of drums with their palms. The crowd began to clap with the beat, and a moment later two columns of hip-swinging Polynesian dancers, male and female, filed in from each side of the stage.

Dressed in bright red and yellow costumes, with wreaths of greenery on their heads and leis about their necks, the performers gyrated with abandon to the native beat. When the opening number came to a dramatic finale, the audience madly applauded, and the program continued with a series of ceremonial dances, some featuring soloists twirling fire and swords.

At the end of the show, the dancers ran into the audience and drew partners from the crowd to join in a group rendition of the traditional hula. "Oh, my gosh," Catherine mumbled as a brawny dancer, whom she remembered from a daring display with swords, rushed toward their table.

Stepping up beside her, the bare-chested man extended his hand in invitation. After a moment's hesitation, and a cheer of encouragement from Jack, Catherine rose from her chair with a laugh and was drawn onto the torchlit beach.

Mesmerized by the sight of the blonde in blue—chuckling as she moved her hips in admirable response to her instructor's lead—Jack was unaware he was totally engrossed in Catherine until a voice over his shoulder made him look around with a start.

"Your lady looks good out there," the photographer

said. "Here's the print," he added, and lay the picture on the table. "You guys could be in the movies."

Jack held up the photo—candlelight, flowers, a couple gazing into each other's eyes. The kid was right. It *did* look like it came straight out of a movie, like it was too perfect to be real. "Good work," Jack complimented, and after amply tipping the photographer, tucked the picture in the breast pocket of his jacket. The crowd-participation hula ended a few minutes later. Joining in the round of applause, he rose to his feet as Catherine arrived at the table—bright-eyed and out of breath.

"If anyone had ever told me I'd get up in front of a crowd of people and do the hula, I wouldn't have believed it," she vowed.

"You looked great," Jack pronounced, and sat back down as she took her seat. "Obviously you're a natural-born hula girl."

She laughed. "For one brief shining moment, I *felt* like one, anyway." Little by little Catherine's expression of merriment settled. "I'm having the best time of my life to-night, Jack."

"Yeah, it's nice," he said. "Real nice."

An air of intimacy bloomed as they looked into each other's eyes. Then the lights came up, the dreamy air dissolved, and the supper crowd began to depart. Catherine sat back in her chair.

"Looks like time is up," she offered, her implication clear.

Jack frowned as the idea of the Volcano Lodge party dawned fresh in his mind. He still didn't like the thought of crashing it, but sensed that if he tried to put his foot down, Catherine would rebel in that quiet way of hers, somehow give him the slip, and end up going on her own. *That,* he would not have.

"All right," he resignedly muttered. "Let's get going."

It was after eleven when they turned onto the rolling road through the foothills of Pali Waipi'o. Bearing right at a fork with a sign to the Volcano Lodge, they rounded a curve and found the drive blocked with a barricade of police vehicles, their blue lights flashing with an aura of emergency against the night.

Jack brought the Cadillac to a short halt. A dozen officers milled about the scene, one of them talking to a couple of reporters beside a TV news van. Beyond the police barricade the lodge was ablaze with light from one end to the other, the shadows of a crowd flickering across bright windows.

"What the hell's going on?" he mumbled.

"An accident?" Catherine suggested.

Jack scanned the hodgepodge of vehicles in their path. One of them was a police canine unit. "No. It's something else." He rolled down the window as one of the men in uniform approached the car. "What's the problem, Officer?"

"I'm afraid I'm not at liberty to say, sir. I'll have to ask you to move along."

"We're on our way to a party at the lodge."

"The lodge is sealed for the time being. No one goes in. No one comes out. You'll have to move along now."

As the officer stepped back, Jack turned to Catherine, who gazed at him in baleful silence. "I'm sorry, baby," he murmured. "I guess it wasn't meant to be." Driving forward, he started to make a U-turn. The headlights swept across the barricade, spotlighting a slender, dark-haired man in a tailored suit. Tanaka. Stomping on the brake, Jack shifted into park.

"Stay here, Catherine," he directed, and strode swiftly toward the lieutenant before other officers could flag him down. Although there had been times when Jack scorned the amount of police support he'd received in protecting Nicki, he'd come to realize that Tanaka had done all he could. He was about Jack's own age, and a mutually respecting camaraderie had sprung up between them at the end of the clown affair.

"Lieutenant!" Jack called as he drew near.

Glancing around, Tanaka excused himself from a couple of patrolmen and greeted him with a smiling handshake. "I didn't know you were back on the island, Casey."

"Just got back yesterday."

"Let me guess. You came for Nicki Palmer's birthday party."

"In a way, yes."

"When did you last speak with Nicki?"

A bad feeling came over Jack as he regarded the lieutenant. The short-lived smile of greeting was gone, in its place the all-business look of an interrogator. "I haven't spoken to Nicki since that day last September when you visited me at the hospital. What's going on? Has something happened to her?"

Tanaka inclined his head in the direction of the TV van. "See those reporters? What I told them is the bare facts as we know them. Sometime between six and eight-thirty this evening, Miss Palmer was abducted from the Volcano Lodge by parties unknown."

"Damn!" Jack bellowed. Spinning around with the impulse to hit something, he kicked futilely at the ground and sent a spray of sandy soil flying.

"As I pointed out," Tanaka said, "the media is here, and there's no keeping a lid on the publicity this time. However, there *were* details that I held back."

Jack quickly turned. "What details?"

"Normally I wouldn't share these things with a civilian. But considering your history with Miss Palmer, I'll make an exception, *if* you can keep your mouth shut."

"Come on, Tanaka. You know me. What happened? Was she hurt?"

"There's evidence to suggest she might have been."

"Damn!" Jack swore again.

"And that's not all. The abductor left behind a calling card, a single wild orchid."

The blue lights of the patrol cars flashed across the lieutenant's face as Jack stared. "It's not the clown, Tanaka," he said finally. "That bastard met up with his maker the night we fell. I'm sure of it."

The lieutenant gave him a piercing look. "There's something else. A few nights ago, after the Waimea Rodeo, Miss Palmer was assaulted by a woman who claimed responsibility for the clown attacks last summer."

"A *woman*?" Jack hooted. "No way. I fought with the guy. It was a man. And he's dead."

"A body was never recovered, Jack. And the woman I'm speaking of is no frail member of any weaker sex. She used to be a *paniolo* at Palmer Ranch. Maybe you met her— Peni Kahala."

"Yeah, I met her, and she's a big, strong-looking girl. But she was *not* the clown I fought with that night on the cliff."

Tanaka shrugged. "I'll take your word for it, but I've gotta say that this thing tonight was pulled off with the same precision that was always the clown's MO. The perpetrator slipped past the surveillance of a four-man police team, and no one saw a thing. No one heard anything. There are no prints. No leads. Miss Palmer returned from a hike with her uncle, laid out a dress for the party, turned on the shower, and vanished.

"Now consider *this:* Four nights ago Peni Kahala confessed to the commission of violent acts against Miss Palmer, then managed to elude police and make a getaway. Kahala even furnished a motive, jealousy over a man. And now *she's* a fugitive, and Miss Palmer is missing. Between you and me, Jack, Peni Kahala makes a damn fine-looking suspect. I just hope the charge doesn't turn out to be murder."

Jack swallowed hard. "You said there was evidence to suggest Nicki was hurt?"

"A hunter's knife is missing from her belt, and there's blood on her hiking shirt. The crime lab has it. I'll give you ten to one that when the results come back, the blood is Miss Palmer's."

Jack rubbed at his aching forehead. "Man, I hate this."

"Sorry to cut this short," Tanaka said, "but it's going to take me all night to finish questioning the extremely pampered guests inside. I can't wait to see what kind of mood they'll be in by dawn." Reaching into his pocket, he produced a business card. "Give me till morning, then page me at this number. I'll fill you in on what we've learned."

"Thanks, Lieutenant."

With a brisk salute Tanaka headed for the entrance to the lodge. Jack walked slowly back to the Cadillac. How the hell was he going to tell Catherine? As it turned out, she already knew.

"It's Nicki, isn't it?" she asked as he got in the car.

"How did you know?"

"I saw how you reacted when you heard the news. Just tell me this much very quickly, Jack. She's not dead, is she?"

"There's no evidence to that effect," he answered carefully. "But the situation isn't good."

Jack had to give her credit. As he recounted what Tanaka said, Catherine sat still as stone. It wasn't until he finished that she spun in the car seat and presented him with her back. Jack placed a hand on her shoulder and felt it rising and falling as she apparently fought for control.

"Will you be okay?" he asked finally.

"We were so close," she whispered. "It isn't fair."

A grim look spread over Jack's face. "No. It isn't." Shifting into drive, he turned sharply away from the police barricade and started down the road to the highway. Catherine looked around.

"Where are we going?" she asked.

"Back to the hotel."

"All the way back to Hilo? No!"

Jack glanced her way, surprised by her adamant tone. "What did you expect? We can't stay here. The lodge is sealed."

"But surely there must be other lodges or inns around here."

"Yeah, I guess there might be. But as it happens, *our* accommodations are back in Hilo."

"We could look for other accommodations."

"Why would we want to do that?"

"Because I don't want to leave."

With a quick look in the rearview mirror, Jack stopped the car in the middle of the deserted road and stretched an arm along the back of her seat. "You're not being logical, Catherine."

"I suppose not," she replied. "I suppose I'm going by instinct, like you always do. Look, Jack, if you don't want to stay with me, I understand. All I ask is that you find me a place nearby for the night."

If his face bore any resemblance to the way he felt, Jack assumed it looked like a thundercloud. "You *know* I won't do that. Dammit, Catherine. All our stuff is in Hilo."

"So we rough it for a night." He stared at her. But she only stared back, then delivered a ringing blow. "Do you recall that first night in Charleston, when I put you up at my place?"

"Oh, yeah. I recall it."

"You *said* you owed me," she curtly reminded.

"How timely of you to remember that at this particular moment," Jack barked. Catherine merely lifted her brows. With a rueful shake of his head, he started the car moving once more.

It was a late Saturday night in one of the most popular resort spots of the world. Nearly an hour of searching elapsed before they found a solitary vacancy in a cheap motel on a back road west of Hawaii Volcanoes National Park. The room was furnished with a double bed, a TV, a phone, and a wooden chair.

"At least it's clean," Catherine announced as she stepped into the tiny bathroom. "And there's a complimentary tube of toothpaste on the sink."

"Great news, honey," Jack chimed from the other side of the wall, where he'd taken a perch on the hardback chair.

Catherine strolled into the bedroom. "This night sure started out differently, didn't it?"

"Yep. And this crackerbox isn't exactly the kind of place I had in mind to spend it."

She emitted a short, giddy laugh. "I guess not. After all your lovely arrangements, we end up here. The lesson of the night seems to be life isn't fair."

"You're getting punchy," Jack replied with a slight frown. "It's almost six in the morning back in Charleston. Why don't you lie down and try to get some sleep?"

Lifting her hands, Catherine tipped her head and swept back her hair. The gesture caused her body to arch, and the silky blue dress to cling. Although Jack was sure she didn't intend it, the effect was one of sheer sexiness. As she looked back in his direction, her hair settled about her face like a golden cloud.

"I can't sleep now."

"No?" he uttered, his throat suddenly dry as the Sahara.

"No," she confirmed, and bent over to remove her sandals.

Jack's eyes zeroed on the curve of her hip. Swiftly rising to his feet, he put his mind on unbuttoning the double-breasted jacket and hanging it about the back of the chair. As he proceeded to yank his tie loose and strip it from his neck, he noted from the corner of his eye that Catherine meandered around the foot of the bed to the window. Pulling aside a curtain covered with giant yellow flowers, she gazed on a parking lot bereft of decoration, save a neon light that flashed alternating glows into the room—blue, white . . . blue, white.

"Hardly an atrium view, is it?" she said.

"Hardly," Jack grunted.

Letting the curtain swish back into place, Catherine left the window and strolled toward him, her hips gently swinging so that the silk shifted in seductive blue streaks with every step. Jack unconsciously freed the top two buttons of his shirt as his heart began to pound. It was flat-out hammering by the time she stopped before him and looked up to meet his eyes.

"Now what?" he mumbled as he peered down at her.

"Perhaps you could page Lieutenant Tanaka and tell him where we are. That way, if something breaks, he could let us know."

Jack's brows rose. "Not bad, Catherine."

"You mean maybe I'm not crazy for wanting to stay nearby?"

"Maybe not," he surrendered, and walked around her to the phone, grateful for the chance to put his mind on something other than how desirable she was.

A quarter of an hour later, Catherine was brushing her teeth with her finger when the phone rang. Turning off the water, she listened to Jack's voice. "Conclusive, huh?" . . . Yeah, I got it . . . Thanks, Tanaka." Patting her chin dry, Catherine laid the towel aside and walked into the room as Jack hung up the phone.

"What is it?" she asked.

He turned and gave her a solemn look. "The crime lab finished the tests on Nicki's shirt. There's no doubt. The blood is hers."

Catching her lip between her teeth, Catherine walked to the bed and sank to a seat on the bright yellow flowers of the bedspread. Jack came over and sat down beside her.

"The lieutenant thinks she's been killed, doesn't he?" Catherine said, her gaze fixed on the wooden floor.

"He . . . fears the worst."

She looked up into Jack's eyes. "And what do *you* think?"

"I don't know what to think. I'd rather not speculate."

"She's not dead, Jack. Somehow I know it."

He smiled as he lifted a strand of hair behind her shoulder. "I'll take your word for it," he answered, and was caught off guard as Catherine turned inside his uplifted arm and leaned her head against his chest.

"First my father, now this," she said. "Suddenly I'm tired."

Jack settled his arm around her and was filled with sensations ranging from the throb of wanting her to the ache of feeling her hurt. "You need to sleep," he said eventually. "In the morning we'll think things through, but neither of us will be worth a damn if we don't get some rest."

Stoically pulling away from her, Jack turned down the covers and beckoned. When Catherine climbed into bed, he briskly tucked her in and turned off the lamp. The room dissolved into shadows that shifted with the rhythm of muted flashes from the neon sign beyond the window. He took a seat in the stiff chair.

Catherine settled on her side. She was weary to the bone, but her mind was painfully alert. Each time she closed her eyes, she saw Nicki's face and was swamped with terror. What she longed for most in the world was to wrap herself up in Jack like a blanket and muffle the fear that thudded inside her with every heartbeat.

"Can I ask you a favor?" she said finally.

"What is it?" his deep voice responded through the darkness.

"Do you think you could just . . . hold me for a while?"

A moment of silence passed before she heard the creak of the wooden chair as Jack's weight left it. Crawling onto the bed behind her, he stretched out atop the covers, put his arms around her, and drew her close. Catherine soaked up the comfort of his solid, bearlike embrace.

"Jack?" she murmured after a few minutes.

"I'm here."

"Nicki isn't dead. I know it. Do you believe me?"

"Yeah, baby. I believe you. Now get some rest."

Stalwartly shutting her eyes, Catherine willed herself to sleep . . . and dream of Nicki.

Early morning mist drifted across the grounds, reflecting the dawn in shifting wisps of pink as the familiar white limousine cruised up the drive to the ranch. Austin was returning with Melrose. The police were holding on to the Ferrari.

Leaving the window, Malia went into the bath and splashed her face with cold water for the countless time

during the past eight hours. She took a few more minutes
to secure her hair in a fresh coil atop her head before
hurriedly departing her chamber. She'd always loved the
rambling halls of the *hale,* but today they seemed intermi-
nably long and dreary. Reaching the study, she paused inside the threshold. Melrose was propped in a chair and
looked exhausted. Austin was pouring himself a Scotch.

"Is there any news?" Malia asked.

"No," Austin replied. "It's a great mystery."

"A great *tragedy,* I'd say," Melrose put in.

"Yes, of course." Turning with his glass in hand, Austin
rested a hip against the bar. "That's what I meant. Malia
said it months ago—hell hath no fury, and so on. It's obvious Peni Kahala has gone completely out of her mind."

Progressing into the room, Malia rested her hands on the
back of a leather chair. "Is there no trail at all?"

"None the police have been able to find," Austin
answered.

"I just don't understand how she could have done this
without leaving a trace."

"Neither can anyone else," Melrose interjected.

"Apparently Peni is more a master at her craft than anyone would have thought."

"You're right, Austin," Melrose swiftly returned. "Peni
would have to be damnably clever, indeed. You were right
there in the same suite of rooms, and yet she managed to
slip in, attack Nicki, and make away with her—all without
stirring your notice."

"As I told the police, she must have waited until I got
in the shower before making her move. At about eight
o'clock, on my way downstairs, I stopped by Nicki's room,
heard the water running, and assumed she'd be down
shortly."

"Leaving it to me to discover that she was missing a half
hour later," Melrose observed.

"That was the way it turned out," Austin remarked, and
tossed down the Scotch.

"I must say you're bearing up remarkably well under the
stress," Melrose said in an odd tone that drew Malia's eye.
His bushy eyebrows were low as he peered in Austin's
direction.

"Each of us handles grief in his own fashion," Austin returned, and started pouring himself another drink.

"Mighty damn convenient, isn't it?" Melrose continued. "Two days before Nicki is scheduled to open her trust, she disappears. If she isn't found, it will take seven years for her to be declared legally dead. And she won't be found, will she?"

"How the hell should I know?" Austin retorted.

"Oh, I think you know," Melrose returned in a cutting tone. "It's clear to me now. I made peace with my fate, but you never did. And now you've got seven years to cover your tracks."

A chill swept over Malia. "What is he saying, Austin?"

"I have no idea. He's gone senile."

"I'm talking about using dormant money to make a fortune for three men with the nerve to use it," Melrose stated. "That was how you put it, wasn't it, Austin? Five million in trust money funneled through a corporate account was all it would take."

"Shut up, old man," Austin said.

"All you needed was Ed Coleman, and me, and Nicki's money. Only just when it started paying off last spring, an earthquake buried the whole damn emerald mine under a Colombian mountain. Ed got panicky, and the next thing you know—bang, he's dead."

Malia's fingers gripped the leather-backed chair in a convulsive clench. "Please, Austin. What is he talking about?" Her golden-haired *kane* sent her a reassuring smile.

"A business deal gone bad," he explained. "Though why Melrose has chosen to bring it up at this moment, I can't imagine." Austin turned a hard look in Melrose's direction. "If I were you, I'd forget about such things. You've earned your retirement. Enjoy it. I suggest a long relaxing trip far away from here."

Pushing out of his chair, Melrose walked toward him. "You'd like that, wouldn't you? You'd like me out of your hair. But it's not going to happen. I'm going to stick around, and nose around, until I figure out *exactly* what happened to Nicki."

Austin lifted his glass. "I wish you the best of luck."

As he tossed down the liquor, Melrose angrily closed

the distance between them. "You're behind this, Austin. I feel it."

Setting his empty glass aside with a clink, Austin faced the older man with flushed cheeks that belied the calm of his voice. "We've been friends for many years, Melrose, and it's obvious you're deranged with grief, so I'll let that pass."

"Yes, we've been friends for many years, but it's only now that I truly know you. You're behind Nicki's disappearance as surely as you were behind what happened to Ed. Who's next? Me?"

"I refuse to listen to this," Austin snapped. "I'm going to bed." He started to turn away, but Melrose caught him by the shirt collar and snatched him nose-to-nose.

"You're a monster," Melrose quietly accused.

Grabbing Melrose's wrist, Austin ripped it from his throat. "And you'd do well to remember it, old man."

After a tense few seconds he released Melrose with a flinging push and stalked away from the bar. He said nothing as he passed the spot where Malia stood rooted, feeling as though her breath had turned to stone within her body.

She mutely watched as her beloved continued from the room toward the hall leading to his chamber. As he passed through shafts of morning sunlight, his hair glistened like gold. She failed to hear as Melrose approached, and looked up with a start when he put a hand on her shoulder.

"I'm going home, Malia."

"All the way back to Hilo?"

"I don't think I'm going to be spending as much time around here as I used to. Will you call me if you hear from the police?"

When Melrose left the house, Malia wandered aimlessly in the path Austin had taken. Perhaps if Jack Casey had not brought back the memory mere hours ago, the brilliance of her love for Austin would have dazzled her eyes like always. As it was, however, a cloud of sadness hung over the halls, overshadowing the old blinding flame, allowing the fearful shades of that long-ago night to take shape and be seen.

As though it were only yesterday, Malia saw herself at a panicked age of nineteen, rushing into the nursery adjoining the mistress's room to grab more towels for the bleeding. The babe she'd hastily deposited in the crib was only minutes old, still heartily crying her lungs out. And Austin was standing over her . . . with a pillow in his hands.

He looked up, and it was as though there was no Austin behind that face. It had been as void of emotion as a painted portrait, as empty of feeling as a hollow shell. "Help me, Malia," he commanded. "Help me regain what's rightfully mine."

The mistress was screaming. The baby was crying. The doorbell rang. The emergency team had arrived. Her lover's eyes froze her like blue ice.

"I'll take care of *them*," he said. "You get rid of *this*."

He'd never asked what she did with the baby. When Malia returned to the ranch that midnight, Austin met her at the door, swept her up in his arms, and made such passionate love to her that her mind became dazed to everything else. The next day, when the surprising news of a second birth reached the ranch, he launched his fantasy, and everyone had lived it ever since. The first twin was stillborn and buried in the family graveyard.

In ensuing days Malia had reconciled things in a fashion that allowed her to live with them. It had been a moment of madness bursting forth one tragic night after years of Austin enduring the pain of being slighted in favor of his brother. His pent-up anger had exploded against Philip's offspring. But the passing moment of insanity would never come again, just as that foreign and chillingly empty visage would never again exist.

But now, after thirty years, the image of that blank face glared at Malia from the shadowed hall. And once again she felt the frigidity of its icy eyes.

Turning into Nicki's room, she crossed to the bed, where the embroidered quilt was carefully folded at the foot. A sob escaped her as Malia covered her face with her hands. Oh, God. How blind had she allowed herself to be?

Managing only to scrape elbows and knees and start the wound in her right palm aching, Nicki must have tried to scale her prison wall a dozen times before accepting the reality that every effort she made only rendered her mission more impossible.

The fissure she'd tumbled down was a rift zone vent that

once released pressure from within the volcano. Centuries of weathering had seeped down the opening, gradually eroding metallic rock into sandy gravel that crumbled away in her hands. Attempting to climb it was like trying to ascend the sheer face of a towering sand dune; the more you clawed, the deeper you dug yourself in.

After giving up, Nicki had sat awhile in the inky blackness, hugging herself in dazed self-pity while the wind whistled eerily through the catacombs surrounding her. Eventually, doing nothing had become more terrifying than leaving the tiny window to the sky that she knew was above. Pushing to her feet, she'd measured the tunnel by feeling her way from one side to the other. It was approximately nine feet wide, and she guessed it was equally tall. Except for the vent that stretched tantalizingly upward like a chimney, the lava tube was a nearly perfect cylinder, bored through the mountain by the molten finger of Mother Earth.

A sense of kinship with that primeval lava had come over her. Its goal had been the same as her own: to get out. There might be miles of labyrinthian tubes winding their way through the volcano, but also there were exits and vents. With nothing but instinct to guide her, she'd gathered her courage, planted her good left hand against the side wall, and started moving.

How long ago that had been, Nicki couldn't begin to estimate. There was no frame of reference on this journey of darkness—no light, no sound except the banging in her head. Only the law of gravity, which mercifully confided which way was up and which was down, seemed to have transferred with her from the bright world above to this hellish, black void.

Behind her was a trail of stubbed toes, blind alleys, and dashed hopes. She felt as though days must have passed, but knew it couldn't be so because she'd have been dead of thirst in two. More than likely the duration of her nightmare could be measured in hours; how many, she hadn't a clue. Her head was spinning as well as throbbing, and once or twice she'd come around to discover she'd passed out and slumped to the tunnel floor.

Now she carried on with the floundering impetus of one lost in a desert—not knowing where she was going, certain only that if she stopped, she would surely die. Nicki tried to lick her lips, but could produce no saliva. The thought of water danced in her head like a seductive dream. And then suddenly, above the internal bang in her ears, there sounded an external roar—like a waterfall rushing over a cliff.

She halted and listened. Nothing. *It was just a damn illusion,* she thought, her eyes scaldingly dry though she longed to cry. But then the sound came again—far away . . . the roar of water. And suddenly she knew it was the blowhole. She was inside the Pali. "Oh, God," Nicki whispered aloud, and started shaking all over as she tried to make her legs move faster.

She could picture the blow-hole clear as day, shooting water high into the air by the craggy foot of the Pali. There was a huge cavern where the volcano met the sea. Although trespassing in the cavern was strictly prohibited, she'd explored it once years ago at low tide. The interior wall was riddled with the mouths of lava tubes.

Nicki hurried blindly toward the sound, tripped and fell, got up and kept going. It got louder and louder. Soon it was like rhythmic thunder. And then, as she peered ahead, she thought she detected a glimmer of light. Hope rose within her until her parched throat nearly choked on it.

Yes! There was light! At first it was only a pinpoint, then a beam. Oh so slowly it began to grow into a circle marking the end of the tunnel. Nicki would have dashed toward it if she'd been able. As it was, she had enough trouble merely keeping herself upright and moving on her trembling limbs.

The circle of light appeared about the size of a silver dollar against the overwhelming blackness when her bare feet stumbled onto wetness. Another matter of yards, and her footsteps splashed into an inch of water. She scooped some up and tasted it. Seawater. Of course. When the blowhole roared as it was roaring now, the tide was coming in.

Alarm gripped her like cruel hands. How far back were the tubes flooded when the tide was in? Were the mouths covered? Had she found a way out only to have it blocked by the damnable sea?

"No!" she cried out, her hoarse voice cracking with terror. Fixing her wild eyes straight ahead, Nicki ran for her life toward the distant light.

Chapter Twenty-two

A sharp cry pierced his sleep. Jack bolted up, his hand reaching by habit for the pistol under his pillow. Just as he realized where he was, his gaze lit on Catherine, who was standing by the bed, hurriedly combing her hair.

"Did you cry out?' he mumbled.

"Probably. You have to get up, Jack."

He squinted in her direction. "What time is it?"

"I don't know. It's morning. Get up. We've got to hurry."

He ran a hand over his tousled hair. "What's the rush?"

"It's Nicki."

Jack came swiftly alert. "What? I didn't hear the phone."

"No one called." Quickly stuffing the comb in her purse, Catherine headed for the bathroom. "I had a dream," she called back. "Nicki's alive. But she's in terrible danger."

He rolled across the bed and stalked to the bathroom door. Splashing her face a few quick times, Catherine grabbed a towel. "Are you sure about this?" he asked.

Patting swiftly at her cheeks, she discarded the towel and looked up to meet his eyes. "I hope you believe in me, Jack, because right now there's no time for doubts."

"Sorry. I'm with you. Okay . . . do you know where Nicki is?"

"That's what scares me. I don't know a location. I don't even understand what all of it means. All I know is that she's trapped inside a volcano, in some black tunnel she thinks of as a lava tube, and she's trying desperately to get to something called a 'blow-hole,' which sounds like thunder because the tide is coming in, and she's afraid she won't make it to the light in time—"

"Whoa, now. Slow down a minute," Jack interrupted as Catherine's words tumbled out more shrilly by the second.

"I *can't* slow down," she insisted. *"Which* volcano? *Where?"*

Blow-hole . . . volcano . . . Malia's voice flashed through Jack's mind: *Nicki and Austin are climbing the Pali . . .* The conclusion banged into place with the impact of falling timber.

"I know *exactly* where Nicki is," Jack stated. "The blow-hole is the Aloha Blow-Hole. She never left the Pali. No wonder the police found no trace. No one would think to look *inside* the volcano, *or* to question the word of Austin Palmer. I'll bet the bastard set up the whole damn thing. I'll bet it's connected to Nicki's birthday, and the trust fund, and all those millions—"

"There's time to figure that out later," Catherine broke in. "Right now we must find Nicki."

The morning was overcast, the clouds gray and puffy and threatening rain as they drove toward their destination of the preceding night. Catherine peered out the window, noting the gusty wind whipping through the palms.

"I hope there's not a storm at sea," she murmured. "When there's a storm, the tide comes in high and fast."

Jack reached over and enclosed one of her hands in his. "Nicki's alive, right?"

"Right," Catherine returned with a small smile.

"So we'll just keep our minds on that, okay?"

They reached the foothills of the Pali in a fast fifteen minutes. Speeding along the deserted, rolling road, Jack turned at the fork leading to the lodge and wondered if the cops would still be there. From the sound of things, he had a feeling the rescue of Nicki Palmer was going to be far from a cakewalk.

As he and Catherine approached the formal drive, however, he saw that the barricade was gone. A solitary unmarked car was at the entrance. As the Cadillac drew near, it moved toward them, and Jack recognized Tanaka behind the wheel. Swiftly lowering his window, Jack flagged him down.

"I've just been finishing up here, Jack," the lieutenant greeted with a weary look. "The search has expanded way beyond my jurisdiction. I'm sorry."

Jack held up a hand. "We know where she is, Tanaka."

"We? Who's *we*?"

"Me and my friend Catherine, here. Nicki's been right

under our noses all along. Right now, at this minute, she's trying to get out of the Pali near the blow-hole."

"Trying to get *out* of the Pali? What the hell is *that* supposed to mean?"

"She's been trapped in a lava tube, Tanaka. And she might not have much time left."

"How do you know?"

"I know. Trust me. Catherine and I are on our way to the beach. Will you come with us?"

"No," Tanaka authoritatively replied. *"You'll* come with *me.*"

Leaving the Cadillac in its tracks, Jack and Catherine transferred to the lieutenant's car, and the dark sedan shot off toward a service road leading to the beach. After taking a look in the rearview mirror, Tanaka glanced to the passenger's seat.

"Hey, Casey," he said quietly. "I've been up all night, and maybe my eyes are playing tricks, but I could swear the lady in back is the spitting image of you-know-who."

"Another story, another time, okay?" Jack returned.

Tanaka shrugged and looked ahead once more. To the left of the car, the Pali rose in grandeur; ahead, the peninsula flanking the mountain arched into the sea and formed one of the boundaries of the horseshoe inlet. When they reached the coast and the service road curved toward the private beach, Tanaka brought the sedan to a skidding halt.

Spilling out of the car, the three of them circumvented a chain and hurried onto the peninsula. The tide was in, the bay tossing with whitecaps. As they turned to look toward the volcano, the blow-hole erupted with a soaring flume that momentarily veiled the gaping cavern at the foot of the Pali.

When the wind swept away the white mist, they beheld a figure plastered against the far wall of the cavern's interior. She was penned on a ledge not much wider than her outflung arms, and waves were smashing all around her.

"Oh, no," Jack muttered, his voice barely audible against the noise of the wind and sea. "It's Nicki, all right."

"How in the world did she manage to get herself stuck out there?" Tanaka shouted, then glanced beyond Jack as he caught sight of Catherine climbing up the craggy incline that bridged the peninsula to the mountain. Some fifteen feet up, it flattened out in a precipice overhanging the horseshoe bay. "Uh, Casey," he added. "Where the hell does your girlfriend think she's going?"

Jack took off after her, with Tanaka close behind. By the time they reached the precipice, which jutted out over the sea like a diving platform, Catherine had discarded her sandals and was stepping out of her dress. Jack's shocked gaze rose as, without modesty in bra and panties, she threw him the blue silk.

"No, Catherine," he commanded.

"I'm sorry, miss," Tanaka joined in. "If you've got any delusions about going into that water, forget them. There are signs posted all around here. The riptide is a killer."

"I've been in riptides before, Lieutenant," she called, the wind whipping her hair about her head like a golden banner.

Jack strode toward her. She backed away and held up a forestalling hand. Something about the look on her face told him he'd better stop or she'd jump for it. He came to a short halt.

"Let me go, Jack," she said, her voice tough as nails. "I can do this. I *know* I can."

"No!" he emphatically returned. "We'll figure another way."

Catherine cast a swift look over her shoulder. Jack's gaze followed hers just as a giant wave rolled into the cavern and swept over the ledge where Nicki was trapped. The wall of water blocked her from view, and when it passed, Jack had the sickening feeling that Nicki must have passed with it. Instead, as the surf drew back in momentary respite, they could see her scrambling to hold on to the rocky wall. Anyone could tell that another wave that strong would take her.

"There's no time to figure another way," Catherine announced, and started to turn.

"Miss!" Tanaka bellowed. "If you insist on this course of action, I'll have to put you under arrest!"

Ignoring the lieutenant's threat, she stepped to the edge and lifted her arms. Jack stumbled after her, searching his mind and unable to think of anything else to shout at her.

"Dammit, Catherine! Don't do this to me! Please!"

She glanced at him long enough to say, "I love you." He read her lips, but failed to hear the words as the blowhole roared.

"No!" Jack yelled. But Catherine was already springing away from the earth, her body spiraling through the air. At that instant the sun broke through the clouds, spotlighting her form as it met the sea, her entrance creating a tiny splash quickly swallowed in the roiling waves. She disappeared beneath the water. A moment later when she surfaced yards away, it was in a porpoiselike dive that cleared the crest of a wave.

"Damn!" Tanaka exclaimed. "Look at her go!"

Jack barely heard. It was as though he'd been frozen—his heart and lungs stopped, his capacity for movement gone. All he could do was watch in horrified silence as Catherine continued like a shimmering fish across the tempestuous bay.

As Catherine drew within a dozen yards of the spot where Nicki clung, a gargantuan swell rolled toward them. The word Jim Whitmore had taught him—*tsunami*—burst into Jack's mind. God, the tower of water appeared like a tidal wave, dwarfing everything in its path as it churned with terrifying momentum toward the barrier of land. The blow-hole spewed like Old Faithful as the wave smashed into the mountain cavern.

Its valleylike lee gave a clear view of the distant cavern wall. There was no one on the ledge . . . no one on the surface of the water. No one. Spinning around, Jack sank to his knees.

"Look, buddy! There she is!" Tanaka boomed a few seconds later. "And she's got Nicki!"

Jack leaped to his feet and bruisingly grabbed the smaller man's shoulder. "Where?" As Tanaka pointed, he gazed anxiously into the distance and spotted the two bobbing dots that were the heads of the women. "What the hell is Catherine doing?" he cried. "She's taking them out to sea!"

"No, look!" Tanaka returned. "She's just getting past the rough surf. Now she's starting to turn. Smart girl. If she can tough it out, she can ride the breakers in to the peninsula. By God, I think she just might make it!" Tanaka went on to say something about getting on the radio for a rescue chopper, but by that time Jack was already scrambling down the promontory.

The violent tides sweeping over her were by far the most powerful Catherine had ever experienced. For the first time in her life, she found it necessary to channel every ounce of her strength into fighting the waves.

She prayed to God for endurance. She called on the mystical spirit of water that had always buoyed her. And all the while that she moved tenuously toward the strip of earth jutting into the Pacific, she gulped down frantic wells of tears. Nicki was too still, and had been ever since she ceased thrashing near the mouth of the cavern.

Please help me, Catherine silently pleaded . . . and received a blessing as she felt the first swell of beach bound sea lift and carry them, however fleetingly, toward shore. She paddled like mad with her free arm to catch the next wave. Soon they were in the breakers. She held tightly on to Nicki, and the two of them rode to ground like body surfers.

As soon as Catherine found her footing, she grabbed Nicki under the arms and pulled her out of the tide. Her head lolled like that of a broken doll. Tears ran down Catherine's face. She paid them no heed as she fought to steady her breathing, and positioned her palms atop Nicki's diaphragm. She gave a sharp push. No response. Again. Still nothing.

Propping her arm beneath Nicki's neck, Catherine pinched her nostrils with shaking fingers, took a deep breath, and gave her mouth-to-mouth. There was a telltale rattle in Nicki's chest. Quickly repeating the process, she drew back as Nicki coughed. Seawater spilled from her lips, along with a gurgling moan. An instant later her lashes parted, and for the first time Catherine met the eyes of her sister.

"Am I dead?" Nicki asked in a laryngitic voice that was barely a whisper.

A short, hysterical laugh escaped Catherine. "No," she managed. "You're not dead."

Nicki blinked several times, as though trying to clear her vision. "What are you doing with my face?" she then asked.

Catherine laughed once more, this time with a dawning sense of joy. "It has to do with genes. We're related, you and I."

"We are?" Nicki rasped. "I don't remember. Suddenly I can't remember anything but being in the tubes, trying to get out—"

"It's okay that you don't remember right now," Catherine broke in, and gave her a scrutinizing once-over. There was a purple swelling the size of a goose egg on Nicki's forehead, plus bruises and abrasions on her face, shoulders, arms, and legs. She was lucky to be alive at all, much less with a perfect memory.

Nicki's eyelids began to drift. "It's hard to keep my eyes open," she reported in the painfully hoarse, foreign voice.

"Don't try to talk," Catherine suggested. "Just rest."

Disregarding the instruction, Nicki peeped up at her. "Who are you, anyway?"

"My name is Catherine." She paused to wipe a stream of salt water from her brow as her heartbeat began to thrum. She'd imagined this moment a hundred different ways—never like this.

"I'm your sister," Catherine added finally.

Nicki smiled ever so slightly as her eyelids dropped. "Be seeing you, Sis," she whispered.

A lump rose to Catherine's throat as a new flood of tears stung her eyes. Leaning down, she pressed a kiss to an unblemished spot on Nicki's forehead.

Catherine was bent over Nicki, cradling her head, when Jack galloped up and dropped to his knees beside her.

"She's not . . .?" he said breathlessly, and was loath to complete the question.

"No," Catherine solemnly answered. "I brought her around with mouth-to-mouth, but now she's unconscious."

Spreading his jacket over Nicki's torso, Jack pressed his fingertips to the side of her throat. "Her pulse is pretty strong, considering everything," he said after a moment.

"You think so?"

"Yeah, I think so," Jack confirmed, his expression turning bleak as his gaze raced over her. "How are *you?*" he added.

"I'm fine. I told her who I am, Jack. She called me 'Sis.' "

He tried to smile, but the most he could force was a stiff grin. "I'm happy for you, Catherine. Really."

Unbuttoning his shirt, Jack stripped it off. The clouds were scattering, the hot sun broiling his naked back. Still, he felt cold clear through as he handed her the shirt.

"Guess I lost your dress. Put this on," he concluded as Tanaka ran up to join them.

"An emergency chopper is on the way," the lieutenant announced, panting to catch his breath. "How is Miss Palmer?"

"Unconscious, but she's got a steady pulse."

As Jack rose to his feet, Tanaka bent to Nicki and pressed his ear to her chest. "Amazing," he mumbled. "This whole thing is truly amazing." His eyes swerved to Catherine. "And *you*," he went on. "I've never seen *anybody* move through water like you do."

"Yep, she's a regular mermaid, all right," Jack remarked in a cutting tone that drew Catherine's eye. As she rolled the cuffs of his black shirt, she regarded him with an injured look. At the moment Jack didn't care. Of *course* he was glad she'd managed to save Nicki in the face of seemingly insurmountable odds. But in the process she'd just about scared the life out of him.

"When did she lose consciousness?" Tanaka asked, his attention back on Nicki.

"Just a few minutes ago," Catherine replied.

"Did she speak to you?"

"Only briefly."

"Did she say anything about what happened to her?"

"No," Catherine answered with a gentle stroke of Nicki's wet hair. "She said there was a lot she couldn't remember."

"Memory loss, huh?" Tanaka muttered, and got to his feet, brushing sand from the knees of his slacks. "I guess she's entitled after *this* ordeal. Sure hope it comes back, though. I want her to be able to point a hard finger at the perpetrator."

Jack's gaze lifted, his eyes narrowing as he glanced toward the Pali. "Nicki hiked the volcano yesterday, and she was found there today. I say she never left it."

"But Austin Palmer—"

"That's right," Jack broke in with a piercing look at Tanaka. "Judging from what you said, I gather he was the only one who actually witnessed Nicki's return to the lodge."

"Damn, buddy," the lieutenant muttered. "I'd have to have rock-solid evidence to accuse a Palmer of *anything*, much less something as sordid as this. There's nothing to implicate him."

"Except Nicki," Jack reminded him. "And if that's the case, he'll have to come after her again—*before* she has the chance to regain her memory." The crash of nearby surf filled an ominous moment, then was joined by the graduating hum of an approaching helicopter. They looked up to see the craft flashing in the sunlight like a metallic bird as it sped in their direction.

"Perhaps we could set a trap," Catherine said, and drew startled looks from both men. "We three are the only ones who know of Nicki's rescue, *or* her condition. Perhaps we could use the situation to lure Austin into incriminating himself."

"No way," Tanaka pronounced. "Considering the condition Miss Palmer is in, there's no way I'd use her for bait."

Dripping wet and wearing nothing more than an oversized shirt, Catherine nonetheless conveyed the regality of a queen as she rose from the sand and encompassed both Tanaka and Jack in her steady gaze. "I wasn't thinking of using Nicki," she said. "You pointed it out yourself, Lieutenant. I happen to be the 'spitting image' of her."

"Damnation!" Jack swore, just before the noise and wind of the descending helicopter cut him off.

As soon as it landed in the grassy area bordering the beach, two medics leaped out and within minutes had covered Nicki with a blanket, strapped her to a stretcher, and planted an oxygen mask on her face. Slinging his jacket over his bare shoulder, Jack silently glared his condemnation at Catherine as they followed the stretcher to the chopper.

While the medics loaded Nicki inside, Tanaka turned and handed his car keys to Jack. "Why don't you drive my car back to your rental?" he cried, lifting his voice above the revving noise of the engine. "Leave the keys in it. I'll have somebody pick it up later."

"Where are you taking Nicki?" Catherine shouted, the wind of the accelerating propeller whipping her wet hair across her face.

"Hilo Medical. The emergency staff is already on alert. They'll be ready for us."

"Can't we all go?"

Tanaka gave her a quick look of apology. "There's not enough room. You've done a hell of a job here today. Now the best thing you can do for Miss Palmer is let us get her to the hospital."

"What about Austin?" Catherine shrilled.

"You mean the idea of setting a trap?" The lieutenant shook his head. "Too dangerous. Besides, I can't swallow the idea that Austin Palmer is involved."

"If you're right," Catherine returned, holding on to the notion like a bulldog, "then it won't be dangerous, *will* it?"

With the sharp arch of a black brow, Tanaka turned to Jack. "You really think Palmer might be behind this?"

"Yes, but—"

"Are you coming, Lieutenant?" the chopper pilot called.

"Be right there!" Tanaka called back. "Where are you staying?" he asked Jack.

"Hilo. Hawaiian Sun."

"Normally, in a case like this, I'd be on the radio to the chain of command as soon as we got airborne, but . . ." The lieutenant paused as he glanced to Catherine and beheld her anxious face. "Considering what I've seen today, I think I owe you the courtesy of thinking this over and calling you first."

"And letting us know how Nicki is," Catherine said.

"Don't worry," he replied, and gave her shoulder a pat. "I'll let you know." With that Tanaka climbed into the helicopter. Shielding their faces against the whipping wind, Jack and Catherine backed away as it lifted off and swooped into the distance. He turned to her with a dark look.

"Would you like to stop at the lodge?" he asked. "I can probably talk somebody into letting you take a shower."

"No, thanks. I'll wait until we get to Hilo."

"So *now* you want to go to Hilo!" She gazed at him with those deep blue eyes that had always—so effortlessly—seemed to reach clear into his soul. At the moment even *they* failed to touch Jack. He continued to glare at her.

"What's the matter?" she softly asked, and set him off.

"What's the *matter?*" Jack repeated with a harsh laugh. "You just brought back the worst moment of my life in spades, Catherine. I thought you were *dead.* Don't you understand? And all I could do was watch. Worse yet, *I* was the one who put you there." He stalked off the grass and onto the glistening sand. Catherine followed in his wake.

"You didn't 'put' me there, Jack. It was my choice."

He whirled around. "*First* you dive into a killer riptide that, by all rights, should have drowned you. And *now* you want to set yourself up as a target for Palmer."

"There's no other way," she said quietly.

"That's what you say every damn time you put your life on the line, Catherine!" he boomed. "There's no other way!"

She hung her head and stared at the sand. Spinning around in exasperation, Jack took a few paces, gazed blindly toward the sea for a few seconds, then looked over his shoulder. She continued to stand that same, forlorn way—looking like a little orphan girl who expected to be beaten. He walked back to her.

"Don't look like that," he said. "You make me feel like your damn Aunt Sybil."

Catherine looked up from beneath downcast lashes. "I believe—and I know *you* believe—that Austin is responsible not only for what happened to Nicki, but also for having me kidnapped thirty years ago. Don't you think I *deserve* the chance to play a part in his comeuppance?"

"Comeuppance?" Jack sharply repeated. "Where did you dig up that word? Never mind. It doesn't matter. The answer is no. Even if Tanaka agreed, which he won't, there is *nothing* you can say that will convince me to endorse the idea of you as bait."

Catherine mumbled something and started walking up the beach. "What did you say?" Jack demanded of her back, at which point she looked around.

"I said, 'Then I'll have to persuade Tanaka on my own.' "

Jack grabbed his head with both hands. "God!" he exploded. "I'm going to be completely insane before this thing is over!"

"I'm sorry," Catherine ventured after a moment. "I don't mean to be difficult. It's just that everything seems so clear—"

"Don't!" Jack said, and held up a swift silencing palm. "Just . . . don't talk to me right now, okay?" Taking a few long angry strides, he grabbed Catherine by the hand and proceeded to lead her at a brisk pace toward Tanaka's sedan.

Two hours later Jack had just stepped out of the shower when Tanaka called. "How's Nicki?" Jack immediately asked.

"Concussion, dehydration, multiple contusions and abrasions. They've got her on fluids and painkillers. She's pretty beaten up, but she's going to be okay. Be sure to tell Catherine."

"Don't worry. It's not likely she'll let me escape with the slightest detail."

"That Catherine is quite a lady. Is she yours?"

Jack cut his eyes toward the phone. "Why do you ask?"

Tanaka chuckled. "Never mind. Your tone says it all. One thing I can't figure—how did you two know that Nicki was in that cavern?"

"That's a question you'll have to ask Catherine."

"Are they twins?"

"Once again—"

"I need to know, Jack. If Nicki has a twin, and it's common knowledge that she's here on the island—"

"No one knows she's here, Tanaka. In fact, no one knows of her existence, and that's the way Catherine wants to keep it until she can talk to Nicki."

"I can respect that," the lieutenant said, his voice suddenly all business. "I'm keeping my mouth shut right now myself. I've been thinking about your theory concerning Austin Palmer."

"And?" Jack prodded.

"Something occurred about an hour ago that's making me look at him long and hard. Peni Kahala turned herself in and confessed to both the assault at the rodeo and one incident last summer. She denies abducting Miss Palmer yesterday, and her alibi is airtight, coming—as it does— from a bunch of nuns at Our Lady of Mercy Convent. Peni also denies responsibility for the acts of the clown last summer, and once again her alibi stands up. At the time of the clown's final attempt on Miss Palmer, Peni was in critical condition in a small hospital on the coast. You were right, Jack. She wasn't the one you fought on the cliff."

"And I'm right about the guy I fought being dead, too,

which means we've eliminated the two primary suspects in this case. It wasn't Peni *or* the clown. So who does that leave? Maybe a man we *know* was on the volcano where Nicki was found? Maybe the sole witness who verified her return to the lodge? Austin Palmer."

Tanaka groaned. "Man, that sure has a bad ring to it."

"Truth sometimes does."

"I only wish we could count on Miss Palmer coming around and telling us, point-blank, what happened. But the one complication the doc can't give a positive prognosis about is this amnesia thing. She might recover her memory right away, or maybe not at all. There's a fifty-fifty chance she may never be able to tell us who tried to kill her."

"But if it *was* Palmer," Jack said in a heavy tone, "he won't be willing to take a fifty-fifty chance."

"Jack, the Palmer name swings a lot of weight on the island. Nobody's going to authorize trying to trap one of them. Even now I'm putting my badge on the line by keeping quiet. There's a statewide search on for Nicki Palmer. Do you realize how much manpower and tax money we're talking about?"

"I used to be a cop, remember?" Jack glumly pointed out.

"And your specialty was covert operations. Believe me, nothing has ever been more covert than *this* has to be. If we do it, it has to be just us—you, me, Catherine. And it has to be *now,* because if it turns out that you're wrong—"

"I'm not wrong. I just don't like being right this time."

"Catherine wants to do it," Tanaka returned.

"Oh, *hell,* yes. I know that."

"If you're right about Palmer, this might be the only way to nail him. Frankly, that's the only reason I'm taking the risk."

Jack stared unseeingly toward the colorful scene beyond the atrium doors. He pictured Nicki, beat up and unconscious. He envisioned Catherine, and imagined her son of a bitch uncle stealing her life away when she was a newborn.

"Catherine deserves a reckoning with Austin Palmer," he said finally. "So I guess it's a go."

"Then we're in business," Tanaka responded. "I've got Nicki checked in as Jane Doe in ICU on the fourth floor. How soon can you and Catherine get to the hospital?"

After hanging up with Tanaka, Jack dialed Catherine's room and told her the news about Nicki. "I think the lieutenant's sweet on you," he added.

She laughed. "What makes you say that?"

"He's gonna fly with your idea to play bait for Palmer," Jack returned, his voice filled with uncontrollable bleakness.

"And you don't want me to do it," she observed.

"No. I don't. But that doesn't make any difference, does it?" Silence. "Well, does it?" he pressed.

"Bottom line," Catherine answered finally, "I suppose not."

"That's what I thought. I'll pick you up in a half hour."

It took Jack half that time to pull on black jeans, black T-shirt, black boots. The color suited his mood. Making a quick trip downstairs to the lobby, he stopped in a flower shop, purchased a freshly made lei of sweet-smelling plumeria, and returned to their floor with minutes to spare. When he arrived at Catherine's room, he found that she'd left the door ajar and was busy in the bathroom. He stepped onto the atrium terrace to wait.

A few minutes later she walked onto the terrace, wearing a yellow shirt and white slacks and looking bright and sunny as a summer day. He turned from the rail. "Come here," he said. When she dutifully approached, he produced the lei. "I happened to realize something a while ago. Happy birthday," he concluded while draping the flowers about her neck.

"Thank you, Jack," she murmured, and looked up with such a brilliant smile that he was momentarily dazzled. When he came around a few seconds later, he found his hands on Catherine's shoulders and his gaze embedded in her eyes. Briskly withdrawing his hands, Jack stuffed them in the pockets of his jeans.

"I'm going to suggest to Tanaka that we limit the time frame on this thing as much as possible," he curtly announced. "Even with no traffic, it still takes nearly three hours to drive from the ranch to Hilo. If Tanaka waits until evening to make the call and dangles the carrot of Nicki's memory being expected to return by morning, that should force Palmer to action sometime between the hours of eleven p.m. and five a.m."

Catherine's brilliant smile gradually faded. "I wish you weren't so angry about this."

"I'm not angry, Catherine," he snapped. "I'm just . . . I don't know what I am."

"Worried," she suggested.

"You *make* me worry, woman. I've been worried ever since I met you. It's making me old."

Catherine stepped up and tousled his hair. "I don't see any gray yet," she teased.

Jack caught her wrist and peered into her eyes. "I want you to be very alert and very careful."

"Same to you," she replied. "Now let's go see my sister."

After spending half the day in bed, Austin had been "hungry as a bear" at suppertime. Malia was able to swallow hardly a bite, not that Austin noticed. Now he was in the study, playing Frank Sinatra music and drinking Scotch. Always before, when she looked upon her lover, shivers of adoration had washed over her. Tonight, there were chills of horrified wondering instead.

Malia was listlessly washing the dishes when the phone rang. Sprinting to the threshold of the study, she stepped just inside and listened breathlessly to Austin's side of the conversation.

"The beach at the lodge? How did she get *there*? . . . What do you mean, you don't know? . . . What exactly *is* hysterical amnesia? . . . No permanent damage. Good. . . . Well, if she's sedated, I suppose that makes sense. I'll plan to be there first thing in the morning. . . . Room 210 in the new wing. Got it. . . . Thank you, Lieutenant."

By the time Austin hung up, Malia's heart was pounding like a frenzied drum. "What did the lieutenant say?"

Austin turned, and she'd never seen such astonishment on his face. "They found Nicki," he answered. "Alive," he added on a note of bewilderment that all but escaped Malia as her knees buckled and she grabbed at the portal for support.

"It's uncanny," Austin continued in a tone of wonder. "Apparently she swam out of the horseshoe bay at the Pali and ended up on the beach at the lodge. Absolutely uncanny."

"Where is she?" Malia tremulously demanded.

"Hilo Medical Center."

"Is she hurt?"

"She has a concussion, some bumps and bruises. She's sedated, and the doctors want her to sleep undisturbed through the night."

"What was that about amnesia?"

Austin's eyes swerved to hers. "Nothing to worry about. A temporary condition expected to clear up by morning. And get this: Peni Kahala didn't do it. She turned herself in to the cops and has an airtight alibi for the time of the abduction. Funny how things turn out, isn't it?"

"Funny? I can't imagine using that word in this situation."

"I meant, *funny* as in 'strange,' " Austin returned on an impatient note. "I suppose you'll want to go with me to the hospital in the morning."

"Oh, *yes*," Malia confirmed.

He walked over to the stereo, turned off the music, and set his empty glass on the bar. "You know, Malia," he began as he looked around, "this thing has drained me. I think I'm going to turn in, and I feel like a little privacy tonight. Do you mind?"

Shattering her sense of relief, chills of horror struck anew. Malia didn't want to think the thought that flashed through her mind, but it formed anyway. By morning Nicki would be able to reveal what happened to her, *and* who did it. By morning . . .

"Of course I don't mind, Austin. We both need time alone."

His gaze turned piercing. "What does *that* mean?"

Malia shrugged. "Worry for Nicki has drained me as well."

Walking up to her, Austin bent to kiss her on the cheek. She caught her lip as she glanced aside. "Good night, then," he said.

"Good night."

"Aren't you going to say anything else? Normally you tell me you love me." Malia looked up to meet his endlessly blue eyes.

"I've always loved you, Austin. I always will."

With a smile he left the room and proceeded down the hall. Malia made her typical rounds of turning off lights on

the way to her room. There she brushed her teeth, washed
her face, and retrieved the loaded pistol Austin kept in her
bedside table. Tucking it in her dress pocket, she waited
until ten before dousing her bedroom lights, slipping out
of the house, and dashing through the moonlight into the
blackness of the garage.

Feeling her way to Austin's expensive sports car, she
climbed into the back and curled up in the cramped confines of the floorboard. She hoped her nightmarish suspi-
cions would dissolve with the darkness. She prayed she
would wake in the morning with nothing to show for a
night's folly except stiff joints.

But it was not to be. The hour was nearly midnight when
the garage door opened and she heard Austin's approaching footsteps. He came around to the driver's side,
and she held her breath. But then a moment later he
changed his mind and walked away. By the time Malia
gathered the nerve to raise her head and peep out the window, she heard the starting of an engine.

Headlights illuminated the garage long enough for her to
see Austin in a plain black company car that was rarely
used, and *never* by him. The lights went out, and the car
rolled stealthily out of the garage. When Austin was past
the house, he turned on the headlights once more and the
car sped into the distance.

After a moment's indecision Malia scrambled to the front
and settled in the driver's seat. Depressing the clutch, she
turned the ignition and pressed the gas. *So far, so good,*
she thought as the engine turned over and proceeded to
rumble with expectancy. She was not an especially good
driver and was particularly poor with a stick shift. Releasing
the brake, she shifted into first, and the car lurched jerkily
out of the garage.

Taking heart from the fact that she was moving at all,
Malia forced the stick grindingly into second gear. If Austin
knew what she was doing with his prize auto, he'd shoot
her. She almost laughed in sheer madness as the ironic
weight on her right side reminded her of the pistol in her
pocket.

Gaining speed, Malia shifted determinedly into third and
shot past the house along the drive toward the seaside
highway.

Chapter Twenty-three

The new wing of Hilo Medical Center had yet to be formally opened and, compared to the bustling main building, was distinctively deserted. The isolation factor had made it the obvious choice when Jack and Tanaka scouted a location.

A solitary nurse was on duty at the second-floor station. She attended patients in two private rooms at the opposite end of the hall from Catherine. Tanaka had swung the weight of his badge to wangle the use of Room 210 for the night and had left the nurse with the impression that he was harboring an official witness.

While Catherine used makeup to create the illusion of scrapes and bruises, Jack had ventured into the main building and pilfered the supplies necessary to complete the image of an injured Nicki. After dressing in the hospital gown he brought, Catherine pinned up her hair, and Jack bandaged her head in a concealing skullcap.

"How do I look?" she asked when he was done.

"Not bad for a mummy," he joked in the only show of levity he'd been able to muster all night.

With the difference of their hairstyles eliminated, the likeness between the twins was amazing. The final touch was the IV Jack taped to Catherine's wrist after she climbed into the hospital bed. Once that was done, and she lay prone beneath the crisp white sheet, he had to admit that if he'd walked into the room expecting to see Nicki, even *he* would have been fooled.

Now, as their vigil crawled into the third hour, they were all at their posts: Tanaka, behind the emergency exit door with the window looking straight toward Room 210; Catherine, on the bed in the dimly lit chamber; and Jack, camped out in the adjoining bathroom with the lights out and the door cracked just enough to maintain clear surveillance.

Innumerable times he'd wished for the pistol he left behind in Chicago, and had even hinted to Tanaka about loaning him one, only to receive a stern reprimand. "I'm already pushing my authority to the limit, Casey," he'd said. "You know all that kung fu stuff. *I'll* pack the heat."

If Palmer showed up tonight, it meant he was a killer. And so Jack stretched in the limited space of his tiny hideout, flexing his muscles to keep them loose and hoping "all that kung fu stuff" would be enough.

"What time is it now?" Catherine whispered.

Jack glanced at the neon digits of his watch. "Almost three," he whispered back.

"Maybe he won't come."

"He'll come," Jack grimly returned.

"I've been thinking about Nicki," Catherine said after a few seconds. "She was so deathly still."

"She's sedated, Catherine. That's part of what being sedated means—stillness. Nicki's going to be fine." *It's you I'm worried about,* he mentally added.

A few minutes of silence passed, and then: "Jack?"

"I'm here."

"What's going to happen when all this is over?"

He hesitated, then skated deftly around the inquiry. "A lot of things," he answered. "A whole new life is opening up for you, Catherine. But now is not the time to talk about it. We've got to be quiet and keep our minds on what we're doing, okay?"

As she murmured her assent, Jack hung his head in the closeted darkness. He'd evaded the true question he sensed she was asking. What Catherine really wanted to know was what was going to happen between the two of them.

The heavy question weighed him down. Jack took a deep breath and slowly exhaled. Damn, he wished he could light up a smoke.

It was almost too easy.

A grocery truck was making a delivery to the service entrance of the cafeteria. Hoisting a box of produce to his shoulder, Austin camouflaged his face as he walked into the kitchen, which was flooded with fluorescence and noisy with the guttural voices of the night crew.

One of the guys was telling a joke. Austin waited for the punch line.

When the group of six or so howled with laughter, he set his box on the counter and slipped through the swinging door to the dark and empty dining room. Making swift progress through columns of tables laden with upturned chairs, he reached the double-door entrance, swiftly turned the latch, and peeped out. A freight elevator was directly across the hospital corridor.

Rubber-soled sneakers muted his footsteps as he walked nonchalantly across the deserted hall. The elevator panel was accompanied by a handy menu, which included a listing for the doctors' lounge. Pressing the corresponding button, Austin clasped his hands behind his back and softly whistled as he rode up four flights.

The doors opened with a *ding!* and he was presented with his first challenge. A nurse was proceeding up the hall not ten yards away, though her back was turned. Austin quickly took charge of a service cart parked by the elevator doors. Keeping his head down, he quietly pushed it along and surveyed the corridor from beneath hooded lids.

The nurse was continuing toward a brightly lit station in the distance. Austin was starting to think he was going to have to ditch the idea of the doctors' lounge when he suddenly came upon it. Casting a precautionary look inside, he found it to be as empty as the cafeteria dining room.

Once again, everything became easy. Taking what he wanted from the supply closet, he dressed in surgical scrubs, cap, mask, and gloves. When he finished, he took an assessing look in the mirror by the door. No one would recognize him, and the loose-fitting garb completely concealed the carved handle of the custom-made bowie knife tucked in the back of his waistband. Not that he expected to use it. A clean and simple pillow should do the trick.

Adopting the air of a physician with much to do, Austin strode briskly out of the lounge and in the opposite direction of the nurses' station. He didn't look back, and it was apparent that no one noticed as he proceeded through the fourth-floor breezeway to the adjoining new wing, which was not yet in formal use. The floor was quiet, the midway station attended by a solitary security guard with his feet propped up. He straightened with a start as Austin approached.

"Excuse me, Doctor—"

Austin held up a hand, passed swiftly by, and the guard didn't try to detain him.

He continued the full length of the hall, his eyes narrowing on the door to the emergency stairwell. It opened with a soft *whoosh.* Once he was on the other side, Austin peered through the tiny window. The guard up the way had propped his feet once more. Austin smiled behind the surgical mask.

Too damn easy, he thought once more, and started noiselessly down the stairwell. Descending one flight, he bypassed the door marked with a big 3, and then came to a short halt as he heard something—a faint scratching noise, almost like someone shuffling his feet. Creeping down the concrete steps, Austin peered below.

Tanaka was posted at the second-floor door. *How diligent,* Austin thought, and silently withdrew the knife. Holding it by the sheathed blade, he lifted the handle of carved oak as he continued down the stairs.

Tanaka must have sensed something at the last instant. He started to turn, but it was too late. Austin brought the knife handle crashing into the back of his skull with a powerful blow that would have brought down a man twice his size.

Tanaka crumpled to the floor and lay sprawled, facedown. Austin checked the oak handle of the bowie. There was a little blood. Bending down, he smeared it on Tanaka's jacket, replaced the knife in his waistband, and took a look through the emergency door window.

Room 210 was dead ahead. Down the way a nurse was standing at the station. Otherwise, the corridor was deserted. When the nurse turned and started in the opposite direction, Austin slipped across the hall, stole into the hospital room, and silently closed the door behind him.

There she was, remarkable as it seemed. His plan had been flawless as always. Of all his targeted adversaries, only Nicki had managed to beat him at his secret game—however fleeting her victory might be. Untying his surgical mask, Austin allowed it to loop about his neck as he strolled to the bed.

"Nicki, Nicki, Nicki," he murmured. "What *am* I going to do with you?" He eyed the bandages covering her skull. "You must have gotten a pretty nasty bump on the head. Temporary memory loss, huh? Unfortunate for you; fortunate for me."

He studied her face. There were a few bruises, but nothing like one might have expected. "Actually, you look quite good, considering." His gaze traveled along her arms. He picked up her limp right hand and turned it over.

"How's that cut—" he began, and broke off. There was no gash from a hunter's knife on her palm. There wasn't even a scratch. Austin's startled eyes rose to Nicki's face and narrowed to slits when he detected movement of her lashes.

"You're not Nicki," he growled, and pulled his weapon.

"Hold it right there!" Jack boomed as he burst into the room. Palmer spun around. He was holding a wicked-looking bowie knife with a curved blade. Acting with instinctive speed, Jack executed a roundhouse kick. His booted foot connected with Palmer's extended hand and sent the knife clattering across the floor.

For a suspended second Palmer gazed at him in motionless surprise. But in the next he'd grabbed Catherine and hauled her off the bed. "Stop!" Jack yelled as Catherine cried out. He started toward Palmer. Wrenching one of Catherine's wrists behind her, the bastard yanked her up in front of him and lodged a threatening forearm over her throat.

"*You* stop!" he warned. "Or I'll snap her neck like a twig!"

Jack halted in his tracks. Maintaining a secure hold on Catherine, Palmer dragged her across the floor and released her imprisoned wrist only to grab his knife. As he straightened, he jerked Catherine up with him, nearly choking her so that she clawed futilely at his arm.

"I said, *stop it*!" Jack bellowed. But when he took a frenetic step forward, Palmer swiftly raised the shiv to Catherine's throat. The silver blade glimmered in the meager light, its tip resting threateningly against her jugular vein.

"It would take me less than one second to inflict a mortal wound," Palmer coldly announced. "You must admit, Casey, that I hold this little lady's life in my hands. Who is she, anyway? She looks enough like Nicki to be her—"

Looking down with blatant curiosity, he yanked Catherine's chin so that she stared up at him. "Well, I'll be damned," he said with a short laugh. "It's the star-crossed twin."

"There's no way out for you, Palmer," Jack desperately stated. "Tanaka is here, and—"

"And is taking a nap in the emergency stairwell at the moment. Did the two of you cook up this little ploy? You, Tanaka, and the little look-alike, here?" He pressed a quick kiss to the side of Catherine's exposed neck. Jack's stomach lurched.

"Come get _me_, Palmer!" he challenged. "I'm the one you want!"

"You are so right, Jack. Tonight wouldn't have been necessary at all if you hadn't butted in last year. I'll get around to you. But for now the girl seems to be pretty good leverage. You see, I want you to answer a question. If you do, she stays alive. If you don't, I'll kill her right before your eyes."

To illustrate his point, he pricked Catherine with the tip of the blade. A scarlet drop of blood marred the creamy skin of her throat, and she never made a sound.

"Dammit, Palmer!" Jack shouted. "What the hell do you want to know?" The hard, unfeeling eyes that leveled on him were so obviously those of a killer that Jack couldn't believe he hadn't see it earlier.

"Where's the real Nicki?" Palmer demanded.

Jack clenched his jaw so hard that it began to spasm. The sadistic bastard lifted Catherine until she was on tiptoe. A moan escaped her constricted throat.

"Well?" Palmer prodded. "Do you want to watch her die, Jack?"

The memory of a blinding explosion flashed before Jack's eyes, but it wasn't as terrifying as the reality that stared him in the face when the vision cleared.

Screeching to a stop by the entrance to the new wing, Malia left the engine running, lights blaring, and door gaping as she ran inside. There was one person in the lobby, a security guard who ambled toward her with an apologetic look.

"I'm afraid you must be in the wrong place, lady," he said.

"Is this the new wing?" Malia asked.

"Yes, ma'am."

"Then I'm in the right place." She started toward the elevator. The guard was quick to hurry after her.

"Sorry, ma'am, but I'm going to have to ask you to leave."

Malia turned, produced the pistol, and pointed it at him. "Would you give me your gun, handle first, please?" His eyes round as saucers, the guard did as she said.

"Now raise your hands." He was quick to comply. "Will this elevator take me to the second floor?" He nodded. Malia pressed the button. The doors instantly opened.

"You may call the police now if you wish," she said as she stepped inside. "I'll be in Room 210."

Malia barely had time to discard the guard's gun on the elevator floor before the doors opened. The second-floor nurse looked up with surprise as Malia walked rapidly out of the elevator and down the hall, taking swift note of the numbers on the doors.

"Excuse me!" the nurse objected, and trotted after her. "No one is allowed down here!"

Room 218 . . . 216 . . . 210 was probably at the end of the corridor.

"Stop!" the nurse called. "I said, no one is—"

Malia turned and raised the pistol. The nurse halted with a look of shock and raised her hands.

"Go back to your station," Malia ordered, and hurried on.

When she banged through the door at the end of the hall, the scene that greeted her seared her brain like a branding iron. Jack Casey, all in black, stood poised at her right, his face drained of color. Austin was costumed in the surgical clothes of a doctor, and holding a knife to Nicki's throat.

Malia brought the pistol to a straight-armed firing stance. "Let her go, Austin," she commanded.

"Malia?" her lover sputtered as though he couldn't believe what he was seeing.

Jack started briskly in her direction and extended his hand. "Give me the gun, Malia."

Swinging the pistol around, she aimed it at his chest. "Back up, Jack."

Austin emitted a short laugh. "I'd do what she says. I taught her to shoot, and if I say so myself, she's not half bad."

When Jack took a few frustrated backward steps, Malia looked back to Austin. "I said, let her go."

"Afraid I can't do that, honey. But guess what. This isn't even Nicki."

In a swift move he positioned the razor-sharp blade beneath the bandage at his captive's hairline and sliced upward through layers of gauze in one fell swoop. The skullcap fell to the floor, and strands of golden hair escaped pins to settle around her face.

"Loot at that," Austin said. "It's the damn bitch I told you to get rid of thirty years ago. This whole thing has been an elaborate ruse to draw me in."

After an astounding look at the girl's face, Malia lifted her gaze to Austin, only to be confronted with the fearful, blank visage of her nightmares. She forced herself to breathe, forced herself to think.

"The police are coming, Austin," she said finally. "We must get out of here."

A single brow shot up. "We?" he questioned. "Are you saying you intend to stick with me?"

"Haven't I always?" Malia replied. "Where you go, I go."

"I can't afford to leave anyone in this room alive," the blank face stated.

Malia swallowed hard. "Then come take the gun. It's faster."

He peered at her, and the ghost of Austin resurfaced on his features. "You surprise me, Malia. You really do," he remarked, and started sidestepping in her direction, holding the girl at knifepoint all the while.

"Don't do this, Malia," Jack begged, and took a frantic step.

She stopped him by cocking the hammer with a distinct click. "Trust me, Jack," she returned with a sharp look. "You need to stay exactly where you are."

When Austin drew within arm's length, Malia jammed the barrel between his ribs and pulled the trigger. The point-blank-range shot knocked him off his feet. Austin released the girl and fell sideways, the knife tumbling from his hand. As Nicki's twin stumbled forward, Jack grabbed her and spun around, putting the shield of his body between her and the gun.

"What happens *now,* Malia?" he shouted.

The hand with the pistol dropped to her side. "Nothing you need worry about," Malia forced through numb lips. "There is something I must know, Jack. Is Nicki truly alive?"

"She's going to be fine," he tersely returned.

Malia's focus shifted to the blonde huddled in Jack's protecting arms. She appeared to be racked with sobs, though she made no sound. "And the twin. What is her name?"

Jack glanced swiftly around. "This is Catherine."

"Catherine," Malia repeated. "She's very lovely and very brave." As Jack turned back to the girl, Malia walked woodenly to Austin's prone form. The pool of blood spreading around him was like a red tide. Mindless of it, she lay down beside him and took his hand. His lashes fluttered like the wings of wounded birds as his blue eyes looked into hers.

"You surprise me, Malia," he rasped. "You really do."

And suddenly the lashes went still and his eyes fixedly stared. Holding tightly to Austin's fingers, Malia turned the pistol to her breast and fired.

Within minutes of the gunshots, a noisy crowd began gathering—hospital security and staff, swiftly followed by the police. Everyone was rushing and shouting.

Doctors hurried in, dropped to their knees, and examined Austin and Malia.

Strapped to a gurney pushed by speeding orderlies, Lieutenant Tanaka went flying by the door.

A horde of police officers closed in.

Catherine witnessed it all through a daze. She couldn't respond to the officers' harried questions. It was as though every ounce of her energy and mind power had been siphoned. Jack, however, was solid as rock. Draping a blanket about her shoulders and pushing her to a seat on the bed, he took over.

In a way the next few hours seemed to go on forever; in another they seemed to pass in the blink of an eye. Melrose was notified and came hurrying over. Catherine met the grandfatherly man from her dreams wearing a hospital gown and blanket, and could barely string sensible words together to say hello to him.

At one point a nurse approached, checked her over, and offered a "mild tranquilizer." Catherine refused. If she became any more tranquil, she wouldn't be able to sit up.

Lieutenant Tanaka showed up, sporting a white strip of bandage around his head and suffering from a headache, but otherwise fine. When the police statements were finally completed and they were free to go, Catherine, Jack, and Melrose went to the ICU to check on Nicki, whose vital signs continued to improve as she rested. Later in the morning, a nurse confided, she was scheduled to be moved to a private room.

"Thank God," Melrose said as he stared at Nicki through the glass partition. "I'll stay with her now," he added. "You two go back to your hotel and get some sleep. You deserve it."

The morning sky was bright as Catherine and Jack drove to the Hawaiian Sun. He walked her to her room, opened the door, and hesitated. As for Catherine, there was no hesitation whatever. Stepping out of her shoes along the way, she headed for the bed and curled up atop the crisply made bedspread.

Jack followed in her path. "At least get *into* the bed," he grumbled. Pulling back the spread on the other side, he turned and covered her. Her eyelids never stirred, and she took him by surprise when she said, out of the blue: "You're quite a hero."

Jack straightened with a start and stared down at her. She appeared so still, so pristine—like a little girl already fast asleep. "*You're* the hero," he countered.

"Do you think so?" Catherine murmured.

"Yeah, I do."

"That makes me happy." A lump gathered in his throat as he sank to a crouch by the bed. "Will you wake me when it's time to see Nicki?" she added, her words beginning to slur as sleepiness thickened her tongue. A smile crept to Jack's lips.

"Sure. I'll wake you." Seconds ticked by. Catherine's breathing settled into a peaceful rhythm. With a parting stroke of her hair, he rose to his feet.

"Be seeing you," she mumbled.

Jack's feelings erupted with such force that they brought tears to his eyes. "Catherine?" No reply. No movement. Just the steady rise and fall of her shoulders beneath the covers. "I love you," he added in a whisper, and quietly withdrew from the room.

Afternoon sunlight streamed through the hospital room window, glimmering on Nicki's hair, mercilessly illuminating the purple bump on her forehead and the black-and-blue shiner beneath it. For the countless time in the past nine hours, Melrose looked at her and was stunned by the wonder that she was alive.

When she came around earlier in the day, it was with a fully recovered memory. He'd stood by her when the police showed up, and Nicki undertook the task of reporting the events that took place two afternoons earlier on the Pali. She faltered only once, and that was when she revealed the moment that Austin—her uncle and lifelong comrade—kicked her over the side of the fissure that dropped dozens of feet into the lava tubes.

The attack would have crushed a lesser spirit, but Nicki had remained undaunted—a quality she apparently shared with her newfound twin, Catherine Winslow. When Melrose considered the two of them, he was so deeply moved he couldn't express how it made him feel . . . except he felt damn lucky to have seen such courage, and known such women, in his lifetime.

He cringed whenever he remembered his link in the sordid chain of events. If only he'd quashed the proposition about the emerald mine. . . . "I can't believe I allowed myself to be part of anything that could lead to this," he mumbled.

"It wasn't the trust fund scheme," Nicki objected with lingering hoarseness. "It was Austin. He was sick, Melrose. He told me things that day I never want to think of again, much less repeat. None of us ever really knew him."

"Decades ago I wondered why your grandparents bequeathed their estate so unevenly—a comfortable, though restricted allowance to Austin, and the bulk of their holdings to Philip. Now I believe they must have suspected there was something not quite right about their younger son."

"None of us knew him," Nicki repeated. "Not even the one who loved him best." Her lips began to tremble, her eyes to burn. "The house is going to be so dreadfully empty without Malia."

"Yes, it is," Melrose soberly agreed. "She cared for you a great deal, Nicki. That's why she did what she did. She protected you to the bitter end."

Covering her tearing eyes with a muffling forearm, Nicki lay quiet and still. When she looked once more at Melrose a few minutes later, she was able to bring a small smile to her lips.

"As I said, the house is going to be empty. That's why I think you should sell that old place of yours here in Hilo and live at the ranch full-time."

"But, Nicki," he said after a startled instant, "I explained the situation about your trust fund. The opening will be delayed until you're well enough to travel to Honolulu, of course, but as soon as the books are audited—"

"Then the entire embezzlement scheme can be laid at Austin's door," she broke in. "He's the one who cooked it up, anyway."

"Well, yes, but—"

"For heaven's sake, Melrose. I can't have you shipping off to prison someplace. I need you. Are you going to come live at the ranch and teach me how to run Palmer International, or not?" He stared at her for another disbelieving moment. Then, with glistening eyes, Melrose took her hand and lifted it to his lips.

"It would be my extreme pleasure," he said.

"Don't worry," Nicki retorted with the arch of a brow. "I'll get my five million's worth out of you before we're done."

"I'll look forward to it," he replied with a chuckle.

Nicki glanced past Melrose to the window. Sunlight was so beautiful. She'd never take it for granted again. Beyond the pane the hospital grounds were lush and green—amazingly, vividly green. She couldn't wait to get outside and breathe the open air. She couldn't wait . . . to see Kimo. Her gaze returned to Melrose.

"Do me a favor, will you? Call Kimo for me."

Melrose's bushy brows lifted. "Kimo?"

"You told me once that if I couldn't love him, I should let him go. Well, I don't want to let him go. I *do* love him."

"Are you sure, Nicki?"

"One benefit of making it through a near-death experience is that your feelings become crystal clear. Will you call him?"

"Of course," Melrose blustered. "But what should I say?"

"Tell him I'm here and that I'd like to see him. Tell him . . . hell, just tell him I love him, will you?"

"*That's* certainly to the point."

Nicki released a heavy breath. "It's been a long time coming. I spoke to Kimo last week, and for the first time I realized how much I've hurt him over the years. He's fed up with being hurt. I just hope I'm not too late."

"If my two cents are worth anything, I say Kimo has the kind of feelings for you that don't change," Melrose returned as he rose to his feet. "I'll get going and let you rest now."

"Melrose!" Nicki chimed as he turned. "When do you think Jack and Catherine are going to get here?"

He bestowed a tolerant look. "For the hundredth time, Nicki, I don't know. They had a long hard night, but they'll be here. Try to be patient."

"Patient," she muttered distastefully as he left her bedside. "Melrose!" she raspingly called once more. "Is there anything at all you neglected to tell me about Catherine?"

He smiled. "I told you everything I know *twice.* However, I *will* add that the two of you make a remarkable pair."

After Melrose departed, Nicki stared at the ceiling and savored the revelation. She had a twin sister, Catherine Winslow of Charleston, South Carolina. And, of all things, it was Jack—*her* Jack—who had found Catherine and brought her to the Big Island. It was wild . . . amazing . . . fantastic!

Nicki willed the hours to fly, but they passed slowly. It was after six when a knock sounded on the door and Catherine stepped in. Her hair was golden blond and chin-length. She was wearing a red shirt and khaki walking shorts that showed off shapely legs.

"Hi," she greeted, and remained hesitantly inside the door.

"Hi," Nicki returned.

"You're looking *much* better."

"You're looking pretty good yourself."

"Jack thought he'd give us a few minutes to talk on our own."

"Wise man," Nicki pronounced, and patted the sheet beside her. "Come on over and have a seat." As Catherine complied, Nicki's hungry gaze settled on her eyes. "When I woke up this morning," she added, "I thought you were a dream."

"That's what I thought about *you* for a very long time."

Pushing up with her good hand, Nicki locked an arm around Catherine's neck. "Thank you for saving my life," she whispered.

Catherine embraced her with matching urgency, and they clung to each other. When they finally parted, both of them smilingly wiped tears from their eyes. Nicki settled back on the pillow, sought Catherine's hand, and clasped it as she studied her.

"Quite an auspicious meeting, wouldn't you say?"

"I can't think of anything much more dramatic," Catherine answered with a warm smile.

"Melrose says that, in addition to everything else, it looks like Austin was behind your kidnapping all those years ago."

Catherine's smile dimmed. "I don't suppose we'll ever know the whole truth about that night. Maybe we should let it go and focus on the fact that we're lucky to have found each other now."

"*Damn* lucky," Nicki agreed. "How the hell did you manage to find me at the Pali?"

Catherine glanced down at their clasped hands before lifting her eyes once more. "You showed me the way."

"I did? How?"

"Ever since I was a child, I've been dreaming about you, Nicki. At least I *thought* I was dreaming. I just found out a matter of days ago that I was actually connecting with *you,* your real life. Somehow, when we connect, everything you see, hear, and feel, *I* experience, too."

"God . . . how does *that* work?"

"Maybe God is the only one who *does* know how it works. I surely don't. Can you imagine what would happen if news of this leaked out? The medical profession would be at our throats—"

"The press would be at our heels like a pack of dogs."

"I can see the headlines now: TELEPATHIC TWINS SHOCK WORLD!"

"This has to remain strictly confidential," Nicki concluded.

"Right. As far as anyone needs to know, we're sisters who managed to reunite. Period."

Nicki's face took on a thoughtful look. "You know, from the earliest days I can remember, there have been times when something came over me. I don't know how to describe it—a warm feeling like a guardian angel was smiling down on me. I used to fantasize that it was Mother. Maybe it was you instead."

"I'd like to think so," Catherine replied. They gazed into each other's eyes for a few solemn seconds before Nicki broke into a mischievous grin.

"Now, on to more important things," she said.

"Such as?"

"Men, of course. Are you married? Got a boyfriend? What?"

"Neither," Catherine answered with a light laugh. "I was engaged last summer. It took me a while, but I finally faced up to the fact that it wasn't right, and I called it off. No regrets."

"No one special in your life?"

Catherine glanced aside. "Not really. What about you? The last I knew, you were very much in love with Jack."

"Yeah, I guess I was."

"Was?" Catherine repeated, her gaze leaping to Nicki's face.

"I cared a great deal for Jack, and I always will, but . . . I'm not the same girl I was when I knew him, Catherine. I see things a new way now. It's like a cloud has been lifted from my eyes, and everything looks different . . . including the man I just found out I'm in love with."

"You're in love with someone *else*?" Catherine questioned.

Nicki slowly nodded. "With someone I've known all my

life; only just now do I see that he's the man I want to be with, and have kids with, and grow old with—you get the picture. The last time I spoke to Malia, I asked her what she thought of a future for Kimo and me. She said that if I truly loved him, there would be no wondering, no choice. And ever since I woke up from this nightmare, that's how I've felt. Kimo is the one."

Nicki paused with a sigh. "Now, if only I can convince *him* of that. I told Melrose to call him for me. But I don't know if he'll come."

"Why do you think he won't?"

"Because the last time I saw him he told me flat out that we were too different and there could never be anything between us," Nicki soberly replied.

"A momentary setback," Catherine remarked. "In a way I've known you a long time, Nicki. And one thing I know for certain: Once you've set your heart on something, you're not likely to give up until you've got it."

A slow grin dawned on Nicki's face. "So I'll try not to be too disappointed if Kimo doesn't show up tonight."

"After all," Catherine returned in an exaggerated Southern accent, "tomorrow *is* another day."

A rap sounded at the door, and Jack poked his head in. "It's getting lonesome out here, ladies. Mind if I come in?"

He sauntered into the hospital room, memorably tall and gorgeous in jeans, boots, and a white shirt with sleeves rolled to the elbow. Nicki smiled up at him as he strolled around Catherine and stopped by the hospital bed.

"Hi ya, stranger," she greeted.

"Hey, baby," Bending down, he pressed a familiar light kiss to the top of her head, then stepped back. "How ya feeling?"

"Better than I look," Nicki replied. As Jack chuckled, her gaze darted from him to Catherine and back again. "How in the world did you two hook up with each other?" she added.

"Did Catherine tell you she's a novelist?" Jack responded.

"Get outta town," Nicki responded, looking quickly to Catherine. "You write *books*?"

"And her most recent is entitled *The Clown Wore Black*," Jack continued. "Ring any bells?"

"Clown?" Nicki piped up. "*My* clown?"

"I had a *lot* of dreams last summer," Catherine commented.

"And they inspired her to write a mystery, which *I* picked up at my favorite bookstore."

Nicki listened, enraptured, as Jack related the tale of tracking Cat Winslow to Charleston, discovering that she was Nicki Palmer's look-alike, realizing that the two of them must be twins. "Anyway," he briskly concluded. "Catherine insisted that we come to Hawaii, and it turned out to be in the nick of time."

"I'll say," Nicki murmured. "When did you arrive?"

"Just two days ago," Catherine answered.

"Have you been to the ranch?"

"Only in my dreams."

"Great. Then I get to show it to you for the first time. They're letting me out of here tomorrow afternoon. Can we all drive up together?"

"Sure," Jack slowly replied. "I think we can handle that."

As he said it, he looped a casual arm around Catherine's shoulders. She looked up at him. He looked down at her. And the two of them might as well have shouted it from the rooftops. They were in love with each other.

Folding her arms, Nicki looked from one to the other. "So, what have *you two* been up to since you got together, hmmm?"

Both their faces proceeded to turn a guilty shade of red as they suffered her probing look. They were spared the discomfort of responding as a commotion of raised voices beyond the door drew their attention.

"Sounds like somebody's raising hell with the police officer posted outside," Jack announced. "I'll check it out."

He stalked away, and Nicki lifted a knowing brow as she perused Catherine, whose cheeks continued to glow. But an instant later, when Kimo walked into the room, all Nicki's attention flooded in his direction.

He was wearing jeans, boots, a denim work shirt, and a cowboy hat, which he respectfully swept from his head. He looked like he'd come straight off the range, and was the most breathtaking thing she'd ever seen. His blue eyes burned across the distance between them, and Nicki's heart started pounding so fiercely she'd have sworn the whole room pulsed with the force of it.

"I would have brought flowers," he said. "But I didn't want to take the time to stop."

"That's okay," Nicki mumbled with a fleet glance to Catherine. *Kimo*? Catherine discreetly mouthed as she rose from her seat on the bed. With a short affirming nod, Nicki said, "Catherine, I'd like you to meet Kimo." As Catherine moved to the foot of the bed, Nicki added, "Kimo, this is my sister, Catherine."

As Kimo's gaze switched to the golden-haired blonde, he was filled with astonishment. Damn . . . they were twins. Catherine offered a hand. "Well, *this* is a surprise," he remarked, and joined her in a shake. "Nice to meet you."

"Nice to meet you, too," she said in a soft Southern voice.

Kimo glanced to Nicki. "Was I the only one in the dark all this time? I never knew you had a sister."

"We were *all* in the dark," Nicki replied with a shaky grin. "Catherine and I have just discovered each other."

"I'll bet there's quite a story behind *that*," he said.

"Yes," Nicki murmured as his gaze captured hers once more. "Quite a story."

Silence bloomed as they stared into each other's eyes. Catherine took the cue. "I think I'll go catch up with Jack while you two visit," she announced, and swiftly withdrew.

Nicki's eyes lifted to maintain their gaze as Kimo walked up to the side of the bed. "Are you all right?" he asked, his voice deep and rumbling.

"I know I look terrible, but I'm going to be fine."

"You're always beautiful to me, Nicki."

"Thanks," she whispered.

"I was on the Parker south range when Melrose called. I couldn't believe it."

"I wasn't sure you'd come. After the rodeo in Waimea, you sounded so dead certain you didn't want me in your life."

"For twenty-four long hours I thought you were dead, Nicki. I had plenty of time to wish I'd done things differently. Even so, I'm not willing to settle for a fling that's going to end. Melrose said you love me. Is it true?"

Her gaze roamed over his face, which was as tense as it was incredibly handsome. "It's true, all right."

"Then will you marry me?"

"*Marry* you?" Nicki repeated with wide eyes.

"You know how I feel about you. If a future between us isn't what you're looking for, then—"

"I didn't say that," she broke in. "I'm just surprised. You seemed so adamant about the princess and the *paniolo,* and never the twain shall meet."

"I don't give a damn about that crap anymore. The way I see it, after we fill up the ranch with our children, I'll feel pretty damn well at home there."

"Children?" Nicki mumbled.

Kimo solemnly nodded. "I'd like a lot of them, *if* you're their mother. So what do you say, Nicki? Are you ready to go all the way with me?"

"Oh, yes," she whispered, tried to shift up to reach him, and winced with pain at the effort.

"No, no," Kimo cautioned, gently pushing her back to the pillow. "Hold on a minute."

"What are you doing?" she asked as he strode away.

"Just ensuring a little privacy for a few minutes." Swiftly locking the door, Kimo returned to her bedside. "Slide over."

Dissolving in a mischievous grin, Nicki slipped over and welcomed him onto the narrow hospital bed. Stretching out alongside her, Kimo gingerly slipped an arm behind her neck and cradled her cheek in his free hand.

"Ya know what?" he murmured, his mouth so close she could feel his breath.

"What?" Nicki dreamily replied.

"As soon as you're physically able, I'm gonna make love to you all night long," Kimo stated, and then proceeded to kiss her in a heart-stopping way that sealed his promise.

Catherine stopped to exchange a few words with a friendly nurse at the nurses' station, then continued along the hospital corridor to the waiting area. A few people were watching TV in one of the alcoves. She spotted Jack beyond the glass doors to the adjoining outdoor terrace. Leaning against the wall by the rail, he was smoking a cigarette as he looked out across the dusky hospital grounds. Stepping out into the breezy Hawaiian twilight, she walked toward him.

"I take it Kimo is keeping Nicki company."

"It was pretty obvious they wanted to be alone," Catherine replied with a small smile.

Jack blew a column of smoke into the gathering darkness. "He's been head over heels in love with her for years. I learned that much last summer."

Turning aside, Catherine rested her hands on the rail. "It appears Kimo is destined to become a big part of Nicki's life. She just told me she's in love with him as well."

"And not with *me,* as I tried to point out a week ago."

Catherine looked around. Fading light glimmered in Jack's eyes. They sparkled at her through the shadows. "Looking back," she quietly began, "I'm sorry now that I—"

"Shhh," he admonished. Cramming the cigarette in a neighboring ash can, Jack straightened from the wall. "You did the right thing, Catherine. I never agreed with your reason, but you did the right thing."

"Did I?" As her soft question hung between them, a frown knitted its way across Jack's brow.

"Are you planning on hanging around here awhile?" he asked.

"Well, yes . . . I thought I'd speak to Nicki one more time before leaving."

"I wonder if you'd mind taking a cab back to the hotel."

A pang of alarm shot through Catherine. "What are *you* going to do?"

"I don't know. I just need a break from all this."

"You need a break?" she mindlessly repeated, at which point Jack released a short laugh and ran his hand over his hair in a show of frustration.

"For God's sake, Catherine. I feel as though I've been on the verge of a heart attack ever since I met you. I'll see you in the morning, okay?"

"Sure," she mumbled, and, as she watched Jack walk out of sight, was consumed by the chilling sensation that he was already thousands of miles away.

Chapter Twenty-four

Tuesday, July 11

The afternoon was bright and sunny, a cheery omen as Jack, Catherine, and Nicki departed Hilo in the rented Cadillac. Nicki was propped in the back on pillows confiscated from the hospital, and Catherine spent the majority of the trip pivoted in the front passenger's seat responding to a barrage of questions. By the time they reached the upcountry, she felt as though she'd recited the entire chronology of her life.

Although Catherine's spirits were high with the contagious ebullience of her sister, below the surface a murky sense of dread gathered. The distance Jack had inflicted between them the previous night remained, and seemed to grow more palpable by the hour. Oh, he was pleasant enough as they motored along, joining in occasionally with a quipping remark or companionable laugh. But mostly he was silent as Catherine and Nicki did the talking. Twice during the journey Catherine glanced over and caught his eye. Both times Jack briskly returned his gaze to the road.

Melrose and Kimo—who had resigned from Parker Ranch that very morning—met them at the ranch. As Catherine surveyed the setting from her dreams, she was consumed with such déjà vu that worries of Jack receded. She thought of the dream journals, pictures she'd drawn as a child, and the many times imaginings of this place had filled dark hours. Now, as the mirages stared her in the face with solid form, she was overwhelmed.

The troop of five went inside, the men hanging back as Nicki and Catherine strolled into the airy receiving area

where opposing French doors overlooked the terrace and
pool. Nicki placed a light arm about her waist.

"Is it the way you pictured it?" she asked.

Catherine mutely nodded as detail after miraculous detail
flooded her memory—overflowing, it seemed, to fill her
throat and still her tongue. She emerged from the dazed
state only when the group proceeded to Nicki's room, and
Jack revealed that the embroidered quilt at the foot of the
bed was a birthday gift from Malia. Wrapping herself in
the quilt, Nicki crawled onto the bed and broke down. The
men withdrew, and Catherine stayed with her while she
cried it out.

When they emerged, it was well past five o'clock. Finding
Catherine's bags deposited discreetly in the hall, they
moved her into the guest room next to Nicki's. After fresh-
ening up, they changed for dinner, Nicki into a flowing
turquoise muumuu, and Catherine into a similarly styled
red floral that Nicki produced from her cavernous closet
and insisted that she wear. The two of them proceeded
through the house to find that Melrose, Jack, and Kimo
had set up bar on the lanai—including a bottle of champagne that chilled promisingly in an ice bucket.

In honor of the ladies, Melrose had mixed up a batch of
daiquiris. Sipping on the tart drinks, Nicki and Catherine
left the males to their socializing on the lanai and retired
to the kitchen, where they put together a homecoming luau
courtesy of Malia's amply stocked pantry. There were platters of glazed ham with pineapple, shrimp salad topped
with crab meat, potatoes au gratin with parsley, fresh avo-
cado, plus a selection of exquisite homemade breads. Setting the dining table with their mother's china, silver, and
candelabra, they called the men to supper.

The food was delicious, and throughout the meal the dinner table conversation remained lively—the topics ranging
from ranch business, including Kimo's return, to the whole
of Palmer International and the changes coming about with
Melrose's retirement. When they all had eaten their fill,
Melrose leaned back in his chair with a sober look.

"I hate to break the festive mood," he began, "but I've
made certain arrangements of which you must be aware.
Private memorial services for Austin and Malia will take
place tomorrow morning at ten. They'll be buried side by

side in the family cemetery. I hope that meets with your approval."

Nicki and Catherine exchanged a somber look before Nicki answered, "I believe that's what they would have wanted. Thank you, Melrose."

An oppressive air lingered over the table for only a moment before Kimo rose from his chair. "And now on to brighter things," he said, and elicited a round of smiles. "I have an announcement to make. I'm proud to say that after years of tormenting me beyond belief"—he glanced down at Nicki with a grin—"this lovely lady has agreed to be my wife."

They all leaped to their feet. Catherine embraced Nicki as Jack and Melrose closed in on Kimo with congratulating handshakes. "Why didn't you tell me?" Catherine demanded.

"Kimo wanted to make a formal announcement." Nicki sighed as she turned to gaze toward her fiancé. "Isn't he thoughtful?"

"Yeah," Catherine agreed with a teasing laugh. "And not too hard to look at, either." The champagne was uncorked, glasses poured, and the celebration continued with talk of the wedding, which was tentatively scheduled for the end of November.

"Kimo insists on waiting until he can pool enough money to foot the bill for the honeymoon himself," Nicki confided to Catherine. "He's never been to the mainland. We're going to start in California and spend a month or so traveling across country."

"And ending up in Charleston, I hope," Catherine returned.

Nicki gave her a sly smile. "I was thinking we might make it just in time for Christmas."

A short while later the doorbell rang. Melrose answered it and returned, surprisingly enough, with a young nun. "Her name is Sister Ann, and she has only a limited amount of time before she must return to the convent," he announced, his eyes on Nicki. "She wants to speak with you about Peni."

"I'm sorry to interrupt," the bright-eyed nun chimed in. "It looks like you're having a party."

"Nicki and I have just become engaged," Kimo stated, and walked up to her.

"Oh, my goodness," she breathed as she stared up at him. "You look just as she described. You must be Kimo."

"That's right," he affirmed as Nicki moved up beside him.

"May God bless the two of you with a lifetime of happiness," Sister Ann pronounced with a glowing smile.

"Thank you, Sister," Nicki said. "What's this about Peni?"

The young nun folded her hands. "Dear me, I know everything she did, Miss Palmer, and I'm sure her outbursts must have been both frightening and painful. Nonetheless, I've come here to beg your mercy. Peni needs *help*, not imprisonment."

"Are you trying to say you want Nicki to drop the charges?" Kimo asked with a frown. "Do you realize that during one of the attacks, Peni actually tried to *drown* her?"

"I believe in my heart that Peni never planned to commit such an act," Sister Ann responded. "I believe it was the horror of what she'd nearly done that compelled her to make an attempt on her *own* life. Do you realize that a mere couple of hours passed after the incident at the pool before Peni drove her truck over a cliff on the leeward side of the island?"

"No, I didn't know anything about that," Nicki murmured.

"She nearly died and spent months in the hospital," Sister Ann continued. "Then she came to live with us at Our Lady of Mercy. I understand that you've been through a terrible ordeal, Miss Palmer, but I believe Peni is worth saving. And it won't happen in jail."

"I'm not so sure about this," Kimo remarked. "I've known Peni all her life. She's always had a temper, and I can't forget the way she looked that night after the rodeo— smiling one minute, out of control the next."

"She needs medical treatment," the nun replied. "I'm aware of that, and so is Peni. There is a fine doctor who donates his services to the needy at Our Lady of Mercy, and he's qualified to administer such supervision." Sister Ann looked to Nicki as she added, "Peni is trying her best to face up to what she's done. That's why she turned herself in. She wants to salvage her soul, Miss Palmer. What she prays for is the chance to return to the convent and devote herself to a life of service. There are people who care for her there, people she cares for in return."

Nicki glanced to Kimo, who regarded her with scowling skepticism. Taking him by the hand, she linked her other arm with the young nun's. "Why don't we go in the study, sit down, and talk this through, hmmm?"

As the three of them strolled out of the dining room, Catherine cast a dismal look to Jack and Melrose. "Sometimes it seems as though the sordid business of everything that's happened is never going to end."

"It's almost over, Catherine," Melrose replied in a comforting tone. "After the funeral tomorrow we can all start putting this nightmare behind us. You'll see—day by day, week by week, it will become more and more a part of the past."

"That's right," Jack joined in. "After tomorrow we can all get on with our lives."

The undertone of his remark cut Catherine to the quick. As the anxiety she'd been burying all day boiled to the surface, she filled her hands with the task of clearing the table.

"Want some help?" Jack asked as she began stacking dishes.

"That's okay," she murmured without looking up.

"I don't mind," he returned, and proceeded to help her carry everything into the kitchen before joining Melrose on the lanai.

When she finished loading the dishwasher, Catherine moved to a strategic window, glanced out to the lanai, and saw that Melrose was sitting alone at the table, the red tip of his cigar glowing against the twilight. Exiting the kitchen, she gave him a passing smile as she walked to the edge of the porch. The exotic fragrance of tropical flowers greeted her as she gazed across the lawns to the distant white landmarks of barn and riding ring still visible in the descending darkness.

"It's so beautiful here," Catherine said. "More so than I ever could have dreamed."

"Kind of like paradise?" Melrose amicably questioned.

"Closer to it than anyplace *I've* seen."

Resting his cigar in the ashtray, Melrose leaned back and

folded his hands over his belly. "It's the Palmer home place, Catherine. *Your* home place."

She turned and propped a shoulder against one of the portico columns. "Beautiful as it is, I don't think I could ever think of the ranch that way. It will always be Nicki's place to me."

"You don't think you could be happy here?"

"I'm sure I'll spend *many* happy times here in the future, Melrose. But my home and life are in Charleston, just as Nicki's are here on the island."

Melrose nodded in understanding. Less than a minute passed before Catherine added, "Where's Jack?"

Melrose stifled a grin as he reached for his cigar. "He brought up an odd subject a little while ago. He wanted to know if there was a grave and headstone in the family cemetery for Nicki's supposedly stillborn twin. 'Why, yes,' I told him. 'It's been there for thirty years.' 'Well, it's not going to be there tomorrow morning,' he announced, and took off."

"What do you think he's going to do?" Catherine asked on a bewildered note.

"Oh, I don't think there's any doubt about what he's going to do. He stopped by the garage and picked up a shovel."

Catherine gazed with round-eyed surprise. In this light, disregarding the hair, Melrose could swear he was looking at Nicki. Rising from his chair, he lumbered to the bar, reached inside the cabinet, and returned to hand her a flashlight.

"Take the path past the garage that curves left through the thicket of banyan," he said as he resumed his seat. "There's a white picket fence around the cemetery. You can't miss it."

"Thanks, Melrose."

"My pleasure." Taking a puff off the cigar, Melrose smiled like the Cheshire cat behind the cloud of smoke. "What a night," he added to himself as the pretty young blonde walked into the gathering darkness.

Catherine emerged from the banyan thicket to see that the white picket fence was dead ahead, and Jack only a matter of ten yards or so beyond the open gate. She paused, turned the flashlight to the ground, and watched for a moment as he labored in the glow of an old-fashioned kerosene lantern. Having discarded his shirt, he was naked to the waist, the skin of his chest and arms glistening with lantern light as he methodically scooped and unloaded shovelfuls of dark earth.

Her focus narrowed on the way his muscles rippled as he worked. She remembered the power of his arms, the provocative weight of his body. Her vision momentarily blurred as Catherine was flushed with a dizzying blend of desire and adoration. As she moved forward, the rhythmic scrape of his shovel drowned out the sound of her footsteps. She was several feet inside the gate when he whirled with a start.

"Damn, Catherine!"

"I'm sorry," she said with a smile.

"You shouldn't sneak up on people like that!"

"I wasn't sneaking," she replied with a light laugh. "Did I spook you?"

Jamming the blade of the shovel into the newly turned ground at his feet, Jack wiped a forearm across his glistening brow. "Well, it *is* a graveyard, you know."

"Yes, I know," she replied as her train of thought shifted. Lifting the flashlight, Catherine shone the beam toward the collection of granite markers neatly laid out within the manicured greens of the cemetery. She walked pensively among the grave sites. Flanking the plot where Jack stood were the resting places of her parents; beyond them, her grandparents; farther on, other ancestors, a few dating back to the nineteenth century.

She returned to the twin headstones of her mother and father: Marie and Philip. These were the people who had given her life, the people whose blood ran in her veins. Catherine drew a long shivering breath as a gut-level sense of kinship invaded her. She turned away with the paradoxical sensations of having both suffered a great loss and received a great gift.

"I'm sorry," Jack said as she walked in his direction. "It must be tough never to have known your mom and dad."

"At least I know them *now*. I have you to thank for that."

"You have *yourself* to thank," he returned as he picked

up the shovel. "It was *your* drive that brought us here."
Jack proceeded to pack down the freshly dug dirt with
sharp smacks from the flat of the blade. "That ought to do
it," he pronounced a few minutes later, and tossed the
shovel aside. "I checked it out. There was a headstone here.
Nothing more."

"What in the world made you think of doing this?" she
asked.

"Ever since I heard about this mock grave, the thought
of it has made my skin crawl." Bending toward the lantern,
Jack retrieved his shirt and draped it carelessly about his
neck. "I didn't want to have to look at it during the service
tomorrow. Didn't want anybody else to have to look at
it, either."

"That's very decent of you."

He shrugged. "Frankly, it gave me a sense of satisfaction
to wipe out a small part of Austin Palmer's lie." Picking
up the shovel and lantern, he added, "Come on. I'll walk
you back."

The path through the banyan was dark and narrow. Jack
led the way with the lantern, occasionally glancing back to
confirm that she was following a few steps behind. But he
didn't say anything, and the trek elapsed in silence. They
emerged from the cloistered woods beneath the openness
of a star-spangled sky. The garage was just ahead, and far
to the right the house where light shone from the windows.
Jack proceeded toward the garage at a loping pace. If she
didn't speak up, the moment would be lost.

"Wait a minute," Catherine said to his back. He stopped
and turned, the glow of the lantern at his side casting his
features in golden relief. A wary look formed on his face
as she drew near. "Could I talk to you?" she added.

"About what?"

"The fact that you haven't looked me in the eye all day."
He cocked his jaw and glanced aside. "You seem so far
away," she added. "It's hard for me to believe we were
ever close."

"We're close," he rumbled.

"I mean it's hard to believe we were ever . . ."

He looked around as a single accusatory brow shot up.
"Lovers? I thought I was supposed to forget we ever *were*."

"When I said that, I was acting on the belief that Nicki was in love with you. A lot has changed since then."

"Some things haven't." Catching the light of the lantern, Jack's eyes glowed like foxfire as he added, "I still want you, Catherine—so much that I'd like to lay you down right here on the grass. But I know it wouldn't be right."

Swallowing hard, she stepped up, took the lantern from his hand, and set it down on the dirt path.

"What are you doing?" Jack muttered as she proceeded to do the same with the shovel. Catherine started to lift her hands to his face. He caught her by the wrists and glared down at her, tension radiating about him like a coat of bristling fur.

"I can be your lover, but not your mate," he growled. "Is that enough for you?"

She gazed up into his frowning eyes. "I don't have the answers to any questions, Jack. All I know is that I'm so terribly weary of hiding what I feel. All I know is that I love you." Rising on tiptoe, she overcame the barrier of her corralled limbs, lifted her mouth to his, and ran her tongue over his lips.

He remained stiff and unresponsive. Catherine kissed him anyway. After a few interminable seconds, Jack emitted a muffled groan and released her wrists. Gathering her up in a fierce embrace, he started kissing her back.

Catherine's hands roamed the bare expanse of his back as his tongue seduced her. Holding her tightly against him with one arm, Jack moved a hand to her hip, gathered up the voluminous skirt of the muumuu, and reached beneath it. She gasped as his fingers slipped inside her panties.

And suddenly he halted. Tearing his mouth from hers, he heaved for breath, withdrew his bold hand, and respectfully smoothed her skirt. "I can't," he mumbled against her forehead, then abruptly backed away. "What Kimo and Nicki have—that's what you deserve. *I* know it even if you don't."

When he stooped to grab up the lantern and shovel, Catherine took a halting step in his direction. "Jack, please wait—"

"Let me go, Catherine!" he erupted in a voice that rang across the grounds. "Just . . . let me go," he quietly reiterated before striding away toward the garage.

Hours later, while Kimo and Nicki cuddled in the room next door, Catherine paced the length of the guest chamber. It was nearly one in the morning when she gave in to the urge to peep across the hall to the room where Jack was staying. The door was open, the bedside lamp burning, the bed empty.

Tucking her hands in the pockets of her robe, she coursed through the dark house on bare feet. When she reached the kitchen, she spotted him on the adjoining lanai. Starlight silvered his silhouette as he leaned against one of the columns, his gaze turned to the unfathomable darkness of the lawns. Either he sensed her impending presence or fate stepped in and took a hand, for just as Catherine mustered the nerve to approach him, Jack ambled down the lanai steps and disappeared into the night.

The next morning's service for Austin and Malia was inescapably sad, although the minister did an admirable job of dwelling on the love they'd shared for decades, rather than the violent way their lives came to an end. When it was over, Jack formally extended his sympathy to both Nicki and Catherine, then walked off with Melrose toward the older man's quarters.

Kimo departed for Hilo, where Peni was being held by the county police. After a long discussion the preceding night, he and Nicki had decided he should talk with her in person. Depending on his judgments after the interview, Nicki was leaning toward the idea of dropping all charges, with the provision that Peni be remanded to the custody of the sisters of Our Lady of Mercy.

"Let's do something to get our minds off all this," Nicki said to Catherine, and proceeded to talk her into taking her first horseback ride. "Don't worry," she persuaded as she decked Catherine out in some of her own riding boots and gear. "I'll saddle up Anika for you. She's the sweetest pony on the place."

After a half hour of basic instruction, Catherine nudged Anika to follow Nicki's pony out of the riding ring. They mosied for a while across the green upcountry range, where cattle grazed picturesquely against a backdrop of distant, cloud-topped volcanoes. "I'm taking you to my favorite lookout atop that ridge up ahead," Nicki said eventually.

"Want to try a canter? It's the smoothest gait there is. All you have to do is sit and rock."

And so they galloped across the sun-drenched range, which seemed to stretch out in length as Catherine peered toward the ridge with windswept eyes. Finally they crested the slope, and Nicki reined in. Anika neatly followed the chestnut pony's lead.

"It's kind of like flying, isn't it?" Nicki asked.

"Yes," Catherine breathlessly answered. "I think I'll stick to the water, where the only thing speeding me along is me."

Nicki laughed. "You swim. I'll fly. It's worked out pretty well so far." She took a sweeping look at the panoramic view. "It's pretty, isn't it?" she added.

"Beautiful. In all the years I envisioned this place, I never realized how truly beautiful it is, or how big."

"And half of it belongs to you."

Catherine shook her head. "I'm really not comfortable with getting into that."

"Catherine," Nicki pronounced in the manner of a scolding mother. "It's not something to feel uncomfortable about. You're rich now, that's all. And you don't have to do a thing except open the trust with me next week. Melrose is arranging the legalities as we speak."

Catherine gazed into her sister's eyes. "Doesn't it bother you at all? The idea of sharing something you've always thought of as being all yours?"

"Are you kidding?" Nicki chimed with a lift of her brows. "Listen, kiddo, you're worth a lot more than a few million *any* day." As Catherine chuckled, Nicki gave her a steady look. "You're a Palmer, Catherine. One of the last two. I wish you'd reconsider and move home where you belong."

A knot of emotion rose to Catherine's throat. "For me, home is Charleston. That's just the way things worked out. I have friends there, and responsibilities. Remember the swim clinic I told you about? I feel as though I'm managing to make a difference. It's a feeling I don't want to give up."

Nicki tipped her head for a considering moment. "Plus, Charleston is more accessible from Chicago."

"Well, yes . . . I guess it is. But that's not my reason for going back."

Relaxing the reins, Nicki allowed her pony to graze. "What the hell's going on with you and Jack?" she demanded, and drew a startled look. "It's obvious you're crazy about each other, but the past two days you've acted like strangers."

"You know how Jack is," Catherine said after a moment. "I suppose there's no difference between what's going on now and what went on between you and him last summer."

"Uh-uh," Nicki was quick to reply. "There's a big difference. Jack was never in love with me, but he *is* with you."

Catherine stared at the fingers she'd curled around the saddle horn. "He's never said that."

"Well, he might not be *saying* it, but he's sure *feeling* it. Geez, the way he looks at you could melt the Mauna Kea snowcap." Catherine glanced up with a small smile. "That's the saddest excuse for a happy face I've ever seen," Nicki added.

Catherine's meager smile disappeared as she released a heavy breath. "The bottom-line fact is that whatever Jack feels for me, it isn't enough to overcome the wall that stands between us. Six years ago his wife died in an explosion meant for him."

"I'm sorry to hear that. It's a tragedy. But that was six years ago, and this is now."

"It doesn't matter. Jack hasn't gotten over it. He feels responsible for his wife's death, Nicki, and he doesn't want another mate. He's told me so point-blank on several occasions, including as recently as last night."

"I don't care *what* he's told you. Jack has been a lone wolf for quite some time. Maybe it'll take him a while to realize he's been caught, but he'll come around."

"I'd like to believe that. But I don't."

"Well, I *do*." Nicki pulled up her pony's head so that the chestnut began to prance. "And I've got a hundred bucks that says he'll carry you off into the sunset sometime in the next few days. He can't last any longer than that."

A smile spread across Catherine's face. "That's a bet I'd be happy to lose." They rode leisurely back to the stables. As they drew near, Catherine spotted Jack's Cadillac parked in the drive by the riding ring. He was propped against the trunk of the car, watching them ride up. Her heart fell to her feet.

"This doesn't look good," Catherine murmured as the ponies came to a stop in the stableyard.

"Don't jump to conclusions," Nicki murmured back. "Dismount and go talk to him. I'll take care of your pony."

Slowly obeying, Catherine got down from the back of the horse, handed the reins to Nicki, and ambled in Jack's direction.

"I was waiting for you," he said as she drew near.

Her heart was hammering to beat the band. "So it appears."

"You know," he began, "watching you ride in here made me realize for the first time that you're half-owner of Palmer Ranch and everything that goes with it. That puts you in a pretty elite class." He paused to bestow a faint grin. "But then again, I always *did* say you're in a class by yourself."

For a few seconds all Catherine could do was stare, although her gaze seemed to take on a life of its own—dropping to his booted feet, racing upward past jeans and belt and open-throated white shirt . . . up to Jack's face and his sun-streaked hair that glistened in the sun.

"You're leaving, aren't you?" she said finally.

He glanced aside and crammed his hands in the pockets of his jeans. "Yeah. I got a flight." Catherine captured her lip between her teeth and tried to still its shaking. "It won't do anybody any good for me to stick around," he added, and met her eyes.

She forced herself to maintain a level gaze. "I suppose I should have known this was coming, after last night."

Withdrawing a hand from his pocket, Jack ran it restlessly over his hair. "When you draw out hard things, it only makes them harder, Catherine. And saying good-bye to you is a tough thing. You have no idea how tough."

The backs of her eyes were scalding. "Oh, I don't know about that. I might have some idea."

He reached into his shirt pocket and offered a business card. "Maybe you could drop me a line sometime and let me know how you're doing."

Catherine looked at his hand. By the time her gaze lifted once more, her face had gone white as a sheet. "I don't want your card, Jack," she uttered in a hollow tone.

His arm fell. "You mean, you don't want to stay in touch?"

"I mean I *don't* want your card, and I *don't* want a phone call every six months or so when the thought of me crosses your mind."

A scowl gathered on Jack's face as he tucked the card back in his shirt pocket. "I was always honest with you, Catherine."

"Well then, you can walk away with a clear conscience, can't you?" she returned with surprising steadiness as her eyes burned like hot coals.

"I'm going to miss you," he said after a tense moment.

"Not enough to make a difference."

Jack's scowl deepened. "I'd like to call you sometime."

"Don't. There was a time when I would have jumped at the chance to hear from you sometime, anytime. But not anymore. The way things are now, that wouldn't be good for anyone."

"It would be good for *me,*" Jack insisted.

"I need a clean break to get past this," Catherine bluntly stated. "If you're a gentleman, you'll respect my wishes." He peered at her, seemingly dumbfounded, as the sting of oncoming tears heightened the burning in her eyes. "I don't like good-byes," she hurriedly added. "Forgive me if I cut this short. I wish you the best, Jack. Always."

Stepping abruptly forward, Catherine pressed a speedy kiss to his cheek, spun on her heel, and walked rapidly in the direction of the house. When she cleared the stableyard, she started running. Jack watched until she disappeared up the steps of the lanai, his heart thundering and mouth dry as dust.

Vaulting into the Caddie, he started up the engine and roared off, leaving a wake of flying dirt behind. He was a good football field's length down the drive when he glanced out the window and saw Nicki streaking along beside him, her pony in a flat-out gallop over the lawns.

She waved her arm for him to stop. He slammed on the brakes. Nicki pulled up on the pony so hard that he reared, whirled, and pranced like a show horse as she urged him toward the car. When she reached the edge of the drive, she hopped down, left the pony snorting, and walked over to the driver's window, where she planted her hands on her hips and glared at him.

"What the hell are you doing, Jack?"

"I got a flight."

"I don't mean that. I mean why the hell are you cutting out on Catherine? Any fool can see you guys love each other."

Jack turned and looked ahead. "How we feel is our business."

"So you just brush her off and leave without so much as an aloha for me?"

His gaze turned to hers once more. "I'm sorry, Nicki. I wasn't thinking straight. I intended to say good-bye."

"Do you think that's why I chased after you? So you could say good-bye to *me?* No, Jack! I'm trying to talk some sense into you about Catherine."

"I never meant to hurt her," he said earnestly.

"But you *did,* and you *are,*" Nicki heatedly pointed out. "And you're going to *keep on* doing it as long as you insist on burying your heart with a dead woman."

"Catherine told you?" Jack snapped.

"Just that you feel responsible for your wife's death. Catherine didn't say much. She didn't have to. I always knew you'd built a wall around yourself, Jack. I just couldn't figure out why. Now that I know, I find it extremely sad—not the part about your wife, although of course I'm sorry she died, but the part about how you're letting one tragic event ruin your whole life *and* my sister's."

"I'm sure you mean well, Nicki, but this is *not* something I talk about."

Nicki's brows rose as she spread her arms. "Well, tough. Maybe you *should* talk about it, and damn well get over it."

"This is none of your concern!" he boomed.

"Catherine is the finest thing you're ever gonna come across!" Nicki shouted back. "And she happens to love you. If you throw that away, you truly are a jerk of monumental proportions."

"Thanks so much for that inspiring farewell," Jack barked, and started to accelerate.

"Hey!" Nicki yelled.

Jack stomped on the brake, poked his head out the window, and glared back at her. "What?"

"Did I mention you're acting like a jerk?"

"Yeah, I think you mentioned that!" he bellowed.

"Good!" Nicki hurled.

As the Cadillac sped out of view, Nicki leaped onto the pony and raced back to the stables. Leaving the horse with one of the hands, she hurried into the house and found Catherine curled up on her bed, hugging Malia's embroidered quilt and crying pitifully—her body heaving and shaking, but making no noise.

Climbing up on the bed beside her, Nicki cradled Catherine's head in her lap. "Men," she muttered on a note of distaste as she stroked Catherine's hair. "Even the good ones are assholes. And I'm not excluding Kimo, either. Much as I love him, there are a couple of times I can recall when he acted like a perfect idiot. It's like they can't help it, or something."

After a few seconds Catherine chuckled.

"Are you laughing?" Nicki asked, peering down at her.

Catherine wiped her cheeks as she met Nicki's eyes. "There's no one else in the world who could make me laugh just now. Even the good ones are assholes, huh?"

"According to my experience, yes," Nicki replied. "And my experience with men has been somewhat wide-ranging in the past."

"I'm aware of your credentials," Catherine said, and managed to produce a valiant, if undeniably forlorn little smile. "By the way," she added. "You owe me a hundred bucks."

Six days later the sisters went to Pacific B&T in Honolulu, and the Palmer trust was opened according to their mother's will. After that they hurried to the airport gate, and embraced each other as Catherine's San Francisco flight began boarding.

"I'll miss you," Nicki mumbled against Catherine's cheek.

"I'll miss you, too. But it doesn't matter how many miles are between us, Nicki. We won't really be apart. Not ever again."

Nicki's impish countenance settled in a look of seriousness. "That's true, isn't it? We *won't* be apart. No matter what."

"No matter what," Catherine confirmed just before the last call for boarding passengers boomed over the speaker. "I'll call you soon," she said as she backed away.

"I'll call you, too," Nicki replied, trailing a few steps as Catherine hurried to the ticketing agent and proceeded onto the ramp. "Hey!" Nicki called. "Be seeing you!" she added when Catherine looked around.

"Be seeing you!" Catherine called back, and boarded the plane with a smile on her face.

The radiance of Nicki remained with her as she flew across the Pacific—warm and cozy and almost bright enough to dispel the clammy darkness that enshrouded Catherine whenever she thought of Jack. There had been times the past week when she longed so much just to hear his voice that she glared at the telephone and mentally gnashed her teeth as she recalled the way she shoved his business card back in his face.

But then a sad sense of calm would return. The explosive decision that spilled from her lips the day he left was the right one. Hard as it was to accept the end and close the book on Jack, it would be worse to live each hour on the edge of hoping she might hear from him—maybe a letter . . . maybe a call. . . .

Turning with a sigh to the airplane window, Catherine gazed across the billowing tops of clouds, wondered what he was doing, and knew she'd wonder the same thing every day for the rest of her life.

Chapter Twenty-five

Sunday, August 13

Grace banged on the apartment door. No answer. She banged again. No answer.

"I know you're in there," she called. "So you may as well open up, unless you want this door-banging to go on all night."

Finally, Jack swung the door wide and flourished a theatrical, inviting hand. His clothes were sloppy, his eyes bloodshot. And he needed a shave.

"Charming," Grace murmured as she breezed by.

"Thank you, madame," he returned in a thick voice, and kicked the door closed.

"It smells like a brewery in here."

"If it offends you, maybe you should return to your flowers."

"Oh, no," Grace parried. "You're not getting rid of me as easily as you've been getting rid of Bobby. He's been holding back out of some macho code of respecting his best friend's privacy. Not me. You've been locked up in here for four weeks. That's too long, Jack."

Stopping by the dining table, where he apparently had been camping out, she noted stacks of unopened mail, overflowing ashtrays . . . and a photo of Jack with a blonde. Grace picked it up. Against a romantic tropical backdrop, the candlelit couple appeared to be positively enthralled with each other.

"What's going on?" she asked, glancing around. "Does this have something to do with it?"

"Give me that," Jack commanded.

Grace lifted the photo out of his reach and took a closer look. "What's her name?"

"Catherine," he supplied hesitantly.

"She's very pretty."

"I know."

"And you're in love with her."

"Give me the damn picture," Jack growled, and made another grab for it.

Grace held it behind her back. "It shows clear as day in this photo, Jack. You're in love with her."

"I'll get over it."

"It doesn't look like you're having much success so far," Grace remarked flippantly.

Giving her a disgusted look, Jack stomped into the kitchen, where he peered out the window over a sinkful of dishes. Grace walked up behind him and put a sympathetic hand on his shoulder.

"I'm sorry," she said. "You're really torn up, aren't you?"

"I didn't know it could be like this," Jack replied without looking at her. "I can't work. I can't sleep."

"Did she break your heart?" Grace gently asked.

Jack hung his head. "I broke hers."

Grace leaned around his shoulder to peer at his profile. "You mean, she loves you and you love her, and you broke it off?"

"Something like that," he mumbled.

"Why?" Grace shrilled so that Jack winced. "Never mind. I know why. And it's pathetic."

He straightened and gave her a glare as he stepped over to the fridge. "Thank you for those comforting words."

"You don't need comfort, Jack. You need to be woken up."

Pulling out a beer, he popped the top and lifted the can.

"And you *certainly* don't need any more of that," Grace added.

He took a belligerent gulp. "And I *certainly* don't need you telling me what I need."

"Insult me if you like. It won't work. I'm not leaving until we have this out once and for all. I care about you, Jack. And I'm not going to stand by any longer while you bury yourself in this shrine to a woman who's been dead six years."

He hurled the can toward a pile of trash in the corner. Beer sprayed the room in a fresh coat of the acrid smell that already permeated the place. "In the short time I knew

Catherine, she put her life in mortal danger twice! Two times, Grace! And all I could do was watch, just like with Ellen!"

"Was it worse than this?" Grace retorted.

Jack's wild eyes bored into hers. The wildness gradually dissipated, leaving him to look exhausted . . . defeated. "Nothing's worse than this," he admitted finally.

"Then *do* something about it!"

He ran a frustrated hand over his unkempt hair. "She told me not to call her. She said she wanted a clean break."

"Maybe you could change her mind if you went to her."

"I don't know," Jack mumbled.

"Is Catherine worth the effort to find out?" Grace demanded.

His eyes slowly lifted as the magnitude of the simple question filled his mind and heart. That's what it all boiled down to: Was Catherine worth the effort?

"Oh, yeah," Jack answered with conviction, and filled his lungs with the first clear breath he'd been able to draw in weeks. "Damn, Grace," he added on a note of surprise. "Thanks."

"I was always smarter than you gave me credit for, Jack," she said with a smiling toss of her head. "Even when we were kids."

Grace and Bobby helped him clear out the apartment. A lot of things went to charity. Personal mementos, including framed pictures and photo albums, Grace lovingly packed and took home. Finally, all that remained was to turn in the keys.

On that last day Jack paused at the doorway, his gaze lingering in the direction of the kitchen with the hand-painted cabinets. He could almost picture Ellen standing before the stove, glancing around with a smile.

If he were the type to talk to empty rooms, he'd tell her he'd never forget her . . . that if he could have changed things, he would have . . . that he'd been granted a second chance at happiness, had blown it, and now he had to do everything in his power to get it back. He just had to.

But then maybe Ellen heard his unspoken words, after all. As Jack opened the door for the final time, he felt a breeze—not the harsh wind for which Chicago was known, but a sweet little breeze that seemed to course from within the apartment—caressing his face, ruffling his hair, and then spiriting on, as though eager to be finally free to escape to the heavens.

Tuesday, August 29

It was two in the afternoon, the sun high and broiling. Catherine was coaching a few proficient swimmers in the water; Kenny was on the beach, demonstrating for the umpteenth time the fluid motion of the butterfly stroke. Normally the girls hung on his every word. He noticed immediately when their attention wandered elsewhere. They began whispering and giggling among themselves as they peered toward the street.

Kenny turned and saw some tall dude in jeans and a black T-shirt looking in their direction. Apparently the girls thought he was quite a stud. "Come on, ladies," Kenny started to say, then did a double-take.

Dammit to hell, he thought, and didn't wait to think any further. Stalking across the sand, he didn't hesitate as Jack Casey extended a friendly hand. Hauling back, Kenny put all his outrage in a punch that knocked the bigger man back a few paces.

"Damn, kid," Jack complained, gingerly testing his jaw. "That's a pretty solid right you've got there." Kenny drew back and would have landed another blow. Jack caught his fist and held it. "But you only get one," he cautioned with a dark look.

"I warned you not to hurt her, man."

"I know. I'm here to try to make things right."

"Again?" Kenny ridiculed.

Jack looked into the kid's angry black eyes, and released his hand. "Not *'again,'*" he retorted. "Once and for all."

"Yeah? Well, why should I believe *you*?"

"Because I've got a ring in my pocket," Jack flatly answered.

Kenny scrutinized him for a long thoughtful moment. "You mean, you're gonna pop the Big Q?"

"For lack of a more dignified way of putting it, yeah."

Finally Kenny grinned and stepped aside. "Cool," he said.

"Great," Jack returned with another tender probe of his jaw. "Where is she?"

"In the water."

"In the water. Of course."

As he drew near the rippling tide, she spotted him. Jack watched, his blood thundering in his ears, as Catherine commanded the swimmers to shore and started toward him. She walked out of the water, sleek and beautiful in a blue swimsuit, glistening like something not of the earth. *The Charleston mermaid,* he thought with awe, and tried unsuccessfully to swallow down the lump in his throat.

"This is a surprise," she said as she came to stand before him. Her voice filled his ears with familiar sweetness. Her eyes captured his, and he felt the shock of it down to his toes.

There had been times in Chicago when he tried to convince himself she wasn't really as amazing as he remembered, that he must be building things up in his mind when he recalled the way Catherine stole his breath. But he hadn't been building up anything. Everything he remembered was true, including the way his heart skipped every time he looked at her.

"You're looking well," she added.

Jack ran a nervous hand over his hair and attempted to smile. "You wouldn't have said that if you'd seen me a few weeks ago."

"Oh? Have you been ill?"

His shaky smile faded. "Just at heart," he replied, and quickly went on to add, "I should say that you're looking great as always."

Folding her arms across the front of her wet suit, Catherine gave him a penetrating look. "It's good to see you, Jack, but I can't help wondering what you're doing here. I thought we agreed on a clean break."

His gaze darted between her eyes. "What we agreed on was wrong," he said in a rush. "I know that now. I thought everything would die down with time, but it hasn't. It only gets bigger, and now I see it for what it is . . . for what it's been all along."

After patiently waiting for him to finish, she lifted a quizzical brow. "I'm sorry, but I have absolutely no idea what you're talking about."

"I'm talking about the fact that I love you, Catherine."

Once the words were out of his mouth, Jack became instantly calm. *She,* on the other hand, appeared startled and taken completely aback.

Stepping forward, he took her cool hand in his. "I hope you can forgive me for walking away in Hawaii."

"You *love* me?" she questioned in a tiny voice.

"Oh, yeah," Jack heartily responded. "And you once said that *you* love *me.* Has that changed?" Her eyes wide and round, Catherine shook her head. "Then will you give me one more chance?" He held his breath as she stared.

"Take as many as you like," she finally mumbled.

Releasing a gusty sigh of relief, Jack broke into a smile and pointed toward the street. "See that wagon up there? It's got everything I own in it."

"You mean you've left Chicago?"

"Yep. Moved down south to get me a bride."

"A *what*?" Catherine whispered.

Jack's expression transformed to one of total sincerity as he looked into her eyes. "I love you, Catherine," he said once again. Pulling the black velvet box from the pocket of his jeans, he flipped open the top to reveal the diamond solitaire. "Will you marry me?"

Her knees buckled, and she sank to the sand. Jack bent quickly to one knee. "Are you all right?" he anxiously asked.

She peered up at him with a dazed look. "Wow."

"Wow?" he repeated with the beginnings of a grin. "Does that mean yes?"

"Um-hmmm," she managed. Jack's grin spread as he took the ring from the box and slipped it on her finger. "It fits," she observed.

"*We* fit," Jack pointed out.

"Um-hmmm," Catherine murmured once more, her eyes sparkling to rival the diamond as she looked up from the ring. One of those warming, glowing, inimitable smiles lit up her face just before she threw her arms around his neck.

Jack caught her under the knees and around her back, and rose to his feet. Throwing back his head, he emitted a ringing war whoop and took off with her into the ocean. He fell in thigh-high depths, where he and Catherine dissolved in jubilant laughter and were swiftly joined by the splashing, war-whooping crowd of kids from the beach.

*   *   *

Four weeks later they were married in a small ceremony in St. Michael's chapel. Bobby and Grace flew in from Chicago, Nicki and Melrose from Hawaii. Before the wedding Catherine dressed in the church anteroom provided for brides. As she stood on shaking limbs before the full-length mirror, Ann Marie helped her with the veil while Marla and Nicki, who had become instant pals, gossiped on the chaise longue.

"Boy, that Aunt Sybil is a gruesome-looking creature, isn't she?" Nicki commented.

"And she's as sweet as she looks," Marla sagely replied.

"There, that does it," Ann Marie declared. Stepping back, she clasped her hands and beamed with maternal joy. "You're breathtaking, Catherine."

"Thanks," she murmured, and couldn't resist putting a hand to her diaphragm, where she could swear a gang of butterflies were banging about in frantic captivity. "But I'm just so nervous. I've never been so nervous in my life."

"Deep breaths, dear," Ann Marie advised. "That's what I did at my wedding. Breathe in, hold it, breathe out. Breathe in, hold it, breathe out."

"I'll try."

"Just don't get carried away," Ann Marie added teasingly. "After the ceremony my husband told me he thought I was going to blow the robe right off the preacher."

Catherine was breathing deeply as she left the side room. And Melrose smiled encouragingly as he escorted her down the aisle. But nothing helped until she looked ahead and focused on Jack, tall and strikingly handsome in a formal tuxedo. He slipped her a wink as she drew near, and when Melrose transferred her hand to his arm, he bent to her ear.

"You're beautiful," Jack whispered. After that, all Catherine was able to absorb were the sight of his sparkling eyes gazing down at her, and the sound of his deep voice stating the vows.

"I, Jack, take thee, Catherine, to be my wedded wife . . ." It wasn't until he smiled and reached over to wipe away a tear that she realized they were spilling down her cheeks.

They spent their wedding night in Ann Marie's beach house on nearby Seabrook Island. After carrying her over the threshold, Jack proceeded straight into the bedroom with her. They didn't emerge until hours later to raid the fridge—Catherine having pulled on his formal white shirt, and Jack with a sheet tucked around his waist. Standing by the kitchen counter, they drank champagne and feasted on an elegant platter of cold cuts stocked thoughtfully for the bride and groom.

"Catherine Casey," Jack said eventually, and smiled. "It has a nice ring, doesn't it?"

Catherine gave him a thoughtful frown. "Now, honey. I'm going to continue to write novels, you know. For professional reasons I think it would be wiser for me not to change my name."

He stared at her, his face entirely crestfallen. "You do? Damn, Catherine. It never crossed my mind that you wouldn't want to take my name." She let him squirm a moment longer before melting into a mischievous grin. Jack cocked a suspecting brow.

"You're kidding me . . . is that it?"

"You've been teasing me mercilessly ever since we met, Jack. I thought it was about time to put the shoe on the other foot."

"You did, huh?"

"Yes, I did," Catherine returned with a lyrical laugh. "You looked so funny."

"We'll just see about that." Jack lunged for her, tripped on the sheet and left it on the kitchen floor as he scrambled after Catherine—who bolted through the doorway, shrieking with laughter. He caught up to her after a swift chase around the dining table.

Sweeping her up in his arms, Jack stalked to the bedroom and tossed her onto the bed. She continued to giggle until he moved on top of her, his nakedness settling sensually against her bare legs. Brushing a strand of hair from her cheek, Jack gazed down at her, his expression transforming to one of seriousness.

"I love you, Catherine Casey."

Her deep blue eyes took on shimmering light. "And I love you. More than I can say."

Capturing her hands on each side of her head, he slid up the front of her body. "You don't have to say it," he murmured as he bent to her lips. "Just show me." Entwining his fingers with hers, Jack possessed her mouth and let passion take over.

Tuesday, December 19

The honeymoon suite of the Mile-High Lodge in the Colorado Rockies couldn't have been more romantic. The motif was rustic, but in the most luxurious of ways, right down to the giant bear rug before the huge stone hearth where a friendly fire blazed.

Having removed their boots, Nicki and Kimo sat side by side on the rug, warming their stockinged feet after taking a midnight walk in the snow. "Man," he said with a shiver. "When you have the tropics as a lifelong frame of reference, you don't realize how cold this planet can actually get."

Stretching her arms around him, Nicki nestled against the thick weave of his fisherman's-knit sweater. "Funny, I don't feel the least bit chilly."

Having learned to ski on the snow-covered peak of Mauna Kea, Kimo had shown her a thing or two as they spent the afternoon negotiating the slopes of the ski resort. She'd known him all her life, but her new husband continued to surprise her . . . as did the depths of feeling it was possible for a human being to reach. Nicki looked up and drew his eye.

"I guess I've got my love to keep me warm," she added.

He bent to her lips with a kiss that started out sweet and chaste, then graduated with building desire. Pushing her back against the fur, Kimo rolled on top of her. Reaching beneath his sweater, Nicki ran her hands over the smooth skin of his back. Suddenly she halted and broke away from the kiss.

"What is it?" Kimo breathlessly asked. "What's wrong?"

A sly grin curved Nicki's lips. "Nothing's really wrong, but it looks like *somebody* can't wait for us to arrive in Charleston on Christmas Eve." With a merry chuckle Nicki spread her arms wide and sang out: "I love you, Catherine!"

Hundreds of miles away Catherine woke with a laugh. Turning on her side, she looped an arm around Jack. "I love you, too," she mumbled, and drifted into peaceful, dreamless sleep.